Thomas Hardy's Vision of Wessex

Thomas Hardy's Vision of Wessex

Simon Gatrell
University of Georgia

© Simon Gatrell, 2003

All rights reserved. No reproduction, copy or transmission of this publication may be made without written permission.

No paragraph of this publication may be reproduced, copied or transmitted save with written permission or in accordance with the provisions of the Copyright, Designs and Patents Act 1988, or under the terms of any licence permitting limited copying issued by the Copyright Licensing Agency, 90 Tottenham Court Road, London W1T 4LP.

Any person who does any unauthorised act in relation to this publication may be liable to criminal prosecution and civil claims for damages.

The author has asserted his right to be identified as the author of this work in accordance with the Copyright, Designs and Patents Act 1988.

First published 2003 by
PALGRAVE MACMILLAN
Houndmills, Basingstoke, Hampshire RG21 6XS and
175 Fifth Avenue, New York, N.Y. 10010
Companies and representatives throughout the world

PALGRAVE MACMILLAN is the global academic imprint of the Palgrave Macmillan division of St. Martin's Press, LLC and of Palgrave Macmillan Ltd. Macmillan® is a registered trademark in the United States, United Kingdom and other countries. Palgrave is a registered trademark in the European Union and other countries.

ISBN 0–333–74834–4 hardback

This book is printed on paper suitable for recycling and made from fully managed and sustained forest sources.

A catalogue record for this book is available from the British Library.

Library of Congress Cataloging-in-Publication Data
Gatrell, Simon.
  Thomas Hardy's vision of Wessex / Simon Gatrell.
    p. cm.
  Includes bibliographical references (p.) and index.
  ISBN 0-333-74834-4
  1. Hardy, Thomas, 1840–1928—Settings. 2. Hardy, Thomas, 1840–1928—Knowledge—Wessex (England) 3. Regional literature, English—History and criticism. 4. Wessex (England)—In literature. 5. Country life in literature. I. Title.

PR4757.S46G37 2003
823'.8—dc21   2003049764

10 9 8 7 6 5 4 3 2 1
12 11 10 09 08 07 06 05 04 03

Printed and bound in Great Britain by
Antony Rowe Ltd, Chippenham and Eastbourne

To Michael Millgate

Contents

Preface viii

List of Illustrations xi

Introduction xii

1 The Conception and Birth of Wessex   1
2 Variations on the Original Theme   27
3 The First Evolutionary Leap   45
4 *Tess of the d'Urbervilles*   61
5 Handling New Wessex   91
6 The Collected Editions 1   112
7 The Collected Editions 2   140
8 The Poetry   164
9 Cider, Mead and Ale   188
10 Sounds   195
11 The Languages of Wessex   202
12 Wessex Rail   226
13 Conclusion: Politics, Guides and Critics   234

Notes   244

Index of Place Names   256

General Index   260

Preface

An important note to the reader

In its original conception this book was to have included all revisions that Hardy made to the various aspects of Wessex. This was found to be economically unviable, and instead much of the material will be found at a website associated with the book: http//www.english.uga.edu/Wessex. Many of the endnotes direct the reader to the website for further information, and indeed the arguments in the book are now supported by only the essential minimum of illustration. The website has three levels, all of which may be accessed from the front page. The first responds directly to the book's endnotes, and also has a full list of books consulted; the second includes a range of secondary material relevant to details of Wessex discussed in the book; the third is an archive listing almost all (to claim completeness would be folly) the revisions Hardy made in his fiction to aspects of Wessex (for the poetry the reader should consult Samuel Hynes's edition, details of which are given in the following section). I welcome lists of errors on the website, for though I have striven to exclude them, they are surely there. Please send them to me at *sgatrell@uga.edu*.

Texts

Hardy's work is quoted, unless otherwise indicated, in its first edition form, with variants where relevant in **bold** face, since it is with the first serial and book appearance, and variants from them, that I am concerned. Prose quotations are identified by volume (v), book or part number and chapter (c, where necessary) number, except where indicated. Three-decker novels often had a separate numeration of chapters in each volume. There will be found on the website a key that will allow readers to adjust the chapter numbers for one-volume reference. Poetry quotations are from *The Complete Poetical Works of Thomas Hardy* Vols I–V, edited by Samuel Hynes (1982–95).

Abbreviations

The most important of these refer to the website. In the notes, references are in this form: **ws** followed by an abbreviation for each chapter. Users should follow the instructions on the front page of the website: http//www.english.uga.edu/Wessex.

The following books are also abbreviated for economy of reference:

Bibliographical Study: *Thomas Hardy: A Bibliographical Study*, R L Purdy (Second edition, 1968).
DCM: Documents in the Hardy collection in the Dorset County Museum. I am grateful to the curator for permission to quote from the collection.
Hardy in History: *Hardy in History: A Study in Literary Sociology*, Peter Widdowson (1989).
Hardy the Creator: *Hardy the Creator: A Textual Biography*, Simon Gatrell (1988).
Letters: *The Collected Letters of Thomas Hardy* edited by Richard Little Purdy and Michael Millgate, vol. I–VII (1978–88). An eighth and supplementary volume will appear soon.
Life and Work: *The Life and Work of Thomas Hardy* edited by Michael Millgate (1984).
Proper Study: *Thomas Hardy and the Proper Study of Mankind*, Simon Gatrell (1993).

Thanks

This book is a product of more than thirty years' work on Hardy's texts, and owes something to everyone I have talked with about Hardy during that period, in Oxford, Coleraine, Dorchester, Athens, and elsewhere, and to the people who have helped me at all the libraries I have visited. I am deeply grateful to you all. But there are some whose influence and friendship has been perpetual, and others who have helped with issues specific to this book, and I must let them know how important they have been. Michael Millgate is *the* Hardy scholar, and has been a good and generous friend to me from our first meeting. Bill and Vera Jesty used to live at Max Gate, the splendid house that Hardy built, and they have given me not just the extraordinary experience of sleeping in the room in which Hardy wrote *Tess of the d'Urbervilles*, but their company on many walks around Dorset, and the benefit of their huge knowledge of the past and present of Wessex. Many of the ideas fleshed out here were first floated in talks with them. It has been wonderful to share all this with such good friends. Pamela Dalziel's scholarship is an inspiration, and her friendship a resource. During the long gestation of the material that underpins this study Dale Kramer was in a sense my partner; he and I worked together on two different proposals for complete critical editions of Hardy's fiction, and both times it was not his fault that the projects fell through. Discussion and argument with Dale have made the issues of Hardy's texts come alive for me. Peter Shillingsburg's gift has been to stimulate me to think harder and faster and more clearly on textual (and all other) matters when I am in his company; I only hope some of that strength and clarity has lasted long enough. The two curators of the Dorset County Museum I have worked with, Roger Peers and Richard de

Peyer, have in their different ways, and under different conditions, made the Hardy collection in the museum a site of pure pleasure; Lillian Swindall was very helpful throughout my specific work on this book. The University of Georgia has been wonderfully supportive, and I have been blessed with a remarkable series of graduate students who have worked on Hardy with me here; each of them has contributed something significant: Jane Gatewood, Sarah Dangelantonio, Frank Mitchell, Russ Greer and Mark Rollins – and to their names I must add that of Kathy Agar. Without the encouragement of Nelson Hilton, the idea of the website that has made the whole project viable would never have got off the ground, and without Alice Kinman's hands-on assistance it would never have seen the light of the screen. Adam Parkes has read parts of the manuscript, a piece of work only less valuable to me than our common enthusiasm for cricket and football. Without the love and encouragement of Tita and Clym neither this nor any other of my work would have seen the light of day.

Simon Gatrell
December 2002

List of Illustrations

1. Illustration that Hardy drew to 'In a Ewelease Near Weatherbury' in *Wessex Poems* (1898). — xii
2. Hardy's map for the first edition of *The Return of the Native* (1878). — 29
3. Alfred Parsons's illustration for 'Wessex Folk'(1891). — 91
4. The first map of Wessex, from the *Bookman* (1891). — 94
5. Map of Wessex in Annie Macdonnell's *Thomas Hardy* (1894). — 101
6. The map of Wessex made for the Osgood, McIlvaine collected edition of Hardy's work (1895). — 113
7. The Raeburn illustration for *Desperate Remedies*. — 116
8. The Raeburn illustration for *Under the Greenwood Tree*. — 117
9. The Raeburn illustration for *A Pair of Blue Eyes*. — 120
10. The Raeburn illustration for *Far From the Madding Crowd*. — 122
11. The Raeburn illustration for *The Hand of Ethelberta*. — 126
12. The Raeburn illustration for *The Return of the Native*. — 127
13. The Raeburn illustration for *The Trumpet-Major*. — 130
14. The Raeburn illustration for *A Laodicean*. — 132
15. The Raeburn illustration for *Two on a Tower*. — 134
16. The Raeburn illustration for *The Mayor of Casterbridge*. — 135
17. The Raeburn illustration for *The Woodlanders*. — 137
18. The Raeburn illustration for *Wessex Tales*. — 140
19. The Raeburn illustration for *A Group of Noble Dames*. — 143
20. The Raeburn illustration for *Tess of the d'Urbervilles*. — 144
21. The Raeburn illustration for *Life's Little Ironies*. — 151
22. The Raeburn illustration for *Jude the Obscure*. — 153
23. The Raeburn illustration for *The Well-Beloved*. — 154
24. The revised Wessex map for the publication of *A Changed Man* in the Wessex edition (1914). — 162
25. Edmund New's map of South Wessex for *Thomas Hardy's Wessex* (1902). — 237

Introduction

'Hardy's Vision of Wessex.' I have to admit that I chose the title partly in order to be able to use for the dust-jacket the illustration that Hardy drew to 'In a Ewelease Near Weatherbury' in *Wessex Poems*. It is such an appropriate emblem for the book. At first for Hardy, Wessex was a real place seen through lenses that distorted, displaced, redistributed details, but which permitted chosen aspects of its culture to pass unhindered; gradually, as his vision changed, the lenses allowed more and more of the environmental detail to come through with only minimal alteration, until, after the publication of the map of Wessex accompanying the first collected edition of his work in 1895, the only distortion of the real caused by the lenses of the imagination worn by the writer was the presence of the lenses themselves, transparent, but not quite imperceptible. Thus the total lack of any visual distortion of the portion of the landscape seen through the glasses drawn in 1898.

It is also important that the ewelease is described as existing near Weatherbury, and thus a genuine Wessex scene, though at the same time, presumably, Hardy sat and drew it near Puddletown.

But when Hardy began writing he had no vision of Wessex, save what he might have heard as a young man in Dorchester from William Barnes, or read in childhood history books. What this book sets out to show is the stages by which Wessex evolved from latency in Hardy's mind to the region which is now bidding for its own althing. The forces driving Hardy through the evolutionary steps were both internal and external, and it seems worth here offering a schematized account of what I provide detailed evidence for in the rest of the book and on the associated website.

1 Early poems offer a distinctive world-view.

2 *Desperate Remedies* Hardy found that he had to write fiction out of places he knew intimately. The known views of family and friends were against any exposure to publicity. Therefore the Wilkie-Collins murder-mystery plot has Dorset places well disguised and manipulated. There is, however, the Dorset dialect.

3 *Under the Greenwood Tree* charts the replacement of something valued in the local community by something imported from outside.

4 In the spring of 1873 Hardy brought together three of his novels, *Under the Greenwood Tree, A Pair of Blue Eyes* and *Far From the Madding Crowd*, along the very slender thread of the town he called Casterbridge. Perhaps slightly less than a year later, but under the influence of his decision to link these novels, he dropped the name Wessex into the manuscript of *Far From the Madding Crowd*, though too late on in the story for him to elaborate the idea. This he did thoroughly in his next novel, *The Hand of Ethelberta*, and Wessex was established as a county which in Hardy's imagination covered parts of south-west Hampshire and south Dorset; apparently it had nothing to do with the much wider range covered by Saxon Wessex.

It was in response to this novel that the first article was published that made connections between Hardy's invented names for places and existing English ones. What effect this had on Hardy's sense of Wessex it is impossible to say. But his next four novels, and most of the stories written during the same period, do not, on the surface, advance Wessex into greater prominence.

5 The move of Hardy and his wife to Dorchester, having previously lived in London and a series of places in approximately a twenty-mile radius from the county town, triggered a new stage in Wessex. In *The Mayor of Casterbridge* Hardy deliberately laid place-name connections to all the previous novels and to some of the stories, and perhaps more importantly, characters from other novels appear at an earlier stage of their lives, one novel for the first time extending the life of another. *The Woodlanders* that followed immediately was important because for the first time the centre of a Wessex novel moved north, into the Vale of Blackmore.

It was at about this time, in 1886 or 1887, that Hardy wrote to the publisher of most of his novels, Sampson, Low, to ask

> 'Could you, whenever advertising my books, use the words "Wessex novels" at the head of the list?...I find that the name *Wessex*, wh. I was the first to use in fiction, is getting to be taken up everywhere: & it would be a pity for us to lose the right to it for want of asserting it.'

Evidently Hardy felt himself under some pressure to go as far as he could towards a de facto copyrighting of Wessex, and an article written by J M Barrie in 1889, entitled 'Thomas Hardy: The Historian of Wessex', will also have had its effect upon the next evolutionary leap taken by Wessex.

6a At some time during the summer of 1890 Wessex ceased to be one county (as it still explicitly was in *The Woodlanders*) of undetermined limits, but including by this time most of Dorset, the western part of Hampshire, southern Wiltshire, and eastern Somerset, and became divided into separate counties, which, by implication, had the same borders as the English counties above-named. This transformation occurred first at the end of the manuscript of *Tess of the d'Urbervilles*, the novel that brought all aspects of Wessex together, geographical, cultural and metaphysical; the new arrangement was also included in short stories written at the same time.

6b The final move in the evolution of Wessex to the form with which we are familiar came in 1895, with the publication in the first volume of the first collected edition of Hardy's work of a map of Wessex, which is a map of a part of England with strange names on it. No one who had followed Hardy's fiction from *Desperate Remedies* onwards could be surprised at this. The pressure of the intensifying tendency in his mind towards the recording of unrecorded history, and recording it as accurately as possible – the local historian clashing with the novelist – forced Wessex towards England. And on the whole the external environment pressed Hardy in the same direction. Almost from the beginning Hardy was exposed to the influence of people wanting to know the reality behind the fiction – people writing to Hardy about it, people writing in the journals about it, and people trying to puzzle out the relationships in private. Once it was clear that Wessex was being taken notice of, then there was the commercial pressure to assert his right to the word; in a different age he would have thought about marketing commemorative T-shirts and mugs. Uniting Wessex and England geographically only increased the pressure; before 1895 he always had a convincing escape-clause if anyone claimed he had got things wrong, historically or culturally or atmospherically or in some other way – 'Well, Casterbridge isn't really Dorchester, you know.' When he continued making that distinction after 1895, as for instance in the speech he gave when he was presented with the freedom of Dorchester in 1910, it was much less convincing.

By the time Hardy began to publish his poetry in 1898 his Wessex had reached the limit of its evolutionary capacity, and while his early volumes of verse add much of interest to the total they do not change anything. After his last revision of all his work for the Wessex edition, though, Hardy wearied of Wessex for a period, as if it were now a meaningless façade that his architect's instinct led him to strip away, and *Moments of Vision* and *Late Lyrics and Earlier* are almost empty of reference to his imagined region. It is perhaps surprising that towards the end of his life Hardy became reconciled again to his creation, accepting that Wessex had gone beyond him into the public world of England, and working with it in that spirit in *Human Shows* and *Winter Words*.

This skeletal reading will be fleshed by the detail and analysis of the earlier and longer part of the book, and its relative simplicity clothed in complexity and ambiguity. But Wessex is not just a place. The society and culture of Wessex evolved too, as Hardy's understanding of his creation expanded, and these chapters also trace that evolution, but they cannot do so in all the detail that the development of some of Hardy's ideas deserve. Thus the book concludes with four thematic chapters, each of which considers a representative or significant constituent of Wessex. From a wide range of possibilities I have chosen drink, railways, language and sounds; the material that would form the basis of separate analysis of other pervasive elements, like fate, the opposition of town and country, class, or work, can be found on the website.

The reader will encounter a number of voices in the text. I had begun this project by wanting to show how Wessex would have seemed for someone reading Hardy's work with intense interest as it was published, someone from the reading middle class, a London lady of some leisure, who was caught in the 1870s by the particularity and unfamiliarity of the environments Hardy created. How it strikes a contemporary, one might say. So I imagined for myself Lucy Stowe, and in particular her notebooks. She is introduced more fully in the first chapter. At one time her voice dominated the early chapters of the book, but I have pruned her contribution to what I hope is sustainable and useful.

It soon became clear that her accounts were not enough. Another kind of reader was abroad in 1870, one who shared with Hardy an intimate knowledge of Dorset and its surrounding country, and could penetrate from the start enough of Hardy's disguise to identify specific details and guess at others. I don't suppose there were more than a dozen of these, but one there was who quite early on went public with his knowledge – Kegan Paul – and I have occasionally imagined his thought on details he did not write about. In thinking about Paul's articles a third contemporary response suggested itself. I had forgotten the immediacy of Hardy's reaction to public criticism of his work, and once I looked at the reviews again, I saw that their comments on Wessex must have had some effect on the directions in which he chose to go. In the end, though, a lot of this material found its way out of the book and on to the website.

And then there is the controlling voice of the modern scholar, informed by a hundred years of writing about Wessex, and by the experience of collating, or having been associated with collations of the available versions of all of Hardy's fiction. Others have published critical or variorum editions of the poems. So here is to hand all, or almost all of the evidence that remains by which one can judge the development of Wessex in Hardy's imagination.

This book of course does not exist in a critical vacuum, and I have read everything that seemed even marginally relevant; but there is not in the body of the discussion much reference to the work of other writers who have thought about this issue. My argument proceeds primarily from the accumulated detail of Hardy's revisions, though it emerges onto the ground more usually fought over. There are two writers, though, whose thoughts have directed my own since I began working with Hardy's texts, and I cannot quit this introduction without expressing my gratitude to them. The first is Michael Millgate, whose *Thomas Hardy: His Career and a Novelist* was published in 1971 (London: Bodley Head) as I was working on the critical edition of *Under the Greenwood Tree* that was my doctoral thesis. Until then I had come across nothing in the way of critical analysis of Hardy that particularly caught my imagination, that seemed necessary, incontrovertible. I had not encountered Hillis Miller's *Thomas Hardy: Distance and Desire*, which might have worked thus, nor had I read David Lodge's wonderful chapter on *Tess of the d'Urbervilles* in *Language of Fiction*; and so Millgate's book became and remains for me the essential work on Hardy as a fiction-writer, and I have always had the uncomfortable feeling that everything I have done in relation to Hardy has been an extension of his ideas. As far as Wessex is concerned, we do differ a little, here and there; but the first two pages of Millgate's chapter 'The Evolution of Wessex' are like a summary of the first 60 pages of this book, and there are scattered throughout the whole of *Career* hints and details that I have taken up and fleshed out with evidence, but not materially altered.

The second critic is Raymond Williams, whose chapter on Hardy in *The Country and the City* (London: Chatto and Windus, 1973) came like a flash of transforming light to me in South Africa as I was preparing my thesis for examination that year. It was the first piece of his writing I had encountered. I did not think then as I do now that the eloquence and conviction of his approach to Hardy derives from the passion of the personal, barely veiled beneath the scholarly. The relevant chapter is called 'Wessex and the Border', which title he explains in the second paragraph:

> The Hardy country is of course Wessex: that is to say mainly Dorset and its neighbouring counties. But the real Hardy country, we soon come to see, is that border country so many of us have been living in: between custom and education, between work and ideas, between love of place and experience of change.

Williams valued Hardy so highly and wrote about him with such controlled intensity because in Hardy he had found a writer who told the truth about the complexity of his own life experience, which was also Williams's life experience. For me, in those formative years, there was a rich contrast between Millgate's cool brilliance and William's strength of feeling barely restrained by integrity of intellect. Between them they touched the sources of my commitment to Hardy as a man and as a writer.

For them both Wessex is a society in change, a long slow change, observed and embodied by a writer who is at once part of it and educated beyond it, and who betrays that double consciousness at every turn, even to understanding the advantages and limitations of the education itself.

There are also two articles which I gladly acknowledge as precursors of this book. It was W J Keith's 'Thomas Hardy and the Literary Pilgrims' (*Nineteenth-Century Fiction* 1969, 80–92) that first argued for a relationship between the mapping of Wessex in the early 1890s and the revisions Hardy made to his fiction for the first collected edition in 1895–6, and every subsequent analyst is indebted to it. Much of the discussion remains valid.

John Fowles has always written brilliantly about Hardy, and he knows Dorset past and present as well as anyone. If I had to recommend only one essay to illuminate Hardy's view of Wessex, it would be the introduction he wrote in 1984 to a book of historical photographs entitled *Thomas Hardy's England* (London: Cape), brought together by Jo Draper and himself. As Keith's article is in the same line of thought as Millgate's work, Fowles is in harmony with Williams, and taken together the two books and two shorter pieces represent the subterranean core of what follows.

1
The Conception and Birth of Wessex

Thomas Hardy was born in 1840 in Higher Bockhampton, Dorsetshire. His mother had been a servant and his father was a mason and builder. His mother's was a dominating personality; she was ambitious for her children and was reluctant to lose control of them as they grew up; she had strong views on many subjects and read voraciously. His father was handsome, easy-going and deeply musical. Also living in the family until her death in 1857, was his paternal grandmother, Mary, who had been born in 1772 and was a 'rich oral source of stories, traditions and folklore, as well as recollections of what Hardy came to perceive as the historical past: the period when the threat of a French invasion seemed very real...'[1]

Hardy went to school in Dorchester and was subsequently apprenticed to John Hicks, a local architect. After serving his time he moved to London, in 1862, to practice in Arthur Blomfield's office, and was there for five years, until (amongst other things) the London climate eroded his health too severely and he returned to Dorset to work again for Hicks, and then for G R Crickmay of Weymouth who took over Hicks's practice.

While he was in London he began writing verse, and though none of it was published at that time, he retained the manuscripts; and when his first collection, *Wessex Poems*, appeared in 1898, a fair number of them were dated 1866 and 1867. It is impossible to know what relationship the poems finally published in 1898 bore to those completed thirty years earlier, and all we can do is to assume that if not identical, revision of them did not amount to rewriting. Two of these dated early poems that are best known and most anthologized – 'Hap' and 'Neutral Tones' – are in their way important antecedents to Wessex.

'Hap' is the lament of a person who would find it easier to deal with personal disaster if it had been engineered by a malicious divine agent against whom he could direct his resentment, rather than by those 'purblind doomsters', 'Crass Casualty' and 'dicing Time'. It is painful to understand that pure chance is the only cause of sorrow or joy. Throughout the development of Wessex the question of what causes things to happen there the way they do is of primary importance.

'Neutral Tones' is still more suggestive. It begins:

> We stood by a pond that winter day,
> And the sun was white, as though chidden of God,
> And a few leaves lay on the starving sod;
> – They had fallen from an ash, and were gray.

And ends:

> Since then, keen lessons that love deceives,
> And wrings with wrong, have shaped to me
> Your face, and the God-curst sun, and a tree,
> And a pond edged with grayish leaves.

To anyone familiar with Hardy's work the idea underlying the poem is a commonplace one, found in his novels from *Desperate Remedies* to *Tess of the d'Urbervilles*.[2] Once a place or an object is associated with an intensely felt emotion it becomes permanently significant; it forever carries a weight of personal history. Naturally, everywhere in the inhabited world is capable of holding such significance for someone; we all love and hate and weep and pray and curse and die in particular places. So when Hardy came to write novels he found that, at the heart of narrative, feeling could not be divorced from environment, and consequently neither could character nor could plot. No Victorian novelist could have written a placeless plot, but for Hardy place (natural or man-made) had a more profound significance than for other writers. What we see is that, as he compiled invented plots, gradually the less personal, more public ideas of the significance of place also became important: he saw the power within family fanes, local pieties and parish histories and within the marks that distinguish a county or a region, like language and work-practices. Thus personal history gradually sponsors public history. The development of Wessex, in this account, is a matter of Hardy making connections from his own intense perception, of the sort expressed so vividly in 'Neutral Tones', to an increasingly more general application – from individuals to community; from small community to larger; and ultimately to the largest community that was, in his mind, able to support the name.

Another way of coming at a similar understanding is through an idea that finds its clearest expression in comments the narrator of *Tess of the d'Urbervilles* makes about Tess Durbeyfield:

> At times her whimsical fancy would intensify natural processes around her till they seemed a part of her own story. Rather they became a part of

it; for the world is only a psychological phenomenon, and what they seemed they were.

Or at least 'what they seemed they were' to her; but the narrator has also a finger on what readers are asked to accept as an objective reality:

> this encompassment of her own characterization, based on shreds of convention, peopled by phantoms and voices antipathetic to her, was a sorry and mistaken creation of Tess's fancy – a cloud of moral hobgoblins by which she was terrified without reason. It was they that were out of harmony with the actual world, not she. (XIII)

We may, if we make the effort to set aside the authority of the narrative voice, argue that this objective reality is in fact no less subjective than Tess's 'mistaken creation'; but for the purpose of gaining an insight into the development of Wessex, the assumed dualism is valuable, for in studying Hardy's work chronologically, we see that what begins as an individual world imaginatively constructed from places of personal importance to him, is gradually, but with increasing emphasis, modified by connection with the external world of apparently objective reality. At any rate, this study provides the detail by which such an argument may be judged.

Hardy could not get his poems published, and, besides, he was well aware that as a poet he would have to subsidize his writing by architecture. Writing was a pleasure, or a necessity for him, and to anyone with half an eye on the literary marketplace it was clear that the most profitable form of successful writing was fiction. So as soon as he left London in 1867, he began work on the manuscript that would eventually be submitted to a number of publishers in 1868 and 1869 as *The Poor Man and the Lady; By the Poor Man*. The manuscript was accepted by Chapman and Hall, but ultimately withdrawn by Hardy, and no trace remains of the text as it stood. The title, however, embodies another essential element of Wessex: a perpetual awareness of class-distinctions; and what we can gather of the narrative from a variety of sources makes it clear that class-conflict was a central thematic strand in the novel. It is also evident that contrasts were drawn in *The Poor Man and the Lady* between rural and urban life, initiating what would ultimately be another important aspect of Wessex, the idea that it provides an opposite pole to the metropolis: that Wessex gains a significant part of its meaning by being not-London.

On the advice of George Meredith, who had read *The Poor Man and the Lady* for Chapman, Hardy abandoned his first novel, and decided to write instead a somewhat sensational mystery story. He borrowed a number of passages from the earlier novel, as Pamela Dalziel has shown (and probably used other episodes now unidentifiable), and he also prosed some of his unpublishable poems.[3] He wrote *Desperate Remedies* quickly, submitting most of the manuscript to Macmillan early in 1870, who again turned it down. Eventually William Tinsley took it and it was published anonymously in March 1871.

Hardy began his public mediation between the world as psychological phenomenon and the world as objective reality by fabricating for *Desperate Remedies* a fictional environment from materials that were close at hand near Dorchester and Weymouth.

However, before I can continue with this analysis I have to interject an essential observation: the last part of the previous sentence, straightforward and unexceptionable as it is nowadays, contains a dilemma intrinsic to this study. I need both to know and not to know such information. I need to be able to be a contemporary reader of the novel's first edition, but also to understand details of Hardy's transformations of topographical realities that would be unavailable to such a contemporary reader. It has seemed therefore worthwhile, for the sake of distinguishing between the perceptions of the twenty-first-century student and the nineteenth-century reader, to invent the notebooks and diaries of Lucy Stowe. The majority of Hardy's early readers will have lived in London (less than four hundred copies of *Desperate Remedies* were sold in 1871, and most of those went to Mudie's huge lending library), and very few would have had more than a passing curiosity about the setting of the narrative. Lucy Stowe, aged fourteen in 1871, was the youngest daughter of a successful barrister and contented widower. She was one of those rare readers for whom the place where any romance occurred was at least as interesting as the story itself. She had been reading parts of *Waverley* as a young girl and in 1871 Scott was her passion. It was not until three years later when, in common with almost everyone else she knew, she began reading *Far From the Madding Crowd* in *Cornhill*, that she became an enthusiast for Hardy, and sought out his earlier novels to read between the *Cornhill* episodes. Her diaries, which I have imagined myself to have inherited, are full of brief comments on all her reading, but *Far From the Madding Crowd* as it developed evidently triggered a powerful response in her sympathetic imagination, and she began to keep a separate notebook for her thoughts about the novel. For the next twenty years, through marriage and other adventures, she maintained this practice as each of Hardy's new fictions were made public; I see these notebooks as ranged on the shelf by my side as I write. The one on *Desperate Remedies* was begun on 6 June 1874, and begins: 'At last Papa has found a copy of "Desperate Remedies," all three volumes bound together, which makes it rather heavy to hold.'

On the first page of the novel she read the following:

> Ambrose Graye, a young architect who had just begun the practice of his profession in the midland town of Hocbridge, went to London to spend the Christmas holidays with a friend who lived in Bloomsbury. They had gone up to Cambridge in the same year...

There is nothing in this sentence and a half to alert her to anything interesting about the world the novel is to inhabit, except perhaps that Hocbridge is an invented name amongst the English ones. Graye's solicitor, she learnt a little later, practises in reading. The first chapters of *Desperate Remedies*, though, are by way of being a prelude to the action, which begins in earnest when Graye's two children, Owen and Cytherea, travel by train from Hocbridge to Creston, 'a seaport and watering-place in the west of England' (vI cI.5), where Owen hopes to gain employment as a clerk in an architect's office. We know now that Hardy was visualizing Weymouth when writing of Creston, but Lucy had no idea of this. On one page she wrote a list of the place names in the novel:

Creston
Lewborne Bay
Humdon Castle
Galworth
Laystead
Carriford
Knapwater House
Froominster
Chettlewood
Buckshead Hill
Peakhill Cottage
Southampton
Palchurch
Mundsbury

Save Southampton, these are all invented names, fictional places. Lucy's knowledge of the west of England was slight, but she had been to Freshwater in the Isle of Wight for a holiday with her family, and they had travelled by rail from London to catch the ferry from Lymington, so she noted a pleasant sense of familiarity when characters in *Desperate Remedies* also travelled to Southampton and to London along some of the same track. This led her to look for Creston along the coast westward from Southampton on a map, but she could not find it. 'It is curious, is it not' she wrote, 'that fictional places and real should be together like this in a story.' But then on the opposite page there is the addendum 'I see that Mr Hardy does this again in the latest episode of "Far From the Madding Crowd" when Bathsheba goes to Bath. Perhaps he likes to give us a point of reference we will recognize – though both are a good many miles from where the action mostly happens.' And underneath this is squeezed in: 'Plymouth in "A Pair of Blue Eyes" too.' Apparently she did no more detective work in 1874, but there was one name in her list that might have helped her, had she been sufficiently interested at that stage, to relate what Hardy described to the map of England. Aside from Creston, the most important town in *Desperate Remedies* is Froominster;

it has the county gaol, the county bank, a corn exchange and a considerable market, while the local newspaper is called the *Froominster Chronicle*. Though nowhere called the county town, it has all the attributes of one, and if Lucy had looked on her map westward from Southampton, she must soon have come across Dorchester, a county town on the banks of the river Frome (pronounced Froom, and so spelled by Hardy almost invariably).

This might have done no more than pique her curiosity; but for readers reasonably well acquainted with Dorchester, the various details of Hardy's description of Froominster would have left them in no doubt that Dorchester was the model (they might also have cited the High Street leading to a bridge that separated town from country, or the fact that the newspaper published in Dorchester was called the *Dorset County Chronicle*). Thus it seems necessary, indeed, to predicate not two, but three classes of readers for the first edition of *Desperate Remedies*: those with at best a passing interest in the environment of the novel (most readers); those, like Lucy, with a stronger interest stimulated by Hardy's detailed descriptions of place, distance and geographical relationship, but without the local knowledge necessary to begin to make connections on the ground; and those (few indeed) with both the interest and the knowledge. (That there was at least one such reader, however, was made clear in 1876; but more of him in due course.)

Once Froominster had been identified with Dorchester by this last kind of reader, all sorts of questions would arise for him, if he had a curious mind. Creston has nothing about it that would prevent it from being based on Weymouth, but what of Carriford and Knapwater House? Knapwater House is a 'country mansion about fifteen miles off' (vI cIV.1) from Creston, and a mile or so from a railway station at Carriford Road. If the railway in the novel is the railway in Dorset, then fifteen miles from Weymouth reaches nearly to Wareham, and there is no village and house at that kind of distance that conforms even approximately to Hardy's descriptions, and even the informed local reader would come to a dead end, despite the wealth of information offered in the narrative. Lucy spent some pages trying to organize all the distances and directions into some sort of coherence, but eventually gave up in mock-despair. She wrote: 'Take this passage:

> Manston was wearing his old garden-hat, and carried one of the monthly magazines under his arm. Immediately they had passed the gateway he branched off and went over the hill in a direction away from the church, evidently intending to ramble along, and read as the humour moved him. The lady meanwhile turned in the other direction, and went along the church path.
>
> Owen resolved to make something of this opportunity. He hurried along towards the church, doubled round a sharp angle, and came back upon the other path, by which Mrs. Manston must arrive. (vIII cV.1)

The important thing here, as it so often seems to be, is the lay of the land, and yet it isn't at all made clear, especially when taken in combination with other paths and roads so fully but incompletely described before. I think Mr Hardy had the whole landscape for miles around vividly present to his mind as he was writing, and gave all the details necessary to follow the movements of the characters at any given moment, but in doing so forgot that the background, so clear to him, was quite opaque to me, so that a passage like this is lit up by the lantern-beam of his description, but the surrounding country is in darkness. I know, for instance, that the church is on the turnpike road that runs through Carriford, opposite the burnt-out ruins of the Inn, but I have never been able to see how one gets from the old Manor to the church. In most novels it wouldn't matter, because there is so much less detail of this sort; but here I long to see it all with Mr Hardy's inner eye; he doesn't leave me the freedom to imagine a scene of my own, but he doesn't fulfil the expectations he arouses. Perhaps no writer could, and still tell a story. I don't know.'

Well, now we recognize, what would have been very hard to understand in 1871, that Knapwater was a version of Kingston Maurward, the big house of Hardy's birth parish of Stinsford, one he knew well from his childhood. The building and its immediate grounds are described in the novel with some accuracy – but it is more like nine or ten miles from Weymouth than fifteen. And when the relationship of the house to the village and church of Carriford is in question, or the relationship of Carriford to the surrounding towns and villages of Froominster, Palchurch and Mundsbury, then it soon becomes clear that Hardy was writing to disguise his borrowings as much as he could. This is the explanation for the impossibility of making a coherent map of the action of the novel. Much that he writes is in detail a recollection of a place or a journey he knew well, but it is placed in an unfamiliar or invented context.[4]

Nevertheless there are clues for an intimately informed reader. When the Three Tranters Inn, which Hardy placed in the middle of his imagined village, burns down, one consequence of the conflagration is the presumption that a Mrs Manston burns with it:

> Two days later the official inquiry into the cause of her death was held at the Traveller's Rest Inn, before Mr. Floy, the coroner, and a jury of the chief inhabitants of the district. The little tavern – the only remaining one in the village – was crowded (vII cIII.2)

There was a small inn called the Traveller's Rest (also the original of The Quiet Woman in *The Return of the Native*), on the road from Stinsford to Tincleton (the same place appears in Hardy's poem 'Weathers'). Here, however, the pub is 'in' Carriford, and the name is common enough; but my hypothetical reader would also have known, and a glance at a contemporary directory for the district tells us, that John Floyer MP lived in the village of West Stafford, hardly two miles from the Traveller's Rest across the Frome valley. Evidently Hardy was having fun. If Mr Floyer read the book, he, for one, would have made the topographical connections, and recognized the borrowings, displacements and disguises.

Before being burnt down, the inn had already been deprived of much of its function as a staging post by the arrival in the neighbourhood of a railway line. As a matter of fact, there has never been a station associated with Kingston Maurward, though the line east from Dorchester does run just across the Frome meadows south of the house, and an imaginary station in Floyer's village of West Stafford would be the right distance away. However, when Cytherea Graye was driven from Carriford Road station to the house, it was along a turnpike road, the same that goes past the Three Tranters; there has never been any such major road running north–south from the railway. And on a larger scale the railway produces similar problems once Froominster is approximated to Dorchester. Indeed, there is no way of reconciling all the information about directions and distances that Hardy provides, of drawing a map which will satisfy all conditions – something that will eventually come to seem unusual in a Hardy novel.[5] At this early stage in his writing, though, he was torn three ways, between the desire to delineate vividly and precisely, the need to write places he knew intimately, and a cautious sense that over all a veil of disguise would be prudent if he did not wish to upset family, friends and neighbours.

Here I want to make a distinction between what might be called narrow Wessex and broad Wessex, between the matters of topography so far examined in relation to *Desperate Remedies*, and the sense of Wessex as an imaginatively conceived and coherent world in which, life is lived according to certain conditions and in certain ways that are not characteristic of the mundane world in general, and not always of that part of the world upon which Hardy based Wessex. The two aspects of Wessex are interdependent, but they grew at different rates as Hardy developed his ideas. Much of the broader Wessex might also be understood as the creation and development of Wessex's society and culture; by the time he was writing *Tess of the d'Urbervilles* this had become a very wide-ranging subject indeed, but in *Desperate Remedies*, written well before any idea of Wessex had emerged from Hardy's creative mind, there are not so many topics to consider. All of them, though, will become constant elements in his design of Wessex once that place is established.

The first of these is work. There *are* people in Wessex who do no work or whom we do not see working; but they are few – the landowners, like Cytherea Aldclyffe in this novel, the daughters of well-off families, like Grace Melbury in *The Woodlanders*, or the unemployed and the old. By the time Hardy had finished writing fiction Lucy had some understanding of the nature of very many rural occupations, and an understanding of their place and significance in

Wessex. In *Desperate Remedies* much of Hardy's attention is given to the working out of his complicated plot concerning a small group of middle-class people. We do not see Owen Graye at work as an architect's clerk; his sister Cytherea makes a half-hearted attempt to be a lady's maid, but she is too independent-minded, has been brought up too fully to see herself in the middle class, for her to endure more than a day in that role. Manston is reported as going about some of the business of an estate steward. But there is not much room in the narrative for the working classes. The one extended passage of labour, which could well stand as a model for most of the accounts of work done in subsequent novels, is the wringing down of apples for cider:

> Edward Springrove the elder, the landlord, now more particularly a farmer, and for two months in the year a cider-maker, was an employer of labour of the old school, who worked himself among his men. He was now engaged in packing the pomace into horsehair bags with a rammer, and Gad Weedy, his man, was occupied in shovelling up more from a tub at his side. The shovel shone like silver from the action of the juice, and ever and anon, in its motion to and fro, caught the rays of the declining sun and reflected them in bristling stars of light. (vI cVIII.3)

The passage as a whole (of which this is a fragment) is by no means a manual nor is it a full account of the process; but it gives a sense of the life within the work, the occasional beauty of it. There is no emphasis on the strenuousness required to perform it, but on the other hand the work is not idealized. Springrove does pack the bags, a whole group of villagers strains at the screw of the press, compressing the apples and expelling the juice. But at the same time it is evident that this is a communal occasion; Farmer/Innkeeper Springrove presumably pays Weedy 'his man', but we don't know if the others are in his temporary employ, or whether they will be rewarded for their assistance in kind, or whether they lend a hand out of good fellowship, the day being fine and the work not particularly arduous. The scene is a long way from Tess Durbeyfield swede-hacking in the winter rain at Flintcomb-Ash.

A second aspect of Wessex culture might be described as the operation of local customs and traditions. Most readers of Hardy will think in this context of club-walking or mumming or skimmity-riding, but in *Desperate Remedies* there is an instance that in one way is more interesting still:

> 'No – don't, please, Cytherea,' said Edward, softly. 'Come and sit down with me.'
> 'O yes. I ought to have asked *you* to,' she returned, timidly. 'Everybody sits in the chimney-corner in this parish. You sit on that side. I'll sit here.' (VIII cII.2)

Cytherea here is distinguishing between the customs of different parishes – aware of something that is done in Palchurch but not in Carriford, say. This implies a stronger parish identity and a greater degree of separation between parishes than is usually found in Hardy, except where the local bands of musicians are concerned. The ringing of the church bells at the end of the novel might perhaps also be thought of as a customary activity, one that has in common with the apple-pressing mentioned before the pleasure of a communal enterprise.

Then there is class. No novel of Hardy's is exempt from considerations of class; indeed it seems a justifiable generalization to say that almost no English novel is exempt from such considerations. But, as is by now well-understood, Hardy is particularly sensitive to the issue, and sharply aware of the small distinctions in rural society that distinguish several social gradations, where a casual middle-class urban visitor would, if pressed, distinguish one, or none. Hardy also, as the vestiges of *The Poor Man and the Lady* suggest, and as *The Hand of Ethelberta* in particular confirms, has strongly held opinions about class-hostility and the reasons for it. In *Desperate Remedies*, for instance, Edward Springrove, the innkeeper's son, speaks to the landowner Cytherea Aldclyffe as an equal, and the narrator comments:

> Miss Aldclyffe, like a good many others in her position, had plainly not realised that a son of her tenant and inferior, could have become an educated man, who had learnt to feel his individuality, to view society from a Bohemian stand-point, far outside the farming grade in Carriford parish, and that hence he had all a developed man's unorthodox opinion about the subordination of classes. (vII cIII.4)

Which reads very much like an autobiographical experience.

From the first, too, Hardy worked with the question of how to represent the indigenous speech of the district. On the whole in *Desperate Remedies* Hardy gives strong indications of accent, and a certain amount of deviation from the grammar of standard English, but not much in the way of lexical variation. This is Gad Weedy, who has the richest local pronunciation: 'Whilst Master Teddy Springrove has been daddlen, and hawken, and spetten about having her, she's quietly left him all forsook' (vII cV.2).[6]

These are all facets of Dorset life that Hardy observed and thought important as early as *Desperate Remedies*. There are also some characteristics of Hardy's own habitual pattern of thought that become as much an element of Wessex as the landscape or the agricultural labour. One instance of this, as I have already noted, is a nexus of ideas about causality, about the validity of concepts like fate, destiny, chance, Hap, providence (divine or otherwise), or the immanent will, when balanced with human agency, intentional or otherwise. It is an issue that many Victorian writers address, but none so richly or insistently as Hardy, not even George Eliot, to whom on occasion Hardy alludes in this respect. And the debate in Hardy's mind becomes an issue for Wessex and its people, placed there by narrator after narrator, in every novel, most notably in *The Dynasts*, and in dozens of poems, so that it becomes part of the Wessex air they breathe. It is so even in *Desperate Remedies*:

> 'I used to think 'twas your wife's fate not to have a liven husband when I sid 'em die off so,' said Gad.
> 'Fate? Bless thy simplicity, so 'twas her fate; but she struggled to have one, and would, and did. Fate's nothen beside a woman's schemen!'
> 'I suppose, then, that Fate is a He, like us, and the Lord, and the rest o' em up above there,' said Gad, lifting his eyes to the sky (vI cVIII.3).

Hardy was always responsive to criticism, and an important element in charting the development of Wessex is the voice of the reviewer. It will be seen that though the notices of *Desperate Remedies* were mixed, embryonic Wessex, as I have outlined it above, was well received:

> The characters are often exceedingly good. The parish clerk, 'a sort of Bowdlerised rake', who refers to the time 'before he took orders', is really almost worthy of George Eliot, and so is the whole cider-making scene at the end of the first volume. The west-country dialect is also very well managed, without being a caricature. (*Athenaeum* 1 April 1871)[7]

> This nameless author has, too, one other talent of a remarkable kind – sensitiveness to scenic and atmospheric effects, and to their influence on the mind, and the power of rousing similar sensitiveness in his readers. (*Spectator* 22 April 1871)

> ... the sketch of [old Springrove] ... reminds us of the close and truthful drawing in Mr. Barnes's delightful *Dorset Poems* and *Hwomely Rhymes*.... We may add that a familiarity with several kinds of manual work adds great point to the author's natural power of vivid description. (*Saturday Review* 30 September 1871)

By contrast with *Desperate Remedies*, Hardy's next novel had barely any plot at all, though it had more in the first edition than it had initially in the manuscript. This time, when Hardy again sent them his manuscript, Macmillan were interested but not really excited; they did not offer to publish *Under the Greenwood Tree* at once, and after waiting a few months for further news, Hardy offered the manuscript to William Tinsley, who had been the man finally to publish *Desperate Remedies*. Tinsley offered £30 for the copyright, and Hardy accepted; it was a sum that would at least cover the loss he had incurred over his first novel. *Under the Greenwood Tree* came out in two volumes in June 1872. Again he used some material from *The Poor Man and the Lady*, and again he used his own parish as the centre of the novel, though in a quite different way. In *Desperate Remedies* he had taken details from south central Dorset and placed them in a totally fictional relationship with each other and the railway line that runs through the county to Weymouth. For *Under the Greenwood Tree* Hardy imagined almost all of the action taking place within a few miles of his birthplace, but gave in the text very few hints that he had done so. This is how Mellstock, the parish that is at the heart of the action, is described:

> Mellstock was a parish of considerable acreage, the hamlets composing it lying at a much greater distance from each other than is ordinarily the case.... There was East Mellstock, the main village; half a mile from this were the church and the vicarage, called West Mellstock, and originally the most thickly-populated portion. A mile north-east lay the hamlet of Lewgate, where the tranter lived; and at other points knots of cottages, besides solitary farmsteads and dairies. (I.iv)

If the names were changed this would accurately describe Stinsford, but the account of the journeys across the parish the choir makes as they play and sing carols is carefully anonymous, and no one but Hardy would know where he had in mind. When Budmouth first enters Hardy's work in this novel, there was nothing that might have made Lucy think of Weymouth.[8] The environment is prominent in the novel, the places people live, the paths they take, the country they travel through are all so vividly given that any reader might say to herself, as Lucy Stowe did, that surely this is a real place; but no hint is given her of where the real place might be. Indeed Hardy again inserts deliberate elements of disguise, as for instance when the vicar, walking from Mellstock to the nearby town Casterbridge, goes across 'dale and heath'; but of course it is only possible to know that this is disguise when the reality behind the fiction is made clear later in Hardy's development of Wessex. For Hardy the story could only have resonance, value – could, indeed only be written – if it was set in the place in which the actual choir at the centre of the narrative had sung and played; but at the same time he was not anxious for anyone else to know this.[9] All Lucy could do was admire and wonder.

On the other hand, she did notice some connections between *Desperate Remedies* and *Under the Greenwood Tree*. She caught the fact that both are set in cider-producing districts, and she copied this comment by Keeper Day on his wife, adding: 'I remember something quite like this about the clerk's wife in "Desperate Remedies", though I can't find it just now' (the interested reader will find it above p. 11):

> 'There's that wife o' mine. It was her doom not to be nobody's wife at all in the wide universe. But she made up her mind that she would, and did

it twice over. Doom? Doom is nothing beside a elderly woman – quite a chiel in her hands' (II.vi).[10]

'Mr Hardy makes you hear things you've never noticed before,' Lucy also noted, before quoting the opening of *Under the Greenwood Tree*: 'It goes with that passage I copied from "Desperate Remedies" about the different sounds rain makes.'[11] At the end of her notes on the novel Lucy commented, '"Under the Greenwood Tree" is like what I have read so far of "Far From the Madding Crowd" in that I have learned much about the right way to do things in the country, like tapping a cider-barrel, making a shoe, or hiving bees (or visiting a member of the superior classes, for that matter, I suppose).'

In *Under the Greenwood Tree* we watch the rapid and ill-motivated extirpation of the church musicians from their time-honoured posts. The members of the Mellstock choir regret very much their dismissal, and though they all accept that the vicar has the right in his own shop to order business as he chooses, still some feel sufficiently rebellious to suggest staying away from church on the Sunday of their supersession. And there are later in the novel other evidences of change in the rural community of no fixed place that is Mellstock, straws in the wind. There is a discussion about what will happen after the marriage service of Dick and Fancy:

> 'And then, of course, when 'tis all over,' continued the tranter, 'we shall march two and two round the parish.'
> 'Yes, sure,' said Mr. Penny: 'two and two: every man hitched up to his woman, 'a b'lieve.'...
> 'Respectable people don't nowadays,' said Fancy. 'Still, since poor mother did, I will' (V.i).

During her teacher-training in London, Fancy has been exposed to and has accepted as normative, the current social conventions of the urban middle-class; the word that captures the spirit of her responses to the 'immemorial' local customs is 'respectable'. Family piety, allied to the overwhelming confirmation of local practice by everyone else except her compliant husband-to-be, ensures for the moment the survival of the wedding tour of the district, and the strength of the old to assimilate the new without losing its identity seems possibly sufficient; but with the railway connection to London – so prominent in *Desperate Remedies* – only a few years away from the world of *Under the Greenwood Tree*, it is evident (though it did not strike Lucy) that the survival of the traditional will at best be precarious.

It is possible to argue from a historical perspective that every generation feels, when a number of things that have been familiar since their grandparents' youth disappear or are destroyed, that a way of life that has existed from time out of mind is threatened or is falling apart. Hardy here, and in narratives to follow, makes us share this feeling and recognize its power – that if experience and memory force people to respond thus, then the response is real and active in their lives, and it does not diminish its force to call such an understanding an illusion. On the other hand some of Hardy's multiple narrative voices are more objective, sometimes commenting directly or indirectly on the limited and subjective nature of the characters' responses, sometimes suggesting (more often in later work) that the nineteenth century, and in particular the half-century from 1840–90, did indeed mark the decisive decline of many of the particular ways of life embodied in Wessex, some of which had existed (not, of course, unmodified) for several centuries.

A final note suggestive of the future: it may be no more than a coincidence that a character in *Desperate Remedies*, of whom we know nothing but his name, is called John Day. A very sharply attentive reader, who remarked upon whatever else there was in common between *Under the Greenwood Tree* and *Desperate Remedies*, might possibly have said to herself on reading of Fancy Day and her family, that perhaps John was her cousin – though in fact Lucy did not.

When *Under the Greenwood Tree* was published, Hardy was working in London again as an architect, and an encounter with his publisher led to him agreeing to provide a serial for *Tinsley's Magazine*, his first attempt in that form. He had very little of the novel written, and he had rapidly to learn the business of writing against continual printer's deadlines. His need to shape the detail of his narrative out of what was immediate to him was a help in this respect. In 1870 he had gone to St Juliot in North Cornwall to execute a church-restoration commission for Crickmay, and had fallen in love with the rector's sister-in-law, Emma Gifford. There is a significant autobiographical element in *A Pair of Blue Eyes*, and again we now are well aware that the environment he created for the novel was a version of one he had become intimately familiar with.

Though Hardy nowhere stated as much in the novel, the combination of the dramatic cliff-bound coastline, names like St Eval's and St Kirr's, and the intervention of Plymouth as a terminal port and railway station between London and that coast meant that contemporary readers who were interested had sufficient information to identify at least the county of the main action of the story. Hardy is once again precise but selective in local detail and sufficiently imprecise in broader topographical relationships to make a close identification impossible. There is a certain amount of disguise, as in earlier novels, and also a couple of outright topographical anomalies. This is Mrs Smith talking of Elfride Swancourt to her son Stephen: 'I see her sometimes decked out like a horse going to Binegar fair, and I admire her for't. A perfect little lady' (vI.cX). Binegar is in the Mendips in Somerset, and it is marginally possible that Binegar horse fair was as well known so far away as Cornwall as it was in Dorset. However a second occurrence of a real name of significance in Dorset rather than Cornwall renders another explanation more probable. The speaker is again Mrs Smith: 'We used to go looking for even-ashes together in Benvill Lane' (vIII cIX). Benvill Lane is in Dorset, south of Toller Down. Tess Durbeyfield walks along it to and from Emminster.[12] Now *A Pair of Blue Eyes* was written under considerable time pressure as a serial story in *Tinsley's Magazine*, and it is certain that Hardy again made use of significant fragments of *The Poor Man and the Lady* to pad out his invention. This is the case with some of the London scenes, and it seems most likely that these two occurrences of English names of places far to the east of the supposed site of the story, in the speech of this one character, come from the same source. Both were removed when the novel was reprinted in one volume in 1877. When Lucy Stowe read *A Pair of Blue Eyes* she was as sure as she had been with the earlier novels that Hardy had a real place in mind, and was paying close attention to this aspect of the narrative for hints, but her knowledge of Dorset and Somerset was much too slender for her to have picked up these details.

On the other hand she did see that Hardy was liberal with what she called travel-guide descriptions. Amongst others she noted that when Knight went to Brittany, he did so 'by way of Weymouth, Jersey and St. Malo', (vIII cII) and thus, though she could not yet make the connection, in Hardy's first three novels the first of these places was known by three different names: Creston, Budmouth and Weymouth.

There is one place name in *A Pair of Blue Eyes*, though, that indicates the beginning of an idea at the heart of Wessex; it occurs in a passage in which Stephen Smith is describing his previous life to Elfride Swancourt:

> I have not lived here since I was nine years old. I then went to live with my uncle, a blacksmith, near Casterbridge, in order to be able to attend a national school as a day scholar; there was none in this remote part then. (vI cVIII)

The choice in the first edition of *A Pair of Blue Eyes* of Casterbridge as the town in which Smith had his education is striking. For readers familiar with details of Hardy's life it adds an extra element to the already clear autobiographical strain in the novel; and this repetition Lucy did notice, especially since the name had already occurred in the serial of *Far From the Madding Crowd* that she was reading at the same time, as well as in *Under the Greenwood Tree*, and she commented: 'I had thought Mellstock and Casterbridge to be further east than this seems to suggest, but it is most interesting to feel that in some way the two earlier stories are also connected in their imaginary worlds.' Lucy did not read the serial version of *A Pair of Blue Eyes*, or she might also have noticed, since her mind was already on such things, that in *Tinsley's Magazine* Smith's uncle lived near Exeter rather than Casterbridge. The fact that Hardy made this change to Casterbridge in revising proof for the first edition, when at the same time he was writing Casterbridge into the early manuscript leaves of *Far From the Madding Crowd*, implies a deliberate motive, and there is justification for speaking of a first conscious gesture towards the embryonic Wessex.

Since substantial chunks of the novel are borrowed or adapted from *The Poor Man and the Lady*, it is scarcely surprising that *A Pair of Blue Eyes* should derive much of its character from the vein in Hardy that led him to write the unpublished novel. In particular he revisits ideas about the essential differences between rural and metropolitan life, and there is also a perpetual undertone, sometimes foregrounding itself, of class distinction and class-hostility. Lucy commented particularly on the second of these, noting the novel's community in spirit in this respect with *Desperate Remedies*. She only quoted, though, the most flagrant piece of bigotry, which is in the vicar Mr Swancourt's voice, after he has learned that Stephen Smith, whom he had welcomed into his house, is the son of a mason in his parish:

> 'What the deuce could I be thinking of! He, a villager's son; and we, Swancourts. We have been coming to nothing for centuries, and now I believe we have got there. <u>What</u> shall I next invite here, I wonder!...It is not enough that I have been deluded and <u>disgraced</u> by having him here, – the son of one of <u>my</u> village peasants – but now I am to make him my son-in-law! Heavens above us, are you mad, Elfride?' (vI cIX)

The underlinings are Lucy's, made without further comment.

Lucy came to think about the contrasts between London and country life through this speech of Elfride:

> there are beautiful women where you live...And you will look at them, not caring at first, and then you will look and be interested, and after a while you will think, 'Ah, they know all about city life, and assemblies, and coteries, and the manners of the titled, and poor little Elfie, with all the fuss that's made about her having me, doesn't know about anything but a little house and a few cliffs and a space of sea, far away.' (vI cX)

'To me Elfride', she wrote, 'sounds rather childish, but she's supposed to be older than I am. But then, I remember, Mr Hardy wrote at the beginning of the novel: "She had lived all her life in retirement...and at the age of nineteen or twenty she was no further on in social consciousness than an urban young lady of fifteen" (vI cI). This made me think of Bathsheba in the first episode of "Far From the Madding Crowd":

> From the contours of her figure in its upper part, she must have had a beautiful neck and shoulders, but since her infancy nobody had ever seen them. Had she been put into a low dress, she would have run and thrust her head into a bush. Yet she was not a shy girl by any means; it was

merely her instinct to draw the line dividing the seen from the unseen higher than they do it in towns. (vI cIII)

And then there is that lovely piece about Keeper Day's silences in "Under the Greenwood Tree":

'You might live wi' that man, my sonnies, a hundred years, and never know there was anything in him.'
'Ay; one o' these up-country London ink-bottle fellers would call Geoffrey a fool.' (2.v)

There is quite a lot of this sort of thing really in "A Pair of Blue Eyes", like Stephen looking as if he could never get on in London, or the idea (one that would never have occurred to me) that workmen specialise in London, but have to be able to turn their hands to anything in the country; and of course there is more in this month's "Cornhill".'

There are also present in *A Pair of Blue Eyes* the earliest notes of a couple of the social themes of Wessex. For the first time the narrator pays some analytical attention to the perceptions of the agricultural labourer:

To those hardy weather-beaten individuals who pass the greater part of their days and nights out-of-doors, Nature seems to have moods in other than a poetical sense: moods literally and really – predilections for certain deeds at certain times, without any apparent law to govern or season to account for them. They read her as a person with a curious temper. (vII cIX)

The voice in this passage, however, is as yet that of an interpreter mediating between those who get soaked and baked at the hands of nature and those happy ones who only read about such misadventures. There are also the first hints of landlordism:

The only lights apparent on earth were some spots of dull red, glowing here and there upon the distant hills, which ... were smouldering fires for the consumption of peat and gorse-roots, where the common was being broken up for agricultural purposes. (vI chII)

To the profit of the local landowner and the loss of grazing and turbary for the peasant, though no such comment is made by Hardy's narrator.

It is possible that when Hardy deliberately linked three novels together through Casterbridge, as noted above, he already had in mind the further unifying detail of an imaginary county; perhaps he was just waiting for the right name. It should at any rate not be surprising that it was in the serialization of *Far From the Madding Crowd* that Hardy first used the word Wessex, though it came late in the novel, in the penultimate episode, almost slipped in edgeways.

At some time in June or July of 1874 Hardy decided to describe Greenhill Fair as 'the Nijnii Novgorod of Wessex' (vII cXX).[13] It is ironic, or at any rate surprising, that the first mention of a nineteenth-century Wessex should be in association with a Russian fair-city that would by itself have seemed exotic to metropolitan readers in the 1870s. Lucy's response was 'Where is Nijnii Novgorod? When was Wessex?' And then 'Why did Mr Hardy introduce Wessex here? Is that where the novel is taking place? But it isn't a historical novel like Sir Walter Scott's.' Then she read a little later: 'The great mass of sheep in the fair consisted of South Downs and the old Wessex horned breeds,' and after writing it out, she added 'Perhaps this is the answer, perhaps there are sheep in that part of the country that have been called Wessex sheep since whenever Wessex existed.' So, in a sense she missed the importance of the big moment, but then, no one who wrote about the novel in public remarked on the word at all.

Hardy never explained why he chose Wessex rather than any other name. It is possible, however, to speculate that the close relationship he had already forged between his fiction and observable reality precluded an invented name, and that eventually, after some casting about, he recalled the enthusiasm of the poet and teacher William Barnes, whom he had known as a young man in Dorchester, for Saxon Wessex as the source of the Dorset dialect. It is certain, though, despite his assertion in the 1895 preface to *Far From the Madding Crowd*, that he had at this stage no concept of his Wessex as a region anywhere near as extensive as that covered by the early medieval kingdom.

Lucy, it will be remembered, was reading *Under the Greenwood Tree* at the same time as the serialization of *Far From the Madding Crowd*, and she began to make the connections between the two that Hardy must have wondered if his best readers would make. By the time she had finished she had noted six details the two stories had in common, one character and five places: Keeper Day, Casterbridge, Mellstock, Yalbury Wood, Budmouth and the Three Choughs Inn at Casterbridge. Reviewing what she had found, she wrote: 'It is in the first chapter of "Far From the Madding Crowd" that Gabriel Oak's farm is placed in connection with the Casterbridge of "Under the Greenwood Tree": "The field he was in this morning sloped to a ridge called Norcombe Hill. Through a spur of this hill ran the highway from Norcombe to Casterbridge, sunk in a deep cutting." And then when his sheep are killed he goes to the hiring fair there. Budmouth is fourteen miles from Lewgate and fifteen from Weatherbury. Weatherbury isn't far from Casterbridge, and can't be very far from Mellstock or Lewgate, because Yalbury Wood is near to both, and Joseph Poorgrass of "Far From the Madding Crowd" has been drinking metheglin with Keeper Day who lives there in "Under the Greenwood Tree". But I can't work out how they all relate to each other. It is as if

Mr Hardy isn't quite sure if he wants to bring the worlds of the two stories together or not. I mean, for example, in "Under the Greenwood Tree" Keeper Day lives "in the depths of Yalbury Wood", which is "intersected by a lane at a place not far from the house" (II.vi) while the Yalbury Wood of "Far From the Madding Crowd" is traversed by a turnpike road. I suppose it might be a very large wood, but I don't get the impression that it is from either novel.'

Lucy's uncertainties were not shared by at least one equally acute and sensitive reader of *Far From the Madding Crowd*, and though he has left no record of his initial response to any of these novels, there is no doubt that Kegan Paul, Dorset man, clergyman, essayist and publisher, recognized some of the places Hardy described, and knew well the kind of people he based his characters on. In 1874 Paul (then forty six) resigned the living of Sturminster Marshall in Dorset, after being vicar there for twelve years, and two years later wrote the article that blew Wessex wide open (see below pp. 23–4). Let me hypothesize his response to Hardy's topography in *Far From the Madding Crowd*.

Paul made the connection between Hardy's Weatherbury and Weatherbury Castle, an earthwork on a hill just outside Milborne St Andrew and some three and a half miles north-east of Puddletown.[14] At first he thought Hardy must have had Milborne in mind, but as details accumulated he began, tentatively, to favour the latter as source; amongst them was a vivid memory of the old Buck's Head Inn near Yellowham Wood. Paul was quite clear, though, that Casterbridge was a version of Dorchester, and he also saw that for some reason Hardy had reversed the town when sending Fanny Robin to the workhouse there. Here is a small example:

> 'One mile more,' the woman murmured. 'No; less,' she added, after a pause. 'The mile is to the Town Hall, and my resting-place is on this side Casterbridge. Three-quarters of a mile, and there I am!' (vII cX)

The Workhouse in Dorchester, however, was on the other, western side of the town from Puddletown or Milborne, out on Damer's Road towards Bridport. When Joseph Poorgrass comes to collect Fanny's body from the same place, Hardy gives the name of the church that would be heard if the workhouse were at the east end of the town – St George's Church in Fordington. To complicate matters still further Hardy also reverses the direction that a cart would take from Dorchester to Puddletown:

> The afternoon drew on apace, and, looking to the left towards the sea as he walked beside the horse, Poorgrass saw strange clouds and scrolls of mist rolling over the high hills which girt the landscape in that quarter. (vII cXII)

Paul could not know that in the manuscript of the novel, Hardy originally wrote 'to the right', and then replaced it with 'to the left'.

Weatherbury is not described in any detail, just a few of the significant buildings, the church, the malthouse, and Bathsheba's farm on the edge (the original of which, as Hardy's 1912 preface explains, was not in any case in Puddletown itself), but Hardy amused himself and puzzled Paul by adding an ironic element of disguise when he described the malthouse:

> In the ashpit was a heap of potatoes roasting, and a boiling pipkin of charred bread, called 'coffee,' for the benefit of whomsoever should call, for Warren's was a sort of village clubhouse, there being no inn in the place. (vI cXV)

In fact there were five pubs in Puddletown, and Paul knew the village's reputation for heavy drinking.

The old maltster relates, during one of the sessions in his malthouse, the story of his working life. At one place he was only hired for eleven months at a time, to keep him from being a charge on the parish if he were disabled – a characteristic piece of employer chicanery, but it was the name of another of the places he worked at that prompted a comment from Lucy: 'I'm really surprised. No-one could imagine Snoodly-under-Drool to be a real name. It's the kind of name I'd expect to find in novels that treat country life farcically, or speak contemptuously of the countryside, and "Far From the Madding Crowd" certainly does neither.'

As we have seen, Lucy also recognized that both *Under the Greenwood Tree* and *Far From the Madding Crowd* are novels that celebrate the proper way to do things. Proper may mean skilful, may mean appropriate, may mean according to long-established fashion (or all three together), and the later novel abounds with such properly performed tasks, mostly done by Gabriel Oak, with or without assistance. There is, for instance, quite a lot about how to be a shepherd. This is the first insignificant example that Lucy noted:

> It came from the direction of a small dark object under the plantation hedge – a shepherd's hut – now presenting an outline to which an uninitiated person might have been puzzled to attach either meaning or use. (vI cII)

She accepted that she was 'an uninitiated person', as were all her friends, but she couldn't quite make up her mind whether she enjoyed being lectured as the narrator went on to do. Passages of overt instruction were rare, she admitted, and the knowledge imparted essential for a full immersion in the alien rural world of the novelist's characters. She noted also the pattern shaped by the novel: the shepherd's year begins with lambing, which we see in two parts, separated by the disaster to Oak's own flock, and from two aspects, the master's and the servant's (Gabriel is not allowed the skins of the dead lambs by the farmer Bathsheba Everdene); then there is the attempt to make a ewe take another's lamb, then washing, shearing, curing bloated sheep and finally selling them at a sheep fair.

Drawing back a little, the same, she saw, was true of the farming year as a whole; interspersed between the sheep affairs are the other activities on a mixed farm of Bathsheba's sort – haymaking, harvesting various cereals, hiving bees, wringing apples for cider – all ending at Christmas. This was the same seasonal cycle as had informed *Under the Greenwood Tree*.

But what struck Lucy most, what seemed to her, reflecting on all four of Hardy's novels, a keynote of a further stage of rural intensity in his last, was the comparison of the great barn with the church and the castle.

> One could say about this barn, what could hardly be said of either the church or the castle, akin to it in age and style, that the purpose which had dictated its original erection was the same with that to which it was still applied. Unlike and superior to either of those two typical remnants of mediaevalism, the old barn embodied practices which had suffered no mutilation at the hands of time. Here at least the spirit of the builders then was at one with the spirit of the beholder now. (vI cXXII)

After inscribing the paragraph of which this is a fragment, Lucy noted: 'It is a strikingly effective and thought-provoking description, but when Mr Hardy writes: "Here at least the spirit of the ancient builders was at one with the spirit of the modern beholder" I must confess I am somewhat concerned at his implied view of the state of Christianity in this country – or at least in his country.' Then she continued, quoting from the same passage:

> This picture of to-day in its frame of four hundred years ago did not produce that marked contrast between ancient and modern which is implied by the contrast of date. In comparison with cities, Weatherbury was immutable. . . . In these nooks the busy outsider's ancient times are only old, his old times are still new; his present is futurity.

'Here', Lucy wrote, 'is a statement of permanence, or of relative permanence, to set alongside the story of enforced change that is told in "Under the Greenwood Tree"; and it contrasts too that dialogue between the old maltster and Gabriel Oak about how things are different in Norcombe. I think perhaps Mr Hardy wants me to smile at the maltster's responding to such small changes as the death of an apple tree with "how the face of nations alter", but in the context of such paragraphs as I have just copied out, the phrase seems more consonant not just with his feelings, but with a reality of a different kind from that which I am used to in London. Though perhaps the fact that a young woman is farming at all might justify the maltster's last comment.

'And – I see how much I am learning – I am struck by the idea of telling time without a clock or a watch like Gabriel, or the labourers at Endelstow.

It seems too that the shoemaker in *Under the Greenwood Tree* who claimed that he could recognize people by their feet was only saying what most countrymen would affirm, that the local craftsman has special knowledge and a special way of doing things.

'Bathsheba and Fancy Day have quite a lot in common – after all Bathsheba was educated to be a school-teacher, and so it is not surprising that she brings a new taste to Weatherbury, what the maltster calls her "strange doings". She tells Liddy that "Samplers are out of date – horribly countrified". But at the same time she has been horribly countrified herself; I remember that in the beginning of the novel Mr Hardy says if she had been put into a low dress "she would have run and thrust her head into a bush." She seems to have become a deal more sophisticated in a very short space of time without my particularly noticing the cause.'

One of the reviews of *Far From the Madding Crowd*, perhaps the most thoughtful, is by R H Hutton in the *Spectator*. He identifies Hardy's region for the first time as 'Dorsetshire probably' and says that Hardy has 'mastered' the landscapes and work of the county, to the degree that the reader 'carries away new images, and as it were, new experience, taken from the life of a region before almost unknown'.

Hutton had almost certainly learned that Dorset was Hardy's county from his brother John, who had published reviews himself in the *Spectator* of Hardy's first novels, and had written to Hardy in 1873 what is the earliest surviving enquiry after the reality behind the fiction:

> By the bye, will you do me the great favour of telling me what places Endelstow, Stranton, St Kirr's &c really are – and also Mellstock & Lewgate? We know something of North Devon & Tavistock & I have been at Taunton – & these neighbourhoods seem to be the scenes of your tales & yet I do not exactly recognize any real places that I know. I picture places to myself very vividly & get disappointed afterwards when I find I have got wrong – I am rather great in locality & the faculty has its disadvantages – I always want a *map* as a frontispiece to a good novel. (DCM H3531 3 July)

Hardy's reply does not survive, but it is likely that he gave away his secrets.[15]

His brother's review goes on, however, to raise an issue which came to be canvassed by critics throughout Hardy's career:

> the reader who has any general acquaintance with the civilisation of the Wiltshire or Dorsetshire labourer, with his average wages, and his average intelligence, will be disposed to say at once that a more incredible picture than that of the group of farm-labourers as a whole which Mr Hardy has given us can hardly be conceived...

The review is at once highly intelligent and very revealing. Hutton expresses with spirit and even passion the attitudes of the highly educated urban elite. Though he might have denied it, it is his instinctive assumption that every agricultural labourer is a clod, and he has to make a perceptible effort of reason to acknowledge that some few at least of the workfolk in the country, or even the county, must be as Hardy displays them. Hutton warns armchair explorers of this *terra incognita* that, should they venture themselves amongst the natives, they would not be so finely entertained as they are by Hardy's invention, or indeed entertained at all.[16]

Hardy's next novel, *The Hand of Ethelberta*, prompted similar attacks. The first notice of Hardy's work to mention Wessex was that in the *Athenaeum*; after quoting part of the dialect-dialogue between an ostler and a milkman at the opening of the novel, the reviewer comments that it: 'might be the language of an ostler in Shakespeare, but would it be heard nowadays at a "Wessex" inn?... It is said that careful examination failed to detect 200 words in the vocabulary of a certain village in Cambridgeshire; is it possible that Somerset and Dorset are so much more eloquent?' (15 April 1876). The last sentence demonstrates the failure of the middle-class investigator to penetrate the obdurate surface of rural culture, an almost inevitable condition of things, noted by Hardy some years later in 'The Dorsetshire Labourer', and also in an article published in the *Examiner* of 15 July 1876, and headed 'The Wessex Labourer':

> Very few, indeed, outside his own rank attain to intimacy with the English labourer; and in Dorset, where the peasant retains a strongly-marked individuality... the labourer and squire feel towards each other as if they were of different races.... It is to this population that Mr Hardy introduces us, with rare insight...

The piece was written by Kegan Paul, and it also contains a thorough defence against the accusation that Hardy's peasants are altogether too eloquent, intelligent and witty to stand as a reasonable likeness of any real peasant that ever existed. He too quotes from the ostler–milkman dialogue, and comments: 'the Wessex man knows that these passages have in them the real ring, all equally true to life and scenery.... the Dorset labourer is... no fool in his own line, but rather very shrewd, racy and wise, full of practical knowledge of all natural things, and of considerable powers of thought.'

So Lucy, reading these reviews, and confronted with such contradictory views, presented to her anonymously as was the custom, had to make up her own mind whether Hardy was fantasizing a whole population, or whether he was essentially reflecting a reality to which he had special access. Thus she was already confronting the dilemma of Wessex: is it make-believe, or is it real, or is it something in-between? In the end she felt that the pleasure she got from the conversation of these people meant that it didn't altogether matter whether their counterparts could be found in Dorset; but the fact that the *Examiner* article was the first to make explicit for her connections between the places in the novels and places in Dorset predisposed her in the author's favour as someone who really knew what he was talking about.

In his topographical revelations Paul was mostly accurate:

> 'The Hand of Ethelberta,' again, is full of Dorset coast scenery, all recognisable, though distance between places is now and then, for artistic purposes, misstated. But Swanage, Corfe Castle, Bournemouth, Lulworth with its cove and castle, are all there...'[17]

The part about distances being altered 'for artistic purposes' was comforting to Lucy, whose efforts to work out the environments of *Desperate Remedies* and *Under the Greenwood Tree* had cost such headaches. She was, however, provoked to wonder what particular artistic purposes might be served by such disguise: 'If a reader recognises the places but the distances are wrong, then the result is confusion, isn't it? And if the reader doesn't recognise the places, then the specific distances are no issue. And if, like me, the reader, not recognising the places, tries to work out the interrelationship of the places, and can't because the distances are not only wrong but inconsistently wrong, then the result is worse confusion. Where is the art in that?'

It seems certain that Kegan Paul wrote without Hardy's authority or knowledge to inform Lucy and anyone else who read the piece; but if so, then how did Hardy respond? Was he irritated or pleased? Did he see it as good publicity or an unwarranted stripping of veils he had intentionally placed? He was still playing with the relationship between his own experiences of place and their fictional representation or disguise; and yet *The Hand of Ethelberta* shows that his imagination was beginning to consolidate disparate elements into a larger environment with what he may have begun to think of as a larger purpose.[18]

At any rate, Hardy and details of Dorset were definitively brought together in public for the first time in Paul's article. It was unsurprising that the occasion for the essay was the publication of the much abused but recently rehabilitated *The Hand of Ethelberta*, for it is in this novel, and in this novel alone of Hardy's first nine, that Wessex as a geographical space is made prominent. It is present from the first sentence: 'The young Mrs. Petherwin stepped from the door of an old though popular inn in a Wessex town to take a country walk.'

Lucy wrote excitedly on reading it: 'I *knew* Wessex was going to be important; it's a new county of England, better than Barsetshire I think, or Loamshire and Stonyshire because it tells you where it is, down in the south-west somewhere, even if you didn't know earlier. But then it isn't necessarily just one county, or at least I don't think it is. Or was. I really shall have to find out.' She noted other occurrences of the word scattered through the novel, and tried to decide exactly what kind of space Wessex was – province? district? county? The form of the address of Ethelberta's family – 'Arrowthorne Lodge, Wessex' – implied a county she thought, but other allusions were unclear: a local newspaper is called the 'Wessex Reflector' (IX), and when Ethelberta Petherwin is discussing musical settings of her poems with acquaintances in London she says: 'It is one which reached me by post only this morning from a place in Wessex, and is written by an unheard-of man who lives somewhere down there...' (X) This is followed by: 'A deaf gentleman...declared...that Wessex was in his judgement as well as hers a very picturesque part of England.'

She discovered that the historical Wessex was a region of some considerable extent; but it did not seem to her that the district encompassed in the novel ranged so wide. There were new place names, Anglebury, Sandbourne, Knollsea, and even before the *Examiner* piece she had worked out that Hardy had probably intended Knollsea to be Swanage, which gave her a clue to the identities of the other places. Melchester, an indeterminate location in *Far From the Madding Crowd*, seemed to her to have become clearly Salisbury; but there was still a lot it was impossible to work out.

Wessex also had an important role to play in the central theme of the novel. In *Far From the Madding Crowd* there had been, despite the general harmoniousness between farmer and workforce, hints of the class hostilities that underlie Hardy's earliest thinking about human relations in fiction, and which have been foregrounded in much modern writing about him. Andrew Randle the stammering farmhand had been turned away from his last place because he said 'his soul was his own, and other iniquities, to the squire'. (X) There is a bitterness too that lies behind Mark Clark's measure of certainty that having a woman to run their farm will result in disaster: 'All will be ruined and ourselves too, or there's no meat in gentlemen's houses!' (XV) This aspect of the relations between the classes was restrained below the surface of narratives that had proved acceptable to the majority of novel readers, but he chose to let it flow in *The Hand of Ethelberta*. The novel illuminates what Lucy later called 'Mr Hardy's experience of not being a gentleman', and one of the ways it does this is by contrasting life in London society with life in Wessex, as in:

'Oh, you are here, Picotee? I am glad to see you,' said the mistress of the house, quietly.

This was altogether to Picotee's surprise, for she had expected a round rating at least, in her freshness hardly being aware that this reserve of feeling was an acquired habit of Ethelberta's, and that civility stood in town for as much vexation as a tantrum represented in Wessex. (XX)

Or when one time Christopher leaves the London house he kisses Ethelberta on the cheek, she demands that he kiss Picotee too:

> 'She is my sister, and I am yours.'
>
> It seemed all right and natural to their respective moods and the tone of the moment that free old Wessex manners should prevail, and Christopher stooped and dropped upon Picotee's cheek likewise such a farewell kiss as he had imprinted on Ethelberta's. (XXVI)

The Hand of Ethelberta is nowadays often thought of as a wholly managed self-conscious satire on the manners and practices of Society, that reveals more fully than any other novel the class-antagonism that drives all of Hardy's writing; there is much to support such a view, and if I had to choose one detail that effectively uses an element of Wessex life to attack a member of Society, it would be the description of the old Lord Mountclere courting Ethelberta, 'the viscount busying himself round and round her person like the head scraper at a pig-killing' (XXXIII) – a deliberately crude and cruel description, and one that gains extra resonance for Hardy's modern readers by association with the pig-killing episode in *Jude the Obscure*. But there are also (as usual) details that leave the reader in uncertainty about Hardy's position. Ethelberta's brother Sol, as we might expect, attacks her marriage to Mountclere because she has betrayed her class:

> 'Berta, you have worked to false lines. A creeping up among the useless lumber of our nation that'll be the first to burn if there comes a flare. I never see such a deserter of your own lot as you be! But you were always like it, Berta, and I'm ashamed of ye. More than that, a good woman never marries twice.' (XLVIII)

The deeply conventional morality of the last sentence suggests that Hardy understands that, though London Society is flawed, the Wessex labourer too has prejudices that might be held to undermine any simple argument about class in the novel.[19]

2
Variations on the Original Theme

In June 1876 the Hardys took a house in Sturminster Newton, where they stayed while Hardy was working on his next novel, *The Return of the Native*. For Hardy, writing in retrospect in his autobiography, this seemed the happiest period of his married life, and the energy caught within the novel perhaps reflects some of his delight. Sturminster was one of the market towns serving the Vale of Blackmore, a district which Hardy knew little of, but which he soon grew to appreciate, and which he made the birthplace of his most intensely envisioned heroine Tess Durbeyfield. For *The Return of the Native*, he kept to the small region of his greatest critical successes so far, *Under the Greenwood Tree* and *Far From the Madding Crowd*, though no one would have known it from reading the first edition of the novel.

From the evidence of Lucy's notes it seems she paid even more attention to the detail of the story than she had in the earlier novels. Hardy could hardly have expected so searching a reader, but the *Examiner* piece on the Wessex labourer had further stimulated her curiosity about the world he was creating. One note was specially triumphant. Quoting Timothy Fairway on the height of Clym Yeobright's now-dead maternal uncles: 'Longer coffins were never made in the whole county of Wessex', she wrote: 'So Wessex *is* a single county. I *thought* it was from *The Hand of Ethelberta*, but it was hard to tell and what I found out about the Saxon Wessex suggested a bigger region so long ago.'

From the first, her interest in place had encouraged her to observe what has not always been noticed by later readers, that Hardy had two ways of seeing Egdon Heath, and that if they were not incompatible, they did keep a reader in uncertainty. The opening chapter of the novel has been thoroughly discussed over the last hundred and twenty years, but, because it was quite unlike anything that Hardy had yet written, just a little of Lucy's response is valuable:

Goodness! I had no idea Mr Hardy thought about places like that. It is quite alive, and almost human; no, it *is* human, only it is too huge; and when he writes about a real human reclining 'on a stump of thorn in the central valley of Egdon' I feel quite uncomfortable, though I'm not sure why. It is a real landscape, with a history – he quotes someone called Leland and the Doomsday Book – but at the same time it is imaginary, or at least I should say, imagined, perhaps. It is like the spirit of man in a nightmarish way, and it has superhuman powers over time and the weather, it has loves (the storm) and enemies (civilisation). How can anyone live in such a place? It would be quite exciting I should think.

Later on though, and particularly when she thought about the map at the front of the first volume of the first edition, she confessed herself confused, for Egdon, she recognized, was not only at once a metaphorical landscape and a titanic and untameable stretch of land, but also a mappable piece of countryside, perhaps six miles by four, with houses on it and villages at its edge, paths and hills and valleys and ponds, furze and heather and animals and insects and birds, thoroughly known and understood, and not at all exciting. 'What', she asked herself, 'is a person to think?' And after some days of thinking, she came to the conclusion that Hardy wanted her to stretch her mind, to see that it was all these, depending on who was experiencing it, and in what frame of mind. For the narrator at the beginning, and for Eustacia often it was one thing; for Clym it was another, for Thomasin, and the narrator in a different mood, yet another. It was the account of Thomasin's response to the storm at the end of the novel that opened her eyes to this:

> To her there were not, as to Eustacia, demons in the air, and malice in every bush and bough. The drops which lashed her face were not scorpions, but prosy rain; Egdon in the mass was no monster whatever, but impersonal open ground. Her fears of the place were rational, her dislikes of its worst moods reasonable. At this time it was in her view a windy, wet place, in which a person might experience much discomfort, lose the path without care, and possibly catch cold. (V.viii)

And then she lists for herself many other examples of the different ways that the heath is seen by different characters, amongst which is this demonstration of the relationship between Eustacia and the Egdon of her mind: 'It is wonderful that Mr Hardy could understand that Eustacia's hair is Egdon too; he writes that to see it "was to fancy that a whole winter did not contain darkness enough to form its shadow. It closed over her forehead like nightfall extinguishing the western glow." (I.vii) This is just the way that Egdon extinguishes the moonlight: "The moon had now waxed bright and silvery, but the swarthy heath was proof against such illumination, and there was to be observed the striking scene of a dark, rayless tract of country, under an atmosphere charged from its zenith to its extremities with whitest light."

(IV.iii)' Landscape, she was beginning to be shown by Hardy, was not, as she had always assumed, an objective reality; in Wessex such truths are shown more clearly than in the ordinary world. But still, Hardy's map bothered her by its factual, limiting juxtaposition to the opening chapter of the novel, and she began to investigate it in relation to the text.

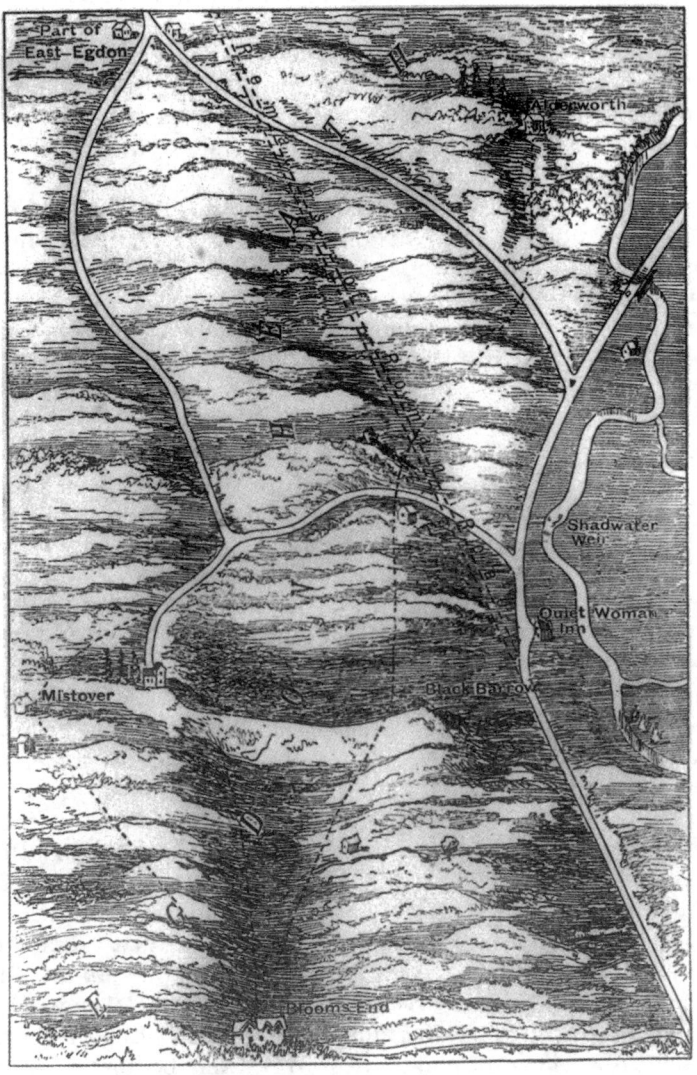

SKETCH MAP OF THE SCENE OF THE STORY.

The first details she noted were absences: absence of a scale and of any indication where north might be. 'I suppose north is at the top', she wrote, 'and I suppose there is no scale because Mr Hardy didn't want to diminish the heath more than was inevitable by having a map in the first place. But then why have the map at all? I suppose it does help with understanding the relationships of the places on the heath, but if you take the details in the text, the map doesn't satisfy all of them, indeed I think no map could, just as with the places in his other novels. It has always been puzzling to me that Mr Hardy should be so precise in his individual descriptions and distances and directions, but when you try to bring them all together, some of them aren't reconcilable; and this map makes the puzzle more acute. I wondered too, at first, why Southerton and Budmouth and Flychett weren't on the map, but then saw that nothing actually happened in the novel in those places – events at them were just talked about; so they aren't part of the "scene" of the story. Though I should like to be sure that Budmouth is Weymouth, because it's in "Under the Greenwood Tree" and "Far From the Madding Crowd" too.'[1]

Let me interrupt Lucy here to mention a detail or two that she could not know. In the original inscription of the early leaves of the manuscript Hardy called the seaside town Cresmouth, which name only became the more familiar Budmouth in revision. At first, then, there was to have been virtually no connection at all between this and earlier novels, and at some time, probably after the novel had been gently turned aside by *Blackwood's Magazine*, there was a tussle within Hardy's creative consciousness between his early conception of the heath and its dwellers as totally isolated, and the insistent sense that was growing in him that his work, all his work, bore just that degree of relationship to the reality about him as Wessex signified, and that it was important to remind the reader that each of his novels came from the same source. The latter argument won, and Cresmouth became Budmouth.[2]

The town of Southerton is universally the town of resort for the heath-folk on occasions of business and pleasure, but of Southerton's location in relation to anywhere else there is no hint. No directions, no distances and no details of description assist the curious in guessing at an original for it; it appears nowhere else in Hardy's work, and it is reasonable to suggest that the town is one of the very few significant places in Hardy's fiction that is purely imaginary.

In tracking the references to Wessex, Lucy noticed that nothing on the heath is explicitly identified as being a part of Wessex; we learn that Grandfer Cantle belonged to the South Wessex Militia during the Napoleonic Wars, and that people in Wessex towns and villages neighbouring the heath were sympathetic to Clym at the end of the novel. 'I can't be sure whether this is coincidental or not, but if not, then perhaps Mr Hardy is saying that here are more different ways to see the heath; it is a place in Wessex, but also it is separate from Wessex. Neighbouring farmers certainly think of Egdon as outlandish, quite untouched by modern agriculture, calling it "an obsolete thing", and bestowing on it "nothing better than a frown". (III.ii) Or there are the reddlemen: they are disappearing from Wessex because of the railways it seems. But there are on railways on Egdon, and things survive there, untouched, like the mumming:

> A traditional pastime is to be distinguished from a mere revival in no more striking feature than in this, that while in the revival all is excitement and fervour, the survival is carried on with a stolidity and absence of stir which sets one wondering why a thing that is done so perfunctorily should be kept up at all. (II.iv)

I know exactly what Mr Hardy means, it's like some of our social rituals here, things that have always been done, and go on being done, though no one seems very enthusiastic about them, because to do without them would be unthinkable. For some people going to church is like that, but Egdon is quite different in that too: "The day was Sunday; but as going to church, except to be married or buried, was phenomenal at Egdon, this made little difference" (I.x). In another bit about things surviving (it's the maypole this time), Mr Hardy says the people on Egdon are really not Christian at heart: "the impulses of all such outlandish hamlets are pagan still" (VI.i). This sounds very good, until you think of Christian Cantle or Timothy Fairway, who don't seem pagan at all. The ordinary Guy Fawkes bonfire was described as a Promethian rebelliousness against winter, or something like that, and certainly the gaiety there was very energetic. Two views again, the ordinary day-to-day characters we see, and the imaginative mind's way of talking about them.'

'It's interesting, isn't it: Mr Hardy invents this place Wessex, it seems, only to use it as a contrast to something else. In "The Hand of Ethelberta" it was London and London people, in "The Return of the Native" it is this boundless wilderness and pagan society within which the story goes on, looking out to Wessex from time to time, but not really part of it.'

And I might add with the benefit of hindsight that in *The Trumpet-Major* Wessex, as the site of the unrecorded past, is contrasted with England as the site of history, that in *A Laodicean* Hardy appears to want to set aside Wessex altogether, but can't quite manage it, and that in *Two on a Tower* the only mention of the county is in the first sentence of the novel – and so conclude that Hardy for ten years or so was satisfied with the place as he had established it in *The Hand of Ethelberta*, and saw it as not much more than a useful fiction which he could make use of when it suited him.

Towards the end of her notes, Lucy speculates briefly on what she saw as another innovation in Hardy's work as she had read it. She begins by transcribing a longish passage that begins with a comment about Clym:

that he and his had been sarcastically and pitilessly handled in having such irons thrust into their souls he did not maintain long.... Human beings, in their generous endeavour to construct a hypothesis that shall not degrade a First Cause, have always hesitated to conceive a dominant power of lower moral quality than their own... (VI.i)[3]

'I can't remember that Mr Hardy has anywhere before this novel been interested in talking about God in this way, though of course he doesn't call it God, but "a First Cause", which I suppose is in keeping with the pagan tone that surfaces here and there in the book. He means, though, a power that makes things happen to us. I can't forget the way that chapter about Eustacia begins:

had she handled the distaff, the spindle, and the shears at her own free will, few in the world would have noticed the change of government. There would have been the same inequality of lot, the same heaping up of favours here, of contumely there, the same generosity before justice, the same perpetual dilemmas, the same captious alternation of caresses and blows as we endure now. (I.vii)[4]

I can't be sure whether he really believes or not that the Greek fates do govern the world, though. He certainly implies that Clym was foolish, or at least in error, in rejecting the idea that sarcasm and pitilessness are appropriate to a First Cause that works in our world – Clym and the rest of us Christians too. But on the other hand he surely doesn't approve of Eustacia's continual blaming of some Colossal Indistinct Prince of the World for her misery, when he makes it clear that so much of it, except her being on the heath in the first place, is her own selfish fault; once he even says that Destiny is a creation of her own mind.[5] No one else tries to shift the responsibility like this from their own shoulders, do they? But in a way I see his point, because if you think that God does act benevolently in the world, because He is a God of love and sacrifice, then it is not such a big step to imagine God to be like the Old Testament Jehovah, and you might be half-way to thinking of Him as an oppressor. I have never thought of this before. It is rather disturbing. I thought it was just chance that Clym's letter didn't arrive in time to stop Eustacia going out to Damon, but perhaps it *was* the First Cause. And now I come to think of it, chance might just be another name for the First Cause.'[6]

In her unprofessional but acute way, Lucy has understood that *The Return of the Native* is the novel in which Hardy first considers seriously and systematically human perceptions of the notion of fate or destiny – another prominent strand in the completed web of Wessex.[7]

One final comment. It has been fascinating to watch how, through the progress of Hardy's first six novels, his awareness has become sharper of the inextricable interrelationship of humans and their environment. Wessex, which is beginning in *The Return of the Native* to become not just a word for a semi-fictional geographic space, but a social and cultural construct, is a place where such perceptions inform, through the narrative structure, the fabric of life. In this respect, the first chapter, in which a stretch of terrain is offered as a metaphor for the current, and future, human condition, even while remaining aloof from individual human activity and concern, establishes a tone which the remainder of the novel sustains. One could quote thirty or forty examples to illustrate this perception, but as it becomes in later novels more and more completely an integral part of his writing, such lists would soon become redundant; however, for the sake of clarity, here are a few examples from the second and third chapters. This is Diggory Venn: 'His eye, which glared so strangely through his stain, was in itself attractive – keen as that of a bird of prey, and blue as autumn mist.' This is (we discover) Eustacia Vye: her figure 'descended on the right side of the barrow, with the glide of a water-drop down a bud, and then vanished'. The men and boys who displace her from the top of Blackbarrow: 'had marched in trail, like a travelling flock of sheep; that is to say, the strongest first, the weak and young behind'. It is, to a twenty-first-century reader of Hardy, one of the essential qualities of Wessex that such interpenetration of nature and human is continuous and often sharply illuminating. That many nineteenth-century readers also understood what Hardy was about is suggested by the generally excellent reviews of the novel. As a representative voice, the notice in the *Observer* (5 January 1879) goes at once to the heart of the issue:

> His first chapter introduces us to none of the characters destined to play parts in the story, unless, indeed, the Heath of Egdon may be considered one of the *dramatis personae*. The frontispiece consists of Egdon Heath's portrait in the form of a sketch-map; passage after passage throughout the three volumes is taken up with the description of the wide waste land of what Mr Hardy calls Wessex; and its various conditions, characteristics, and appearances are carefully studied for their own sake.

And the reviewer is also the first to take up Hardy's awareness that parts of the life he embodies in his novels of Wessex are disappearing:

> [The talk of Grandfer Cantle, the conception of Christian Cantle, the portrait of Diggory Venn] all these are full of life, and would be worth attention, if only because they deal with a type of existence fast being improved off the face of the earth by railways, building operations, compulsory education, and other agencies of destructive as well as creative tendency.

When *The Return of the Native* had fairly begun its run in *Belgravia* Hardy and his wife moved again to a suburb of London, and he began serious research in the British library in the period of the Napoleonic Wars in preparation for his next novel.[8] But the first fruit of this close attention to recorded history was a long short story called 'The Distracted Young Preacher'. It was published in the *New Quarterly Magazine* and *Harper's Weekly* in the spring of 1879, and it shares with *The Trumpet-Major* a new departure for Hardy, the presence of Dorset names throughout, save for the central village which is called Nether-Mynton, and which, by geographical relationship with the Dorset places (as well as by the clearly allusive fictional name) is a version of Owermoigne. Thus Swanage, Ringstead, Holworth, Lulworth, East Chaldon, Weymouth and Bere, and the countryside in between, form the landscape of the story. The narrative – a smuggling story of 1835 – is based on historically verifiable fact, but is heightened by a fictitious romance. For Lizzy Newberry, the heroine, smuggling is an essential, but also a traditional occupation: it takes three generations, she implies, to establish such a tradition – 'My father did it, and so did my grandfather' – an important perception in the Wessex system of things.

Lucy found in the story confirmation of her thought that it was also the way of things in Wessex that women were by and large altogether more independent-minded and freer to act as they wished than she had been accustomed to think them in England – a thought, however, not reinforced in *The Trumpet-Major*, first published in 1880. The first sentence of the novel announces the time and place of the narrative:

> In the days of high-waisted and muslin-gowned women, when the vast amount of soldiering going on in the country was a cause of much trembling to the sex, there lived in a village near the Wessex coast two ladies of good report, though unfortunately of limited means.

And yet, *The Trumpet-Major* is unique amongst Hardy's novels in that, like 'The Distracted Young Preacher', with a few exceptions all places are given their English rather than new Wessex names.

'It is true that the village the ladies live in has the fictitious name Overcombe, and that Overcombe does not even approximate to any English village, so far as I can tell; so to that extent we are', Lucy's concluding note ran, 'in Wessex. And there is one link in the novel with the Wessex I have become familiar with, when Festus refers to 'thread-the-needle at Greenhill Fair' (XXVII) – the same place Timothy Fairway's wife used to run for a gown-piece, the place where Wessex started in 'Far From the Madding Crowd'. And when John Loveday referred to 'the bandmaster of the North Wessex Militia' (XI) I remembered that Grandfer Cantle talked of himself as having belonged, at this same period, to the South Wessex Militia in 'The Return of the Native'. But they, and others who live in or near Overcombe, move from Overcombe to Weymouth and Dorchester, Portland and Abbotsbury, Bere and Blandford, Puddletown and Portisham. As you read, you don't notice this going from a place that doesn't exist to one that does as anything strange, but when you stop and think about it, it ought to be quite confusing. It only isn't, I think, because the two kinds of places aren't described any differently – they both seem just as real.[9]

'I have worked out two reasons why Mr Hardy might have used both Wessex and English names; the first I thought of because of his contrast of "the unwritten history of England (II)" to which everyone at Overcombe belongs, with "the stream of recorded history...outside which...the general bulk of the human race were content to live on as an unreckoned, unheeded superfluity (XIII)", and recorded history is present quite often in Weymouth and the rest, where it could not be in Budmouth'.

'The other reason is that I think he liked the idea of his invented characters (and his historical characters) moving in and out of reality, he liked the idea of Wessex existing parallel to Dorset (though Dorset is never named). He is able to suggest more clearly in this novel what I have always felt, that Wessex exists in such a close relationship with Dorset and bits of surrounding counties, that people can move from one to the other without anyone noticing the change.'

This is an important insight, in its way, and though Hardy did not write another historical novel, and did not have historical characters present *in propria persona* in any more of his prose, in his poetry and in *The Dynasts* in particular, these issues will be raised again.

Most of the reviews of the novel wrote of the scene being laid in Dorset, but several, influenced perhaps by the first sentence of the novel, or perhaps by the fact that this was Hardy's fourth novel in a row to be set in his version of the Saxon kingdom, spoke rather of Wessex. Most interesting is the review in *John Bull* (13 November 1880), in which Dorset and Wessex mingle freely: '...the action passes entirely on the Dorsetshire coast, not far from Weymouth....the scenes upon the esplanade at Weymouth, where the loyalty and patriotism of the inhabitants of Wessex were so deeply stirred'.[10]

It was at Tooting in 1880 that Hardy began writing his next serial, something of a special commission, since he had been chosen to open the new European edition of *Harper's Monthly Magazine*. That he fell seriously ill after completing no more than three or four serial episodes must thus have been irritating as well as distressingly painful. Nevertheless he continued to write through the illness and the long convalescence. Under such circumstances it is hardly surprising that his achievement in *A Laodicean* did not in any way match his conception.

'Do you think Mr Hardy has got tired of Wessex?' Lucy wrote: 'This novel has only one mention of Wessex, and that is a very casual one, a reference to the "most popular quadrille band in Wessex" (III.vi). Someone keeps some horses at Budmouth, and someone else goes to Casterbridge, so the novel keeps contact with the others, so to speak, but only just. There is almost none of the pattern of life that there was in "The Return of the

Native" – the imagery, the intimate relationship of humans with the rest of nature, the local history, the customs, the story-telling. Instead at Paula's garden party we get "some young people who were so madly devoted to lawn-tennis that they had set about it like day-labourers at the moment of their arrival" (I.xv). It is so strange to think of Mr Hardy and lawn-tennis together; but the comparison of the tennis-players with day-labourers is unmistakably his. And speaking of day-labourers, who had a part even in "The Hand of Ethelberta", they exist here only to show how remote they are from the people in the novel. I marked this when I read it, though I wasn't quite sure why it bothered me:

> It being the month of August, when the pale face of the townsman and stranger is to be seen among the brown skins of remotest uplanders... few of the homeward-bound labourers paused to notice him further than by a momentary turn of the head. They had beheld such gentlemen before... (I.i)

Now that I've finished the story I see that what made me uncomfortable is the unbridgeable gap between Somerset and the passing labourers; perhaps that is true to life, but I feel betrayed by a Wessex that has nothing to do with working people.'

It might by now be possible for a modern reader to think that Lucy has become an original Wessex-enthusiast, creating her own rather romantic urban-middle-class idea of what Hardy was doing, or ought to be doing. Her disgust at another passage from the novel is further symptomatic. She transcribed the whole of it:

> On the neat piers of the neat entrance gate were chiselled the words 'Myrtle Villa.' Genuine roadside respectability sat smiling on every brick of the eligible dwelling.
> 'How are the mighty fallen!' murmured Somerset, as he pulled the bell.
> Perhaps that which impressed him more than the mushroom modernism of Sir William De Stancy's house, was the air of healthful cheerfulness which pervaded it. Somerset was shown in by a neat maidservant in black gown and white apron, a canary singing a welcome from a cage in the shadow of the window, the voices of crowing cocks coming over the chimneys from somewhere behind, and sun and air riddling the house everywhere.
> Being a dwelling of those well-known and popular dimensions which allow the proceedings in the kitchen to be distinctly heard in the parlours, it was so planned that a raking view might be obtained through it from the front door to the end of the back garden. (I.v)

Lucy commented 'How I hate this in Mr Hardy. It has nothing to do with Wessex. I don't want to read about the kind of thing I can see in the suburbs from the train. I understand that it's supposed to contrast with the castle, but that isn't really part of Wessex either.'

Lucy can't pay attention to the passage, fixed as she is on her view of what Hardy might be doing. She cannot hear the really interesting conflict going on in the description: how the almost savage irony in 'genuine roadside respectability' is countered by 'healthful cheerfulness', and the sarcasm of 'those well-known and popular dimensions which allow the proceedings in the kitchen to be distinctly heard in the parlours' is countered by 'sun and air riddling the house everywhere'. The reader ought not to know whether she is expected to despise or admire. Hardy is in control of such ambiguity, as usual; it is his intention to produce in the reader the confusion of opposed but simultaneously held thoughts to echo that felt by Somerset. In a passage of this sort, in a novel of this sort, Hardy is ironizing his own Wessex celebration of old customs and the dying way of life in *The Return of the Native* and *Under the Greenwood Tree*. We might also think in this context of the delapidation of Overcombe Hall through the deliberate neglect of a miser, given us in comic detail in *The Trumpet-Major*.

Lucy's view, though, that the novel really has nothing to do with Wessex, gains support from Hardy himself, in a revision he made to the proofs of the serial. The question: 'You saw the second letter in the morning papers?' appears thus in all published versions. But on the uncorrected proof it read: 'You saw the second letter in the *Wessex Mail*?' (I.xv) This alteration is a small piece of evidence that Hardy was not entirely sure about *A Laodicean*'s Wessex connection with the rest of his work, and it is reasonable to speculate that if someone had drawn his attention to the other passing references to Wessex, he would have discarded them also.[11]

Hardy's next novel, *Two on a Tower*, was written in 1882 for the *Atlantic Monthly*, the only one of his novels to be first published as a serial in America alone. It is not discussed much, and might seem to have more in common with *A Laodicean* than, say, *The Return of the Native*, when the idea of Wessex is in question, especially when it is noticed that Hardy opens it with a statement of Wessex, and finds no need to mention the county again: 'On an early winter afternoon...a gleaming landau came to a pause on the crest of a hill in Wessex' (vI cI). But such a view would not at all meet the case.

The parish of Welland, in which most of the action takes place, hardly has a nucleus of houses worth calling a village, and we experience it as a carefully arranged disposition of a few buildings: the tower on its earthwork and surrounded by trees, the hut built beside it, Mrs Martin's farmhouse, all grouped together on one side of the 'old Melchester Road'; and on the other, within Welland Park, are the great House and the Church.

Lucy wrote out this piece about the hut on the earthwork next to the tower:

> It was a strange place for a bridegroom to perform his toilet in, but, considering the unconventional nature of the marriage, a not inappropriate

one. What events had been enacted in that earthen camp since it was first thrown up, nobody could say; but the primitive simplicity of the young man's preparations accorded well with the prehistoric spot on which they were made. Embedded under his feet were possibly even now rude trinkets that had been worn at bridal ceremonies of the early inhabitants. (vII cIV)

And commented 'I thought of Blackbarrow when I read this. It is good to be reminded of "The Return of the Native", to have this line of continuity drawn again between the present and the remote past; it had been one of the important things about Wessex, and I have missed it recently.' Later in her reading she came upon this:

An hour after that time Louis entered the train at Warborne, and was speedily crossing a country of ragged woodland, which, though intruded on by the plough at places, remained largely intact from prehistoric times, and still abounded with yews of gigantic growth and oaks tufted with mistletoe. (vIII cX)[12]

'The word "prehistoric" made me think back to the earthwork and its tower, and the absence of the plough reminded me of Egdon similarly immune. But here Mr Hardy is drawing a contrast rather than making a connection – the railway and its passengers slice through woodland untouched since the Celts, leaving it untouched still – but there is no railway through Egdon, and more than the landscape remains as it was on the Heath. In "Two on a Tower" we are, but for these reminders, in the modern world.'

Not quite as modern though, she might have added, as Sir William de Stancy's bijou bungalow. She delighted in the first account of Welland House:

This drive...was also the common highway to the lower village, and hence Lady Constantine's residence and park...possessed none of the exclusiveness found in some aristocratic settlements. The parishioners looked upon the park avenue as their natural thoroughfare, particularly for christenings, weddings, and funerals, which passed the squire's mansion with due considerations as to the scenic effect of the same from the manor windows. (vI cIII)

'This is good: connection between the gentry – the aristocracy should I say – and the working people, the big house as a familiar part of the social life of the parish. How different from "A Laodicean".'

Near the beginning of her notes Lucy had expressed surprise at a similar connection: 'This exchange between Lady Viviette Constantine and Amos Fry – I love his self-description: "a homely barley driller, born under the very eavesdroppings of your ladyship's smallest out-buildings" (vI cI) – this exchange only takes place because Amos has some information that Lady Constantine wants, but how many aristocratic ladies would ever have started it? Few, I think, and even fewer would have gone out across a ploughed field on foot in the first place. An independent-minded woman, evidently, as usual in Wessex.

'The way Mr Hardy describes Amos, like a moving piece of Lady Constantine's estate, also brings back "The Return of the Native":

> a moving figure, whom it was as difficult to distinguish from the earth he trod as the caterpillar from its leaf, by reason of the excellent match between his clothes and the clods. He was one of a dying-out generation who retained the principle, nearly unlearnt now, that a man's habiliments should be in harmony with his environment. (vI cI)

In his way he is like the reddlemen, vanishing from Wessex because superseded by fresh fashions brought in by the flashing engines of the railway. And Mr Hardy is sad about it.'

One relationship with an earlier novel Lucy did not remark upon: the working parishioners of Welland are members of the parish choir, but, unlike the Dewys and their associates in *Under the Greenwood Tree*, they are labouring men rather than artisans, and their commentary has a distinct class-bias. They assert, for instance, the value of the old tuning at choir-practice and quite overcome their vicar, who is made to seem ridiculous, inept.

In another example, some of the workfolk come to look at a comet through Swithin's telescope, and in passing bring the novel's astronomical theme into context with their own lives for a moment. But this is not the main emphasis:

> 'And what do this comet mean?' asked Haymoss. 'That some great tumult is going to happen, or that we shall die of a famine?'
> 'Famine – no!' said Nat Chapman. 'That only touches such as we, and God only concerns hisself with the best breeds [**concerns himself wi' the upper classes MS; concerns himself with born gentlemen 1v**]. It isn't to be supposed that a strange fiery lantern like that would be lighted up for folks with ten or a dozen [**with ten MS**] shillings a week and their gristing, and a load o' thorn faggots when we can get 'em.' (vI cXII)

Hardy evidently wanted in revision to suggest that Wessex wages weren't quite as mean as report would have them, but Nat's point remains essentially the same: we are too insignificant to attract attention from divine admonitions. Later on Hezzy Biles says in the face of the possibility of meeting Sir Blount Constantine's ghost: 'I've not defied the figure of starvation these five-and-twenty year, on nine shillings a week, to be afeard of a walking vapour, sweet or savoury' (vII cVIII), which makes one wonder who it is that gets so much as twelve shillings a week.

This is an appropriate moment to pause and consider a possible development in the attitude of Hardy's narrator towards the workfolk into whose mouths he places such dialogue. Lucy makes no comment, but it is quite possible that many readers, urban, middle-class, would be led to relate the superstitious and ignorant savages of Wessex to those in some tropical fragment of the Empire, terror-struck by an eclipse or a comet or some similar phenomenon. The question is, how far was Hardy aware of the possibility of such a comparison, and how far did he encourage it? It might be argued that Hardy knew that Haymoss would be well aware, from frequent iterations in Bible narratives, of what extraordinary celestial manifestations might portend, that many educated people in England might well also feel that comets carry consequences in their train. Both possibilities are there. But there are some moments in the novel that seem less ambiguous.

The description of the approach to Welland House quoted approvingly by Lucy continues with a sentence that she left out:

> Hence the house of Constantine, when going out from its breakfast, had been continually crossed on the doorstep for the last two hundred years by the houses of Hodge and Giles in full cry to dinner. (vI cIII)

It is not just the use of the conventional generic and dismissive Hodge when he might as easily have used Biles or Chapman, specific families of workfolk in the district, but the tone in which they are written of – 'in full cry to dinner' – that marks a remoteness from the whole class, of the sort Lucy had noted in *A Laodicean*. In *Under the Greenwood Tree*, for instance, Hardy had observed the choir with humour, had encouraged the reader to smile at them as well as with them from time to time; but there was never this treatment of the whole class as a foreign species, howling and hustling for its food. Later on there is this: '... a very tolerable, well-wearing May, that the average rustic would willingly compound for in lieu of Mays occasionally fairer, but usually more foul' (vII cX). Could Hardy have had his narrator use the phrase 'the average rustic' in his earlier novels?[13] Not without some attendant irony. The same remote generalization turns up in Hardy's next substantial piece, the novella *The Romantic Adventures of a Milkmaid*:

> Jim ... was a village character, and he had a villager's simplicity; that is, the simplicity which comes from the lack of a complicated experience. But simple by nature he certainly was not. Among the rank and file of rustics he was quite a Talleyrand, or rather had been one, till he lost a good deal of his self-command by falling in love. (VII)

The first two sentences make a point that Hardy has made in his novels since *Under the Greenwood Tree*, and which is one of the principles which had seemed to underlie the developing Wessex; but when he writes 'the rank and file of rustics', he seems to express everything that is alien to Wessex, alien to a desire to understand Wessex. There had always been in Hardy's narrative voice a split between the storyteller who is the intimate and equal of the characters, and the commentator who adopts the position of the detached informed cultivated observer, interpreting foreign rites and customs for us.[14] But this latter presence did not normally treat the objects of his scrutiny with patronage or implied contempt.

It seems thus reasonable at this point to wonder whether Hardy's success in mediating an unfamiliar culture to the average upper-middle-class urban novel-reader by imagining what such a reader needed to understand, has not led him on occasion unconsciously to adopt that point of view himself.[15]

A primary source of material relevant to this issue is the paper that Hardy wrote the following year for *Longman's Magazine*, which he called 'The Dorsetshire Labourer', with an echo of Kegan Paul's earlier article 'The Wessex Labourer'. The piece begins:

> It seldom happens that a nickname which affects to portray a class is honestly indicative of the individuals composing that class.... when the class lies somewhat out of the ken of ordinary society the caricature begins to be taken as truth.... Thus when we arrive at the farm-labouring community we find it to be seriously personified by the pitiable picture known as Hodge... This supposed real but highly conventional Hodge is a degraded being of uncouth manner and aspect, stolid understanding, and snail-like movement. (*Orel* pp.168–9)

This is ironic in the light of his own use of the objectionable word in *Two on a Tower*, but here as everywhere he shows himself capable of taking opposing positions more or less simultaneously. He says that, to an explorer from cultivated London in darkest Dorset, this Hodge might on first contact appear as he is commonly represented. If, however, the explorer remains with the labourer and his family for six months he will discover the untruth of the caricature in every respect. Hodge

> has become disintegrated into a number of dissimilar fellow-creatures, men of many minds, infinite in difference; some happy, many serene, a few depressed; some clever, even to genius, some stupid, some wanton, some austere... (170–1)

This is what Hardy shows through his characters in *Two on a Tower*, despite the different view of one narrative voice. He goes on to say what he had also demonstrated in the novel, that their language, which at first seemed 'a vile corruption of cultivated speech' will be understood as a tongue with grammatical inflection rarely disregarded by his entertainer, though his entertainer's children would occasionally make a sad hash of their talk. Having attended the National School they would mix the printed tongue as taught therein with unwritten, dying, Wessex English that they had learnt of their parents, the result of this transitional state of theirs being a language without rule or harmony. (170)

Here Hardy writes (it is the only time in the essay) of Wessex as the equivalent of Dorset, perhaps drawing attention to the ancient roots of the tongue, and perhaps also giving a straw's weight extra to the speculation that he decided on Wessex as a name for his fictional county because of William Barnes's advocacy of historical Wessex and its language.[16]

The main point that Hardy makes in the remainder of the essay is that the labouring workforce of Dorset has recently changed from predominately static to predominately mobile, which fact brings a train of consequences:

They are losing their individuality, but they are widening the range of their ideas, and gaining in freedom. It is too much to expect them to remain stagnant and old-fashioned for the pleasure of romantic spectators.

But, picturesqueness apart, a result of this increasing nomadic habit of the labourer is naturally a less intimate and kindly relation with the land he tills than existed before enlightenment enabled him to rise above the condition of a serf who lived and died on a particular plot, like a tree. (181)

Thus, while their pecuniary condition in the prime of life is bettered, and their freedom enlarged, they have lost touch with their environment, and that sense of local participancy which is one of the pleasures of age. (182)

After an interlude in which he discusses the nature and effect of Joseph Arch's intervention in Dorset agricultural employment practices, noting that wages have risen by thirty or forty per cent as a result of agitation stimulated by Arch's movement, he returns to another effect of the voluntary deracination of the labouring workforce, and the improvement in their rates of pay:

A depopulation is going on which in some quarters is truly alarming. Villages used to contain, in addition to the agricultural inhabitants, an interesting and better-informed class, ranking distinctly above those – the blacksmith, the carpenter, the shoemaker, the small higgler, the shopkeeper... who had remained in the houses where they were born for no especial reason beyond an instinct of association with the spot. (188)

The pressure on the landowner to find space for his workfolk has meant the dispossessing wherever possible of this class of people, who are thus forced 'to seek refuge in the boroughs. This process, which is designated by statisticians as "the tendency of the rural population towards the large towns," is really the tendency of water to flow uphill when forced.' (188)

The essay was to prove a useful quarry for details in two of his subsequent novels, and this is perhaps why the very fine piece was never reprinted during his lifetime.[17] In the context of the predominately elegiac tone of Hardy's treatment of Wessex in his fiction, it is instructive to note the balance he strikes in 'The Dorsetshire Labourer' between regret for the loss of rural practices that both the observer and the participant valued, and the advantages for many of the participants of the practices that replaced them.

The essay was the first product of Hardy's decision to live again in the immediate neighbourhood of his birthplace, to live in Dorchester, which place he had kept away from ever since his marriage. This return of the native was intended to be permanent. He designed, and his father's firm built a house, which he called Max Gate, on an open down just to the south-east of the town. It is perhaps surprising then, that the first piece of fiction that he wrote in Dorchester, the story 'Interlopers at the Knap', which appeared in the *English Illustrated Magazine* in 1884, is also the first Wessex narrative to have its focus to the north of the turnpike road from Bridport through Dorchester to Wimborne:

> The north-west road from Casterbridge is tedious and lonely, especially in winter time. Along a part of its course it is called Holloway Lane, a monotonous track without a village or hamlet for many miles, and with very seldom a turning. (I)

It is not clear whether Hardy wished the reader who was aware of the identity of Casterbridge as Dorchester to think of this as the road to Yeovil, or the road to Crewkerne, which diverge some five miles north-west of the county town. We learn more about the road a little later:

> They were travelling in a direction that was enlivened by no modern current of traffic, the place of Darton's pilgrimage being the old-fashioned village of Hintock Abbas, where the people make the best cider and cider-wine in all Wessex, and where the dunghills smell of pomace instead of stable refuse as elsewhere. The lane was sometimes so narrow that the brambles of the hedge, which hung forward like anglers' rods over a stream, scratched their hats and curry-combed their whiskers as they passed. (I)

Hintock-Abbas is a new Wessex name, and at once the eager mind of Lucy turned over the possibilities. Cerne Abbas immediately caught her eye on the map, but she reflected that the road from Dorchester to Sherborne that serves that village is much more north than north-west of the county town.[18]

The story was the only piece published in 1884, and he only had time to write one in 1885, 'A Mere Interlude', which was not collected until *A Changed Man* in 1913. It has some unique features. It is set in a part of Cornwall which, as far as we know, Hardy never visited. Though it is not a historical narrative all the names are English names, so that like 'Benighted Travellers' it is not a Wessex story at all (it is perhaps no coincidence that like the earlier story too, 'A Mere Interlude' was sold to Tillotson's the fiction syndicators, and thus never appeared in London).

Baptista Trewthen, the heroine, 'was the daughter of a small farmer in St Mary's, one of the Scilly Isles', and after training as an elementary teacher she went to 'a school in the country near Exeter'. An elderly but wealthy bachelor who lives 'at Hugh Town, St Mary's' wishes to marry her. To get to her home she goes by packet from Penzance, but on this occasion she becomes stranded in the town for several days, and wonders if she should return to 'the Devonshire village' or stay in Penzance. She decides to stay, and pretends to be a tourist; all the places she visits are accurately named. Subsequently Truro and Redruth, St Michael's Mount, Mousehole and St Clement's Isle are mentioned; and when she gets home their ship 'touched the pier of Hugh Town' and 'Mrs Trewthen and her daughter went together along the Hugh, or promenade.'

In a small way this story is an enigma; it is quite alien from Hardy's habitual practice for him to set a story in a place he had never visited. There is indeed nothing in the details of Penzance or of any of the other named locations that he could not have derived from a guidebook to the district, or that he could not have learned from a friend or acquaintance who had been there, but there is no evident reason why he should have done either. This situation is so unusual that it gives rise to speculation: did Hardy in fact visit these places at some time before 1885? It is highly unlikely that such a visit would have gone unrecorded in *The Early Life*, unless there were some good reason for keeping it concealed – to suggest which is really to be mischievous without much cause. But it does not seem enough metaphorically to shrug the shoulders and say 'Who knows why authors do things – they don't write to please critics with their consistency.' Careful research amongst the travel literature and the periodicals of 1884 and early 1885 might turn up a quarry from which Hardy knocked out his descriptions; but in the event of such a discovery the question, why break a lifetime habit now, would still remain.

There is another detail, by no means significant enough to prove anything, that might indicate some personal experience on Hardy's part. In *The Woodlanders*, Hardy will experiment with a representation of the North-west Dorset dialect in the mouth of Grammer Oliver; in this story the elderly Scilly merchant David Heddegan twice uses in speaking to Baptista Trewthen the unique locution 'mee deer'. No Wessex speaker's accent is ever represented thus, and it is a reasonable assumption that Hardy is attempting to give some sense of the sound of a Scilly speaker. It may of course be that he is doing no more than recalling the accents of North Cornwall he heard on his visits to St Juliot. But it is in some ways extraordinary that this enigmatic story should be the immediate precursor of a novel that marks a new stage in the evolution of Wessex.

3
The First Evolutionary Leap

By 1886 everyone who cared to know was aware that in Hardy's fiction, Casterbridge stood for Dorchester and was the county town of Wessex. *The Mayor of Casterbridge* is the only one of Hardy's novels to have a place name in its title, and as we read we are forced to consider the town with the same kind of intensity that we were made to experience Egdon Heath in *The Return of the Native*. But the novel begins at a place we have never heard of, indeed the scene was 'one that might have been matched at almost any spot in any county in England at this time of the year', (vI cI) though we learn later the village is many miles to the north of Casterbridge. 'Thus Weydon Priors is probably', Lucy wrote, 'but not certainly, outside Wessex. Before this, whenever Wessex people have wanted to refer to or remember a fair-day, it has been at Greenhill Fair. It comes with the surprise of novelty to find another fair in one of Mr Hardy's novels.'

    Though we have followed characters to Casterbridge in *Under the Greenwood Tree* and *Far From the Madding Crowd*, and the town is mentioned in other narratives, we have been given no particular sense of its individuality. Now in a series of sharp and rich passages of observation it is the focus of Hardy's recreative imagination; Dorchester becomes Casterbridge – a process that is at the heart of Wessex, the real transformed by Hardy's assimilative vision into something that is at once more and less than the real. Wessex is the consequence of Hardy's strong and developing thoughts about places, and their relationship with people, applied to his past and present experience. No one person's reported impression of Dorchester would be identical with another's, even if they were all sworn to objectivity and had similar powers of expression, but Hardy feels no pressure to be objective. He tries to find the best words to express his understanding of things, the way things seem to him. And gradually that understanding has become more and more inclusive of all that he has known and thought of life in the district in which he first came to independent observation and thought.[1]

We first encounter the town when Susan Henchard and her daughter reach it, and though Elizabeth-Jane has the first words, the account rapidly shifts through several points of view in a remarkable sequence of impressions with as rapidly shifting tonal qualities, all held together by Casterbridge's geometry. This is the Wessex impulse at work. Metaphor and simile run rife, but in the end there is made present a distinct, coherent, and highly individual image of the town (vI cIV). Most of the other paragraphs and sequences of paragraphs that build up the mosaic of impression and information that is Casterbridge, show a similar variety of points of view. Wessex is not (if anyone ever thought it was) just the creation of an authoritative mono-vocal narrative voice, and this is one of the reasons why it is so rich with possibility and variety and range and depth; why it is still alive for readers after more than a hundred years with more than the life of a nostalgic indulgence, why Wessex has withstood the attrition of a similar period of increasingly intense professional scrutiny.

It would be self-indulgence to quote each of the paragraphs strung through the early part of the novel in which Hardy, from the range of perspectives that his imagination has at command, fills out his vision of the nature and history of the town. Those in which he reveals the Roman foundation of the town, and surviving evidences of its Roman occupation stand somewhat in the same relationship to the narrative as do the evocations of the Celtic barrow-builders in *The Return of the Native*. Though there have been surface changes, still the bones of the town are very old. What shapes Casterbridge is not (as with many towns) what separates it from the surrounding farmland, but rather the opposite, the permanent intricate and organic relationship between town and country, between townsfolk and countrymen. There is the interaction of the country come to town on market day with the urban merchants and craftsmen, offered at considerable length from several vantage points at different times; there is the image of the 'red-robed judge' who, 'when he condemned a sheep-stealer, pronounced sentence to the tune of Baa, that floated in at the window from the remainder of the flock browsing hard by' (vI cXIV); there is the paradox that in the 'eastern purlieu' of Dummerford lived 'burgesses who daily walked the fallow; shepherds in an intramural squeeze'. (vI cXIV)[2]

To admire the particular flexibility and grace of Hardy's writing about Casterbridge, even to feel the occasional banalities, is to do the same for Wessex, for Wessex is not only a place and a culture, but it is also a style, a way of seeing and understanding the world, which has its banality as well as its grace. At the same time, Casterbridge *is* a place, and it *is* evidently based on Dorset's Dorchester, and this relationship poses Hardy the usual problems that the conversion from Dorset to Wessex has posed him from his first novel; but these are secondary to a more important issue.[3]

At work during the period between 1883 and 1885 on the files of the *Dorset County Chronicle* of sixty years earlier, he was quite evidently pondering

Wessex. A new impetus of development is to be found everywhere in *The Mayor of Casterbridge*, but it is evident in two areas in especial, both tending towards the same end. In the first place, moments in the novel make it clear that a sense was rapidly growing within him that much of his fiction represented a single ongoing account of the conditions of things in Wessex – at different times, and in different places and with different characters, yes – but he was beginning to see more clearly how the times were interconnected, how the places were more than isolated fragments of an otherwise empty county. In a single instance in *Far From the Madding Crowd*, he had already allowed characters in one novel to recall a character from another, but such interactions happen on a different scale here. There is, for instance, a list of the places from which carriers came to Casterbridge: they 'hailed from Mellstock, Weatherbury, Hintock, Sherton-Abbas, Stickleford, Overcombe, and many other villages round' (vI cIX). For the first time, therefore, a series of places already familiar to Hardy's contemporary readers is brought together. They were quite deliberately taken back to *Under the Greenwood Tree*, *Far From the Madding Crowd*, 'Interlopers at the Knap', 'The Romantic Adventures of a Milkmaid' and *The Trumpet-Major*. Sherton-Abbas is a new name, which first appears in the first edition; in the manuscript and the serial, the list at that point read: 'Weatherbury, Hintock-Abbas, Stickleford'. For the first edition he reduced Hintock, even though it had been 'Hintock-Abbas' in 'Interlopers at the Knap', because, in the early spring of 1886, while he was reading proofs for this version of *The Mayor of Casterbridge*, he was already at work on the manuscript of his next novel, *The Woodlanders*, in which Sherton-Abbas was from early on the main urban focus. It is perhaps not surprising that Markton from *A Laodicean* does not appear in the list, since it is quite unidentifiable with any existing place; Welland and Warborne of *Two on a Tower* are perhaps a little too far away. The only book absent from this list that might have been expected is *The Return of the Native*. The omission of Southerton gives some strength to the argument that Hardy wished Egdon to be untied to any specific Wessex place, while embodying, in the conditions and habits of life upon it, a substantial fragment of Wessex culture. However, at the end of *The Mayor of Casterbridge* the heath does enter the novel:

> a forking highway which crossed Egdon Heath. Into this road they directed the horse's head, and soon were bowling across that ancient country whose surface never had been stirred to a finger's depth, save by the scratchings of rabbits, since brushed by the feet of the earliest tribes. (vII cXXII)

In these paragraphs the connection through repetition with *The Return of the Native* is very strong.

Thus Casterbridge is the centre from which trading routes and passenger routes radiate to the centres of other novels and stories. *The Mayor of*

Casterbridge is the site Hardy chooses to gather together the separate maps of his previous work into one map of Wessex. He even finds room to add Port-Bredy, though in the manuscript it was once Portwich (and in the serial also), and once Bridwick. Port-Bredy is one of the Wessex names, rare so far, that is more or less transparent, in that it takes little interpretive skill with a map of the region to guess that he had Bridport in mind.[4] Perhaps more importantly, for the first time places prominent in other novels – Mellstock from *Under the Greenwood Tree* and Egdon Heath from *The Return of the Native* – are also scenes of action in this one. Before this, with the exception, indeed, of Casterbridge itself in *Under the Greenwood Tree* and *Far From the Madding Crowd*, Hardy had made less intimate Wessex connections by having characters just mention places like Budmouth. It will be remembered how in *The Return of the Native*, for instance, he had been scrupulous in avoiding the adjacent settings of *Under the Greenwood Tree* and *Far From the Madding Crowd*.[5]

Secondly, in a parallel striking innovation, he introduces, *with speaking parts*, characters from another novel (in this case *Far From the Madding Crowd*):

> The creditors, farmers almost to a man, looked at the watch, and at the money, and into the street; when Farmer James Everdene spoke.
> 'No, no, Henchard,' he said warmly. 'We don't want that. 'Tis honourable in ye; but keep it. What do you say, neighbours – do ye agree?' ...
> 'Let him keep it, of course,' murmured another in the background – a silent reserved young man, named Boldwood; and the rest responded unanimously. (vII cVIII)

It is a major step in the creation of a unitary Wessex when one novel involves the past of another. By the time of *Far From the Madding Crowd* James Everdene is all but dead, and Boldwood is a middle-aged man. Thus *The Mayor of Casterbridge* writes a fragment of the earlier novel's history, unimagined till now, and thereby extends the life of *Far From the Madding Crowd*. This is symbolically a highly significant event.

It is evident that Wessex has become more than a convenient device. But once the novels begin to be accepted as parts of a larger whole, much of which is yet unwritten, certain problems begin to arise with the earlier texts – in particular matters of consistency. If Wessex were not beginning to accumulate in this way it would be less worthy of note that there are, for instance, several places in which what is said in *The Mayor of Casterbridge* conflicts with what has already been established in *Under the Greenwood Tree*.[6]

It is not surprising that *The Mayor of Casterbridge* is influenced by 'The Dorsetshire Labourer'. It is in the account of the inhabitants of Mixen Lane that there is a direct resonance from the essay:[7]

Yet amid so much that was bad needy respectability also found a home. Under some of the roofs abode pure and virtuous souls whose presence there was due to the iron hand of necessity, and to that alone. Families from decayed villages – families of that once bulky but now nearly extinct, section of village society called 'liviers,' or lifeholders – copyholders, and others whose roof-trees had fallen for some reason or other, compelling them to quit the rural spot that had been their home for generations – came here, unless they chose to lie under a hedge by the wayside. (vII cXIII)

In the essay Hardy wrote of the movement of village people to the towns as 'the tendency of water to flow uphill when forced'; here we see the result of that process. Hardy had scarcely used more bitter irony than is embodied in the 'chose' of 'unless they chose to lie under a hedge by the wayside'. And this is toned down from his original manuscript inscription, which had, instead of 'decayed villages', with its implication of some kind of organic natural process, 'demolished villages', which implies very clearly the hand of the landlord at work. Did Hardy at the last minute, in proof for the *Graphic*, soften his hostility towards the rural landowner because many of them (or their families) bought his novels? The phrase 'for some reason or other' covers much. The comment of the turnip-hoer to the young Michael Henchard at the beginning of the novel is also to the point:

Pulling down is more the nater of Weydon. There were five houses cleared away last year, and three this; and the fokes nowhere to go – no, not so much as a thatched hurdle; that's the way o' Weydon-Priors. (vI cI)

This destruction of living-space, and the community that goes with it, affects Hardy strongly, for it is a notation of such an action that stimulates him to his first crossover from the fictional to the real – the first note in his fiction that implicitly accepts that readers like Lucy have made connections between Wessex and the real world, and that they might visit the real, hoping there to find also Wessex:

Though the upper part of Dummerford was mainly composed of a curious congeries of barns and farmsteads, there was a less picturesque side to the parish. This was Mixen Lane, now in great part pulled down. (vII cXIII)

In the manuscript the last sentence ended at 'Lane', but in reading proof for the *Graphic* Hardy realized that some who read the serial might actually go to Dorchester to look for the equivalent of Mixen Lane, which no longer existed; so he forewarned them. This is another decisive moment in the development of Wessex marked by *The Mayor of Casterbridge*.

Mixen Lane is a sort of social common-denominator, in which all who are unfortunate in different directions are brought together; this is made most vivid by Hardy in the reminiscences of poacher and gamekeeper, side by side in the pub:

> ex-poachers and ex-gamekeepers, whom squires had persecuted without a cause (in their own view), sat elbowing each other – men who in past times had met in fights under the moon, till lapse of sentences on the one part, and loss of favour and expulsion from service on the other, brought them here together to a common level, where they sat calmly discussing old times. (vII cXIII)[8]

The game laws, that privilege the 'sport' of the landed gentry over the most fundamental needs of working people, set men of the same class against each other until, in another kind of sport, the gentleman throws his law-enforcement officer towards Mixen Lane.

The new sense of the general harshness of some aspects of life in both Dorset and Wessex, present in *Two on a Tower*, and represented here by the demolition of cottages and other forms of class-oppression, is paralleled by an intensification in this new attitude to Wessex evident in the mouths of some of the characters in the novel, who have at least a nodding acquaintance with Mixen Lane. This outburst comes from a glazier as a response to a sentimental Scottish song of exile:

> 'Danged if our country down here is worth singing about like that!... When you take away from among us the fools and the rogues, and the lammigers, and the wanton hussies and the slatterns, and such-like, there's cust few left to ornament a song with in Casterbridge, or the country round.'

Christopher Coney adds:

> we be bruckle folk here – the best o' us hardly honest sometimes, what with hard winters, and so many mouths to fill, and God a'mighty sending his little taties so terrible small to fill 'em with. (vI cVIII)

The ordinary people in Hardy's novels have only just begun to speak like this; there is an uncomfortable darkness in such responses. When revising the manuscript Hardy added 'the passons and the lawyers' to the glazier's list, between the lammigers and the wanton hussies. As before, Hardy shied away at the last from such provocation; he cancelled his addition before it could get into print. It was not just the addition of professions to the ranks of those to be cast out as unornamental, but also their careful placement just before the whores, that we have lost.

'The Dorsetshire Labourer' gave Hardy a new confidence in using the voice of the rural economic and social historian, who had informed his readers of the fate of reddlemen in *The Return of the Native*, or of the relative permanence of rural fashion in *Far From the Madding Crowd*. Hardy was always fond of fairs, and in this novel he gives a vivid vignette of an evening at the one at Weydon with which the novel opens. Susan Henchard and her daughter revisit the place seventeen years later, and Hardy notes the changes the space of time has brought about:

> Certain mechanical improvements might have been noticed... But the real business of the fair had considerably dwindled. The new periodical great markets of neighbouring towns were beginning to interfere seriously with the trade carried on here for centuries. The pens for sheep, the tie-ropes for horses, were about half as long as they had been. The stalls of tailors, hosiers, coopers, linendrapers, and other such trades had almost disappeared... (vI cIII)

Another mechanical improvement offered in *The Mayor of Casterbridge* is the horse-drawn seed drill 'till then unknown, in its modern shape, in this part of the country, where the venerable seed-lip was still used for sowing as in the days of the Heptarchy'. He makes the machine one of the many points of contrast between Henchard and Farfrae, the former rejecting it as useless, the latter commenting: 'It will revolutionise sowing hereabout. No more sowers flinging about their seed broadcast, so that some falls by the wayside, and some among thorns, and all that.' It is Elizabeth-Jane who regrets, with an eye to Bible-stories, the passing of 'the romance of the sower', and adds:

> 'How things change.'
> 'Yes, yes – It must be so!' Donald admitted... 'But the machines are already very common in the east and north of England,' he added, apologetically. (vII cI)

Henchard is bound to be against any sort of innovation that he does not understand. Elizabeth-Jane's response is perhaps sentimental, but she only regrets the fact of change, not its inevitability. We are becoming accustomed in the novel to feel that what Elizabeth-Jane thinks is in many respects close to what Hardy himself thinks, and perhaps it is in this instance also. Her view is still closely related to the attitude to social change expressed many years earlier in *Under the Greenwood Tree*. The reference to the Heptarchy Hardy added as an afterthought in the manuscript – a deliberate association of historical Wessex with his own, and striking evidence of his new confidence in his creation; as is the placement of Casterbridge and fictional Wessex in the same continuum as 'the east and north of England'. Hardy has always written of Wessex as if it were a part of England, but he has until now avoided such direct allusion to other areas of the real place.

In *The Mayor of Casterbridge* Hardy returns in a novel, for the first time since *The Return of the Native*, to an action which is centred on an examination of the whole of his idea of what might be involved in Wessex life, and the narrative amplifies and extends that idea in other directions than have been noticed here – in particular he takes up again his investigation, that had lain in abeyance since *The Return of the Native*, of causality, the way things happen in Wessex.[9]

Though the reviews were clear about the identity of Casterbridge, none spoke of the increased presence of interrelationship between novels. R H Hutton in the *Spectator* 5 June 1886 is representative:

> And though the scenery of Dorsetshire, and especially of Dorchester – which is obviously enough the original of Casterbridge – is admirably given, Mr Hardy's art in describing the scenery of the South-West is too well-known to need illustration.

It was *Vanity Fair* 4 September 1886 that (despite its topographical inaccuracies) came closest to understanding the new links that Hardy was making in public between elements of his created world:

> Mr Hardy draws from life. That is in some part the secret of his success. What he writes he knows of, as well as daily communion with it can make him know it. From the window of Mr Hardy's study in Dorsetshire you may see the Galbury Woods of 'The Greenwood Tree' and Bathsheba Everdene's farm, as well as one or two other bits of country which have been 'adopted' into other novels.

The next novel, *The Woodlanders*, followed hard on the heels of this one. The first sentence places Wessex firmly and openly in England:

> The rambler who, for old association's sake, should trace the forsaken coach-road running almost in a meridional line from Bristol to the south shore of England, would find himself during the latter half of his journey in the vicinity of some extensive woodlands, interspersed with apple-orchards.[10]

This could have been the opening of a novel by anyone, if it were not for the exquisite sense of the road's loss of vocation and the interest in apples. The initial reference to the map of England made it relatively easy for Lucy to establish to her satisfaction the relationship between most of the Wessex places in the novel and their English equivalents; but one in particular bothered her, and she was stimulated to the following thought:

> I think I have discovered a pattern in Mr Hardy's books. It is one I might have identified earlier I suppose. I feel fairly confident of Sherborne and

Melbury Osmond and Milton Abbas and the rest, but Little Hintock, and its surrounding woodlands, where almost everything happens, eludes me. It isn't even certain where it ought to be on any map, but there is no settlement in any of the spots that might be indicated by distances and relationships. So I have had to accept that the heart of the action is imaginary. Then I remembered 'The Trumpet-Major' and 'The Distracted Young Preacher' and the way that fictional Overcombe and Nether-Mynton nestled in England, and saw again Egdon Heath as an island of isolation in Wessex, and Casterbridge walled four-square against the countryside, despite the wealth of other details that unite the two. So here's what I think. Mr Hardy needs to focus on a very small part of Wessex for the heart of his stories, and he often needs to make that place more imagined than real, because it is where his imagination is most powerfully at work. But often he also wants, for other reasons, to place that centre in the context of something more like England, though not quite identical to it. That's why Mr Percombe finds it so hard to find Little Hintock – it's Mr Hardy's (and Mrs Dollery's) secret. And I think this is also the explanation of something I noticed earlier, that as the narrative of 'The Return of the Native' made me experience Egdon Heath as the size of Dartmoor, so I have been forced to feel that much of 'The Woodlanders' takes place in a kind of temperate Amazonia. But the given facts of distance and the relationships of place tend to undermine this sense of vast wilderness.[11]

What Lucy noticed is part of the paradox of Wessex, as it is part of the paradox of Hardy's narrators – that each is able to contain, and express vividly, two apparently conflicting ideas at the same time. Wessex, *The Woodlanders* demonstrates again, is both limitless and bound by distance, both timeless and bound by the smallest historical events, simultaneously a country of the imagination and of reality.

The second sentence of the novel introduces to the unsuspecting reader what is the most important contribution of the novel to the growth to maturity of Hardy's understanding of Wessex:

> Here the trees, timber or fruit-bearing, as the case may be, make the wayside hedges ragged by their drip and shade, their lower limbs stretching in level repose over the road, as though reclining on the insubstantial air.

From the beginning Wessex has been a place where there has been a stronger, more intense interrelationship between humans and the world about them than is usually observed in life or in the fictions of others. In *The Woodlanders* this interinvolvement is a part of the air we breathe. This sentence moves from the objective distinction between kinds of tree, to an indication of their power to change elements of their environment, to an image that stimulates the imagination to view the large branches as human sleepers magically resting on couches of air. The trees in the novel are becoming human, and the humans are arborescent. Another example is the very well-known passage in which Hardy says that the competition for survival amongst the trees is identical to that amongst men (vI cVII). It is an important contribution to this perception that all the local crafts and trades (without which Wessex would hardly exist) are tree-work – planting, harvesting, cutting and shaping the dead wood, pressing the fruit. A sentence from the account of the business of removing the bark from recently felled trees brings work, worker and tree into an intimate and ultimately confounding relationship:

> Marty South was an adept at peeling the upper parts; and there she stood encaged amid the mass of twigs and buds like a great bird, running her tool into the smallest branches, beyond the furthest points to which the skill and patience of the men enabled them to proceed – branches which, in their lifetime, had swayed high above the bulk of the wood, and caught the earliest rays of the sun and moon while the lower part of the forest was still in darkness. (vII cIII)

This is at first a characteristic Wessex moment, instructing city dwellers in a rural craft with grace and delicacy. Marty's care and dedication are celebrated, as we have come to expect, and she is totally involved with the tree, she is a 'great bird' trapped by it as well as a girl. But then we are forced to recognize that the tree she is operating upon is dead, that was just now vividly alive, bursting into bud, catching the sunlight; and, through the power of Hardy's imagination, Marty (of all people) incredibly, for a second, is a vulture stripping a slaughtered human carcass. In choosing Marty for this revelation, Hardy ensures that no reader can evade responsibility for the violation.

Even when the narrative voice is the one that might speak of 'Hodge' and 'rustics', this way of seeing the world is in control:

> The battle between frost and thaw was continuing in mid-air: the trees dripped on the garden-plots, where no vegetables would grow for the dripping, though they were planted year after year with that curious mechanical regularity of country people in the face of hopelessness. (vII cI)

The trees destroy the vegetation at their feet competing for nourishment, it is natural; but when people enter the adjective 'curious' detaches the narrator from them, and 'mechanical regularity' reduces them to automata. If the observation is accepted as accurate, then the question is, what does the narrator believe might make Wessex folk act so foolishly? Are they merely stupid? Or unimaginative? Do they, because of the narrow poverty of their lives, live moment to moment and pay no attention to the past, to history? Is it blind hopefulness – that they believe that *this* year things will be different?[12]

An answer of the kind that might have been expected is available in the same chapter:

> To people at home [in the woods] these changeful tricks had their interests; the strange mistakes that some of the more sanguine trees had made in budding before their month, to be incontinently glued up by frozen thawings now; the similar sanguine errors of impulsive birds in framing nests that were swamped by snow-water, and other such incidents, prevented any sense of wearisomeness in the minds of the natives.

Hintock people observe the profligate behaviour of birds and trees, that have no memory, no power of calculation, and so repeat these foolish acts. Being human, they should learn from their observation. But the narrator, filled with his sense of the identity between woodland and woodlanders, implies that this harmony is so thorough that they too go on building their nests – or rather planting their vegetables – in the same place where it is likely to get flooded year after year because it is a law of their nature.[13]

The next sentence of this passage is:

> But these were features of a world not familiar to Fitzpiers, and the inner visions to which he had almost exclusively attended having suddenly failed in their power to absorb him, he felt unutterably dreary.

Fitzpiers is not 'at home' in Hintock, and a page or two earlier Hardy had described some of the consequences of this fact:

> Winter in a solitary house in the country, without society, is tolerable, nay, even enjoyable and delightful, given certain conditions; but these are not the conditions which attach to the life of a professional man who drops down into such a place by mere accident.... They are old association – an almost exhaustive biographical or historical acquaintance with every object, animate and inanimate, within the observer's horizon.

This is a condition for happiness that Hardy saw in 'The Dorsetshire Labourer' being eroded by the new social mobility which has not yet penetrated, isolated and imagined Wessex hamlets like Little Hintock. The past alone can keep a solitary country place alive in winter. From *Under the Greenwood Tree* and *The Return of the Native* it is evident that Hardy in part created Wessex out of one of his deepest needs, to express the associations of the human past with places he had touched or grown with or learned. This need is more than nostalgia for the golden age of one's youth, it is present knowledge working with past association – it is the difference between the sentimental revival of old customs and the unenthusiastic survival of the same, as distinguished in *The Return of the Native*. Later, while

Fitzpiers sits round the tree-barkers' tea-fire with Melbury and his daughter, he begins to learn some of the history that could have made the country alive for him. He 'drew from her father and the bark-rippers sundry narratives of their fathers', their grandfathers', and their own adventures in these woods; of the mysterious sights they had seen – only to be accounted for by supernatural agency; of white witches and black witches...' (vII cIII)

It is part of the matter of Wessex, but Fitzpiers cannot absorb it this way. And indeed the class-separations always present in Wessex are articulated particularly clearly in this novel. Winterborne's contempt for Mrs Charmond – he asks Grace: 'How can you think so much of that class of people?' (vI cIX) – is matched by Fitzpiers's comment to Grace about Winterborne and his cider-makers: 'I do honestly confess to you that I feel as if I belonged to a different species from the people who are working in that yard.' (vII cIX) Both refuse to see the other as anything but a member of an undifferentiated mass. It is a measure of the distance that Hardy has come in this respect from *The Hand of Ethelberta* that in both instances the presence of Grace, socially mobile like her creator, forces the man to consider the individual rather than the undifferentiated mass.

The Woodlanders is the last novel Hardy published in which Wessex is a county – Fitzpiers asserts 'there's nobody can match me in the whole county of Wessex as a scientist' (vIII cII). He signed an agreement to write another novel almost as soon as *The Woodlanders* appeared, but it would be four years before *Tess of the d'Urbervilles* began to appear in the *Graphic*, a period that was filled with short stories, intermittent work on the manuscript of the novel, and some hard thinking about Wessex. A final detail from *The Woodlanders* shows the direction Hardy's thoughts were taking. In an action from the same source of bitterness as had informed *The Mayor of Casterbridge*, Giles Winterborne's house has been pulled down on the orders of Mrs Charmond. As he wanders the space where it had been there comes the observation:

> The apple trees still remained to show where the garden had been, the oldest of them even now retaining the crippled slant to north-east given them by the great November gale of 1824 which carried a brig bodily over the Chesil Bank. (vII cX)

It is hard to imagine that this is the reported thought of Giles. It is rather the richly informed narrator whose interest in the facts of the past of Dorset has, for a moment, got the better of his imaginative control of the situation.[14]

Something similar occurs in 'The Withered Arm', first published at the beginning of 1888. The action mostly takes place in the valley of the Swenn that runs below the heath, familiar from 'The Romantic Adventures of a Milkmaid', but a few important scenes are set on Egdon. At first the waste, with its 'dark countenance' is fully in harmony with its presence in *The Return of the Native*, and when Hardy introduces the idea that it is 'not improbably the same heath which had witnessed the agony of the Wessex King Ina, presented to after-ages as Lear' (V), the impression is intensified, and the allusion to historical Wessex is at once transmuted into appropriate Shakespearean tragedy. But a third encounter moves from imaginative connections with the remote past, to something quite different:

> Though the date was comparatively recent, Egdon was much less fragmentary in character than now. The attempts – successful and otherwise – at cultivation on the lower slopes, which intrude and break up the original heath into small detached heaths, had not been carried far: Enclosure Acts had not taken effect, and the banks and fences which now exclude the cattle of those villagers who formerly enjoyed rights of commonage thereon, and the carts of those who had turbary privileges which kept them in firing all the year round, were not erected. Gertrude therefore rode along with no other obstacles than the prickly furze-bushes, the mats of heather, the white water-courses, and the natural steeps and declivities of the ground. (VII)

Of all of Hardy's places Egdon had seemed the least susceptible to his growing interest in Dorset history. But now the anxious topographer and local historian chooses to demystify Egdon, to represent it for a while as part of England; and we can sense in this decision his view of the relationship between Wessex and Dorset changing, a substantial fragment of dream crumbling before reality.

It is, however, not just in environment that the story is related to *The Return of the Native*; it centres around the possibility of witchcraft, and in this respect, as before, belief and scepticism are held in balance. In Wessex people at that date believed in witchcraft and sorcery, what the narrator called 'smouldering village beliefs' (VII), and perhaps they were right to do so, or perhaps they were merely superstitious.[15]

In the same year, 1888, Hardy collected some of his stories together (including this one) for a book, which he called *Wessex Tales*. In 1886 the publisher Sampson Low, Marston and Co. had begun to issue eight of Hardy's novels, and in an undated letter Hardy wrote 'Could you, whenever advertising my books, use the words "Wessex novels" at the head of the list?... I find that the name *Wessex*, wh. I was the first to use in fiction, is getting to be taken up everywhere: & it would be a pity for us to lose the right to it for want of asserting it.'[16] This is the first evidence of Hardy setting out to copyright Wessex, and the title of the collection of stories is a logical consequence. Hardy made many revisions for *Wessex Tales*, and in our context it is particularly interesting to see what he did with the geography of 'The Distracted Preacher', one of those historical stories, it will be remembered, set mostly in Dorset rather than Wessex. It is hard, in fact, to know what he had in mind. Swanage becomes Knollsea, Ringstead becomes Ringsworth, Lulworth becomes Lullstead and Weymouth becomes Budmouth. On the other hand, though, Holworth remains Holworth, Bere remains Bere, Warm'll remains Warm'll, and Chaldon remains Chaldon. There is no apparent pattern, and what the evidence suggests is either much haste or much uncertainty about the relationship between Wessex and England and the historically verifiable. Another historical story, 'The Melancholy Hussar', published a year or so later, also indicates uncertainty, for in it Weymouth has its English name, as also does Bath (rather than the Pumpminster of *Two on a Tower*).[17]

At the end of 1888 'A Tragedy of Two Ambitions' came out, and there is one proof-revision Hardy made that again shows him thinking about the geography of Wessex: the coroner for the County of Wessex in the manuscript became the coroner for the north-west division of Wessex in the *Universal Review*. He made this change, it seems likely, because for the first time the centre of an action pushed westward into (English) Somerset. Lucy commented that the range of Hardy's Wessex was growing to meet the size of Alfred's.[18]

For most of 1889 he was at work on the manuscript of what would become *Tess of the d'Urbervilles*, but when he sent half of it to the publisher, it was rejected as unsuitable for family journals. As a consequence Hardy turned for a time to stories about the aristocracy of Wessex, six of which he put together for the *Graphic* as *A Group of Noble Dames* at the end of 1890. The following spring he added four that had already appeared elsewhere to make a volume of the same name. The stories themselves have a fascinating textual history, and, together with the frame-narrative Hardy developed in the *Graphic* to link the stories together, are a site of Wessex change. We learn (in different places in the magazine and the book versions) that members of the Mid-Wessex Field and Antiquarian Club were forced by bad weather – snow in the *Graphic* and rain in the first edition – to entertain themselves by storytelling. Lucy had remarked upon Wessex divisions before, in the North and South Wessex militias, and in the coroner's division of the county just mentioned, so she assumed, and probably correctly, that Hardy intended the meeting to take place in some town like Blandford Forum, near the centre of Dorset-based Wessex. In the first edition the frame is introduced thus: 'It was at a meeting of one of the Wessex Field and Antiquarian Clubs...' (I.i), and a few lines later the narrator of 'The First Countess of Wessex' is thanked 'for such a curious chapter of the domestic histories of the *county*' (my italics; the story ranges across the boundaries of the English counties of Somerset and Dorset). For the most part the changes Hardy made to Wessex aspects of the stories are local, but several are of interest because they show (what would be expected) how Hardy's thought on Wessex when handling the story-sequence moved in parallel with his simultaneous work on the manuscript of *Tess of the d'Urbervilles* – in particular there are the first appearances of Marlott, Shaston, Wintoncester and Trantridge.[19] But it was in reading the last story of the sequence in the book, 'The Honourable Laura', that Lucy began to feel that things were changing. The environment was transformed from its magazine appearance in 'Benighted

Travellers'. There (see below p. 247) it was Scottish; now, in order to bring it into Wessex Hardy had to find an appropriate setting that would fit the melodrama of the story with the minimum of alteration. He chose the district about Coomb Martin on the North Devon coast, calling it, transparently enough, Cliff-Martin. Details are altered to suit a cliff-top, seaside situation, but there is one particularly significant change.[20] What originally read: 'The Prospect Hotel, a building standing quite alone on the verge of one of the most picturesque glens in Great Britain' becomes 'The Prospect Hotel, a building standing near the wild north coast of Lower Wessex'. 'North coast! Lower Wessex!' Lucy wrote after looking at her maps. 'Cliff-Martin must be Coomb Martin, so we are in Devon, for goodness sake. What does Mr Hardy have in mind? Wessex has become too big, I suppose, and he has to divide it up for his convenience.' In fact she had missed the story 'For Conscience' Sake' that had appeared in the *Fortnightly* a couple of months earlier, or else she might have been more confused. In the manuscript Hardy had Exonbury as county town of Lower Wessex, but then changed Exonbury to Toneborough (the borough on the river Tone, i.e. Taunton) without changing Lower Wessex. In fact the origin of this county division can be found at the end of the manuscript of *Tess of the d'Urbervilles*, on which he was at work in the summer of 1890.

In the first chapter of the manuscript (and the serial) John Durbeyfield exclaims: 'There's not a man in the county o' Wessex that's got grander and nobler skellingtons in his family than I'; by the penultimate chapter Wessex had changed. As Angel and Tess are attempting to escape from 'justice' the narrator says: 'At dusk Clare purchased food as usual, and their night march began, the boundary between Upper and Mid-Wessex being crossed about eight o'clock' (LVIII). When Lucy read the first chapter in the *Graphic* she didn't think anything much about it, but the last episode set her off: 'The New Forest, where they must have come from, is in Hampshire, and Stonehenge, where they end up, is in Wiltshire, and it looks as if Mr Hardy has after all decided to subdivide Wessex into different counties, based on the English ones. So Hampshire would be Mid-Wessex and Wiltshire Upper Wessex. Or vice-versa I suppose. And Lower Wessex in "A Group of Noble Dames" *is* Devon.' It was with some eagerness that she turned to the beginning of the novel in volumes (published at about the same time as the last serial instalment), where she found her conclusion reinforced by a revised version of Durbeyfield's exclamation: 'There's not a man in the county o' South Wessex that's got grander and nobler skellingtons in his family than I.' This development is possibly the most significant in the history of the progress of Wessex through Hardy's imagination, and it leads directly to the authorized map appended to the first collected edition of his work four years later. Lucy wrote about it thus:

So South-Wessex must be Dorset. There is another altered speech a little further on. By referring back I see that in the magazine it was 'I've got a great family vault at Kingsbere-sub-Greenhill, and finer skellingtons than any man – in the county o' Wessex!' Now it reads 'I've got a great family vault at Kingsbere-sub-Greenhill, and finer skellingtons than any man – in the counties o' Wessex!' (I)

Over the last few shorter stories Mr Hardy has written, and in 'The Woodlanders', and now in 'Tess', I have felt that it has been getting more and more easy to be instantly certain of the real place upon which he has based his fictional place, the gap between novel and reality in this respect has become as tenuous as possible without quite ceasing to exist. If I am correct about the subdivision of Wessex into counties which have identical borders to those in England, then the idea of Wessex as I had understood it begins to lose its shape and validity. Presumably the whole of Mid-Wessex, the whole of Upper Wessex and the whole of Lower Wessex, as well as the centre in South Wessex, are now to be thought of as part of Wessex. Before this the borders of Wessex were appropriately shifting and uncertain; some of Somerset, a little of Wiltshire, quite a lot of Hampshire, perhaps a strip of Devon, perhaps not; it was a fiction, an imagined place, which selected some aspects of life as they might be thought to be lived in those districts, ignored or overlooked others, and made no claim to represent the whole as it exists in England, or particularly to represent precisely space or time as they were experienced in England. Now I feel the situation has changed. The history of Egdon was a straw in the wind, and these county names are the grains that tip the balance away from fiction and towards fact. They help also to account for the Baedeker language that I have complained of as slipping into this wonderful novel from time to time. I am worried that if the scales weigh any heavier in this direction Mr Hardy will actually begin to write guidebooks and antiquarian essays, and give up writing novels altogether.

4
Tess of the d'Urbervilles

Tess of the d'Urbervilles is *the* Wessex novel. It could not have been achieved without the long sequence of novels and stories that preceded it, but if they were all to vanish from human consciousness overnight and *Tess of the d'Urbervilles* were saved, then Wessex would survive, not intact, but in essence. For this reason the novel is here given unusually full treatment.

For the first time Hardy gives to the whole of the county of Wessex (or South Wessex as it becomes by the end of the manuscript), through representative places and activities, the intense attention of his observing eye and ear and his recreative imagination. Blackmoor and the Froom valley and the chalk uplands between – the routes from Marnhull to Cranborne, from Alton Pancras to Beaminster, from Bournemouth to Stonehenge – these are all present to the reader in this one novel as immediately as the single districts and briefer journeys of his earlier novels and stories. The text is full of places and landscapes and work and stories and dances and sounds and rituals, all in consciously constructed harmony with the narrative into which Hardy put his strongest feelings and his most passionate thought. It is amazing that anyone might suggest that Hardy wrote a finer novel; or indeed that any English novelist has.

The first sentence of the novel in the manuscript gave the contemporary reader clear topographical information:

> On an evening in the latter part of May a middle-aged man was riding homeward from Stourcastle town by a lane which led into the recesses of the neighbouring Vale of Blakemore or Blackmoor.

Blackmoor was familiar from *The Woodlanders*. That Stourcastle might stand for Sturminster Newton would have been less evident, but in the event the question of its identity was never raised, for Hardy thoroughly revised the sentence for the opening of the serialization of the novel in the *Graphic*:

On an evening in the latter part of May a middle-aged man was walking homeward from Shaston to the village of Marlott, in the adjoining Vale of Blakemore or Blackmoor.

The time remains, the man is still there, and the Vale of Blackmoor is still his goal; however, in the manuscript Hardy thought of the man riding north, in the *Graphic* he is walking south from what, if we have any local historical knowledge, we recognize as Shaftesbury, to a named but unidentifiable village. At the moment when Hardy effected the change on the proofs for the magazine, he was giving a different shape in his mind to young Tess's world – only on the page of a critical edition, though, can they coexist as part of the continuous history of the text. To lose the word 'recesses' is sad, for it gives a clear idea of the kind of landscape that composes the vale; but he had used it at the beginning of the second chapter also, and one occurrence had to go:

> The village of Marlott lay amid the north-eastern undulations of the beautiful Vale of Blakemore or Blackmoor aforesaid – an engirdled and secluded region, for the most part untrodden as yet by tourist or landscape-painter, though within a four hours' journey from London.
> It is a vale whose acquaintance is best made by viewing it from the summits of the hills that surround it except perhaps during the droughts of summer. An unguided ramble into its recesses in bad weather is apt to engender dissatisfaction with its narrow, tortuous, and miry ways. (II)[1]

Not, perhaps for the first time, but with more candour than before, Hardy encourages a reader like Lucy to literary tourism by providing information about the time it would take her to get there, and by warning her of possible dissatisfaction in dry guidebook tones – tones that recur from time to time throughout the novel.

After speculating about Shaston and Marlott, Lucy noted 'Parson Tringham, the antiquary, of Stagfoot Lane' (I), finding the hamlet of Harefoot Lane in her survey map of North Dorset, and remarking on the good man announcing both his hobby and his home in one breath for the convenience and information of readers; and then she jotted down 'Kingsbere-sub-Greenhill' (I), with the comment that 'it is the first time Mr Hardy has given the place so extensive a name, one that brings in associations with "Far From the Madding Crowd" and all those earlier novels that mention Greenhill fair. And then the parson talks of the ancient d'Urberville manors: "In this county there was a seat of yours at Kingsbere, and another at Sherton, and another at Millpond, and another at Lullstead, and another at Wellbridge" (I)'. Lullstead she knew to be Lulworth, since Hardy had made that change when 'The Distracted Preacher' appeared in *Wessex Tales*, but Millpond and Wellbridge were new to her, and she had no idea where to look for equivalents. 'Does this spread of places', she wondered, 'so early in the novel mean anything? It's very unusual'. In fact it would come to seem inevitable that the novel should begin with a journey, and it is at this date by no means original to suggest that in structural terms *Tess of the d'Urbervilles* consists of a series of journeys and pauses between them, almost all Tess's journeys. These journeys also shape the new Wessex that comes to birth in the novel after a long gestation in less determinate forms. Before she sets out, Hardy describes Tess's geographical understanding:

> The Vale of Blackmoor was to her the world, and its inhabitants the races thereof. From the gates and stiles of Marlott she had looked down its length in the wondering days of infancy, and what had been mystery to her then was not much less than mystery to her now. She had seen daily from her chamber-window towers, villages, faint white mansions; above all the town of Shaston standing majestically on its height; its windows shining like lamps in the evening sun. She had hardly ever visited it, only a small tract even of the Vale and its environs being known to her by close inspection. Much less had she been far outside the valley. Every contour of the surrounding hills was as personal to her as that of her relatives' faces; but for what lay beyond her judgment was dependent on the teaching of the village school (V)[2]

It is this intimate familiarity that she exchanges for a more transient knowledge of the world beyond, which exchange is, amongst other things, a metaphor for the changing experience of the Dorsetshire labourer.

From Marlott towards Casterbridge and back

Tess's first journey is with the horse Prince and some beehives in the direction of Casterbridge. There is an attractive brief description of what might or might not have been identifiable as Sturminster Newton – a single covering roofing it all in sleep:

> When they had passed the little town of Stourcastle, dumbly somnolent under its thick brown thatch, they reached higher ground. Still higher, on their left, the elevation called Bulbarrow or Bealbarrow swelled into the sky, engirdled by its earthen trenches. (IV)

This is the *Graphic* version; in the first edition after 'Bealbarrow' there is, 'well-nigh the highest in South-Wessex'. This factual detail is characteristic of the new Wessex; Hardy could not have written 'the highest in Wessex', in earlier novels, nor even in the early version of this one, for he had no idea of how far Wessex ranged, it was an imaginative rather than a finite space, and moreover later developments of Wessex might have proven his statement wrong.

This is a first tentative and unsuccessful feeler beyond Blackmoor. We do not know how far beyond Stourcastle the journey extended before the life-blood of Prince on the roadway brought it to a close, and Tess returned full of shame and of sorrow.

From Marlott to The Slopes at Trantridge and back

The manuscript leaves that describe Tess's outward journey are missing, and Hardy's earliest version of it can only be inferred from her return. From The Slopes: 'Tess went down the hill to Trantridge and automatically took her seat in the as yet unhorsed van.' So originally the carrier's van stopped at Trantridge. There are, though, also second and third thoughts visible on the manuscript: 'Tess went down the hill to Trantridge Cross and automatically waited to take her seat in the van passing here from Ranborough.' This finally becomes: 'Tess went down the hill to Trantridge Cross and automatically waited to take her seat in the van returning from Ranborough to Shaston' (VI). Ranborough becomes Chaseborough in proof for the *Graphic*, while 'automatically' becomes 'inattentively' for the first edition. It may be that Hardy decided to introduce Ranborough at this point to make it natural that later on the farm-workers from the Trantridge neighbourhood should go there to market and take pleasure, but it also serves the function of placing Trantridge more clearly on a map of Wessex. The names Ranborough and Chaseborough taken together make an identification with Cranborne almost mandatory, and they in turn make Pentridge as Hardy's intention behind Trantridge equally probable. That Hardy had another Dorset village in mind when at first he made the carrier's van stop at Trantridge is shown to be possible during Tess's second journey to The Slopes. As it is, the *Graphic* account of this first outward journey remains unchanged through all the printed versions:

> Rising early next day she walked to the hill-town called Shaston, and there took advantage of a van which twice in the week ran from Shaston eastward to Chaseborough, passing near Trantridge, the parish in which the vague and mysterious Mrs d'Urberville had her residence. (V)

When she reached her goal, the house she had expected to be aged and hoary, she found was brand new and bright red, reflecting the very recent elevation to wealth of its owner, and the falsity of any claim to the name he had annexed. To make more emphatic the contrast between interloping pretension and continuity with the Wessex past, Hardy added, after describing The Slopes:

Far behind the bright brick corner of the house – which rose like a red geranium against the subdued colours around – stretched the soft azure landscape of The Chase – a truly venerable tract of forest land, one of the few remaining woodlands in England of undoubted primaeval date. (V)

When, on Tess's way home, with the blood of Alec's rose on her chin, the carrier gets to his terminus, the narrator notes the fact in picturesque terms: 'The van travelled only so far as Shaston, and there were several miles of pedestrian descent from that mountain-town into the vale to Marlott' (VI). It is somewhat romantic, even a casual reader might say, to call any place in Wessex a 'mountain-town'; but, indeed, a pedestrian, already somewhat fatigued by the walk from Marnhull, on ascending Gold Hill from the Vale to the town of Shaftesbury might well have accepted the epithet.

From Marlott to The Slopes at Trantridge again

When Tess leaves home to go to work at The Slopes, we are told that 'far away behind the first hills the cliff-like dwellings of Shaston broke the line of the ridge' (VII). This, however is in the first edition and there is an interesting sequence of changes in the manuscript which show Hardy revisioning the scene. Originally the manuscript read here: 'Above them the tall wart-like protuberances of Bulbarrow broke the line of the ridge.' Subsequently this begins: 'Behind the first hills the wart-like...' and later still it is: 'Far away behind the first hills the wart-like', which it remains in the magazine.

Investigating topographers have found it difficult, if not impossible, to find a site for The Slopes as it is described in relation to Trantridge Cross and the Chase, and some at least have assumed that the place is purely imaginary. Such investigations are not the purpose of this book, but it is interesting to take the first manuscript reading here, in which Bulbarrow appears tall above Tess and her mother and sisters as they wait for the cart from Trantridge to appear on the ridge, and add to it the information that on her first journey Tess had at first alighted at Trantridge rather than Trantridge Cross, from a carrier's van that ended its journey there. Bulbarrow is eight miles directly south of Marnhull/Marlott, and it seems possible that when Hardy first conceived of the relationship between Marlott and The Slopes and Trantridge, the last was further south and larger than Pentridge, perhaps somewhere like Tarrant Hinton – which name might also possibly have suggested Trantridge as a Wessex equivalent. At any rate he decided in the first edition to direct the reader's attention northward rather than southward.[3]

From Trantridge to Chaseborough and back

It is fairly clear that by the time the story reached print Hardy did intend Pentridge behind Trantridge, for when Tess and the other farm-workers go to the 'decayed old market town' of Chaseborough we are told it is two or three miles they walk – which is the distance from Pentridge to Cranborne (X). Interestingly enough in the manuscript the town was here originally Crankhollow and then Crankholt; but this portion of the manuscript never went to the *Graphic*'s printers, nor did the more painful detail of her return thence through the Chase.

From Trantridge to Marlott

Of this journey there is nothing to say except that for the first time she walks most of the way, until Alec d'Urberville catches up with her. The longer the novel progresses, the more often Tess walks long distances across Wessex, not, as here, through choice, but through necessity. Again she returns to Marlott with sorrow.

From Marlott to Talbothays

After Tess's return to Marlott and the birth and death of her baby, she leaves Blackmoor again:

> She went through Stourcastle without pausing, and onward to a junction of highways, where she could await a carrier's van that ran to the south-west; for the railways which engirdled this interior tract of country had never yet struck across it. While waiting, however, there came along a farmer in his spring-cart... He was going to Weatherbury, and by accompanying him thither she could walk the remainder of the distance instead of travelling in the van by way of Casterbridge.
>   Tess did not stop at Weatherbury, after this long drive, further than to make a slight nondescript meal at noon at a cottage to which the farmer recommended her. Thence she started on foot, basket in hand, to reach the wide upland of heath dividing this district from the low-lying meads of a further valley in which the dairy stood that was the aim and end of her day's pilgrimage. (XVI)

Within the manuscript there is evidence that Hardy could not make up his mind about the farmer's destination; at first it was Weatherbury, but then it was 'Millpond, near Weatherbury'. This time the new version was retained for the *Graphic*, but was returned to Weatherbury in the first edition. Perhaps Hardy made the initial change because Parson Tringham had said that there had been a d'Urberville manor at Millpond, and he had thought to make something of Tess going there, but then decided against it. However it was, a more intimate connection with *Far From the Madding Crowd* than the place name was lost for good when Weatherbury went temporarily unvisited, for the cottage at which Tess ate there had belonged to 'a person named Smallbury', and this detail was not restored for the first edition.

The passage continues:

> The journey over the intervening uplands and lowlands of Egdon, when she reached them, was a more troublesome walk than she had anticipated, the distance being actually but a few miles. In two hours, after sundry wrong turnings, she found herself on a summit commanding the long-sought-for vale, the Valley of the Great Dairies, the valley in which milk and butter grew to rankness, and were produced more profusely, if less delicately, than at her home – the verdant plain so well watered by the river Var or Froom. (XVI)

Though Egdon Heath also connects *Tess of the d'Urbervilles* with earlier novels and stories, the more interesting detail here is in the name of the river. The valley was a familiar one to those who had read all of Hardy's work, but until now, the river in the valley, if it had been given a name, had been known as the Swenn; it is not named at all in *The Mayor of Casterbridge*, or *Under the Greenwood Tree* or *The Return of the Native*. In fact, it is only in 'The Withered Arm' in *Wessex Tales*, and there only once, that it is called the Swenn in a published volume – otherwise the occurrences were in as yet uncollected stories. Only the most careful reader of Hardy's writing would have been in a position to make a connection between the Swenn and the Frome, and only a few of those would have noticed that Hardy had changed the name in *Tess of the d'Urbervilles*.

Indeed very few natural features at all are named in Wessex before 1891; what is evidently a version of the hill Rainbarrows is called Blackbarrow in *The Return of the Native*; some readers will have recognized in the Greenhill of several pieces Woodhill near Bere Regis; but that is all – otherwise Hardy describes but does not name. It is in *The Woodlanders* that this particular geographical reticence in relation to Wessex begins to change, for there Blackmoor is plainly called Blackmoor, and Bubb-Down is lightly disguised as Rubdon Hill. At the same time, when working on 'The Waiting Supper', Hardy was still happy to use the Swenn for the Frome; but in the year or two between the writing of the story and this part of *Tess of the d'Urbervilles*, the evolution of his new attitude to the naming of natural features in Wessex was complete. Thus, as noted earlier, Bulbarrow, one of the hills enclosing Blackmoor, has its English name in this novel; but Hardy gives also an alternative and more ancient name: 'Bulbarrow or Bealbarrow'. With the river his first thought was to use only what he thought of as its ancient name, the Var. It may have been from Hutchins that Hardy derived his idea that this was an early English name for the river, a version of the ancient Celtic for 'dark river' or Blackwater as he called a portion of it in *The Mayor of Casterbridge*. At any rate he was not prepared to call it by its modern name until he revised the manuscript, and it becomes 'Frome'. In proof for the serialization Hardy decided to link old and modern versions of the name, but in doing so altered the spelling of the latter from 'Frome' to 'Froom'. A glance at early maps of Dorset shows that, until the Ordnance Survey fixed the name at Frome, both Froom and Froome were in use; and by reverting to an earlier spelling Hardy was able at once to fulfil his new Wessex vision, but also to preserve an almost intangible veil of difference between modern England and Wessex.[4]

As Tess looks over the valley from the north, the narrator compares the river to the one with which Tess was familiar:

> The river itself, which nourished the grass and cows of these renowned dairies, flowed not like the streams in Blackmoor. Those were slow, silent, often turbid; flowing over beds of mud into which the incautious wader might sink and vanish unawares. The Var waters were clear as the pure River of Life shown to the Evangelist, rapid as the shadow of a cloud, with pebbly shallows that prattled to the sky all day long. There the water-flower was the lily; the crowfoot here. (XVI)

In this passage at first the name of the river was not given at all ('These waters were as clear...'), but Hardy altered 'These' to 'The Frome' in the manuscript and as before to 'The Froom' in the *Graphic*; in the first edition the earlier name replaced the later. The last sentence offers a distinction which, though Hardy was doubtless capable of observing for himself, had been made memorably by William Barnes in his poem 'The Water Crowfoot':

> O small feäc'd flow'r that now dost bloom
> To stud wi' white the shallow Frome,
> An' leäve the clote to spread his flow'r
> On darksome pools o' stwoneless Stour

The river name recurs throughout the novel, and later in the manuscript Hardy tried out Froome as a possibility in a couple of instances. He standardized the name to Froom in the serial, and more often than not preferred Var in the first edition, though Froom remains occasionally, or has Var attached to it.

In the manuscript, Tess, who was then Rose-Mary, visits the tombs of her ancestors at Greenhill Regis before going on to Talbothays. The name connects *Tess of the d'Urbervilles* again to earlier novels with its direct allusion to Greenhill Fair. Later Greenhill Regis was revised to King's-Bere (which incidentally demonstrates that the manuscript of the opening of the novel was written later than this passage). The whole visit gets moved to the end of the novel in the first edition.

From Talbothays to Mellstock

Hardy establishes another connection with existing Wessex soon after Tess becomes settled at Talbothays Dairy in the Valley of the Var or Froom or Froome or Frome:

> Tess and the other three were dressing themselves rapidly, the whole bevy having agreed to go together to Mellstock Church – which lay some three or four miles distant from the dairyhouse. (XXIII)

Mellstock is in *Under the Greenwood Tree* and *Far From the Madding Crowd* and *The Mayor of Casterbridge*, and it was by this time possible to work out, from Hardy's background as revealed in interviews, that Mellstock was probably based on Stinsford. Lucy had tentatively fixed on Lewel as standing in the most probable location for Talbothays.[5]

From Talbothays to Emminster and back

Angel rides home to talk with his parents about Tess. Hardy offers no distinctive detail of the journey either way, but there is one interesting fragment in the description of Emminster when he arrives: 'His father's hill-surrounded little town, the Tudor church tower of red stone, the clump of trees near the vicarage, came at last into view beneath him' (XXV). At first in the manuscript the second phrase read simply 'the church tower'; then Hardy added the 'Tudor', and 'with its decapitated pinnacles' after tower. Next 'decapitated' was cancelled and 'mended' put in its place, and it was only for the first edition that the pinnacles disappeared altogether, and the red stone put in their place. It seems most probable that Hardy revisited Beaminster between the two manuscript revisions, and found that his memory of the most striking feature of the tower was no longer accurate, and then when he came to revise for the book version he realized that the mended pinnacles were purely a response to his earlier inaccuracy, and that no one save the local people would know they were mended, and that some other salient feature would be preferable.

From Talbothays to a station and back

This journey, also in the Froom Valley, is in the opposite direction from Mellstock; Tess and Angel take milk churns to a railway station:

> In the diminishing daylight they went along the level roadway through the meads, which stretched away into gray miles, and were backed in the extreme edge of distance by the swarthy abrupt slopes of Egdon Heath. On its summit stood clumps and stretches of fir-trees, whose notched tips

appeared like battlemented towers crowning black-fronted castles of enchantment. (XXX)

In the manuscript the meads were backed by Egdon 'in the extreme left-hand distance', in the *Graphic* 'in the extreme mist of distance' – which obscures the direction in which they were driving – perhaps evidence that even at this stage Hardy was wavering between concealment and revelation. Rain comes on:

> Remote Egdon disappeared by degrees behind the liquid gauze. The evening grew darker, and the roads being crossed by gates it was not safe to drive faster than at a walking pace.

'Remote' is a late addition to the manuscript, Hardy trying to preserve some of the isolation of the heath he had so vividly generated in *The Return of the Native*. On the way back Tess talks of the urban recipients of the milk, who: 'don't know anything of us, and where it comes from; or think how we two drove miles across the moor to-night in the rain that it might reach 'em in time'. It is the 'moor' here that is interesting, apparently suggesting that their journey is not entirely, or even mainly through water-meadows; but also 'miles' seems to suggest that they went to a station placed somewhere at the distance of Wool rather than Moreton (apparently the nearest station if identity between Wessex and England is assumed – hardly more than two miles from wherever they might have been in the vicinity of Talbothays). It is perhaps as a belated support of this eastward stretching of the dairy's produce that in the first edition Dairyman Crick wonders, when he hears of the engagement of Tess and Angel: 'Who would make the ornamental butter-pats for the Anglebury and Sandbourne ladies?' (XXXII) In the manuscript and serial it was the Casterbridge ladies who might have to do without.

From Talbothays to Wellbridge

After their wedding Angel and Tess drive to the house in which he has taken rooms – which house certainly is at Wool, as every reader of the novel knows now:

> They drove by the level road along the valley to a distance of a few miles, and, reaching Wellbridge, turned away from the village to the left, and over the great Elizabethan bridge which gives the place half its name. Immediately behind it stood the house wherein they had engaged lodgings, whose exterior features are so well known to all travellers through the Froom Valley; once portion of a fine manorial residence, and the property and seat of a d'Urberville, but since its partial demolition a farm-house. (XXXIV)

The passage, though, had gone through several stages of evolution from the apparently fictional to the evidently factual, thus offering a microcosm of the changes taking place in Wessex over the years of the novel's composition. The distance they had to drive in the manuscript varied from 'seven or eight', to 'six or seven', and the final vaguer 'few' miles; but more interesting than such variation is that in the first manuscript version it was not Wellbridge but Stickleford that they reached, and when they did the whole passage was different. They

> turned at once over the old bridge to the farm-house in which they had engaged lodgings. Like so many of the farm-houses hereabout it had originally been a manorial residence; it had, moreover, been the property and home of a D'Urberville; a fact by no means singular in this district, where there were few old houses of the kind which had not at some time or other been the home of a branch of that important family.

Hardy then made sundry small changes, including altering Stickleford to Wellbridge, so that the compositors of the *Graphic* were faced with:

> turned straight away from the village to the lonely farm-house in which they had engaged lodgings, once part of a manorial residence and the property and home of a d'Urberville; an adaptation by no means singular in this district, where there were few old farmhouses which had not at some happy time or other been the home of a modest landowner, before ten estates were merged in one.

In sending copy to America for *Harper's Weekly* Hardy added a new sentence that highlights his growing attachment of significance to Tess's aristocratic forebears: 'Not that the d'Urbervilles, however, were of the latter description; but some member of the family seems to have resided on each of their estates.' But this sentence, like others unique to the American serial, was lost to the English transmission of the story.[6]

It is striking to note the tone of the guidebook that again predominates in the first edition version of this paragraph. There is a similar instance in a one-volume revision to a passage a few pages later, during Angel's nocturnal sleepwalking ramble with Tess in his arms. He enters the ruins of the nearby abbey and we are told in the first edition: 'Against the north wall was the empty stone coffin of an abbot, without a lid. In this he carefully laid her' (XXXVII). In the one-volume edition, the edition read by the large majority of contemporary readers of the novel, Hardy altered the sentence to read: 'Against the north wall was the empty stone coffin of an abbot, in which every tourist with a turn for grim humour was accustomed to stretch himself. In this Clare carefully laid Tess.' This change has two effects. It tends to destroy whatever symbolic force the whole episode had generated, and it openly provokes emulation by readers of the novel, who thus are enabled with the writer's authority to share a space with Tess. Fiction and reality, Wessex and England, can come no closer without merging.

From Wellbridge to Talbothays and Marlott

When Tess makes it easy for Angel to abandon her by saying that she will go home to her parents, they first go together to Talbothays, and then start towards Marlott:

> They re-entered the vehicle, and were driven along the roads to distant Weatherbury and Stagfoot Lane, till they reached Nuzzlebury, where Clare dismissed the fly and man. They rested here awhile, and entering the Vale were next driven onward towards her home by a stranger who did not know their relations. At a midway point, when many miles had been passed over, and where there were cross-roads, Clare stopped the conveyance, and said to Tess that if she meant to return to her mother's house it was here that he would leave her. (XXXVII)

The strangeness here is to read of Weatherbury as 'distant' from Talbothays, for we have already seen the distance described as only 'a few miles' (XVI). It is stranger still, in that the first part of the sentence was different in the manuscript; what Hardy initially wrote was very bare:

> They re-entered the vehicle, and were driven along the roads till they reached Weatherbury, where Clare dismissed the fly and man.

He fleshed this out in revision to:

> They re-entered the vehicle, and were driven along the roads through Weatherbury and Stagfoot-Lane, till they reached Nuttlebury, where Clare dismissed the fly and man.

He altered Nuttlebury to Nuzzlebury on the proofs for the serial. Lucy's speculation that Haselbury Bryant – as it was called on her Survey map – was intended seems a good one; she would have been more convinced had she known Hardy's first version, and the modern name Hazelbury Bryan. But the question still remains, why in the first edition did Hardy alter 'through Weatherbury' to 'to distant Weatherbury'? It is almost the first topographical revision which appears to make no sense however it is considered.

The rest of the journey was also described in less detail when Hardy first wrote it:

They rested here awhile, and were next driven onward by a stranger who did not know their relations. At a midway point, where there were crossroads, Clare stopped the conveyance, and said to Tess that if she meant to return to her mother's house it was here that he would leave her.

It is as if Hardy did not realize while he was writing the significance of this journey to Tess; that she would have marked all the points that were leading to this moment of pure pain – 'he would leave her' – and so had to go back and fill in the route. A romantic view of Hardy's relation to his heroine might suggest that as he wrote he wished to get it over with as quickly as possible, for it was painful for him also. Eventually she gets, alone, to Marlott.[7]

From Marlott via the Marshwood Vale to Flintcomb-Ash

Tess leaves her parents' home to work until the autumn at dairies in the west of Wessex beyond Port-Bredy (which in the manuscript was once Ivell), but she finds no permanent position. The next we see of her is walking from the unnamed Marshwood Vale towards a farm where her friend Marian is working, on the chalk uplands that divide the Froom Valley from Blackmoor.

> She had preferred the fertile country of the south-west to the upland farm for which she was now bound, because, for one thing, it was nearer to the home of her husband's father; and to hover about that region unrecognized, with the notion that she might decide to call at the Vicarage some day, gave her pleasure. But having once decided to try the higher and drier levels, she pressed on, marching afoot towards the village of Chalk-Newton, where she meant to pass the night. (XLI)

For the one-volume edition Hardy decided that 'the south-west' was too vague in the light of the new county-based Wessex – it might mean Devon, or rather Lower Wessex – so he altered the phrase to 'the country west of the River Brit', and made 'pressed on' more explicit as 'pressed back eastward'. Chalk-Newton is easily identifiable by its name as representing Maiden Newton. She trudges on towards Marian:

> Towards the second evening she reached the irregular chalk tableland or plateau, bosomed with semi-globular tumuli, which stretched between the valley of her birth and the valley of her love.
> Here the air was dry and cold, and the long cart-roads were blown white and dusty again within a few hours after rain. There were few trees, or none, those that would have grown in the hedges being mercilessly plashed down with the quickset by the tenant-farmers, the natural enemies of tree, bush, and brake. In the middle distance ahead of her she could see the summits of Bulbarrow and of Nettlecombe Tout, and they seemed

friendly. They had a low and unassuming aspect from this upland, though as approached on the other side from Blackmoor in her childhood they were as lofty bastions against the sky. Southerly, at many miles' distance, and over the hills and ridges coastward, she could discern a surface like polished steel: it was the English Channel at a point far out towards France.

Before her, in a slight depression, were the remains of a village. She had, in fact, reached Flintcomb-Ash, the place of Marian's sojourn. (XLVI)

Lucy noted the information given her about the habits of tenant-farmers, wondering why they so disliked trees; but she was more interested in puzzling over where exactly Flintcomb-Ash might be on the tableland. She could not work it out at this stage, and if she had had access to the manuscript she might at first have wondered if Hardy knew either, for Bulbarrow and Nettlecombe Tout appeared to Tess in the far, then in the near, and only finally in the middle distance. On the other hand she would also have noticed that Flintcomb-Ash was originally called Altland-Ash, and that a little later it appears first as Alton-Ash. This would have given her a clue, as the village of Alton was on her map, north of Piddletrenthide.

Flintcomb-Ash to Emminster and back

The work at Flintcomb-Ash was of the hardest, and Tess was compelled to make the journey to Emminster, to Angel's parents, to ask for their assistance. Hardy is remarkably careful and full in his account of her walk:

> She soon reached the edge of the vast escarpment below which stretched the loamy Vale of Blackmoor, now lying misty and still in the dawn. Instead of the colourless air of the uplands the atmosphere down there was a deep blue. Instead of the great enclosures of a hundred [**of fifty or sixty MS, G**] acres in which she was now accustomed to toil there were little fields below her of less than half-a-dozen acres, so numerous that they looked from this height like the meshes of a net. Here the landscape was whitey-brown; down there, as in Froom Valley, it was always green. Yet it was in that vale that her sorrow had taken shape, and she did not love it as formerly. Beauty to her, as to all who have felt, lay not in the thing, but in what the thing symbolized.
>
> Keeping the Vale on her right she steered steadily westward; passing above the Hintocks, crossing at right-angles the high-road from Sherton-Abbas to Casterbridge, and skirting High-Stoy or Rubdon Hill. Still following the elevated way she reached Cross-in-Hand, where the stone pillar stands desolate and silent, to mark the site of a miracle or a murder, or both. Three miles further she cut across the straight deserted Roman road called Long-Ash Lane; leaving which as soon as she reached it she

dipped down the hill by a transverse lane into the small town or village of Evershead, being now about half-way over the distance. She made a halt here, and breakfasted a second time, heartily enough – not at the Sow-and-Acorn, for she avoided inns, but at a cottage by the church.

The second half of her journey was through a more gentle country, by way of Benvill Lane.... about noon she paused by a gate on the edge of the basin in which Emminster and its Vicarage lay. (XLIV)

The route as it stands in the first edition is coherent enough, though it implies that the Hintocks of *The Woodlanders* are around the Dorchester–Sherborne road rather than, as in that novel, the Dorchester–Yeovil road. Hardy may well deliberately have used this opportunity to redirect readers' attention from Melbury Osmond and its neighbourhood – certainly Lucy made a puzzled query to herself along these lines; she notes with greater puzzlement that apparently Rubdon is another name for High-Stoy, and so she would have to revise all her inferences based on Bubb-Down as the Dorset version of Rubdon. She did not read the one-volume text, which is a pity on this occasion, since the alteration there of 'skirting High-Stoy or Rubdon Hill' to 'skirting Dogbury Hill and High-Stoy, with the dell between them called "The Devil's Kitchen"' might have assured her that Hardy had used the parallelism of the first edition as a fiction to move the landscape of *The Woodlanders* eastwards.

Hardy had decided on Evershead as the Wessex version of Evershot (as against Verton in 'Interlopers at the Knap') in 'The First Countess of Wessex', which was almost certainly written before this part of the manuscript of *Tess of the d'Urbervilles*; but King's Hintock in the story was certainly Melbury House, on the Dorchester–Yeovil road.[8]

In the manuscript, after the description of Cross-in-Hand, there is a mystery of sorts, for the passage originally read:

Three miles further she cut at right angles into Long-Ash Lane; leaving which as soon as she reached it she dipped down the hill by a transverse lane into the village of Chalk-Newton, and being now about half-way over the distance, she made a halt here, and breakfasted a second time heartily enough.

The second half of her journey was through a more gentle country.

This part of the journey in this version does not mesh at all with the earlier part; it is the way Tess would have gone if she had passed by the Cerne Abbas giant rather than Cross-in-Hand, and (tracing her journey farther back) if she had come from somewhere near Dole's Ash and Piddletrenthide rather than further north. However, there is no evidence on the manuscript leaf that the walk along the escarpment overlooking Blackmoor was an addition. The only hint at what might have happened is in an error in the passage that suggests he was copying in some haste (he originally wrote 'miracle or a miracle' rather than 'miracle or a murder'). Perhaps then in an earlier draft of this part of Tess's life he had imagined Alton-Ash near Plush, or further south, and he wrote the journey to Emminster with that placement in mind; but then the symbolic value of Cross-in-Hand occurred to him, and he had to have Tess pass by it. So he placed Flintcomb-Ash further north so that she might reasonably go along the crest of Batcombe on her way to Emminster; but he was in too much of a hurry to alter the remainder of the journey to match the new part. Hence the discrepancies that had to be fixed in further revision. It is at least possible to be clear that the general area is the correct one from another passage:

> as the evening light in the direction of the Giant's Hill by Abbot's-Cernel dissolved away, the white-faced moon of the season arose from the horizon that lay towards Middleton Abbey and Shottsford on the other side. (XLVIII)

Tess's nerve fails in face of the Clare's closed door and Angel's brothers' tone of voice. She walks more slowly back again over the same lanes in her best thin shoes, and, for further punishment, encounters Alec d'Urberville preaching at Evershead. She hurries away from him, but not before he has seen her. So Tess has walked thirty miles across some of the highest hills in Wessex to worse than no purpose; as with so many of her journeys, it would have been better for her if she had not taken it.

From Flintcomb-Ash to Marlott

Tess is forced to walk this road on hearing from her sister of the illness of her mother:

> She plunged into the chilly equinoctial darkness as the clock struck ten, for her fifteen miles' walk under the steely stars.... Tess pursued the nearest course along bye-lanes that she would almost have feared in the daytime... she proceeded mile after mile, ascending and descending till she came to Bulbarrow, and, about midnight, looked from that height into the abyss of chaotic shade which was all that revealed itself of the vale on whose farther side she was born. Having already traversed about five miles on the upland she had now some ten or eleven [**eight or nine MS only**] in the lowland before her journey would be finished. The winding road downwards became just visible to her under the wan starlight as she followed it.... It was the heavy clay land of Blackmoor Vale, and a part of the Vale to which turnpike-roads had never penetrated.... At Nuzzlebury [**Copsebury MS1; Nuttlebury MS2**] she passed the village inn... At

three she turned the last corner of the maze of lanes she had threaded, and entered Marlott (L)

This route offers another mystery to folk like Lucy. There is no reason for Tess to go from Bulbarrow to Hazelbury Bryan to get to Marlott. So it is possible that when Hardy wrote in the manuscript that it was at Copsebury that she 'passed the village inn', he might have intended Wooland, which *is* on the direct route from Bulbarrow to Marlott. On the other hand the more direct route from Flintcomb-Ash to Marlott *is* through Nuttlebury/Hazelbury, but then she would have gone nowhere near Bulbarrow, and would actually have crossed a turnpike road. It seems that Hardy was still anxious to keep the uncertainty alive that prevented Wessex from becoming simply Dorset and the rest.

From Marlott to Kingsbere

Tess's mother recovers, but her father dies, and the family has to leave the Marlott house. At first, in the manuscript they went the few miles to Stourcastle; then in the serial it became Shottsford Forum. Not until the first edition was their goal fixed upon as Kingsbere; and it was this change that prompted (or was prompted by) the removal of Tess's visit to her ancestors' tombs from her journey to Talbothays to this place in the novel. There are several versions of this house-ridding journey, though the earliest destination of Stourcastle had already been forgotten when Hardy came to describe it:

> The distance was great, and though they had started so early it was quite late in the day when they turned the flank of an eminence which formed part of the upland called Greenhill. While the horses stood to stale and breathe themselves Tess looked around. Under the hill, and just ahead of them, was the half-dead townlet of their pilgrimage, Kingsbere, where lay those ancestors of whom her father had spoken and sung to painfulness: Kingsbere, the spot of all spots in the world which could be considered the d'Urberville's home, since they had resided there for full five hundred years. (LII)

It is perhaps because Hardy is interested in ancient tombs more than anything else that he allows himself to call Kingsbere a 'half-dead townlet'. It was not until the one-volume edition that Hardy finally understood all the implications of the change to Kingsbere; there the first sentence was 'The distance was great – too great for a day's journey – and it was with the utmost difficulty that the horses performed it.' In the manuscript and the *Graphic* the whole passage was quite different:

> Later in the day they reached the top of a hill which formed part of the upland dividing the Vale from Shottsford-Forum. They had all walked up

because of the steepness, and while the horses stood to breathe themselves Tess looked around. The country was more open now; high downs had taken the place of the small fertile fields, and a great deal of the country was uninclosed.

When they reach Kingsbere they are told that their lodgings have been let to someone else, and so all their belongings are unloaded in the lee of the parish church. Tess looks at the pile of furniture, but the narrator has a wider context to show us:

> Round about were deparked hills and slopes – now cut up into little paddocks – and the green foundations that showed where the d'Urberville mansion once had stood; also an outlying stretch of Egdon Heath that had always belonged to the estate. Hard by, the aisle of the church called the d'Urberville Aisle looked on imperturbably.

In the manuscript version their waggon is stopped at the side of the road above Shottsford by the man who tells them the lodging is let. Tess similarly gazes at 'the waggon of goods', but the environment is different: 'Round about, Hod Hill, Hambledon, Bulbarrow, and other surrounding eminences, looked on imperturbably.' It is striking how prominent, in this novel, are Wessex Heights.

From Chalk-Newton to Emminster, and thence to Sandbourne

When Angel returns to England, he takes a train to visit his parents at Emminster; they wait for him:

> 'Plenty of time yet,' said the Vicar. 'He doesn't reach Chalk-Newton till six, even if the train should be punctual, and ten miles of country-road, five of them in Crimmercrock Lane, are not jogged over in a hurry by our old horse.' (LIII)

This helped to confirm for Lucy the near certainty that Emminster was Beaminster, and Chalk-Newton Maiden Newton. The name Crimmercrock Lane seems designed for a poem, and Hardy later made it better known through his often-anthologized ballad 'The Dark-Eyed Gentleman', which begins

> I pitched my day's leazings in Crimmercrock Lane,
> To tie up my garter and jog on again...

This narrator, however, jogs on foot rather than in a pony chaise.

When Angel sets out from Emminster to find Tess, he unconsciously follows the route of her abortive journey there (see below p. 249). Then from Flintcomb-Ash he retraces her steps to Marlott, where he is at last given some positive information from the family that had inherited the d'Urberville cottage, though the information is different in different texts. This is the manuscript:

> Clare learned that John Durbeyfield was dead; that his widow and children had left Marlott, declaring that they were going to live at Shottsford-Forum, but instead of doing so they had gone on to Chaseborough....
>
> The distance was a long one for a walk, but Clare felt such a strong desire for isolation that at first he would neither hire a conveyance, nor go to a circuitous line of railway by which he might eventually reach the place. At Shaston, however, he found he must hire; but the way was such that he did not enter Chaseborough till about seven o'clock in the evening, having traversed a distance of over twenty miles since leaving Marlott.
>
> The town being small he had little difficulty in finding Mrs Durbeyfield's tenement, which was in the small upper floor of a house in Whitcliff Street, where she had stowed away her clumsy old furniture as best she could. (LIV)

Thus Angel more or less follows another of Tess's journeys, receding unconsciously, as he does so, further back into her past. In the serial the parallel is exact, as Trantridge becomes the village he travels to, and Tess's mother's tenement becomes 'a house in a walled garden, remote from the main street'. Hardy gave himself the pleasure in the first edition of having Alec on a d'Urberville tomb, but he also effaced altogether the place Joan ended up:

> Clare learned that John Durbeyfield was dead; that his widow and children had left Marlott, declaring that they were going to live at Kingsbere, but instead of doing so had gone on to another place they named....
>
> ... he did not enter Joan's place till about seven o'clock in the evening, having traversed a distance of over twenty miles since leaving Marlott.

In the one-volume edition he altered 'street' in the *Graphic's* last sentence to 'road', implying that the village was indeed a small one; but this does not help answer the question: why did Hardy not want the reader to know where Alec put Joan and her family? Is he no longer interested in the quite powerful symbolism of Angel's search through Tess's past? The answer seems to lie in Clare's actions after being told by Joan Durbeyfield that Tess was at Sandbourne:

> Without entering the house Clare turned away. There was a station three miles ahead, and paying off his coachman he walked thither. The last train to Sandbourne left shortly after, and it bore Clare on its wheels. (LIV)

When Joan was at Cranborne/Chaseborough the nearest station was four or five miles away; if she is at Pentridge/Trantridge it is seven or so. Clearly Angel has to get on a train for Sandbourne, and such a distance was perhaps too much for him to be expected to walk at that stage. So Hardy made the place from which he walked anonymous, and the exigencies of the new Wessex are paramount.

Sandbourne has grown since *The Hand of Ethelberta*:

> This fashionable watering-place, with its eastern and its western stations, its piers, its groves of pines, its promenades, and its covered gardens was, to Angel Clare, like a fairy place suddenly created by the stroke of a wand, and allowed to get a little dusty. An outlying eastern tract of the enormous Egdon Waste was close at hand, yet on the very verge of that tawny piece of antiquity such a glittering novelty as this pleasure-city had chosen to spring up. Within the space of a mile from its outskirts every irregularity of the soil was prehistoric, every channel an undisturbed British trackway; not a sod having been turned there since the days of the Caesars. Yet the exotic had grown here, suddenly as the prophet's gourd; and had drawn hither Tess. (LV)

This, apart from the characteristic Wessex comparison of the magical mushroom town with the land's ancient and undisturbed past, is also an interesting gloss on *The Return of the Native*; by this account Egdon really is substantial by English standards – twenty miles or more in length.

From Sandbourne to Stonehenge and Wintoncester

It is in keeping with the rest of the novel that after being sent away by the Tess whose body and soul do not recognize each other, Angel thinks to take a train somewhere, but ends up walking away from Sandbourne. In turn Tess thrusts a knife into her problem and hurries off on foot to find Angel. Together they walk on more or less northwards; near the end of the day they pass a large building:

> Through the latter half hour of their walk their footpath had taken them up a hill, and turning the corner of a lane, they saw behind an ornamental gate a large board on which was painted in white letters, "This desirable Mansion to be Let Furnished"; particulars following, with directions to apply to some London agents. Passing through the gate they could see the house – an Ionic stone building of regular design, in ashlar.
>
> 'I know it,' said Clare. 'It is Martley Manor-house. You can see that it is shut up: and grass is growing on the drive.' (LVII)

This is how the description began in the manuscript; Hardy had no idea yet where it might be, or what kind of house it was. After the first stages of revision the reader would have had more to go on:

> Through the latter miles of their walk their footpath had taken them into the depths of the New Forest, and, towards evening, turning the corner of a lane, they perceived behind an ornamental... the house – a dignified building of regular design, faced with ashlar.
> 'I know it,' said Clare. 'It is Ferly Manor-house. You can see that it is shut up: and grass is growing on the drive.'

Hardy had fixed in his imagination on some house design; perhaps even on a specific house – the change of name seems to suggest that he had – perhaps Burley Manor, though that was predominately brick. He was, however, not satisfied, and he again made the architecture more anonymous, changing 'faced with ashlar' to 'and large accommodation'; he also altered the name again – to Bramshurst Manor-house. The 'hurst' element of the new name suggests Brockenhurst or Lyndhurst; the 'Brams' part hints at Bramshaw House, six miles north-west of Lyndhurst. This is how the *Graphic* had the passage.

The two travellers passed by the deserted place initially, but Tess soon grew tired and Angel 'was growing weary likewise, for they had been walking more than five hours'. So the first manuscript version. Again Hardy developed a clearer idea of where they might be in revision: 'He was growing weary likewise, for they had wandered not less than twenty miles,' a distance which would apply to Bramshaw. In default of other suitable shelter, they return to the shut-up house, and spend the time of their lives there.

After they are disturbed and leave, Angel plans their further escape:

> We shall get to some port in two or three days. But perhaps it will be best to avoid London after all; and Southampton too, although it is near. Suppose we try Bristol?
> Having thus desultorily thought of a new course he adopted it, bearing approximately towards the last-named port. Their long repose at the manor-house lent them walking power now; and towards mid-day they approached the steepled city of Melchester, which lay directly in their way. He decided to rest her in a clump of trees during the afternoon, and push onward under cover of darkness. At dusk Clare purchased food as usual, and their night march began, the boundary between Upper and Mid-Wessex being crossed about eight o'clock.
> Their course bowed to the right of a direct line, by reason of the intervening city. To walk across country without much regard to roads was not new to Tess, and she showed her old agility in the performance. One townlet, ancient Ambresbury, they were obliged to pass through in order to take

advantage of the town bridge for crossing a large river. It was between two and three in the morning when they went along the deserted street, lighted by an oil lamp here and there, and bordered by no pavement to echo their footsteps. The massive church-tower rose on their right hand, and beyond it was the stone bridge they sought. Once over this they followed the turnpike-road which plunged across an open plain. (LVIII)

This account is notable primarily because, as mentioned earlier (above p. 59) it is the first time in the manuscript that county divisions within Wessex are in the initial inscription. The leaf is almost entirely fair copy, unlike those surrounding it, and may well date from October 1890, when Hardy was making final revisions to the second half of the manuscript before sending it to the *Graphic*. The decision to align Wessex with England in this way may have seemed to Hardy no more than a step in a process of thought that extended back over many years, but looked at from the outside it represents a demarcation line; as Lucy recognized, Wessex had become something new, though the full implications would not be understood by most of Hardy's readers until five years later.

Hardy only gave a name to the 'townlet' that Angel and Tess were forced to pass through in the first edition; Ambresbury is transparently Amesbury (for which place it was the Saxon Wessex name), but it only lasted a year, because for the one-volume edition he changed the route of the pair altogether, so that the relevant sentence began 'The intercepting city, ancient Melchester, they were...' He must have decided that they would necessarily have chosen the most direct route to Bristol, and that walking through Melchester/Salisbury at the dead of night was not such a great risk. So Ambresbury has never made it on to any of the lists of Hardy's Wessex places, and indeed the whole passage is different in the one-volume edition:

'We shall soon get out of this district altogether. We'll continue our course as we've begun it, and keep straight north. Nobody will think of looking for us there. We shall be looked for at the Wessex ports if we are sought at all. When we are in the north we will get to a port and away.'

Having thus persuaded her the plan was pursued, and they kept a bee line northward. Their long repose at the manor-house lent them walking power now; and towards mid-day they found that they were approaching the steepled city of Melchester, which lay directly in their way. He decided to rest her in a clump of trees during the afternoon, and push onward under cover of darkness. At dusk Clare purchased food as usual, and their night march began, the boundary between Upper and Mid-Wessex being crossed about eight o'clock.

To walk across country without much regard to roads was not new to Tess, and she showed her old agility in the performance. The intercepting city, ancient Melchester, they were obliged to pass through in order to take advantage of the town bridge for crossing a large river that obstructed them. It was about midnight when they went along the deserted streets, lighted fitfully by the few lamps, keeping off the pavement that it might not echo their footsteps. The graceful pile of cathedral architecture rose dimly on their right hand, but it was lost upon them now. Once out of the town they followed the turnpike-road which after a few miles plunged across an open plain.

Hardy needed to retain the adjective 'ancient' when altering Ambresbury to Melchester, for the design he had imagined for Tess and Angel's journey required it. They walk from the brand new seaside resort to a manor-house perhaps a hundred, perhaps three hundred years old, to an 'ancient' settlement (it is relevant here that Hardy gave Amesbury its Saxon name) to Stonehenge, the most striking of the prehistoric monuments in the region. This is a pattern he repeated somewhat more economically and memorably at the end of his poem 'Channel Firing':

Again the guns disturbed the hour,
Roaring their readiness to avenge,
As far inland as Stourton Tower,
And Camelot, and starlit Stonehenge.

The progress in both is inland through space and backwards through time. In the poem's quite wonderful last lines the temporal distance covered hints at the perpetual nature of the human desire for violence and revenge; on the other hand, Hardy's choice as markers of a folly, a romantic legend, and a religious and cultural monument, includes a very wide range of human creative enterprise to stand against the destructiveness of the naval weaponry sounding about them. In *Tess of the d'Urbervilles* the journey inward and backward is part of the dense texture of the novel that reveals Wessex as alive in the present and the past, that shows part of the past still active in the present, and that also sometimes contrasts present with past. One of the conflicts dramatized in Tess's nature is between an instinctive paganism, pantheism, and a learned Christianity, and it is no coincidence that Hardy makes sure we are aware of the church she passes at Ambresbury, or the cathedral at Melchester, in order to reach the pagan place – indeed it may have been in part to obtain the more impressive Christian monument that he changed their route. To make sure that we do not miss the point Tess says as she lies on one of the fallen pillars of Stonehenge: 'you used to say at Talbothays that I was a heathen. So now I am at home' (LVIII). Tess, one might say, has been searching throughout Wessex for a home, and the journey from Alec d'Urberville's Sandbourne to Stonehenge is her life experience in microcosm. Wessex in this context assumes another relevance, in that historically it began pagan and became Christian (to be destroyed by the

Normans who were Tess's ancestors); and it is notable that the last chapter of the novel begins with the narrator's comment that Wintoncester (like Ambresbury for Amesbury, this was the Saxon Wessex name for Winchester), where Tess is to die, was 'aforetime capital of Wessex', laying historical Wessex consciously alongside his fictional creation sharing the same name.

Wintoncester is described in rich language, but again, as more often in this novel than before, with some of the redundant detail of a guidebook to the city:

> The prospect from this summit was almost unlimited. In the valley beneath lay the city they had just left, its more prominent buildings showing as in an isometric drawing – among them the broad cathedral tower, with its Norman windows and immense length of aisle and nave, the spires of St Thomas's, the pinnacled tower of the College, and, more to the right, the tower and gables of the ancient hospice, where to this day the pilgrim may receive his dole of bread and ale. Behind the city swept the rotund upland of St Catherine's Hill, farther off, landscape beyond landscape, till the horizon was lost in the radiance of the sun hanging above it.

This medieval cityscape fills in the temporal space after historical Wessex, but it is within the modern that Tess will be executed:

> Against these far stretches of country rose, in front of the other city edifices, a large red-brick building, with level gray roofs, and rows of short barred windows bespeaking captivity, the whole contrasting greatly by its formalism with the quaint irregularities of the Gothic erections. (LIX)

It is with the view over the capital of ancient Wessex that this episode in Hardy's account of his modern imagined Wessex ends. It is the fullest account he ever offered, and it is perhaps most striking for the relationship it offers between the old and traditional and the new and 'progressive'. Paula Power's problem – castle or modern house, de Stancy or Somerset – which is explicitly unresolved for her at the end of *A Laodicean*, is also posed here, and it is true that when, for instance, a grasshopper-like horse-drawn reaping-machine is balanced against a sinister steam-driven threshing-machine, there is no doubt which we are expected to prefer. Every reader will be able to think of other examples. But the question is not quite so clear cut. It is evident that the usurper of Tess's ancestral name, the modern family of trade or usury, is initially regarded with contempt by the narrator, and as represented by Alec, is held up to be despised. But the narrator also comments of the Stoke d'Urbervilles that 'this family formed a very good stock whereon to regraft a name which sadly wanted such renovation' (V), and Tess's own d'Urberville ancestry is purely a liability for her.

It is a feature of Wessex, as we have seen, that lives are lived constantly against a background of work carefully and effectively described. An example of this in *Tess of the d'Urbervilles* is how to bind a sheaf of corn:

> Her binding proceeds with clock-like monotony. From the sheaf last finished she draws a handful of ears, patting their tips with her left palm to bring them even. Then stooping low she moves forward, gathering the corn with both hands against her knees, and pushing her left gloved hand under the bundle to meet the right on the other side, holding the corn in an embrace like that of a lover. She brings the ends of the bond together, and kneels on the sheaf while she ties it, beating back her skirts now and then when lifted by the breeze. A bit of her naked arm is visible between the buff leather of the gauntlet and the sleeve of her gown; and as the day wears on its feminine smoothness becomes scarified by the stubble, and bleeds. (XIV)

It is characteristic of the fruitful density of Hardy's writing that in such a detailed and practical description he can include the irony of Tess, the mother of Alec d'Urberville's child, embracing a straw lover; and it is also characteristic of this novel that the account should end with Tess bleeding. It is not only that she is, as many commentators have pointed out, continually associated with shed blood, but also that in *Tess of the d'Urbervilles* for the first time in a novel much of the work undertaken is not only arduous but also painful. Around most of the dairying is wrapped the glamour of love that hangs over the Frome valley, though the search through the meadow for garlic is back-breaking enough; but at Flintcomb-Ash the reader of Wessex experiences vicariously the misery of arable fieldwork, of dealing in harsh winter weather with the swedes and the reed-drawing and the machine-threshing. That Marian sustains herself with pulls at the liquor flask is entirely unsurprising; that Marian, Tess and Izz manage to sustain themselves through communal friendship is remarkable. In fact, though, the assiduous reader of Hardy would have been prepared to a degree for these intense hardships by a passage in 'The Dorsetshire Labourer':

> In winter and spring a farm-woman's occupation is often 'turnip-hacking' – that is, picking out from the land the stumps of turnips which have been eaten off by sheep – or feeding the threshing machine, clearing away straw from the same, and standing on the rick to hand forward the sheaves....
>
> Not a woman in the county but hates the threshing-machine. The dust, the din, the sustained exertion demanded to keep up with the steam tyrant are distasteful to all women but the coarsest. I am not sure whether, at the present time, women are employed to feed the machine, but some

years ago a woman had frequently to stand just above the whizzing wire drum, and feed from morning to night – a performance for which she was quite unfitted, and many were the manoeuvres to escape that responsible position. (*Orel* pp. 186–7)

Hardy wishes us to be clear that life in the 'secluded world' of Wessex is for many not idyllic; Marty South's work in *The Woodlanders* offers the same warning against the too easy pastoral assumptions of an urban readership, assumptions that perhaps *Under the Greenwood Tree* or *Far From the Madding Crowd*, or Clym Yeobright cutting furze for pleasure in *The Return of the Native*, had fostered.[9]

Hardy had always pointed out to his metropolitan readers the differences between their experience and that of the characters he describes, but in *Tess of the d'Urbervilles* this kind of instruction shares from time to time the polemical edge of 'The Dorsetshire Labourer'. At other times he is particularly interested in distinguishing the closeness to nature of the Wessex workfolk, particularly of the women:

> But those of the other sex were the most interesting of this company of binders, by reason of the charm which is acquired by woman when she becomes part and parcel of outdoor nature, and is not merely an object set down therein as at ordinary times. A field-man is a personality afield; a field-woman is a portion of the field; she has somehow lost her own margin, imbibed the essence of her surrounding, and assimilated herself with it (XIV).

In the first version in the manuscript 'acquired by' was 'imparted to'; Hardy has come to understand that their assimilation with their environment is a matter of will and not of inevitability. In harmony with this perception is the picture of Tess coming closer and closer to Flintcomb-Ash:

> Thus Tess walks on; a figure which is part of the landscape; a fieldwoman pure and simple, in winter guise; a grey serge cape, a red woollen cravat, a stuff skirt covered by a whitey-brown rough wrapper, and buff-leather gloves. Every thread of that old attire has become wire-drawn and thin under the stroke of rain-drops, the burn of sunbeams, and the stress of winds. (XLII)

Angel observes the dairymaids at Talbothays:

> All the girls drew onward to the spot where the cows were grazing in the farther mead, the bevy advancing with the bold grace of wild animals – the reckless unchastened motion of women accustomed to unlimited

space – in which they abandoned themselves to the air as a swimmer to the wave. It seemed natural enough to him now that Tess was again in sight to choose a mate from unconstrained Nature, and not from the abodes of Art. (XXVII)

It is interesting that when Hardy first wrote it the last sentence ended: 'to choose a mate from naked Nature, and not from disciplined Art' – a rather more sexually charged distinction which it is sad to loose. But in either case the image of the young women in a state of nature is vivid and powerful, and the distinction between them and most of their contemporary female readers is strongly drawn – as Lucy confessed. The same is true when Hardy discusses Wessex courtship customs:

> That she had already permitted him to make love to her he read as an additional assurance, not fully realizing that in fields and pastures lovemaking is more often accepted for its own sweet sake than in the carking anxious homes of the genteel, where a home for the body is more thought of than a passion for the heart. (XXVIII)

Thus the first inscription: here is what Osgood, McIlvaine published:

> That she had already permitted him to make love to her he read as an additional assurance, not fully trowing that in fields and pastures to 'sigh gratis' is by no means deemed waste; love-making being here more often accepted inconsiderately and for its own sweet sake than in the carking anxious homes of the ambitious, where a girl's craving for an establishment paralyses her healthy thought of a passion as an end. (250)

The fundamental difference between the two is the addition of the idea that to think of a passion as an end in itself (with all the possible consequences of such a thought) is healthy. In revision to the manuscript and in the *Graphic* 'healthy' was 'natural'. What is natural is not always healthy, and Hardy is making a distinction here for the first edition along the same lines as the assertion of Tess's purity on the title-page. Not only is sexual passion natural, it is good for you – even unto pregnancy and childbirth – if only you are able to view it rightly. And the passage becomes part of the quarrel which new Wessex proposes, by example and by argument, with the established social order of Britain – most particularly in this novel and in *Jude the Obscure*. Take, for instance, the astonishment of Angel Clare's brothers that he can think of joining the Marlott Club-walkers:

> 'No – no; nonsense!' said the first. 'Dancing in public with a troop of country hoydens – suppose we should be seen!' (II)

Or Alec's comment on Tess wiping away his 'kiss of mastery': 'You are mighty sensitive for a farm girl!' (VIII). Though Alec perhaps wouldn't be aware of the distinction, Hardy felt it sufficiently strong (in the light of 'The Dorsetshire Labourer') to alter 'farm' to 'cottage' in the one-volume edition. Tess offers (amongst many other things) an example of the ease with which cottagers can become farm-labourers, though also she might as easily have settled down as a gentleman-farmer's wife, had not circumstances willed it otherwise.

This last conventional phrase, though, blandly masks another issue that has become of considerable importance in Wessex. In responding to *The Return of the Native* or *The Mayor of Casterbridge* it is has been necessary to talk about fate, destiny, providence, chance. In *Tess of the d'Urbervilles* the question of agency in Wessex moves to a different plane, while retaining all the old understanding. In *The Mayor of Casterbridge* there is the conflict between the idea of personal responsibility for one's destiny – 'character is fate' – and the unexpressed idea of the novelist as fate. In *Tess of the d'Urbervilles*, though it seems otherwise, the investigation of causality moves further away from the human. Casual commentary rests on notorious details such as Tess's letter to Angel explaining about her baby sliding under carpet as well as door; but Hardy's investigation has really moved away from coincidences. The only chances outside her control that irretrievably affect Tess's life are that Simon Stoke took the name d'Urberville, that Angel should be at Talbothays at the same time as her, and that Alec should be at Evershead when she passed by – and perhaps the death of the horse Prince, which lays a sense of responsibility on Tess sufficient to force her to accept the idea of claiming kin, though in this case it would be possible to argue that but for his moral and physical weaknesses her father would have been driving the cart.

But these few chances are enough. However much personal responsibility Tess might take for her actions is not the most important point any more. It is the way of things on our planet that preoccupies Hardy in *Tess of the d'Urbervilles*; and more precisely what we are to make of a world in which Tess is not permitted to meet and love Angel before meeting Alec – in which such acts of cruelty are commonplace. In such enquiries, Wessex has no relevance; the concern is universal – or rather, in this area Wessex offers an example, a controlled experiment, one might say, to test this universal (but perhaps not irreversible) law.[10]

There is also in the novel more instruction about the nature of farmers, farms and villages in Wessex; about the tenure and destruction of cottages, and similar matters.[11] The reflection of the truth as he saw it about rural life in Dorset and surrounding counties embodied in such passages, like the universalization of the causality issue, placed forcibly before him a central paradox of Wessex. It began, so to speak, as a disclaimer and a trademark, as if he should have said: 'This is *my* perception of how things are in the culture and society I know best; but because it is personal, it is not to be taken as impartial or objective. The perception has truth, but not necessarily the truth of a photograph or a magazine article.' Wessex gave him freedom to select, to invent, to imagine, not just the characters and their actions, but aspects of the culture they are imagined to live in. And so the invented names, the wrong directions, the conflation of details, disguising to some degree to all readers, and completely to most, his borrowings from England – but even if these borrowings had been obvious to all, still the adoption of Wessex would have provided for Hardy the creative freedom he required within his need to represent his own environment and culture.

What we have seen, though, is that as he matured as a writer, he found most elements of disguise less and less necessary. In his explicitly historical novel *The Trumpet-Major*, Hardy effectively destroyed the broadest level of disguise by using English names for all but the heart of the fiction in Overcombe. In doing so, as we have seen, he embodied a distinction between recorded and unrecorded history. In *The Mayor of Casterbridge* the pressure of reality, of his own past experience of Dorchester as a boy and young man, and his present observation of it as a successfully returning native, threatens to drive out Wessex. That he is forced to tell the historical truth in the midst of the narrative about the destruction of Mixen Lane/Mill Lane is a small manifestation of a strong force in Hardy's maturing creative personality that wants his readers to understand that what he describes is accurate – is how things really were. He begins, as I have said, to see that he is caught in the paradox of Wessex – that if it gives him freedom to adapt and use as he wishes elements of his experience in Dorset and neighbouring areas of other counties, or of life itself, it also gives readers freedom to treat what he says about the culture and society there, or his perceptions about human existence in general as fictional, as belonging to a different order of things than their own.[12]

The problem comes to a head in *Tess of the d'Urbervilles*: hence the decision to use transparent names for places that began just before the novel was started; hence the division of Wessex into counties like those of England; hence the use of Saxon Wessex names; hence the announcement that Wintoncester was once the capital of Wessex. Wessex is effectively no longer a disguise; it is simply a trademark. And yet he clings to the last veil, not just because it is good business – because Wessex has become synonymous with Hardy for the reading public – but because it still does offer a vestige of freedom; it does still give him protection from attack. But, as he would find when it came to *Jude the Obscure*, the protection was very flimsy.

Tess of the d'Urbervilles stimulated a very large number of reviews, and most of them concentrated on the issues of purity and of morality in general; but they were also aware to a greater or lesser degree that it was impossible to talk about the novel without saying something of Wessex; very few, however, took Hardy so seriously in this respect as had Paul and Barrie before them. At one extreme of pastoralism Richard le Gallienne wrote approvingly of Hardy's 'Arcady of Wessex', and called him 'our modern Theocritus' which would perhaps have been apposite in the 1870s; in a hostile notice Mowbray Morris decided that the 'Tess of Mr Hardy's inner consciousness is as much a creature of fantasy as Titania or Fenella.'

The class-issue is unconsciously raised by other reviewers; for the *Speaker* Hardy has so fully embodied Wessex and its people that the reader 'falls to their level' and shares their experience. Richard Hutton wrote of Tess that she 'was pure enough in her instincts, considering the circumstances and class in which she was born'. From similar elevation *Punch* commented on the reality of Hardy's Wessex folk, based on the 'thousands and thousands of genuine Pagans, superstitious Boeotians, with whom the schoolmaster can do little, and the parson still less', while Margaret Oliphant's dismissive piece includes these comments: 'Everybody knows what Mr Hardy's peasants in Wessex are. They are a quaint people, given to somewhat highflown language, and confused and complicated reasoning', and 'Wessex is a very primitive country, we allow...'

Oliphant did distinguish between the fictional Wessex and the English Dorset (she wrote of John Durbeyfield 'If he is not good Dorsetshire, he is at least good Hardy'), but the notice in the *Times* moves indifferently between the two as if no distinction were necessary. It is the *Pall Mall Gazette*, though, that touches in an innocent way on the full complexity of the novel:

> it is Tess who fills one's mind and haunts one's imagination, and in the heart-rending pity of her story one is little able to pause and do justice to the bits of rustic chorus, the wonderful descriptions of Wessex scenery in the changes of the seasons, never better done by Hardy than in this book, and to all the social and natural circumstance with which her story is interwoven.

The cliché of 'rustic chorus' and the primacy given to landscape description are offset by the awareness of the intricate web of interconnection between Tess, her environment, and her culture.[13]

5
Handling New Wessex

As is reasonably well known by now, the sequence of stories and anecdotes at first called 'Wessex Folk', written as soon as he had finished *Tess of the d'Urbervilles*, exists in a draft manuscript version – the only substantial piece of Hardy's fiction for which this is the case. Hardy's friend Alfred Parsons

drew for *Harper's New Monthly Magazine* an illustration to the opening paragraph, which makes it clear that the market town intended is Casterbridge/Dorchester, though Hardy does not name it.

> It is a Saturday afternoon of blue and yellow autumn-time, and the scene is the high street of a well-known market town. A large carrier's van stands in the quadrangular fore-court of the White Hart Inn, upon the sides of its spacious tilt being painted, in weather-beaten letters: 'Burthen, Carrier to Longpuddle'. These vans, so numerous hereabout, are a respectable if somewhat lumbering class of conveyance, much resorted to by decent travellers not overstocked with money, the better among them roughly corresponding to the old French *diligences*.
>
> The present one is timed to leave the town at four o'clock precisely, and it is now half past three by the ancient dial face in the church tower at the top of the street.

Parsons's illustration also shows clearly that the clock visible from the White Hart is on the Corn Exchange and not on the church. The draft manuscript sketches in a few of these details, often with alternative readings – thus 'market town' might indeed have been 'county town', the White Hart might have been the Black Hart, and the carrier's destination was at first Upper Trentripple, and then either Upper Joggingford or Joggington, before the 'ton' was also cancelled. Interestingly, just before 'market/county town', there are two abbreviated indications of possible names for the town: 'Tone' and 'Mex'. The former must represent the Toneborough of 'For Conscience Sake'; the latter may intend Melchester, or may represent some new name Hardy had in mind; in any case both were soon cancelled.

When Hardy finally decided where Burthen was going, he chose, in keeping with his new approach to Wessex, a name that is transparent, though not without its internal ambiguity. As Lucy was clear, Longpuddle is a village along the river Puddle or Piddle – but did, she asked herself, Mr Hardy intend Piddletrenthide, Piddlehinton, Puddletown, or Tolpuddle? The draft manuscript's Upper Trentripple suggests the first of these, but she had no access to that. Soon Longpuddle splits itself into Upper and Lower villages, and since Weatherbury is mentioned, she speculates that neither can be Puddletown, which seems to be confirmed by the end of the sequence when 'the van descended the hill leading into the long straggling village'. 'That certainly isn't Puddletown', she wrote. 'Perhaps Mr Hardy thinks of Longpuddle as both villages, with White Lackington connecting them into one? The houses on the map certainly seem to wander up the valley without a break. Then Upper Longpuddle, where they seem particularly to be going, would be Piddletrenthide.'

Her book is packed with notes of other places too. She has Mellstock and Yalbury Wood and Lewgate from *Under the Greenwood Tree*, and the new

Climmerston, that she suspects, searching the area on the map, must be Waterstone. Then there is Scrimpton, which she can't place – the only helpful detail is that the parish church is a mile and more from the houses of the village, and Monksbury, where someone goes to take a farm, and which is obviously Abbotsbury, she thinks. Abbot's-Cernel is mentioned again, and, though she has no idea of what the figure looks like, she is surprised to read of the 'Cerne Giant', than whom Andrey Satchel knew no more of music, rather than the Cernel Giant. And finally there is Tranton on the road between Woodyates Inn (given its real name) and Shottsford/Blandford, which she thinks, having traced the road on the map, must stand for Tarrant Hinton. One might add what Lucy did not write, that the map of South Wessex is rapidly filling in.

Besides the proliferation of new Wessex places, 'Wessex Folk' is also filled with music and dance. These have always been privileged elements of Wessex, of primary significance not just for their own sakes but also as indicators of character and conveyors of action. Few would now or in the nineteenth century associate Dorset with music, but it is impossible to bring Wessex before the mind and not hear a dance band or a group of church musicians. In 'The History of the Hardcomes' a dance is the cause of all; 'Old Andrey's Experience as a Musician' is a mere anecdote, but 'Absent-mindedness in a Parish Choir', though comic, shares the serious theme that ran through *Under the Greenwood Tree*; the connection is made clear by the narrator's judgement that the Longpuddle band was 'almost as good as the Mellstock parish players that were led by the Dewys; and that's saying a great deal' (270) – indeed in the manuscript he held that they *were* as good.

The last story in the sequence, 'Netty Sargent's Copyhold' turns on the issue that had driven part of *The Woodlanders*, and was discussed in *Tess of the d'Urbervilles*, the falling in of the last life on which possession of a property depends. It was possible to extend tenure by the payment of a small 'fine', but there had been delay in paying it, and the narrator of the story comments:

> How that wretched old Squire would rejoice at getting the little tenancy into his hands! He did not really require it, but constitutionally hated these tiny copyholds and leaseholds and freeholds, which made islands of independence in the fair, smooth ocean of his estates.

In Wessex all landlords are opposed to extending such arrangements. Indeed hostility like this between the gentry and the workfolk or the cottagers is a feature of 'Wessex Folk'.[1]

In *The Bookman* for October 1891 there appeared an article entitled 'Thomas Hardy's Wessex'. It was unsigned, but correspondence in the Dorset County Museum from the editor of the journal, Robertson Nicholl, makes it clear he was the author. Almost half of the first page is taken up with a map of south-western England, from the Isle of Wight to Exeter and from Bristol to

Andover, the English counties – Somerset, Wilts, Devon, Dorset, Hants – marked thereon. Most of the place names, however are double, a Wessex name, with an English name in parentheses below.

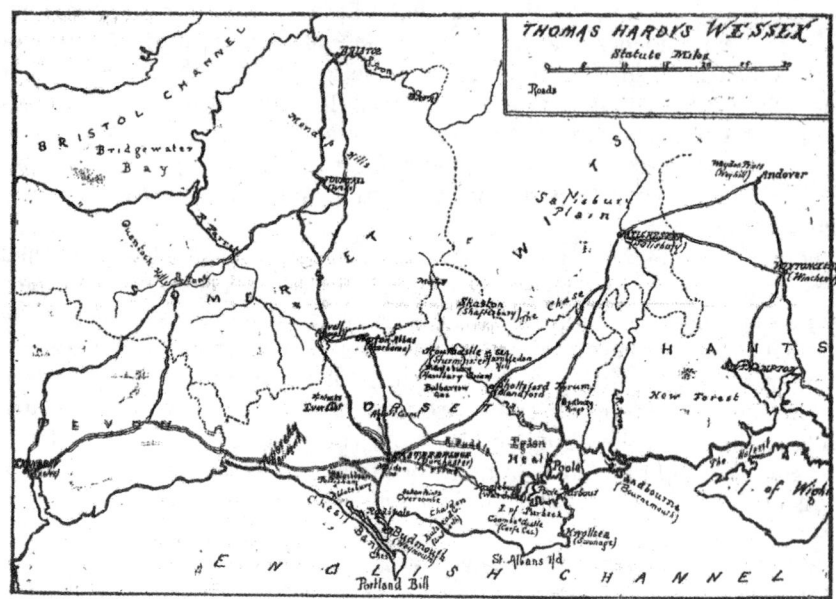

No one has discovered an earlier published map, so far as I know. The first surviving letter from Nicholl to Hardy begins: 'You very kindly said that you would give me some guidance to the scenes of your novels in a key on a map.' (14 August 1891, DCM H4570). Hardy was evidently not disinclined for the map to appear, though in a subsequent letter he made what would become his usual stipulation about identifications not being said to be authorized by him. Nicholl was happy enough with the help he received, and added in a subsequent note:

> I am so very much obliged to you. I shall be very careful not to impute to you the identifications: in fact I am putting in some of my own wh may be wrong. I know no place within [five] miles of Dorchester but there will I presume be no objection to calling it Casterbridge. As of course your letters have made my article much more valuable you must pardon me for enclosing cheque on a local bank. (Friday nd, DCM H4572)

He seemed to enjoy the identification game. It is of symbolic interest that Hardy got paid for betraying Wessex to the media. As far as I can see the only mistakes Nicholl made were to put the Chase in Wiltshire and Marlott to the north-west of Shaston, rather than the south-west; the village is not identified as Marnhull (nor is Abbot's-Cernel identified as Cerne Abbas). The Hintocks are more or less right, and Egdon Heath is further east than Hardy's own later maps have it, but there was geographical authority for such a placement. It is interesting that he gives Overcombe as Sutton Poyntz, rather than Bincombe, and it seems likely that he did so because Hardy gave him warrant. In terms of the maps we are now accustomed to, however, it is striking that the county names are English and not Wessex (Hardy hadn't yet given Somerset a name, or at least not in public).

The essay itself begins: 'Wanderers through our south and south-western counties... will find few better guides than Mr. Hardy'. It is brief, and links the places found on the map with a narrative of a journey through Wessex, just mentioning incidents that occurred in novels and stories at each place as it is touched. There is nothing much to it, but it is the first of a substantial stream of such productions, still flowing more than a hundred years later. It is impossible to judge how much the publication of the slender piece, and more particularly of the map that accompanied it, affected Hardy's thoughts about what he had done and would do with Wessex; but he cannot have seen his names thus stuck publicly to England without feeling something.

Hard on the heels of the map came a new Wessex county in 'The Son's Veto':

> In a remote nook in North Wessex, forty miles from London, near the town of Oldbrickham, there stood a pretty village...

North Wessex, Lucy thinks, must be Berkshire, given the distance from London, and that Hampshire is already spoken for; as for Oldbrickham, she has no idea, since unusually at this stage of Wessex, it is not a transparent equivalent of anywhere on a map, and Hardy gives no further details of the place.

The story is about the evil that certain kinds of education can do, and though Sophie Twycott was 'a child of nature herself', her son is nurtured out of nature into the urban upper-middle-class – 'His education had by this time sufficiently ousted his humanity to keep him quite firm' – firm in objecting to the marriage of his widowed mother to a former admirer from her home-village. When Randolph exclaims of his mother's prospective husband: 'A miserable boor! A churl! A clown!' that is presumably how Hardy imagined a good many of his prospective audience thought of most of his characters (and perhaps of himself).

'On the Western Circuit' was also published at Christmas of 1891, a Melchester story, which has a connection with *Tess of the d'Urbervilles* through the steam-roundabout which so fascinates the servant girl Anne. This machine is a (mostly) beneficent version of the threshing-machine in the novel. The intoxicating undulations of the horses are in direct opposition to the juddering debilitation of the thresher, and indeed for Hardy the ride has the same effect on the senses as a dance, he uses the same language to describe it:

> The riders were quite fascinated by these equine undulations in this most delightful fair-day-game of our times.... She was absolutely unconscious of everything save the act of riding; her features were rapt in an ecstatic dreaminess... Dreading the moment when the inexorable stoker, grimily lurking behind the glittering rococo-work, should decide that this set of riders had had their pennyworth... (I)

The roundabouts and organs of the fair are set alongside the massive silence of the cathedral and its close (which is perhaps the reason for the choice of Melchester), and Hardy comments that the lawyer Raye 'might have searched Europe over for a greater contrast between juxtaposed scenes' (I). There is a characteristically acute passage on the noise made by the fair: 'It was compounded of steam barrel-organs, the clanging of gongs, the ringing of hand-bells, the clack of rattles, and the undistinguishable shouts of men' (I) – a cacophony rather more intense than the sounds he usually records. But in every respect the occasion for the meeting of Anna and Raye is part of contemporary Wessex; Raye is an 'end-of-the-age young man' (II), and Wessex too in this story is at the end of an age.[2]

Meanwhile Hardy was also working on a short and idealising novel, *The Pursuit of the Well-Beloved*, which began to appear in The *Illustrated London News* in October 1892. As is well known nowadays, Hardy did not revise this story for book publication while the story was still running in the magazine – the only serialized novel for which this is the case. He waited four years, and then rewrote parts of the text so substantially that recent editors have seen *The Pursuit of the Well-Beloved* and *The Well-Beloved* (as the title became when it was published as part of Osgood, McIlvaine's collected edition in 1897) as separate works; and I too am considering the serial version separately.[3]

From the wide range of *Tess of the d'Urbervilles* this novel contracts again (if excursions to London are set aside) into a small circumscribed area of the kind Hardy has mostly preferred. From the second chapter a quick glance at a map is all anyone would need to see that the unnamed island can only be Portland:

> he was ascending the steep roadway which led from the village of Slopeway Well to the summit of the rocky peninsula, called an island, that juts out like the head of a flamingo into the English Channel, and is connected with the mainland of Wessex by a long, thin beach of pebbles, representing the neck of the bird.

Lucy wrote about this: 'Slopeway Well' will be Fortuneswell I suppose, and the beach of pebbles is Chesil Bank, but what I can't get out of my head is the picture of the flamingo. I can only suppose that Mr Hardy has not read that wonderful book 'Alice in Wonderland,' or else he would surely not have allowed his readers to make the connection with Mr Tenniel's drawing of Alice carrying her flamingo to play croquet with.

'Mr Hardy is fond of showing us places through the eyes of returning natives, for these people, if they have any eye and sensibility at all, are intensely affected by what was once of daily familiarity but now comes with unexpected freshness:

> What had seemed natural in the isle when he left it now looked quaint and odd amid these later impressions. The houses above houses, one man's doorstep rising behind his neighbour's chimney, the gardens hung up by one hedge to the sky, the unity of the whole island as a solid and single block of stone four miles long, were no longer familiar and commonplace ideas. All now stood dazzlingly clean and white against the blue sea, the sun flashing on the stratified façades of rock. (II)

Since reading this first episode I have gone back to "The Trumpet-Major", because I thought I remembered Anne Garland noticing something of the same effect; and indeed it is so (XXXIV). The only detail that rather surprises me that the gardens on this precipitous rocky slope are divided by hedges; but I have only seen Portland from the distance, so it may be true.'[4]

At the end of her notes on the serial there is this summary: 'The effect that Mr H gains in his recreation of Portland for us is more like that of "The Woodlanders" than that of "The Return of the Native" – it is cumulative, made up of very many little touches, so that I am reminded of an impression-painting when I put it like that. There is no single chapter that immerses us in a powerful vision of the place and its significance, but by the end we have a sharp impression of uniqueness. Now that the strange story has ended, what I specially remember is the rock itself, continually being chipped away. Just once, I think, Pearston himself goes beneath the surface-impression to find a life like that we are forced to see in Egdon Heath:

> He stretched out his hand upon the rock beside him. It felt warm. That was the island's personal temperature. He listened, and heard sounds: nick-nick, saw-saw-saw. Those were the island's voice – the noises of the quarrymen and stone-sawyers. (II)

I shall always think of this as one of the true signs of Wessex, when you feel a place, however large or however small, to have a life of its own, an identity as humans have identity. How is it possible not, for the moment of reading these sentences, to feel the implied pain that the rock feels in being cut away from the mass? And thus to extend the range of your experience, to stretch your sympathies. It is only in Wessex that I have found out that this is possible.'

A map of Hardy's island would include most of the existing settlements under Wessex names: Fortuneswell has already been mentioned, Easton and Wakeham become East Wake; Reform (as it was in Lucy's Ordnance Survey map) or Reforne is Forne 'where the church was' – but there are also ruined castles and another churchyard, lighthouses and quarries, and the southernmost point of the peninsula called the Beal. Off the island would be a lightship, and the crucial confluence of currents he calls the Race. The new conception of Wessex urges Hardy also to add fragments of history for their own sake, as in:

> The descent soon brought him to the pebble bank, and leaving behind him the last houses of the isle, and the ruins of the village destroyed by the November gale of 1824, he struck along the narrow thread of land. (IV)

A piece of information he had already used in *The Woodlanders*.

Hardy is careful to use words unique to the peninsula when he can – 'lerret', a kind of small boat, is an example – and though his handling of Wessex dialect in general is the subject of another chapter, it is perhaps worth noting that this novel is the site of his only attempt to catch the phrasing and accent of an Irishman.

Portland, presumably by reason of its isolation, had retained to the middle part of the nineteenth century, as well as a unique vocabulary, also a series of unique customs – of which the tradition of testing the fertility of a union before marriage is the one most prominent. But these words and practices were fast disappearing. Pearston reflects on Avice Caro:

> He observed that the aim of those who had brought her up had been to get her away mentally as far as possible from her natural and individual life as an inhabitant of a peculiar isle: to make her an exact copy of tens of thousands of other people, in whose circumstances there was nothing special, distinctive or picturesque; to teach her to forget all the experiences of her ancestors; to drown the local ballads by songs purchased at the Budmouth fashionable music-sellers', and the local vocabulary by a governess-tongue of no country at all.... By constitution she was local to the bone, but she could not escape the tendency of the age. (ch III)

As in 'On the Western Circuit', the tendency of the age surfaces as an important consideration in Wessex, as something new, something alien, something to be understood and combatted. It has always been present in Hardy's thinking, from *Under the Greenwood Tree* onwards, but until the 1890s it has not been so objectified. In this, though, Hardy may well be doing no more than reflecting the self-consciousness about *fin-de-siècle* that was present in some article or other in almost any magazine you might pick up.

The serial took up 1892, along with revisions to *Tess of the d'Urbervilles* for the one-volume edition, but in the spring of the following year Hardy published one of the best of his stories, 'The Fiddler of the Reels'. Two adjacent passages bring together the history of Dorset and the history of Wessex in a particularly vivid way:

> For South Wessex, the year formed in many ways an extraordinary chronological frontier or transit-line, at which there occurred what one might call a precipice in Time. As in a geological 'fault,' we had presented to us a sudden bringing of ancient and modern into absolute contact, such as probably in no other single year since the Conquest was ever witnessed in this part of the country.[5]

This is the year of the Great Exhibition at Hyde Park in London, 1851, and though the first person narrator of the story talks of South Wessex, the history is Dorset's. A page or so later he introduces Mop Ollamoor, the fiddler of the title:

> His date was a little later than that of the old Mellstock quire-band which comprised the Dewys, Mail, and the rest... In their honest love of thoroughness they despised the new man's style. Theophilus Dewy (Reuben the tranter's younger brother) used to say there was no 'plumness' in it – no bowing, no solidity – it was all fantastical. And probably this was true. Anyhow, Mop had, very obviously, never bowed a note of church-music from his birth... All were devil's tunes in his repertory. 'He could no more play the Wold Hundredth to his true tune than he could play the brazen serpent,' the tranter would say.

This is pure Wessex; and when Reuben Dewy is brought to witness, the illusion of the continuity of the fictional world in a reality parallel with the historical world is very strong. Much of the environment of *Under the Greenwood Tree* is brought to life again, as well as details from *The Return of the Native*, and at last it seems to be made absolutely clear that Hardy intends Stickleford to represent Tincleton in the Wessex scheme of things. It will be remembered that even in *Tess of the d'Urbervilles* there was some uncertainty on this question.

But the subject of the story, as of the best of the 'Wessex Folk' sketches, is music and dance, and in particular the power of Mop Ollamoor's fiddling. Car'line Aspent is especially susceptible to it, and at the climax of the story she is led to dance for hours against her will by the spell of music he casts over her, until he seizes their illegitimate daughter and vanishes with her. This theme was very close to Hardy's own heart; his own response to music had always been powerful, and he wrote of it with an intensity that is rarely found in his short stories.[6]

Now Hardy had enough new stories to put together in a volume, and in 1894 *Life's Little Ironies* was published. Almost all the relevant changes were alterations to Wessex place names, of which details will be found in **wsCh5**. The exception is 'Wessex Folk' in which the revisions are of some interest.[7]

The first thing that gets changed is the title. Possibly Hardy was reluctant to use the word Wessex again in a collection of short stories; at any rate the sequence becomes 'A Few Crusted Characters'. He took the hint from Parsons's illustration to the serialization (see above p. 91), and altered 'it is now half-past three by the ancient dial face in the church tower at the top of the street' to 'it is now half-past three by the clock in the turret at the top of the street'. He makes a connection between this set of short stories and *A Group of Noble Dames* by naming two of the guests at the squire's Christmas party in 'Old Andrey's Experience as a Musician' as Lord and Lady Baxby. Perhaps stimulated by the inclusion of the same information in 'The Fiddler of the Reels', he added that the Hardcomes were able to go by train from Casterbridge to Budmouth 'the line being just opened'; but the most remarkable change, in a small way, comes in 'Incident in the Life of Mr George Crookhill', when he changes the name of the place where George and his fellow-traveller put up at an inn from Tranton to Trantridge.

Lucy had worked out that Tranton represented Tarrant Hinton, but now her calculations were thrown into disarray. Evidently this was a further alteration designed to link *Life's Little Ironies* more closely with other Wessex narratives, but if her work on *Tess of the d'Urbervilles* was right, Trantridge was a version of Pentridge, and though Pentridge was in the general area that Mr Crookhill rode through, it could not by any stretch be thought of as on the direct road between Melchester and Shottsford. Furthermore there was no mention of an inn at Trantridge in *Tess of the d'Urbervilles*, and it seemed that the farm workers went into Chaseborough to do their drinking. She didn't in the end know what to think, and was quite surprised, since she felt that Mr Hardy was clarifying rather than obscuring the relationships between Wessex and England these days.

One review of the collection, in the *Times* of 30 March 1894, made the connection between Hardy's inventions and the medieval origins of Englishness, discussing the stories as 'the life-tales of his Wessex folk – a race in which we seem to recognise the bed-rock of our Anglo-Saxon nature, stripped of the artificialities of complex life'. But soon *Jude the Obscure* began appearing in *Harper's New Monthly Magazine*, and thereafter talk of Wessex simplicity would dry up. Before it did, though, the establishment of Hardy as an author to be reckoned with in the pattern of English literature reached a new stage, with the publication in 1894 of the first two books on his work. Both devote space to new Wessex, one enthusiastically, the other reluctantly.

Scattered throughout Annie Macdonell's *Thomas Hardy* (London, Hodder and Stoughton) are sentences like '"A Pair of Blue Eyes" is not a Wessex novel, the scene lying in a remote Cornish parish and in London' (34), or

'In "The Trumpet-Major", save for Overcombe, he has given the real [names]' (179–80), which were accurate when written, but were invalidated by the wholesale revision that Hardy was to undertake a year later for the Osgood, McIlvaine collected edition. The map introducing the chapter entitled 'Wessex' was similarly out of date almost as soon as issued. It was still possible for her to begin the chapter with: 'It need hardly be said that Mr Hardy's Wessex does not coincide with the old West Saxon kingdom.' And, though her map does include the English county boundaries, she believes that the Wessex counties are not coterminous with the English ones: 'Outer Wessex has Taunton for its chief centre. Lower Wessex lies along the coast of the Bristol Channel, Upper Wessex along the south-eastern coast of Hampshire' (175–6). Unlike Lucy, she had not read *Tess of the d'Urbervilles* closely enough, and she was confused by 'For Conscience' Sake'(see above p. 59). Hardy's map for the collected edition will put her right – it was in part to correct this sort of misconception that he decided to produce one of his own. The rest of the chapter is a guided tour of Wessex through the novels and stories such as Lucy herself might have made, prefaced by a caution she would have endorsed:

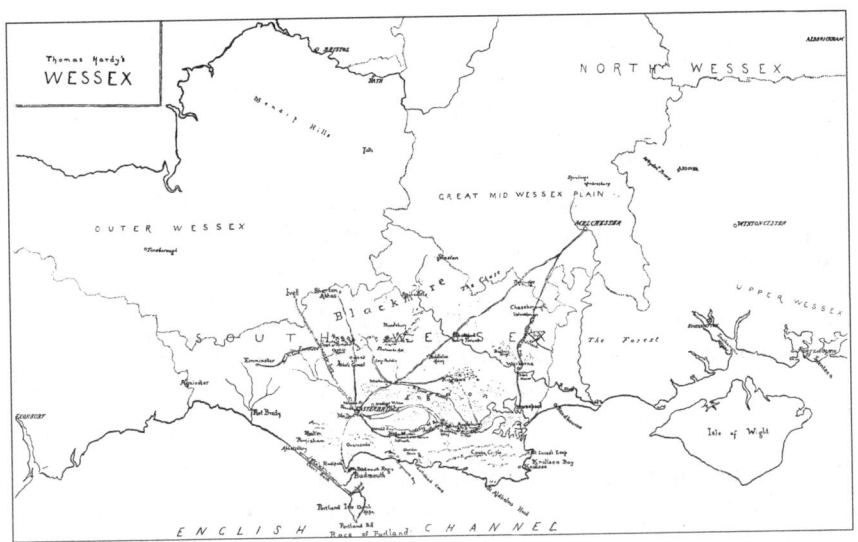

With regard to the identification of the scenes of Mr. Hardy's stories, I should say they have mostly been made by means of maps and personal recognition on the spot, and, as such, are fallible. Besides, Mr. Hardy is an artist, not a photographer: and he does not write guide-books. (179)

Again much of her analysis was overtaken almost at once by Hardy's revisions.

Lionel Johnson's *The Art of Thomas Hardy* (London: John Lane) was the other critical study published in 1894, and it also has a chapter titled 'Wessex'. He addresses Hardy's resuscitation of the word in general terms, and then expresses his own sense of what distinguishes Wessex:

> It is not with any mere desire to make an open secret of his choice, that he has given an ancient name to the country, where the people of his imagination live: *Wessex* is full of significance, and no outworn appellation of antiquity, without a living force. In calling the land of his birth and of his art after its ancient name, the Land of the West Saxons, Mr. Hardy would have us feel the sentiment of historical continuity from those old times to ours... (83)

Though he would like to, Johnson cannot altogether avoid mentioning the topographical game, but he makes his opinion of it clear:

> Critics have already identified Mr Hardy's localities with their originals; a map of them has been published... It is impossible, not to feel some regret at this publicity: innocent as it is, it savours of intrusion.... Granted that Mr Hardy's Casterbridge is Dorchester; his Melchester, Salisbury; his Sherton Abbas, Sherborne: Mr Hardy has not pledged himself to the literal fidelity of a guidebook. (88–9)

And he refuses to play. He makes in the last sentence the same point as Macdonnell, but where she pursues Wessex through south-western England in spite of it, Johnson uses it as a reason to refrain from doing so. It is fascinating to see expressed in the only critical studies to be published before the collected edition, these opposing approaches to new Wessex. Meanwhile Hardy was at work on what would become *Jude the Obscure*.

In the preface to the one-volume second edition of *Tess of the d'Urbervilles* of 1892, Hardy wrote concerning hostile critics of the first edition of that novel:

> Others dissent on grounds which are intrinsically no more than an assertion that the novel embodies the views of life prevalent at the end of the nineteenth century, and not those of an earlier and simpler generation – an assertion which I can only hope may be well founded.

Hardy's last novel provokes such an assertion even more forcibly. However, *Jude the Obscure* begins as a rural Wessex novel, and though there is, to alert readers of Hardy, at once a new edge to the narrative and perhaps occasionally a surprising cynicism, none would have reason to suspect from the first few chapters that he intended to lead them decisively out of the Wessex they had become familiar with.

The opening of the novel in the manuscript shows that as usual Hardy had considerable trouble with the name of the hero (he is Jack before he is Jude, and England, Head, Stancombe and Hopeson before he is Fawley), and with the name of the village to which he has come. Before it settled to Marygreen, it was Shawley, Cawley, and Fawn Green. Here is Hardy's process of naming made clear. At first, by calling Jude/Jack England it appears that he was thinking of him as a representative English figure; Head, as Michael Millgate points out (*Biography* p. 350) is the name of Hardy's grandmother who came from the village of Fawley, and whose given name was Mary; I can offer no guess as to the significance of Stancombe, but Hopeson was clearly intended to be ironic. Jude could not become Fawley until Hardy decided not to go for the transparent Wessex equivalent for the name of the village, but for the personal allusion. He had transferred place name to personal name elsewhere – with Melbury in *The Woodlanders*, for instance – and would do the same with the pig-killer Challow and Phillotson's friend Gillingham later in this novel. It certainly allowed Lucy to identify Marygreen with Fawley on her map fairly quickly.[8]

His initial description of Marygreen is angry:

> It was as old-fashioned as it was small, and it rested in the lap of an undulating upland adjoining the North Wessex downs. Old as it was, however, the well-shaft was probably the only relic of the local history that remained absolutely unchanged. Many of the thatched and dormered dwelling-houses had been pulled down of late years, and many trees felled on the green. Above all, the original church, hump-backed, wood-turreted, and quaintly hipped, had been taken down, and either cracked up into heaps of road-metal in the lane, or utilized as pig-sty walls, garden seats, guard-stones to fences, and rockeries in the flower-beds of the neighbourhood. In place of it a tall new building of German-Gothic design, unfamiliar to English eyes, had been erected on a new piece of ground by a certain obliterator of historic records who had run down from London and back in a day. The site whereon so long had stood the ancient temple to the Christian divinities was not even recorded on the green and level grass-plot that had immemorially been the churchyard, the obliterated graves being commemorated by ninepenny cast-iron crosses warranted to last five years. (I.i)

The paragraph begins in regret, for the ruin of the past through present change is not new in Hardy, nor, more specifically is the pulling down of cottages; but the destruction of the old church stimulates a new bitterness that goes beyond the pained irony of earlier texts that deal with a similar subject. The ninepenny crosses are a final insult. Squires who pull down cottages have the bad excuse that they are fulfilling some plan for their own estates, that however heartless and selfish it may be, they have responsibility for the land and will have to live with the consequences of what they do to the people in some way or another. Hardy compares these destroyers of their own with the architect who comes for a moment from the outside, destroys similarly the old and valuable, but does so without a moment's responsibility to anything other than the fee he is getting. He does not have to walk by the new every day. Hardy had himself originally called the man responsible for the awfulness an 'architect', but he soon decided that he would not wish so directly to malign his old profession. Another change, though not at first sight relevant to Wessex, is worth remarking. In the first inscription of the manuscript 'the ancient temple to the Christian divinities' was 'the ancient temple of God'. It is striking how effectively the revised version detaches the narrator from any presumption of a commitment to Christianity or adherence to its doctrines. That religion is placed on an equal footing with any other from classical Paganism to Positivism. This is a new feeling in Wessex. Though there have been intellectual sceptics; though the ministers of the church have not always been treated with respect, though many of the workfolk are indifferent churchgoers, there has always in Wessex been an underlying acceptance of the authority and value of the established Church. This began to change in *Tess of the d'Urbervilles*, in which the heroine's too ready acceptance of the moral and social teaching of the Church is clearly seen as part of her weakness, while her instinctive pantheism is stressed; in *Jude the Obscure* the comfortable Church takes a battering – so that the destruction of Marygreen's ancient church and its replacement by an alien monstrosity is symbolic also of the change in the Wessex attitude to the institution.

During the opening book of the novel centred on the village, everyone walks or travels by horse and cart, through a small part of the new county of North Wessex, just introduced in 'The Son's Veto'. The county town had eventually been established there as Aldbrickham, but now, as well as Marygreen, there are Cresscombe (Cresvale at first in the manuscript), Alfredston and Fensworth (or Fenworth), and somewhat later there is Kennetbridge. After Jude leaves Marygreen for Christminster, and launches himself out of Wessex into England, the railway becomes an intimate presence, and travelling by rail is a matter of course for all in a way not seen before in Hardy's work. In 'The Dorsetshire Labourer' Hardy had written of the effect the new means of transport had on the mobility of rural workers, whether from district to district or from country to city. In *Jude the Obscure* he shows the effect at work.[9]

Consequently *Jude the Obscure* is, like *Tess of the d'Urbervilles*, a peripatetic novel; this is especially evident when the narrator describes the period of Jude and Sue's great happiness together:

Sometimes he might have been found shaping the mullions of a country mansion, sometimes setting the parapet of a town-hall, sometimes ashlaring an hotel at Sandbourne, sometimes a museum at Casterbridge, sometimes as far down as Exonbury, sometimes at Stoke-Barehills. Later still he was at Kennetbridge, a thriving town not more than a dozen miles south of Marygreen, this being his nearest approach to the village where he was known. (V.vii)

The topography of Wessex is amplified again. In Upper Wessex we are introduced to Stoke-Barehills and Quartershot, and in South Wessex there is Leddenton.[10] Melchester is the scene of more action than heretofore, perhaps in part as a consequence of the story 'On the Western Circuit'; but two towns are specially treated, Shaston and Christminster. The latter of these is outside Hardy's version of Wessex, even though only a stone's throw across the Thames from it. Hardy needs an ancient university city for his narrative, and hence the slight stretch. Hardy could have taken Tess Durbeyfield to Shaston, and he perhaps regretted that he had not. At any rate he manufactures the opportunity to explore the town in *Jude the Obscure* by making it the place where Richard Phillotson was born, and therefore a probable place for him to take a school.

The description of Shaston is in Hardy's best guidebook tone – outlining its medieval Wessex greatness of which only 'vague imaginings' survive, telling some amusing stories about its troubled journey to the present, and giving some sense of its stunning hilltop position overlooking the Blackmore Vale and beyond. In summary he calls it a 'breezy and whimsical spot', and it is not the least of its whimsicalities that it is also the winter home of the 'proprietors of wandering vans, shows, shooting-galleries, and other itinerant concerns, whose business lay largely at fairs and markets'. Hardy goes on to characterize their presence in Shaston through a brilliant natural image, quite in the manner of other Wessex novels:

> As strange wild birds are seen assembled on some lofty promontory, meditatively pausing for longer flights, or to return by the course they followed thither, so here, in this cliff-town, stood in stultified silence the yellow and green caravans bearing names not local, as if surprised by a change in the landscape so violent as to hinder their further progress; and here they usually remained all the winter till they turned to seek again their old tracks in the following spring. (IV.i)

These travelling folk are thematically of the first importance to the novel, and their presence, historically speaking, at Shaftesbury (though I have been unable to find any confirmation that Hardy's statement is indeed based on fact), may well have been a primary reason for the inclusion of the town so prominently in the novel.

Shaston is a Wessex town, not just by location, but by history and context, involved with the surrounding countryside as a market and crossroads, despite its relative inaccessibility from all but the north. Christminster is much more marginal to Wessex, even apart from its geographical position.[11] Like Shaston it has a history, but its past is an English past; the university and those associated with it in Jude's mind are of national, international significance; the cityscape along Chief Street is world-renowned. Even when Jude has a rare insight into the life of the city as distinct from the university it is in a context of receding English history, and of humanity in general:

> It had more history than the oldest college in the city. It was literally teeming, stratified, with the shades of human groups, who had met there for tragedy, comedy, farce, real enactments of the intensest kind. At Fourways men had stood and talked of Napoleon, the loss of America, the execution of King Charles, the burning of the Martyrs, the Crusades, the Norman Conquest, possibly of the arrival of Caesar. Here the two sexes had met for loving, hating, coupling, parting; had waited, had suffered for each other; had triumphed over each other; cursed each other in jealousy, blessed each other in forgiveness. (II.vi)

At the beginning of the novel there is a comparable paragraph concerning not a city or even a village, but a field in the neighbourhood of Marygreen:

> The fresh harrow-lines seemed to stretch like the channellings in a piece of new corduroy, lending a meanly utilitarian air to the expanse, taking away its gradations, and depriving it of all history beyond that of the few recent months, though in every clod and stone there really lingered associations enough and to spare – echoes of songs from ancient harvest-days, of spoken words, and of sturdy deeds. Every inch of ground had been the site, first or last, of energy, gaiety, horse-play, bickerings, weariness. Groups of gleaners had squatted in the sun on every square yard. Love-matches that had populated the adjoining hamlet had been made up there between reaping and carrying. Under the hedge which divided the field from a distant plantation girls had given themselves to lovers who would not turn their heads to look at them by the next harvest; and in that ancient corn-field many a man had made love-promises to a woman at whose voice he had trembled by the next seed-time after fulfilling them in the church adjoining. (I.ii)

In both passages there is a powerful and vivid sense of continuity; the difference between the two is in the purely parochial history evoked by the fragments of clay. Christminster, though not especially large, is a national centre in a way nowhere in Wessex is. This last passage is interesting too because it expresses an early stage of an idea that had begun to become important to

Hardy – that intense emotions, powerful actions, or even perpetual presence, are in some form retained by the places they occurred at, and are accessible to sensitive people years or generations later. The poetry of Wessex is full of places that retain such charges.

In fact it might not be too much to suggest that fictional Wessex can no longer be made to contain with ease the ideas about which Hardy wishes most strongly to write. Jude's thwarted attempts to find a vocation and a community within which to practice that vocation; Sue's antipathy to marriage, and her attitude to the Church; the narrator's analysis of the way the world works: these are the most important themes of the novel, and their significance is nationwide, culturewide; they go to the roots of Western civilization, and, despite the Wessex locations for the action, it is evident that Hardy's context has become wider. Much of the power of *Jude the Obscure* resides in the cumulative effect of passages like this in Sue's voice:

> I am certain one ought to be allowed to undo what one has done so ignorantly! I daresay it happens to lots of women; only they submit, and I kick.... When people of a later age look back upon the barbarous customs and superstitions of the times that we have the unhappiness to live in, what *will* they say! (IV.ii)

It has been the tendency of Hardy's novels to this date to show how things are different in Wessex from the metropole in the present, and to show how they are different in the present from the past. In *Jude the Obscure* what we mostly get is argument and discussion about contemporary English attitudes, conventions, principles. Wessex is for the most part merely a convenience. Here is a perception of Phillotson's of which the same is true:

> To indulge one's instinctive and uncontrolled sense of justice and right, was not, he had found, permitted with impunity in an old civilization like ours. It was necessary to act under an acquired and artificial sense of the same, if you wished to enjoy an average share of comfort and honour; and to let loving-kindness take care of itself. (VI.iv)[12]

We have become accustomed to occasional comments of this sort from the narrators of Hardy's novels, but not from the characters – from almost all of the characters. Here is an example from early in Jude's married life:

> There seemed to him, vaguely and dimly, something wrong in a social ritual which made necessary a cancelling of well-formed schemes involving years of thought and labour, of forgoing a man's one opportunity of showing himself superior to the lower animals, and of contributing his units of work to the general progress of his generation, because of a momentary surprise by a new and transitory instinct which had nothing in it of the

nature of vice, and could be only at the most called weakness. He was inclined to inquire what he had done, or she lost, for that matter, that he deserved to be caught in a gin which would cripple him, if not her also, for the rest of a lifetime? (I.ix)

Whenever Sue and Jude are together it is likely that some question of universal or at least national significance will be debated between them; otherwise it is more common to find these issues presented as indirect discourse, as the workings of the character's mind. But either way they come to dominate the novel.

There are many allusions in the novel to 'the times', something else that distinguishes it from other novels – and the issues of 'the times' are country-wide, not Wessex issues, as for instance Sue's: 'I hate to be what is called a clever girl – there are too many of that sort now!' (II.v) Or Jude's 'It is just one of those intrusive, vulgar, pushing, applications which are so common in these days...' (II.vi) The climax of this kind of analysis of English society at large comes when Jude reports a doctor's view that boys like little Jude, who seem to see all the terrors of life 'before they are old enough to have staying power to resist them' represent 'the beginning of the coming universal wish not to live'. (Vi.ii)

If readers look for evidence of the concerns that have defined Wessex heretofore, they will find them. For example, the town and country contrast that is a part of every Hardy novel is attenuated here, but there is one particularly interesting example. Sue and Jude are benighted in the country, having missed the last train back to Melchester, and are put up in a cottage:

'I rather like this,' said Sue, while their entertainers were clearing away the dishes. 'Outside all laws except gravitation and germination.'

'You only think you like it; you don't: you are quite a product of civilization,' said Jude... (III.ii)

Sue's remark reveals her as urban and indeed 'a product of civilization', ruralizing a little. Any reader of Hardy's work would know that, despite appearances, most 'laws' operate as fully in rural working-class society as in the urban middle-class. Compare her facile view with Angel Clare's genuine understanding of the complexities and simplicities of such a life.

There are accounts of work, too, in the novel – a little bit of baking, some mason's work, a hint at school-teaching – but only one extended and thoroughly presented activity: how to slaughter a pig. There has been nothing like it in Hardy's writing so far; when Tess wrings the necks of the dying pheasants, there is a painful sentence describing their plight and another simply noting Tess's action. Here, however, the passage is much too long to quote, and the detail ultimately devastating:

> The dying animal's cry assumed its third and final tone, the shriek of agony; his glazing eyes rivetting themselves on Arabella with the eloquently keen reproach of a creature recognizing at last the treachery of those who had seemed his only friends. (I.x)

Hardy infuses horror into the whole killing.[13] He gives those who see the animal only as a source of money or meat a hard time, and he does so, unsurprisingly, by giving the pig consciousness. Nevertheless, Arabella's materialism in the face of this *tour-de-force* is striking, and (if a reader has the strength of mind to resist the rhetoric that has preceded her response) is not without weight:

> 'Thank God!' Jude said. 'He's dead.'
> 'What's God got to do with such a messy job as a pig-killing, I should like to know!' she said scornfully. 'Poor folks must live.'

One of the witness to the preparations for the killing is a robin, who is granted as much consciousness as the pig himself; it 'peered down at the preparations from the nearest tree, and, not liking the sinister look of the scene, flew away, though hungry'. There is a parallel with the poem 'Wagtail and Baby', and there are other moments when this preoccupation of earlier novels, the interaction of man and nature, is vividly flashed across the narrative, as in a description of little Jude: 'The child fell into a steady mechanical creep which had in it an impersonal quality – the movement of the wave, or of the breeze, or of the cloud' (V.iii), or the way trees weep for the remarriage of Sue and Richard: 'The fog of the previous day or two on the lowlands had travelled up here by now, and the trees on the green caught armfuls, and turned them into showers of big drops. The bride was waiting, ready; bonnet and all on'. (VI.v)

There are even a few characters of some importance who retain a Wessex point of view – in particular Vilbert and Mrs Edlin.

> Vilbert was an itinerant quack-doctor, well known to the rustic population, and absolutely unknown to anybody else, as he, indeed, took care to be, to avoid inconvenient investigations. Cottagers formed his only patients, and his Wessex-wide repute was among them alone. (I.iv)

He is a walker, and walks across the whole of Wessex; he is a fraud, and a fit mate for Arabella, but he makes up an element in the individuality of Wessex. Dialect-speaking Mrs Edlin remains a staunch friend to both Jude and Sue, but also she is the advocate of a common sense, ordinary attitude to marriage as simply something that should done as it has always been done:

> What–and ha'n't ye really done it? Chok' it all, that I should have lived to see a good old saying like 'marry in haste and repent at leisure' spoiled like this by you two! 'Tis time I got back again to Marygreen – sakes if tidden – if this is what the new notions be leading us to! Nobody thought o' being afeared o' matrimony in my time, nor of much else but a cannon-ball or empty cupboard! Why when I and my poor man were married we thought no more o't than of a game o' dibs. (V.iv)

Her final memorable comment, however, acknowledges that, like so much else in Wessex, old attitudes no longer suffice:

> Weddings be funerals 'a b'lieve nowadays. Fifty-five years ago, come Fall, since my man and I married! Times have changed since then! (VI.ix)

Jude the Obscure is a powerful and disturbing novel, as commentators since 1896 have demonstrated; but the only sense in which it is fully a Wessex novel is that the action takes place there. In every other respect there are just vestiges of the elements that have up to now constituted Wessex. Perhaps then the new Wessex, fully inaugurated in the Osgood, McIlvaine collected edition, is merely a fragment of England; maybe what is true in England is true in Wessex; maybe Wessex now is just a copyright mark, assuring the reader that this is a genuine Hardy novel. When he introduces the Wessex equivalent of Basingstoke, he writes that 'the town may be called Stoke-Barehills' – a tacit admission that it is all an illusion, and that in the end Wessex names are unimportant, could be anything else he chose. One final quotation symbolically represents these possibilities:

> It was one of those cloudless days which sometimes occur in Wessex and elsewhere between days of cold and wet, as if intercalated by caprice of the weather-god. (II.iii)

The sentence reads as if he first intended just 'in Wessex', as if it were his dream-country, and such things happened there; but then he recognized that such things of course happen everywhere, and so Wessex is reintroduced to the real world. It is not just realism that has become for Hardy an imaginative straitjacket, but Wessex too.

It is evident that the reviewers of *Jude the Obscure* understood, not just that there was not much of Hardy's usual Wessex background (as they thought of it), but that he was handling issues that made Wessex irrelevant. Most notices of *Tess of the d'Urbervilles* mentioned Wessex. Only two of *Jude the Obscure* did. The reviewer in the *Pall Mall Gazette* (12 November 1895) makes his regret at the paucity of rural life and work and landscape in a brief conventional way: 'The gloomy whole is unrelieved to any material extent by the painting of country-scenes, such as we have learned to expect from him... when treating of that great grave gracious Wessex-land that he and we both love'. Edmund Gosse, Hardy's friend, was more explicit and more self-revealing; he wrote in *Cosmopolis* (January 1896) that Hardy was 'happiest in the heart of' Wessex. 'When Mr Hardy writes of South Wessex (Dorsetshire) he seldom goes wrong.... In choosing North Wessex as the scene of a novel Mr Hardy wilfully deprives himself of a great element of his strength'. His peroration climaxed in the celebrated 'What has Providence done to Mr Hardy that he should rise up in the arable fields of Wessex and shake his fist at his Creator?' The less often quoted sequel is relevant here too: 'His early romances were full of calm and lovely pantheism... We wish he would go back to Egdon Heath and listen to the singing in the heather'. Probably many of the novel's first readers, made uncomfortable by its subject and its bleakness, wished so too.

While he was still completing 'Hearts Insurgent' (as the *Harper* serialization of *Jude the Obscure* was ultimately called), towards the end of 1894, he began the far-reaching work of revision to his whole of his fiction for a collected edition to be published by Osgood, McIlvaine and Co.

6
The Collected Editions 1

History

Even before James Ripley Osgood set up his partnership with Clarence McIlvaine in London he had been interested in publishing a collected edition of Hardy's works, as may be seen from a letter Hardy wrote to him in December 1888: 'with regard to the other matter, I think I told you that my publishers have the right to print my books till the end of copyright, unless I give notice to the contrary. Perhaps, however, it will be the better plan to wait till I can see you on this' (*Letters* I.182). Evidently they did talk about it, perhaps more than once, and soon after establishing the house of Osgood, McIlvaine & Co., Osgood wrote to Hardy on the subject again (4 December 1890, DCM): 'You will recall our conversation of some months ago when I suggested the plan of a new and uniform edition of your books. I shall be glad to hear if you are ready to discuss this.' At that time Hardy's agreements with other publishers, in particular Sampson Low, Marston & Co., who owned temporary rights over most of his novels, had nearly four years to run, and so the project was shelved, to reappear in 1893, when Hardy could look forward to gathering his whole output in the near future, with the exception of *Under the Greenwood Tree*, the copyright of which he had sold outright.

Ward and Downey's rights to *Desperate Remedies*, sold in 1892 to Heinemann, expired at the same time as Sampson Low's in their novels, but Hardy had some difficulty in extracting *The Woodlanders* and *Wessex Tales* from Macmillan; eventually a compromise deal was worked out by which Macmillan would issue all Hardy's novels in a colonial edition in exchange for the novel and the volume of short stories. In May 1894 Clarence McIlvaine arranged terms (a 15 per cent royalty) with Percy Spalding, a partner in Chatto and Windus, who held the copyright, for the inclusion of *Under the Greenwood Tree* in the new edition, and all was complete. He had undertaken to write a preface for each of the volumes, and they make fascinating reading for the student of Wessex. Henry Macbeth-Raeburn was engaged to draw and engrave landscape scenes from each novel (he visited every setting under advice from Hardy, as the form in which the title of each drawing was given makes clear: THE '*******' OF THE STORY / Drawn on the spot, ('where '*******' is the Wessex name of a place in the narrative') while Stanford was given the task of redrawing Hardy's own map of the region; their version appeared at the end of each book (except for *Tess of the d'Urbervilles*, in which it is tipped to page 129 for no accountable reason), and is reproduced here. In it, set out neatly, is a part of England with Wessex names in italics (except for the counties), the county boundaries corresponding exactly to those of England; it is the icon of the new Wessex.

In 1900 Harper (who had taken over the publication of the collected edition after Osgood, McIlvaine foundered) issued in Britain a slender double-column paperback of *Tess of the d'Urbervilles*, printed on cheap paper, costing 6d (2.5p in current coinage); the edition was 100,000 copies, but it has sunk into oblivion, almost without trace. I know of seven copies that survive, and certainly there are more, but even when compared with the first edition of *Desperate Remedies*, of which perhaps 400 copies found their way into general circulation, and well over a hundred are still around, it is an exceptionally rare book. What makes it worth searching for and preserving is that Hardy revised the text quite substantially, as he did for the similar edition of *Far From the Madding Crowd* published a year later – more is known about the latter, since pre-publication witnesses have been preserved in Edinburgh. These issues might have made the start of a new collected edition, but Harper themselves got into financial trouble, and Hardy decided he wanted to change publishers. There was a certain amount of acrimony involved in the transference of his books from Harper to Macmillan, but it was achieved in 1902, and the Wessex novels were reissued at once as the Uniform edition. Hardy revised many of them in a small way, anxious to avoid expense by requiring resetting of type.[1]

The next stage in the development of Hardy's reputation as an author was the production of a limited luxury edition, and this was mooted in 1910, only for the deal to fall through. Instead Macmillan came up with a collected edition of their own, the Wessex edition of 1912–13, for which Hardy (at the age of 72) made sometimes substantial revisions, many of which had a bearing on Wessex. The edition had photographs by Hardy's friend Hermann Lea as frontispieces. The *edition de luxe* came in America first, in 1915 (Harper's Autograph edition), for which Hardy made a handful of changes, and then in Britain in 1920, the Mellstock Edition. Again Hardy altered a few pages. There were separate collected editions of Hardy's poetry, but they will be considered in a subsequent chapter.

In what follows the reader will find material from all of these revisions brought together. The basic rationale for this procedure has two elements: it is more convenient so, but more importantly, once the major overhaul of Wessex was undertaken for the Osgood edition, almost all other changes to this aspect of Hardy's work follow the same pattern. In general terms that pattern was to bring all of his fiction into the framework of Wessex that had been established in his imagination since 1890, and as each novel or collection of stories published before that date is examined, the thoroughness and economy with which Hardy managed this will emerge. Each work is examined in the order of its original publication. Exigencies of space mean that most novels and collections of stories are discussed in an analytical paragraph or two, while the wealth of material on which the discussion is based, essential to a complete understanding of what Hardy accomplished in these revisions, will be found on the associated website. When revisions are noted, **O** indicates the Osgood, McIlvaine edition, **W** the Wessex edition, **O2** the Uniform edition, **TH12** the study copies of the volumes of the Wessex edition in which Hardy made occasional manuscript revisions; other editions significant for individual novels are identified as necessary. The Raeburn illustrations are reproduced within the discussion of each book.

Desperate Remedies
Osgood: Volume XII, Preface: February 1896, Illustration: Knapwater House.
Wessex: Volume XV, as a Novel of Ingenuity, Preface: August 1912. Illustration: Knapwater House.

> in the present edition of 'Desperate Remedies' some Wessex towns and other places that are common to the scenes of several of these [**several of this series of W**] stories have been called for the first time by the names under which they appear elsewhere, for the satisfaction of any reader who may care for consistency in such matters.

This bland preface, with its disingenuous implication that a few name changes had done the business, and equally disingenuous implied disclaimer of a personal commitment to consistency, masks the special problem Hardy faced with this book, a problem that lay essentially in the fact that it was the first novel he wrote. In almost every respect Hardy had tried to make it hard to identify any of the reality behind the setting of the novel, and he had taken details to suit the action from all over the neighbourhood of his birthplace, without particularly considering their consistency. The reality underlying the environment of his second novel *Under the Greenwood Tree* was much the same as in *Desperate Remedies*, but the names were different and the fiction mostly consistent with that reality. As Wessex developed, Hardy used *Under the Greenwood Tree*'s names in other novels and stories. So, when he allowed the novel to be reissued in 1889, he had to make changes, in particular to the one name that was by now quite penetrable – Froominster. Casterbridge had been thoroughly established as the name of the county town of Wessex, and the fictional version of Dorchester. There were two solutions: the more difficult would have been to reshape the whole landscape of the novel around Casterbridge and Mellstock – which would have required considerable rewriting, and would have connected the novel intimately with *Under the Greenwood Tree*; the easier was to change the name, and to remove the (now anonymous) county town further away – this he did, the former by changing the initial letter, and Froominster becomes Troominster, and the novel is (topographically at least) turned away from Wessex.[2] Other inland places, Carriford, Knapwater and Mundsbury, are unchanged in name or description, and on the coast Creston would also have remained unaltered were it not that in Manston's escape from justice at the end of the novel he is tracked to that town, where his pursuers expect him to take the steam-packet to the Channel Islands. Many of Hardy's readers would in 1889 have put together the facts that the Channel Islands boat left from Weymouth, and that in Wessex Budmouth is Hardy's name for Weymouth; so here, and here only, he altered Creston to Budmouth. Though this necessary change had what Hardy must have thought of as the extra benefit of assuring readers that Creston was not Budmouth, whatever they might hitherto have suspected, nevertheless it does tie the novel to Wessex.

When he was faced with the novel again for this collected edition, he must have been tempted to permit it to remain in its 1889 guise; but the overriding logic of new Wessex, in particular that all his fiction shared the same physical and cultural environment, would not allow it. Carriford, however, still did not become Mellstock, though the illustration of Knapwater House shows Kingston Maurward, in the heart of the parish of Stinsford/Mellstock. Buckshead Hill, the one name that had appeared to form a link with *Far From the Madding Crowd*, ought to have become Yalbury Hill, but was instead erased altogether, and almost all the other substantial changes to Carriford saw the simple removal of details appropriate to Stinsford and

Knapwater House

thus Mellstock, but not to Carriford.[3] Creston did become Budmouth throughout, though, and Hardy, accepting the Mellstock/Carriford anomaly and confident that few people would notice, did his best to throw them off anyway by altering the distance between Knapwater and Budmouth from 'about fifteen miles' to 'not twenty miles' (ch IV.1). The distance between Weymouth and Kingston Maurward is less than ten miles; nineteen miles would put the house actually in Wareham/Anglebury.

Elsewhere, too, Hardy encountered problems correlating times and distances of journeys, once the places had become anchored not just to the map of Wessex, but to that of England. Hardy declined here also to perform the substantial rewriting that would have been required to solve the problems satisfactorily, and so the reader, if paying close attention, is asked to imagine some almost superhuman walking. The railway line too became fixed as a result of new Wessex, and also necessitated some subtle fudging of the Dorset/Wessex identification; for instance, at different times in the Osgood edition the stations originally at Troominster, Galworth and Mundsbury are all replaced by Anglebury. Once Troominster becomes Casterbridge it has also to be Dorchester and the county town, and this too requires complicated and not altogether satisfactory reorganization.

Thus *Desperate Remedies* is reluctantly dragged into Wessex. *Under the Greenwood Tree*, however, was much more satisfactory.

Under the Greenwood Tree
Osgood: Volume XVI, Preface: August 1896, Illustration: Mellstock Church. Wessex: Volume VII as a Novel of Character and Environment, Preface: April 1912. Illustration: Mellstock Church.

The preface Hardy wrote for *Under the Greenwood Tree* in 1896 was characteristic of one motive that informed the writing of these introductions. It is essentially the work of a local historian, one who has intimate knowledge of church musicians, laying out some of the conditions of their service, and assuring the reader that reality underlies the narrative.[4] Hardy added two

Mellstock Church

paragraphs in 1912 for the Wessex edition, the second of which is one of the most emotional notes he appended to any of his work:

> In rereading the narrative after a long interval there occurs the inevitable reflection that the realities out of which it was spun were material for another kind of study of this little group of church musicians than is found in the chapters here penned so lightly, even so farcically and flippantly at times. But circumstances would have rendered any aim at a deeper, more essential, more transcendent handling unadvisable at the date of writing...

Revisions to one passage made in both editions hold a hint of this quite passionate regret:

> Then passed forth into the quiet night an ancient and well-worn [**and time-worn O**] hymn, embodying [**embodying a quaint W**] Christianity in words peculiarly befitting the simple and honest hearts of the quaint characters who sang them so [**words orally transmitted from father to son through several generations down to the present characters, who sang them out right O**] earnestly. (I.iv)

It is the Christianity that is quaint now, not the characters. Hardy also adds here an antiquarian note of the sort that is a mark of the new Wessex; the tonal changes in 'Time-worn' and 'right earnestly' also contribute to the new effect.

Bringing *Under the Greenwood Tree* into new Wessex was a straightforward task, since (despite the occasional attempts at disguise) the framework was already there in the first edition text. The number of revisions is considerable when both Osgood and Wessex editions are taken into account, and almost invariably, when a passage is revised in both editions the progression is towards closer identification with the reality of Stinsford and Dorchester.[5]

There are a few details other than topographical that get altered that have significance for Wessex. Hardy was always interested in apples, and for the Osgood edition he changed the names of some of the varieties – presumably to represent more accurately what was actually grown in that place at that time:

> 'This in the cask here is a drop o' the right sort' (tapping the cask); "tis a real drop o' cordial from the best picked apples – Horner's and Cadbury's [– **Sansoms, Stubbards, Five-corners, and such-like O**] – you d'mind the sort, Michael?' (I.ii)

I have found records of Cadburys – also to be called White Jersey (they originated near Cadbury Castle), Horners – also to be known as Hangy Downs (a mild bittersweet cider apple) and Michaelmas Stubbards (yellow-green with a brownish-red flush, more of a desert apple from Devonshire), but not the other two.

Throughout the Wessex edition Hardy scattered antiquarian footnotes for the better information of his readership, and there is one in *Under the Greenwood Tree*:

> 'Very well; we'll let en come in,' said the tranter feelingly [**tranter W**]. 'You'll be like chips in porridge, [*add footnote*: **This, a local expression, must be a corruption of something less questionable. W**] Leaf – neither good nor hurt.' (II.iv)

Perhaps motivated by the same impulse, he added a good anecdote about the new vicar's reaction to the habits of the old:

> [*add* 'No sooner had he got here than he found the font wouldn't hold water, as it hadn't for years off and on; and when I told him that Mr. Grinham never minded it, but used to spet upon his vinger and christen 'em just as well, 'a said, "Good Heavens! Send for a workman immediate. What place have I come to!" Which was no compliment to us, come to that.' W] (II.ii)

Whether this was a story Hardy remembered of the old Stinsford vicar, or just one that he had heard told of somewhere and thought appropriate, cannot be known.

A final point in relation to *Under the Greenwood Tree* has relevance to other texts also. In the Osgood edition he altered the name of one of the Casterbridge butchers from Sabley to Haylock (IV.iv). A little work with directories of the period shows that in Dorchester there were butchers William Hayward and William Lock, and the new name was Hardy's joke. But this matter of Casterbridge naming is a little more complicated. Earlier in the novel we are introduced to the two clocks in Keeper Day's house, one made by Thomas Wood, the other by Ezekiel Sparrowgrass; in 1896 Sparrowgrass was changed to Saunders (II.vi). The same directories yield Thomas Saunders as the name of a clockmaker in Dorchester. The same kind of thing happens in *Far From the Madding Crowd*, where the surgeon who looks at Troy after Boldwood has shot him is in the first edition called Granthead; in the Osgood edition he becomes Aldritch (vII cXXIV) – John Aldridge was a Dorchester surgeon. On the other hand, in *The Mayor of Casterbridge*, the landlord of the King of Prussia was called Stannidge from the start (vI cVII), when the landlord of the Three Mariners in Dorchester, on which the King of Prussia was based, was called Standish – another small piece of evidence that in 1885–6 Hardy was becoming more confident about narrowing the gap between Wessex and England.

A Pair of Blue Eyes
Osgood: Volume IV, Preface: March 1895, Illustration: Castle Boterel Harbour.
Wessex: Volume X in Romances and Fantasies, Preface: June 1912, Illustration: Castle Boterel Harbour.

Castle Boterel Harbour

HK indicates readings found in the one-volume edition published by Henry King in 1877.

W20 indicates readings found in the 1920 reimpression of the Wessex edition.

Hardy's preface, like that for *Under the Greenwood Tree*, is intensely personal. The first paragraph is part of his ongoing penance for his involvement in the restoration of ancient churches, among them St Juliot near Boscastle, where he met his wife. It is their courtship that colours the last two paragraphs – Hardy used some of the imagery from the penultimate paragraph in his poem 'Beeny Cliff', commemorating her death. In between there is an interesting second definition of his Wessex project (coming soon after the preface to *Far From the Madding Crowd*), with a justification for including North Cornwall in the scheme:

> The shore and country about 'Castle Boterel' is now getting well known, and will be readily recognized. The spot is, I may add, the furthest westward of all those convenient corners wherein I have ventured to erect my theatre for these imperfect little [**imperfect W**] dramas of country life and passions; and it lies near to, or no great way beyond, the vague border of the Wessex kingdom on that side, which, like the westering verge of modern American settlements, was progressive and uncertain.[6]

This account implies that Hardy was still slightly embarrassed at having to include *A Pair of Blue Eyes* in Wessex. In the first chapter he made this change:

> Her father, the rector of the parish [**of a parish on the sea-swept outskirts of Lower Wessex O**]. (vI cI)

And reference to the Osgood map above p. 113 shows that the boundary between Devon and Cornwall was only marked by the river Camel (not itself named), and that Lower Wessex then included both Devon and Cornwall. At a place later in the novel he had (most unusually) added the English county name to the text in the one-volume edition, and had to modify it in Osgood:

> The possibility is that Mrs. Smith was getting mollified, in spite of herself, by these remarkably friendly phenomena among the people of St. Kirrs [St. Kirrs [*St. Launce's O*]. And in justice to them it was quite desirable that she should do so. The interest which the people of this unpractised Cornish [*the unpractised ones of this O*] town expressed so grotesquely was genuine of its kind, and equal in intrinsic worth to the more polished smiles of larger communities HK]. (vIII cIX)

Omitting all reference to a county was perhaps the wise thing to do. At another place, too, Hardy decided not to use Wessex in an Osgood revision, when he might well have:

> To those hardy weather-beaten individuals [**those musing weather-beaten West-country folk O**] who pass the greater part of their days and nights out of doors... (vII cIX)

Eventually he decided to call Cornwall Off-Wessex, but this was not until after 1912, after the death of his first wife. It seems likely that in 1895 Hardy was under some pressure not to offer the inquisitive any unavoidable indication of the exact scene of the novel, the scene also of his courtship of Emma. Indeed, *A Pair of Blue Eyes* is the only novel which Hardy revised at all considerably after the Wessex edition. By 1920, after he had come to terms with Emma's death, he felt free to make it clearer that West Endelstow was a version of St Juliot, and to add some personal reminiscences of journeys made there fifty years earlier. A number of changes make the situation of the church approximate to that of St Juliot, a process he had begun in 1912. Finally there are some class-details to be noted, evidence of the gentrification of the Smiths.[7]

Far From the Madding Crowd
Osgood: Volume II, Preface: February 1895, Illustration: Weatherbury.
Wessex: Volume II in Novels of Character and Environment, Preface: 1895–1902, Illustration: Weatherbury.

O1 indicates Harper's sixpenny edition published in 1901.

Weatherbury

The preface to *Far From the Madding Crowd* defines Wessex and lays out a history of its development.

> In reprinting this story for a new edition I am reminded that it was in the chapters of 'Far from the Madding Crowd,' as they appeared month by month in a popular magazine, that I first ventured to adopt the word 'Wessex' from the pages of early English history, and give it a fictitious significance as the existing name of the district once included in that extinct kingdom. The series of novels I projected being mainly of the kind called local, they seemed to require a territorial definition of some sort to lend unity to their scene. Finding that the area of a single county did not afford a canvas large enough for this purpose, and that there were objections to an invented name, I disinterred the old one.

This is the history of Wessex as Hardy would have liked it to be, looking back from the perspective of 1895 over twenty-five years of writing; or perhaps it was how it seemed to him then it must have been. But the evidence as this study has presented it suggests otherwise, that Wessex only slowly grew in Hardy's imagination to the scale it had in 1891 when *Tess of the d'Urbervilles* was published. It is hard to imagine, though it may be true, that Hardy projected a 'series' of novels in 1874. It is barely true that 'the area of a single county did not afford a canvas large enough' even for the new Wessex of 1891-5, if the county is Dorset. To start with Wessex included bits of Hampshire and Wiltshire, but did not include all of Dorset; only in *The Mayor of Casterbridge* and *The Woodlanders* did the north-western part of the county enter Wessex, and only in *Tess of the d'Urbervilles* the south-western part. The eastern section of Somerset joined through some short stories in the late eighties, and Exeter had a sort of honorary position as a base of operations, perhaps in Wessex, perhaps not. *A Pair of Blue Eyes* was outside Wessex altogether. It was really only in *Jude the Obscure*, and in revisions for the present edition that Wessex reached the Saxon proportions that Hardy claims for it in this preface.

It would be interesting to know what objections Hardy had to inventing a name for his fictional district; after all he was happy enough to invent names for the places that he used. If one were to speculate, it would be to suggest that George Eliot's Loamshire and Stonyshire and Anthony Trollope's Barsetshire were models that he really did not wish to emulate. From the very beginning, in reviews of *Desperate Remedies*, Hardy's work was linked with Eliot's, and it was perhaps partly in reaction that he chose Wessex rather than Downshire, or some such name. On the other hand the construction of Trollope's names Barchester and Barsetshire so clearly followed the pattern of Dorchester and Dorsetshire, that he must have been wary of following that example either.

The preface continues:

> The press and the public were kind enough to welcome the fanciful plan, and willingly joined me in the anachronism of imagining a Wessex population living under Queen Victoria, – a modern Wessex of railways, the penny post, mowing and reaping machines, union workhouses, lucifer matches, labourers who could read and write, and National school children. But I believe I am correct in stating that, until the existence of this contemporaneous Wessex [**Wessex in place of the usual counties W**] was announced in this present story, in 1874, it had never been heard of [**had never been used in fiction 01** *copy*; **had never been heard of in fiction, if at all 01** *proof*; **had never been heard of in fiction and current speech, if at all 02**], and that the expression, 'a Wessex peasant', or a 'Wessex custom', would therefore have been taken to refer to nothing later in date than the Norman Conquest.

In the list of Victorian accomplishments there are many of the forces that drove the changes in village life that his novels record.[8] The implication of the sequence of revisions for the sixpenny edition is perhaps that between 1895 and 1901 someone had told him that they thought they had heard of someone who had anticipated his usage, in an essay in a magazine for instance, though without coming up with the precise reference (thus the 'if at all'). I have found no earlier fictional account of a modern Wessex. The preface goes on:

> I did not anticipate that this application of the word to a modern use [**word to modern story 01**] would extend outside the chapters of my own chronicles [**of the chronicles themselves 01; of these particular chronicles W**]. But the name [**But it 02**] was soon taken up elsewhere as a local designation. The first to do so was [**elsewhere, the first to adopt it being 02**] the now defunct *Examiner*, which, in the impression bearing the date July 15, 1876, entitled one of its articles 'The Wessex Labourer,' the article turning out to be no dissertation on farming during the Heptarchy, but on the modern peasant of the south-west counties, and his presentation in these stories [**counties 02**].
>
> Since then the appellation which I had thought to reserve to the horizons and landscapes of a merely realistic [**a partly real, partly 02**] dream-country, has become more and more popular as a practical provincial definition; and the dream-country has, by degrees, solidified into a utilitarian region which people can go to, take a house in, and write to the papers from. But I ask all good and gentle [**and idealistic W**] readers to be so kind as [**readers W**] to forget this, and to refuse steadfastly to believe that there are any inhabitants of a Victorian Wessex outside the pages of this and the companion [**outside these 02**] volumes in which they were first discovered [**which they were first generally known 01** *first proof*; **which their lives and conversations are detailed 01** *second proof*, **02**].

Perhaps the most important revision of all is to the first clause in the second paragraph here, in which Wessex changes from a 'merely realistic dream-country' to a 'partly real, partly dream-country'. It must be remembered that in February 1895 when Hardy wrote this preface he had not yet made the long sequence of revisions that culminated in *Under the Greenwood Tree* a year and a half later, and though he must have had a good idea of what would be involved, it seems likely that the experience itself forced him to make this alteration to the preface at an early opportunity. In the original wording Hardy intended readers to understand his surprise that what was merely a dream-country presented as if it were real, or presented in realistic terms, should have been taken as absolutely real – in other words, his meaning would have been clearer if 'merely' had come before 'a'. The new wording, whatever the motivation for the change, is entirely different in effect from the earlier, in that it acknowledges that part of the 'horizons and landscapes' of Wessex are in fact real: that some towns and cities, and all rivers and heights, are given their real names. It may go further, and imply also that much described under fictional names is also real (and that, as a consequence of the revision for the Osgood edition, much more is real than had been the case before that revision). Thus the new version reflects accurately what

Hardy did in 1895–6 to some, if not to all, of his novels, acknowledging the inevitability of the further solidification of Wessex into a utilitarian region.

When Hardy first wrote *Far From the Madding Crowd* he made no consistent effort to disguise the environments of the novel, with the exception of the relationship of Weatherbury to Casterbridge; on the other hand nor was he at all concerned with the kind of accuracy that new Wessex now demanded from him. Consequently he had to alter much detail for the Osgood edition, and found more to change or add in 1901 and 1912. Weatherbury becomes a version of Puddletown, the road from Weatherbury to Casterbridge (with villages along the route) is clarified, Casterbridge itself is reoriented, and the wider context of the action is brought into Wessex.[9] The result is to place the action on maps of both Wessex and England; but nothing essential to the narrative is lost thereby. What is gained, in general, here as elsewhere, is a closer connection through place with the rest of Hardy's fiction – a sense for the reader, strong by the end of the novel, of an environment shared, a continuity. There is one change to the environment that also changes in a small way our understanding of a character:

> In the ashpit was a heap of potatoes roasting, and a boiling pipkin of charred bread, called 'coffee,' for the benefit of whomsoever should call, for Warren's was a sort of village [**sort of O**] clubhouse, there being no inn in the place [**clubhouse, used** [*used by Bathsheba's set 01* **only**] **as an alternative to the inn O** [*inn, where it would have been awkward for them to be seen by her sharp eyes 01* **only**]]. (vI cXV)

The idea before 1895 was to make Weatherbury different from Puddletown, which had a reputation for heavy drinking – and five pubs. Two further implications of the paperback revisions noted here are that Bathsheba was more interfering than most farmers with her workfolk, and that she was down on drink. The phrase 'Bathsheba's set' is also interesting, in that for a fraction of time it gives the village an alternative life – the inhabitants who aren't in her 'set'. There is less sense of a complete village life in this novel than there is in *Under the Greenwood Tree*, though Puddletown was thriving then, and Hardy knew it intimately.

It is a feature of revision in this novel that Hardy paid considerable attention to Wessex when he worked on the text for the Harper paperback edition of 1901, and that the details added or amended then were not, for the most part, incorporated into any subsequent version of the novel. The few that were adopted (or adapted), Hardy made for the reissue of the Osgood plates by Macmillan in 1902 as their Uniform edition.[10]

The Hand of Ethelberta
Osgood: Volume X, Preface: December 1895, Illustration: Corvsgate Castle. Wessex: Volume XVI in Novels of Ingenuity, Preface: August 1912. Illustration: Corvsgate Castle.

Corvsgate Castle

Neither preface has any material relevant to Wessex. *The Hand of Ethelberta* was the first novel Hardy wrote with Wessex in his mind, and he had relatively little trouble in making the rural parts of the novel conform to the new Wessex scheme of things. Every place in the region described in the novel except Knollsea has some changes to bring it closer to what a visitor to the English equivalent might find – but sometimes the change is only to a name or a distance.[11] There is only one mild surprise in the revisions for either edition. This is when Ethelberta thinks of Neigh's country estate:

> All she knew was that its name was Harefield [**Farnfield O**], that it lay from twenty to [**lay thirty or O**] forty miles out of London in a south-westerly direction... (XXVII)

Farnfield is the second Wessex transparent name for a place that is outside Wessex, though like the first, Christminster, it is very close to the border. Farnham is 38 miles from London, but still just in Surrey; the difference between the two is that the plot of *Jude the Obscure* meant that Christminster had to be Oxford, but Hardy could have put Neigh's estate anywhere. Why he did not push it across the border into Upper Wessex is not at all clear, especially when other places beyond Wessex are carefully brought within its boundaries. Ethelberta's father writes to her about Ladywell, whose 'family own a good bit of land somewhere out Norfolk [**Aldbrickham O**] way' (VII); the Petherwins lived in Connaught Crescent in the first edition, in Osgood it becomes Exonbury Crescent (VIII): and Christopher says: 'Do you remember, when father was alive and we were at Scarborough [**Solentsea O**] that season' (II). These examples give some sense of the total Wessex pressure of mind under which Hardy was working in 1895.

The Return of the Native
Osgood: Volume VI, Preface: July 1895, Illustration: Egdon Heath.
Wessex: Volume IV as a Novel of Character and Environment, Preface: April 1912. Illustration: Egdon Heath.

Egdon Heath

The rather brief Osgood preface is almost entirely historical and topographical. To this he added a paragraph in 1912, apologizing to 'searchers for scenery' for the imperfections in detail of the relationship between fiction and reality.[12] In fact, when Hardy came to handle *The Return of the Native* in the early summer of 1895, he faced the new Wessex dilemma in its most serious form. In 1878 he had pulled off the trick of persuading the reader that Egdon was at once immense and fathomless and a mappable patch of land a few miles square. As long as no one could be sure where those square miles of heathland existed outside Hardy's imagination, the double power of the mystery and the realism were held in balance, each nourishing the other.

But since then Egdon had appeared in *The Mayor of Casterbridge*, in 'The Withered Arm', in *Tess of the d'Urbervilles* and in 'The Fiddler of the Reels'; and though much in these later representations was in harmony with *The Return of the Native* – though it was an 'ancient country whose surface never had been stirred to a finger's depth', though 'thick clouds made the atmosphere dark, though it was as yet only early afternoon; and the wind howled dismally over the hills of the heath', though it was called 'the enormous Egdon Waste' and a 'tawny piece of antiquity', 'a place of Dantesque gloom at this hour' – yet each reference in a subsequent text tended to make the place more familiar, less mysterious.[13] It was, however, the passage in 'The Withered Arm' discussed earlier (p. 57) that decisively began the work carried on in 1895 and 1912. The story is a different kind of narrative from *The Return of the Native*. As Hardy makes clear in the 1896 preface to *Wessex Tales*, it is a retelling of history, or at least folk history, and thus Hardy feels an obligation to the reality out of which the narrative sprang. It is only because, in the past of Dorset, the heathland had stretched unbroken for ten miles or more, that a horsewoman, understood to be living in the 1820s, might in the story traverse it unhindered. Without this explanation the veracity of the piece of oral history might be compromised.

Once thought and written, such a passage could not be ignored. Even though Hardy was aware of the generic difference between novel and story, he could not permit two versions of Wessex. Between 1878 and 1895 Egdon had been demystified and located in relation to surrounding Wessex places, and for good or ill he had to accept the consequence when he came to revise the novel; but there is evidence that he was not glad to do so, that he did so with a sense of constraint, and even of irritation that he had written himself into an untenable position. His boyhood sense of the heathland beyond his birthplace was intimate, strong, ever-present to him, and was the source of the power within his representation of Egdon. To be forced by another strong compulsion to limit this dimensionless, timeless arena was painful, and in 1895 he changed as little as he could, and even then ambiguously.[14]

He made a number of alterations to distances and directions, but they were not made consistently throughout the novel, and, highly unusually, he made more such changes in 1912 than in 1895. All these revisions, including discussion of other anomalies they give rise to, are given in the website, and it will be seen there that most of the Osgood revisions occur at the beginning and the end of the novel, as if Hardy began with appropriate intentions, but could not sustain them, until prompted by the diminishing number of pages before him to a renewal of effort. It is notable for instance that the revision in the following passage was left until 1912:

> 'I knowed her brothers well. Longer coffins were never made in the whole county of [**of South W**] Wessex, and 'tis said that poor George's knees were crumpled up a little e'en as 'twas.' (II.vi)

And even in the first book there are places where in any other novel the revisions made in the Wessex edition might have been expected in 1895:

> Maybe you can call to mind that monument in [**in Weatherbury W**] church – the cross-legged soldier that have had his nose [**his arm W**] knocked away by the school-children? (I.iii)

Part of Egdon is in Weatherbury/Puddletown parish and Sir William Martyn's memorial in alabaster there is thoroughly battered about. Much later in the novel Hardy replaced Southerton with Weatherbury in the Osgood edition (V.iv) without any particular motive in the text for doing so, whereas it seems quite likely that he had Puddletown church in mind in this description all along.

It also happened very rarely that Hardy altered in 1912 a topographical revision he had made for the Osgood edition, but there is an example in *The Return of the Native*:

> '...Now, can you tell me if. Bottom [**Rimsmoor W**] Pond is dry this summer?'
> 'Bottom [**Rimsmoor W**] Pond is, but Parker's [**Moreford O; Oker's W**] Pool isn't, because he is deep, and is never dry – 'tis just over there.' (IV.vi)

Moreford had a double existence prior to 1895; it was (as Moreford St. Jude's) one of the places where the maltster had worked in *Far From the Madding Crowd*, 'north-west-by-north' from Weatherbury; and it was six miles east of Lower Mellstock in *Tess of the d'Urbervilles* (thus making it the equivalent of the Dorset village of Moreton). The occurrence in *Far From the Madding Crowd* was replaced in the Osgood edition with Millpond St Jude's/Milborne St Andrews, a place which corresponds more or less to the direction from Puddletown indicated, and was perhaps where Hardy was thinking of in 1873. It is less clear what Hardy had in mind here in *The Return of the Native*, for the *Tess of the d'Urbervilles* identification as Moreton does not work particularly well, since the whole of the Frome valley lies between the part of the Heath described in the novel and the village. It seems at least possible that he was not concentrating very hard when making this revision. The Wessex edition's Rimsmoor Pond and Oker's Pool both exist in Dorset a couple of miles north of Moreton, evidence that for the Wessex edition Hardy was content, or at least resigned, finally to fix *The Return of the Native*'s Egdon.[15]

The Trumpet-Major
Osgood: Volume IX, Preface: October 1895, Illustration: Budmouth Harbour. Wessex: Volume XI in Romances and Fantasies, Preface: October 1895. Illustration: Budmouth Harbour.

Budmouth Harbour

The preface, like those for *Under the Greenwood Tree, A Pair of Blue Eyes* and *Wessex Tales*, is personal, and relates some of the unrecorded, local history that lies behind the narrative. Hardy also explains about the newspapers and other documents he consulted, and in this way the preface reflects the primary distinction in the novel between recorded and unrecorded history. [16]

As the texture of *The Return of the Native* was fundamentally altered when it was brought into new Wessex, so too was that of *The Trumpet-Major*. It was, as we have seen, a historical novel that named all the places touched by recorded history with their English names, and left a few (no more than three or four) as opaquely Wessex – in particular Overcombe, where most of the purely fictional action of the novel took place. He could have left the novel thus in 1895, but that would have run counter to his desire (or need) to integrate all his work into his new fictional reality. Thus Dorchester becomes Casterbridge, Salisbury becomes Melchester, Abbotsbury becomes Abbotsea and so on.[17] The effect is transformative, but it leaves, as so often, some puzzles. Why, for instance in chapter XXVII should 'the Puddletown volunteers' be altered to 'the Longpuddle volunteers' and not 'the Weatherbury volunteers'? [18]

He also had trouble with Overcombe. In the early editions the village is a mixture of sites and buildings from all over the district to the north-east of Weymouth, brought together in the approximate location of Dorset's Bincombe; for new Wessex Hardy tries (through both collected editions) to reorganize the details around the mill that he had taken from Sutton Poyntz. He succeeds to a degree, but, as was inevitable, leaves also confusion. [19]

In altering English places to Wessex ones, Hardy treated Weymouth as a special case. There is a parallel here with his treatment of the town in 'The Melancholy Hussar' when he had collected it in *Life's Little Ironies* a year earlier. Whenever Weymouth was mentioned in the magazine version of the story Hardy replaced it not with Budmouth, but with a phrase like 'the watering-place'. He does the same as far as possible in *The Trumpet-Major*, though it is hard to use such periphrasis in dialogue and make it convincing.[20] There is some evidence that he grew weary of finding alternatives to Budmouth about half way through revising the novel, for the name occurs much more frequently later on. The obvious reason for attempting to avoid using Budmouth, or at least to use it as little as possible is an aesthetic one. Weymouth is so far the focal point of the novel's attention that the name occurs very often in the text – so often, Hardy may have thought, as to jar on the sensitive reader. But this could not really be true of 'The Melancholy Hussar', and it is also the case that in, say, *The Mayor of Casterbridge*, the name of the county town appears frequently, but Hardy makes no attempt to find ways around it.

Other places close to Weymouth also disappear; Radipole goes entirely, as do Lodmoor and Broadwey. Perhaps Hardy could not be bothered to invent Wessex names for them, and they are included in greater Budmouth. Portesham, a little further away, does survive as Pos'ham – which approximates to the local pronunciation. There are a couple of changes to Portland, though none to prepare for the radical revision to *The Well-Beloved* in 1897. Two Wessex changes were made to the Osgood plates when Macmillan issued their Uniform edition in 1903.[21]

Finally there are a couple of revisions that relate to other aspects of Wessex:

> She, too, had a very nice appearance in her best clothes as she walked along – the sarcenet hat, muslin shawl, and tight-sleeved gown being of the newest Overcombe fashion, that was only about two years old in Weymouth [**about five years old in Weymouth MS; about a year old in the adjoining town O**], and in Paris three or four [**Paris about eight or ten MS; London three or four O**]. (XIII)

This compares with the cut of a smockfrock passage in *Far From the Madding Crowd*. Hardy also alters the apples that go to make the cider for Bob's wedding:

> It had been pressed from fruit judiciously chosen by an old hand – Horner and Cleeves apples for the body, a few Crimson-Kitties [**& just a dash of early Pippins... MS1; a few Tom-Putts O**] for colour, and just a dash of Old Fivecorners for sparkle. (XVI)

This may be compared with the revision to *Under the Greenwood Tree* above p. 118.

A Laodicean

Osgood: Volume XI, Preface: January 1896, Illustration: Stancy Castle.
Wessex: Volume XVII as a novel of Ingenuity, Preface: October 1912. Illustration: Stancy Castle.

Stancy Castle

There is a certain irony inherent in having an illustration of Stancy Castle as frontispiece to both editions, since it is supposed to have burned down at the end of the novel. The Osgood preface has nothing much to do with Wessex, but the postscript added for the Wessex edition does have a sentence of interest:

> Looking over the novel at the present much later date [than the first publication in 1881], I hazard the conjecture that its sites, mileages, and architectural details can hardly seem satisfactory to the investigating topographist, so appreciable a proportion of these features being but the baseless fabric of a vision.

As we shall see, Hardy ultimately did his best to make all these details fit together without doing substantial rewriting, but his conjecture is an accurate one. In the first edition there was no possible way of knowing where the English part of the action was set, though a couple of details of Markton, the main town, were suggestive of Dorchester. In the revisions for the Osgood edition Hardy tried (not very hard) to convince himself and his readers that the scene is laid in Somerset – primarily through Macbeth-Raeburn's illustration depicting Dunster Castle and labelled Stancy Castle. Indeed Hardy made remarkably few alterations in 1896, doing the absolute minimum required to suggest a setting in Outer Wessex rather than South Wessex. The inn at Markton changes its name from the King's Arms to the Lord Quantock Arms; an unidentifiable place (Helterton) is turned into the county town of Outer Wessex (Toneborough), and so is Casterbridge; the number of counties a telegraph message must go across to reach London from Stancy Castle is increased. This is the sum total of the adaptation of the novel to Outer Wessex, and it may well only have been his hero's name (Somerset) that suggested the county to Hardy when he took up the novel to revise.[22]

One change in 1896 seems to be part of Hardy's attempt to relocate every extraneous place to Wessex. Havill speaks of Paula:

> 'In something over six weeks – a fortnight before she returns from Brighton [**from the Scilly Isles O**], for which place she leaves here in a few days.' (II.i)

This is worth noting because, it may be recalled, the Scilly Isles are the partial setting of 'A Mere Interlude', the only narrative to run its course in places that Hardy had, so far as we know, never visited. Should one speculate that (hitherto unknown to all) Hardy went there with someone like Paula around 1880? No, of course not, what an idea!

Hardy felt in 1912 that he had to try more seriously to make the novel fit Dunster, but I imagine it was with some reluctance that he undertook the necessary changes. The attempted transformation of the environment begins with the belated recognition that Dunster castle does not have a keep. Other details of the castle also change. Because the village of Dunster nestles beneath the castle, Hardy had to decide what to do with Markton, two or three miles away in the Osgood edition. He could have abandoned it altogether, and chosen a new Wessex-name like Dunwich for the settlement attached to the castle, but that would have been a touch too radical for what he felt he could do in 1912. Instead he decided to split Markton, move half of the references to within a short distance of the castle, and the rest twenty miles away to Toneborough.[23] This leads him into the description of feats even more amazing than those in *Desperate Remedies*. For instance, Dare and Havill take a stroll of an evening out of Toneborough (which until the Wessex edition had been Markton):

> They went down the town, and along the highway. [**highway. The evening being tempting they walked further and further till they were unexpectedly near Markton and the Castle above. W**] When they reached the entrance to the park a man driving a basket-carriage came out from the gate and passed them by in the gloom. (II.ii)

This is revision contemptuous of probablities; it is no wonder that Havill asks: 'Well, what was the use of coming here [**of tiring ourselves by walking these miles W**]?' Hardy never states the distance between Toneborough and Markton in the novel, and had he not created the precisely mapped Wessex, such fiddling around with the text might have been acceptable.

Two on a Tower
Osgood: Volume V, Preface: July 1895, Illustration: Welland House and park. Wessex: Volume XII in Romances and Fantasies, Preface: July 1895. Photograph: Welland House and tower.

The preface has two sentences relevant to Wessex:

> The scene of the action was suggested by two real spots in the part of the country specified, each of which has a column standing upon it. Certain

Welland House and park[24]

surrounding peculiarities have been imported into the narrative from both sites [**sites, and from elsewhere W**].

Again Hardy covers himself from the topographers, though he doesn't give specifics or details. In fact, because he is content to let the environment remain sharply defined but openly an amalgamation of features from various places, there are remarkably few alterations to aspects of Wessex in this novel in the two major revisions.[25]

The Mayor of Casterbridge

Osgood: Volume III, Preface: February 1895, Illustration: The High Street, Casterbridge.

Wessex: Volume V as a Novel of Character and Environment, Preface: February 1895–May 1912, Illustration: Looking up the High Street of Casterbridge.

The High Street, Casterbridge

All that the preface contains that is relevant to Wessex is an assertion that the story got its donné from real events in Dorchester. And in fact the revision to the novel overall is not as substantial or significant as might have been expected.

Hardy went back to his first instinct and returned local landmarks in Casterbridge to their real names, as for instance in:

> I shall return through Casterbridge, and Budmouth, where I shall take the steamboat [**the packet-boat MS1, O**]. Can you meet me with the letters and other trifles? I shall be in the coach which changes horses at the Stag [**Antelope MS1, O**] Hotel at half-past five Wednesday evening. (vI cXVIII)

It is interesting that in this example also Hardy preferred another original manuscript reading. In the Wessex edition he introduced into Casterbridge names that had been superseded in Dorchester itself: 'Newson's back was soon visible up the road [**road, crossing Bull-stake W**].' (vII cXVIII), or 'when they reached the Town Pump [**reached Crossways, or Bow W**]' (vII cXX). Some other names were changed, some added, and some descriptions revised – in particular the location of Lucetta's home – one example is: 'The house I am going into is that one they call High Street Hall [**High-Place Hall O**] – the old stone one overlooking [**one looking down the lane to W**] the Market' (vI cXX) – and of the place where Henchard attempts to persuade Farfrae to return to his dying wife – 'In a cutting on the summit of the last [**In Yalbury Bottom, the plain *[Bottom, or Plain, W]* at the foot of the hill O**], he listened.' (vII cXVII)[26]

Some of the character-links to *Under the Greenwood Tree* are revised or altered, as when old Dame Ledlow is identified not as farmer Penny's sister, but, in Osgood as 'farmer Shinar's sister' and in Wessex as 'farmer Shinar's aunt'. Finally there is the reinstatement, with a few changes, of Henchard's return to Casterbridge for Elizabeth-Jane's wedding at the end of the novel, which had been excluded from the first edition as redundant.[27]

The Woodlanders
Osgood: Volume VII, Preface: September 1895, Illustration: The country of the Woodlanders.
Wessex: Volume VI as a Novel of Character and Environment, Preface: April 1912, Illustration: The country of the Woodlanders.

The Osgood preface extols the setting of the novel in a fashion sufficiently broad to apply to any version of the text, but the Wessex edition's supplement addresses the problems investigating topographers would have in pinning down the chief location of the story, even in the newly clarified 1912 account:

> I have been honoured by so many inquiries for the true name and exact locality of the hamlet 'Little Hintock,' in which the greater part of the action of this story goes on, that I may as well confess here once for all

The country of The Woodlanders

that I do not know where that hamlet is more precisely than as explained above and in the pages of the narrative. To oblige readers I once spent several hours on a bicycle with a friend in a serious attempt to discover the real spot; but the search ended in failure; though tourists assure me positively that they have found it without trouble...

He adds also a characteristic note marking the decay of pre-industrial Wessex:

In respect of the occupations of the characters, the adoption of iron utensils and implements in agriculture, and the discontinuance of thatched roofs for cottages, have almost extinguished the handicrafts classed formerly as 'copsework,' and the type of men who engaged in them.[28]

A considerable number of revisions in both editions go to effecting the removal of Little Hintock from under Bubb-Down to the vicinity of High-Stoy. For Osgood Hardy really just replaced Rubdon with High-Stoy and did not pay very close attention to the consequences. In revising for the Wessex edition he thought harder about the real landscape to the north of Dogbury Gate, and altered some topographical details in the light of his investigation. But even so he remained judiciously vague about the precise location of most places in the novel in relation to Dorset. To give just one example, Grace accompanies her husband Edred on the beginning of a journey from Little Hintock:

> Thus they proceeded to the turnpike road, and ascended Rubdon Hill to [**ascended towards Dogbury Hill and High-Stoy, till they were just beneath O; ascended towards the base of High-Stoy and Dogbury Hill, till they were just beneath W**] the gate he had been leaning over when she surprised him ten days before....
> With these words he mounted his horse, passed through the gate [**through a wicket O**] which Grace held open for him [horse, **turned into a branch road by the turnpike W**], and ambled down the steep bridle-track [**the incline W**] to the valley.
> She closed the gate [**She ascended the slope of High-Stoy O**] and watched his descent, and then his journey onward. His way was east, the evening sun which stood behind her back beaming full upon him as soon as he got out from the shade of the hill....
> And so the infatuated surgeon went along through the gorgeous autumn landscape of White-Hart Vale... Soon he rose out of the valley, and skirted a high plateau of the chalk formation on his right, which rested abruptly upon the fruity district of deep loam, the character and herbage of the two formations being so distinct that the calcareous upland appeared but as a deposit of a few years' antiquity upon the level vale.
> He kept along the edge of this high, uninclosed country, and the sky behind him being deep violet she could still see white Darling in relief upon it. (vII cXII)

It is remarkable really that the latter part of this quotation was unchanged in either revision, that what Hardy imagined Grace seeing from the eastern slope of Bubb-Down he was quite happy for her to see from the top of High-Stoy, even though in the Wessex edition he added a branch road for Edred to ride down, and decreased the slope of its descent (there is such a road, now only a track, going south-east, skirting Minterne Park and Little Minterne Hill).[29]

There are, naturally enough, changes consequent upon the relocation. Mrs Dollery's van runs to Abbot's-Cernel and not Great Hintock now, and the Hintocks themselves are internally modified, though it is worth noting how little one knows about the arrangement of any Hintock at any stage in the novel's development. Sherton has a few details expanded or emended, and some other names and distances are altered.[30] Finally there are a few changes relevant to Wessex culture rather than geography, the most important of which generalize on the fate of Giles Winterborne's cottages:

> 'Her lawyer is instructed to say that Mrs. Charmond sees no reason for disturbing the natural course of things, particularly as she contemplates pulling the houses down,' he said, quietly.

'Only think of that!' said several. [several. **'Pulling down is always the game.' W**]

Winterborne had turned away, and said vehemently to himself, 'Then let her pull 'em down, and be d – d [**be damned O**] to her!' (vI cXV)

Coming here one afternoon on his way to a hut beyond the wood, where he now slept, he noticed that the familiar brown-thatched pinion of his paternal roof had vanished from its site, and that the walls were levelled [**levelled according to the landlords' principle at this date of getting rid of cottages whenever possible W**]. (vII cX)

7
The Collected Editions 2

The arrangement of Hardy's stories between volumes was altered for both the Osgood edition (when *Wessex Tales* gained 'An Imaginative Woman'), and the Wessex edition (when 'An Imaginative Woman' was transferred to *Life's Little Ironies*, and 'The Melancholy Hussar' and 'A Tradition of Eighteen Hundred and

Wessex Tales
Osgood: Volume XIII, Preface: April 1896, Illustration: Higher Crowstairs.
Wessex: Volume IX in Novels of Character and Environment, Preface: May 1912 (also an addition for the Mellstock Edition Vol XV, June 1919). Illustration: The Hangman's Cottage at Casterbridge.

Higher Crowstairs

Four' were placed in *Wessex Tales*). The preface to *Wessex Tales* is essentially the same in both editions, but Hardy had to alter certain passages to take account of the altered contents of the volume. Thus the beginning:

> An apology is perhaps needed for the neglect of contrast which is shown by presenting two consecutive stories of hangmen [**two stories of hangmen and one of a military execution W**] in such a small collection as the following.

Hardy justifies himself with a characteristic new Wessex appeal to existing cultural history, asserting that 'in the neighbourhood of county-towns tales of executions [**towns hanging matters W**] used to form a large proportion of the local traditions'. Presumably he thought this true at least of Dorchester, and he supports his view by reference to his own experience, thus striking at once the note of the whole piece, which is to bring before the reader the personal and historical foundation for some of the stories. The basis for 'The Withered Arm' is next given a personal twist:

> In those days, too, there was still living an old woman who, for the cure of some eating disease, had been taken in her youth to have her 'blood turned' by a convict's corpse, in the manner described in 'The Withered Arm'.

Hardy goes on to rewrite the story a little:

> Since writing this story some years ago I have been reminded by an aged friend who knew 'Rhoda Brook' that, in relating her dream, my forgetfulness has weakened the facts out of which the tale grew. In reality it was while lying down on a hot afternoon that the incubus oppressed her and she flung it off, with the results upon the body of the original as described. To my mind the occurrence of such a vision in the daytime is more impressive than if it happened in a midnight dream. Readers are therefore asked to correct the misrelation, which affords an instance of how our imperfect memories insensibly formalize the fresh originality of living fact – from whose shape they slowly depart, as machine-made castings depart by degrees from the sharp hand-work of the mould.

There could be no more eloquent demonstration of Hardy's frame of mind in 1895–6; he does not suggest that 'The Withered Arm' is a record of fact, a historical or cultural document – there is the saving phrase 'facts out of which the tale grew' – but he is quite concerned at having got one at least of those facts wrong, and thinks the error important enough to tell the reader about it.[1] Sometimes, in the Wessex edition, this sort of 'correction' gets made in a footnote to the text, but those notes mark a further stage in

Hardy's double vision of his novels as tales and historical documents which he had not reached in 1896. He could doubtless have rewritten the two-page episode in the story, but he rethought and recast in the collected editions no passage of comparable length in any novel or story published before 1890. It is not that he would not meddle at all with the narrative once it had become fixed in volume form, for there are numerous examples in which the emphasis of an episode or an incident is altered, or in which a sentence of decisive clarification is added to an ambiguous situation (as, for instance, in Bathsheba Troy's responses to her husband's absence, presumed drowned, or in Alec d'Urberville's conversion to evangelical fundamentalism), but rather that he would not enter the text to such an extended degree. He made the required changes in the examples given, and in all others, by the alteration of single words, phrases and at the most by the addition of a sentence.

It is fruitless perhaps to speculate whether it was simple disinclination or weariness that prevented Hardy from doing the kind of work required to incorporate the daytime dream into the Osgood version of 'The Withered Arm', or whether he felt – consciously or unconsciously, prompted by morality or historicity or aesthetics – that there was a limit to the amount of disturbance he should make to a story written years before. At any rate, he requests the reader to do the work for him – an invitation to collaborate in the recreative enterprise of reading to an unusual degree.

The preface goes on in the Osgood version to give authority for other stories – for details of the smuggling in 'The Distracted Preacher', and for the hard-to-swallow physical resemblance between a mother's child and a man, not the child's father, whom she has intensely desired at her child's conception and birth, found in 'An Imaginative Woman'. In the Wessex Edition, naturally enough, the latter disappears with the story, and in its place are three new paragraphs, the first two of which give some more of the historical background to the action of 'The Distracted Preacher', and refer also to a note appended to the story itself, for which see below.

The third new paragraph begins with a sentence intended to undo the effect of everything that has gone before: 'However, the stories are but dreams, and not records.' This sentence is a counter to the alteration in the 1902 preface of *Far From the Madding Crowd* of Hardy's description of Wessex from 'a merely realistic dream-country' to 'a partly real, partly dream-country' – and seems disingenuously inaccurate. In the last part of the account of his 'error' in 'The Withered Arm' he had written of memory and fact in terms which emphatically privileged 'living fact' through the terms of the comparison with mechanical reproduction; and the whole paragraph, indeed the whole Preface, privileges 'living fact' over the product of the imagination. It is thus slightly ironic that the note added for the Mellstock edition, which refers to 'A Tradition of Eighteen Hundred and Four', explains that though the story was a figment of his imagination, he was told several years after its first publication 'that it was a real tradition'. 'Great was his surprise!' Whether it was a tradition of Sussex, where the story was originally set when he wrote it in 1882, or of Dorset, whence it moved in the first edition of *Wessex Tales* of 1888, does not appear.

As far as revision to the stories is concerned, it was with 'Interlopers at the Knap' and 'The Distracted Preacher' that Hardy was most concerned. Alterations to the environment of *The Woodlanders* meant consequent changes to the former – one of which, unusually, was made for Macmillan's Uniform edition. The substantial environmental change to the latter had already taken place on its collection into *Wessex Tales* – the change from Dorset to Wessex – though there remained some work still to be done. It is further support of the idea that by 1912 Hardy had become more interested in fact than fiction derived from the fact that he adds substantial notes indicating the 'true' conclusion to the smugglers' story – returning Wessex to Dorset, one might say.[2]

A Group of Noble Dames
Osgood: Volume XV, Preface: June 1896, Illustration: King's Hintock Court.
Wessex: Volume XIV in Romances and Fantasies, Preface: June 1896 Illustration: Wintoncester Cathedral.

These stories are almost untouched in any way relevant to this study in either of the collected editions; it is only in 'The First Countess of Wessex' that there is anything substantial to report, and that only of the Wessex edition.

King's Hintock Court

Tess of the d'Urbervilles

Osgood: Volume I, Preface: January 1895, Illustration: Wellbridge Manor-house. Wessex: Volume I in Novels of Character and Environment, Preface: March 1912, Illustration: The Froom Meadow.

00 indicates the paperback edition published by Harper in 1900

Wellbridge Manor-house

Tess of the d'Urbervilles already had a substantial preface, written for the one-volume edition of the novel in 1892 (the plates of which were used to set the Osgood edition text); to this (as *Tess of the d'Urbervilles* was the first volume of the edition to appear) Hardy added paragraphs that are a commentary on the map that was appended to each volume, a verbal concession of what the map displayed. In the Wessex edition these paragraphs were somewhat expanded and removed to a 'General Preface to the Novels and Poems', which appeared at the beginning of *Tess of the d'Urbervilles*:

> In the present edition it may be well to state, in response to inquires from readers interested in landscape, pre-historic antiquities, and especially old English architecture, that the description of the backgrounds in this and its companion novels has been done from the real [**real – that is to say, has something real for its basis, however illusively treated W**]. Many features of the first two kinds have been given under their existing names; for instance, the Vale of Blackmoor or Blakemore...The rivers Froom or Frome, and Stour, are, of course, well known as such. And in planning the stories the [**And the further W**] idea was that large towns and points tending to mark the outline of Wessex – such as Bath, Plymouth, The Start, Portland Bill, Southampton, &c. – should be named outright [**named clearly W**]. The scheme was not greatly elaborated, but, whatever its value, the names remain still.

When in 1895 Hardy wrote that the 'backgrounds' of his fiction had 'been done from the real', he was using a painterly metaphor that gave his audience warrant for anticipating the kind of accuracy they would expect from a topographical artist – or the compiler of a guidebook. Hardy, however was neither, as we have seen, and he found it necessary to qualify his initial confident statement – ironically so, since revision in 1912 to aspects of Wessex was almost entirely in the direction of making his accounts of buildings and landscape conform more closely to the real.

It might be making too much of the second change to the paragraph to argue that in removing the idea that the stories were planned, Hardy, for once, was acknowledging (to himself at least, and to anyone who bothered to compare the texts) that Wessex geography grew rather than came into existence as the result of a premeditated plan. He goes on to write of the settlements of Wessex:

> In respect of places described under fictitious or ancient names – for reasons that seemed good at the time of writing [**writing them – and kept up in the poems W**] – discerning persons [**discerning people W**] have affirmed in print that they clearly recognize the originals: such as Shaftesbury in 'Shaston', Sturminster Newton in 'Stourcastle'...and so on. I shall not be the one to contradict them; I accept [**on. Subject to the qualification above given, that no detail is guaranteed – that the portraiture of fictitiously named towns and villages was only suggested by certain real places, and wantonly wanders from inventorial descriptions of them – I do not contradict these keen hunters for the real; I am satisfied with W**] their statements as at least an indication of their real and kindly [**their W**] interest in the scenes.

Hardy does not tell his readers why he chose to give (presumably real) places fictional or ancient names, just that it seemed like a good idea at the time, which is not very helpful. But what is more striking is the transformation in the tone of the end of the paragraph. He is considerably less good-humoured in his acknowledgement of the activity of investigating topographists – apart from anything else they have forced him at the age of seventy-two, into more investigation of his own into such details (and consequent revision) than he was happy to perform. He can no longer consider their interest kindly, and he seems to doubt whether it is even real.

The list of places indicated by the suspension points in the passage above is quite long, but (naturally enough) it does not include names of shifting identity, like the Hintocks, Trantridge, or Overcombe. The map, however, is not so reticent (though Hardy could, perhaps, have chosen to leave them off the map also); it shows Trantridge in the place of Pentridge, Overcombe more in the place of Upwey than of Bincombe, and the Hintocks scattered about the western Vale of Blackmoor.

These paragraphs are embedded in the General Preface to the Wessex edition, which begins by explaining the new classification of the novels that Hardy had introduced, and goes on to consider Wessex, rather as he had in the Osgood preface to *Far From the Madding Crowd*, but in a more theoretical, less practical way:

> I would state that the geographical limits of the stage here trodden were not absolutely forced upon the writer by circumstances; he forced them upon himself from judgement. I considered our magnificent heritage from the Greeks in dramatic literature found sufficient room for a large proportion of its action in an extent of their country not much larger than the half-dozen counties here reunited under the old name of Wessex, that the domestic emotions have throbbed in Wessex nooks with as much intensity as in the palaces of Europe, and that, anyhow, there was quite enough human nature in Wessex for one man's literary purpose. So far was I possessed by this idea that I kept within the frontiers when it would have been easier to overleap them and give more cosmopolitan features to the narrative.

The unspoken assumption behind the eloquence, especially in 'I considered... there was quite enough human nature in Wessex for one man's literary purpose', is still that the idea of Wessex was fully present to his mind from the beginning – which, literally speaking, it was not. It does seem that Hardy wanted his readers to understand that the concept of Wessex found in the revised novels had always been present to shape his fiction, and I think that what lies behind that desire is his awareness that from the first he was compelled to write about the people and environments that were intimately familiar to him, and if he did not know in 1870 to call this impulse Wessex, that was just a matter of identification. A paragraph later he describes a quality of his fiction that gives weight to such an interpretation, for it is as present in *Desperate Remedies* as in *The Well-Beloved*:

> At the dates represented in the various narrations things were like that in Wessex: the inhabitants lived in certain ways, engaged in certain occupations, kept alive certain customs, just as they are shown doing in these pages.

It is the triumph of the power of Hardy's creation that he can write with certainty 'things were like that in Wessex'. But he goes on to add a description of what he has done since he wrote the novels, of what he has done for their revised editions:

> if these country customs and vocations, obsolete and obsolescent, had been detailed wrongly, nobody would have discovered such errors to the end of Time. Yet I have instituted inquiries to correct tricks of memory, and striven against temptations to exaggerate, in order to preserve for my own satisfaction a fairly true record of a vanishing life.

Wessex had become by 1912 a commonplace contemporary regional name requiring no explanation, of which Hardy was the historian. To a much greater degree than when he made the claim in the 1895 preface to *Far From the Madding Crowd*, Wessex had become a place to write to the papers from. This is another way of understanding that by 1912 Hardy had become a victim of his own invention; Wessex is not exactly a monster, but Frankenstein does come to mind. The moment he decided to publish the 1895 map was the moment when he lost control over Wessex. Though he says that it was for his own satisfaction that he did all the work required by these editions, it might be argued that his will was now subordinate to the independent dynamic of his creation. As we have seen, by 1912 he had become rather weary of investigating topographists, and the next chapter will show that his poetry reflected that weariness for a while.

Like *A Group of Noble Dames*, *Tess of the d'Urbervilles* was first published in book form by Osgood, McIlvaine, and it was revised plates of the second edition in one volume that were used for the first collected edition three years later. It is not surprising, therefore, that Hardy made relatively few alterations in 1895. When at the turn of the century Harper, who had taken over the ailing Osgood list, proposed a paperback edition of *Tess of the d'Urbervilles*, Hardy made a substantial number of revisions, since the text was to be reset. Only a few of these changes of 1900 found their way into Macmillan's Uniform edition three years later, since again the second edition plates were used to print it. By 1912 and the Wessex edition, as we have seen, Hardy's desire to conform Wessex to England had intensified, and so it was there that he made most changes to the topographical elements of the novel – some of which, indeed, seem of the minutest significance. One such example is an adjustment to Crick's dairy house:

> Between Clare and the window was the table at which his companions sat, their munching profiles rising sharp against the panes; while to the rear [**the side W**] was the milk-house door... (XVIII)

It is clear that Hardy had a particular building in mind, though commentators and topographists cannot agree which. It is a detail he changed for his own satisfaction alone. Another good example is in the account, such as it is, of the route Tess and Abraham took with the beehives from Marlott to Casterbridge:

> on their left, the elevation called Bulbarrow or Bealbarrow, well-nigh the highest in South Wessex, swelled into the sky, engirdled by its earthen trenches. From hereabout the long road declined gently for a great [**road was fairly level for some W**] distance onward. (IV)

Did Hardy, in preparation for the revision, yet again, of all his work, attune his mind to pay attention to this kind of detail, or was it that, rereading *Tess of the d'Urbervilles* in the winter of 1911, his description triggered a visual memory of the road between Sturminster and Hazelbury Bryan and... well, I was about to write Hartfoot Lane, but in fact Hardy doesn't indicate which way Tess would have taken to Casterbridge, and several are possible. It must be supposed that for Bulbarrow to swell into the sky for them, they were reasonably close beneath it (did he think of Rawlsbury with its earthworks as part of Bulbarrow?), and though the road south through Hartfoot Lane and Cheselbourne is not perhaps the most direct, 'fairly level' does describe its course reasonably accurately. A further revision suggests that in the Wessex edition they had not got much beyond Hazelbury (if they went that way), which is seven miles from Marnhull:

> in the setting sunlight he retraced the dozen miles [**the eight or nine miles W**] to Marlott. (IV)

It is impossible to tell exactly where the fatal collision took place, though these revisions imply that Hardy was himself visualizing the spot as he made them. It is paradoxical, and perhaps significant for a thorough understanding of Hardy's complex feelings about Wessex, that he should evidently be anxious to represent the lay of the land and the location of the incident more accurately in relation to Dorset, but that at the same time he does not give enough detail to allow a reader to make the same identification. Was he still torn between revelation and concealment (which would indeed be paradoxical, but which is suggested by certain changes to *The Return of the*

Native also), or was it that he was (as proposed earlier) just unable or unwilling to do the rewriting that would have been necessary to put the reader in possession of all the necessary facts? The same questions must be asked of the next change, which is to the route Alec d'Urberville took with Tess between Marlott and Trantridge:

> With a dim sense that he was vexed she looked steadily ahead as they trotted on for a further half-hour [**on near Melbury Down and Wingreen W**], till she saw, to her consternation, that there was yet another descent to be undergone. (VIII)

The addition of these Wessex heights in place of the vague time reference certainly narrows things down, but is still vague enough to allow of different possibilities. It seems improbable that Hardy was deliberately teasing the topographist by offering her nearly enough information to enable her to follow the journey exactly – but not quite. But if he could be bothered to make any more detail available, why not make sufficient detail available?

When at the end of the novel Tess and Angel walk away north from Sandbourne we find Hardy still fiddling with the identity of the house they first pass and then make their love bower:

> Through the latter miles of their walk their footpath had taken them into the depths of the New Forest, and towards evening, turning the corner of a lane, they perceived behind an ornamental gate [**behind a brook and bridge W**] a large board on which was painted in white letters, 'This desirable Mansion to be Let Furnished;' particulars following, with directions to apply to some London agents. Passing through the gate they could see the house, a dignified [**an old brick W**] building, of regular design, and large accommodation.
> 'I know it,' said Clare. 'It is Bramshurst Manor-house [**Bramshurst Court W**].' (LVII)

Presumably some time after 1895 but before 1911, he was pressured in some way to find a real place for them to be, and so altered just enough details so that Denys Kay-Robinson can write that it:

> has been identified with Moyles Court, north of Ringwood. Correctly defined as 'an old brick building of regular design and large accommodation', the ancient manor had by 1860 decayed to a mere shell.... The brook and bridge are easily recognisable, despite the presence of a new concrete bridge nearby. (*The Landscape of Thomas Hardy* 153)

The distance they had walked had also to be changed:

they had walked not less than twenty miles [**had wandered a dozen or fifteen miles 00, W**], and it became necessary to consider what they should do for rest. (ch LVII)

Moyles Court is twelve miles from Bournemouth as the crow flies more or less; but it is hardly deep in the New Forest, rather on the edge.

There was no food on the premises, but there was water, and he took advantage of the fog to emerge from the mansion, and fetch tea, bread, and butter, from a shop in the little town [**in a little place W**] two miles beyond. (LVIII)

In the Wessex edition he might have had Ibbesly in mind, which is slightly less than two miles from Moyles Court by the lanes. When they leave they travel northwards again; originally they crossed the (unnamed) River Avon at Ambresbury/Amesbury, but Hardy changed the place to Melchester/Salisbury for the one-volume edition, and with it the church of the former became the cathedral of the latter; he neglected, however, to envisage accurately enough every detail of the change, for there remained one to be altered later:

The graceful pile of cathedral architecture rose dimly on their right [**their left 00, W**] hand, but it was lost upon them now. (LVIII)

For those of his novels written before the nineties, Hardy was able where he wished in the collected editions to be more open about sexual relations, and was able to introduce allusions to crude or vulgar matters that he knew would have been censured and censored by Leslie Stephen and his fellow executors of public morality and taste. Such additions are for the most part not relevant to this study, except in so far as they help to make more full and more accurate Hardy's account of how things were in Wessex; but it is worth noting that Hardy thought one addition of the latter sort sufficiently important to warrant the plate-disturbance it would create in 1895 – an example that embodies a detail of agricultural life in Wessex and elsewhere that he would have found impossible to mention twenty years earlier:

Clare's mind flew to the impassioned, summer-saturated [**summer-steeped 1v**] heathens in the Var Vale [**Vale, their rosy faces court-patched with cow-droppings O**] (XXV)

Another similarly unmentionable addition Hardy intended, it seems from annotations in his study copy of the first printing of the Wessex edition of the novel, to be included in subsequent printings:

''Tis years since I went to Conjuror Trendle's son in Egdon – years,' said the dairyman bitterly. 'And he was nothing to what his father had been.

I have said fifty times, if I have said once, that I don't believe in him. And I don't believe in him [**in en O; in en, though 'a do cast folks' waters very true TH12**]. (XXI)

Life's Little Ironies
Osgood: Volume XIV, Preface: June 1896, Illustration: A view in Melchester. Wessex: Volume VIII in Novels of Character and Environment, Preface: May 1912, Illustration: The White Hart at Casterbridge.

The preface Hardy wrote for the Osgood edition has a family resemblance to that he wrote for *Wessex Tales*. It begins:

A view in Melchester

A story-teller's interest in his own stories is usually independent of any merits or demerits they may show as specimens of narrative art; turning on something behind the scenes, something real in their history, which may have no attraction for a reader even if known to him – a condition by no means likely.

Again there is the balancing of the fictional against the real, and the balance coming down in favour of the real in Hardy's eyes at least. In this case the sequel is a discussion of elements of the reality behind 'The Melancholy Hussar':

she who, at the age of ninety, pointed out the unmarked resting-place of the two soldiers of the tale, was probably the last remaining eyewitness of their death and interment; that the extract from the register of burials is literal, to be read any day in the original by the curious who recognize the village.

Several of the other stories are true in their main facts, if there should be anybody who cares to know it. In respect of the tale of 'Andrey Satchel', some persons still living may discern in Parson Toogood one to whom they, or at least their fathers, were not altogether strangers.

And there follow other details of Toogood's activities, which themselves sound more like fiction than fact. What is surprising is that Hardy should wonder if any of his readers would be interested in the reality in the fiction.

As has already been noted with regard to *Wessex Tales*, Hardy slightly rearranged stories between the two collections for the Wessex edition, and amongst other things 'The Melancholy Hussar' was transferred to *Wessex Tales*. As a result the Osgood preface was entirely scrapped, and instead he wrote in 1912 a bare account of the rearrangement.

There were no revisions to the stories in this volume for either collected editions that are relevant to this study.

Jude the Obscure
Osgood: Volume VIII, Preface: August 1895, Illustration: Christminster.
Wessex: Volume III as a Novel of Character and Environment, Preface: April 1912, Illustration: Christminster.

It will be recalled that the Osgood edition of *Jude the Obscure* was also the novel's first edition. In the preface Hardy provides, in an amplification of the weight given to facts in these preliminaries in general, some of the salient facts of the process of writing and publishing the novel, which he follows by the rather hopeful suggestion that there is nothing in its subject matter 'to which exception can be taken'. The postscript that he added for the Wessex edition relates at considerable length the controversy that followed the novel's publication; but none of the relation is relevant to Wessex (except insofar as it shows that Wessex has become the vehicle of more truth about human nature and English society than much of contemporary society finds easy to bear).

Christminster

The novel was discussed slightly out of sequence before the collected editions (above pp. 102–11). It was there suggested that the novel moved in a register beyond or against the developing Wessex so fully embodied in *Tess of the d'Urbervilles*, and it is scarcely surprising that Hardy needed subsequently to make extremely few alterations relevant to this study.

Before Hardy set to work to revise 'The Pursuit of the Well-Beloved', he executed a couple of commissions for short stories, both of which appeared at Christmas 1896. As the title of 'A Committee-Man of the "Terror"' suggests, this is another narrative of the period of the Napoleonic Wars, and though it takes place in Weymouth/Budmouth Regis (of which there are one or two fresh details), in keeping with Hardy's practice in revising *The Trumpet-Major* and *Desperate Remedies* for the Osgood edition, he goes out of his way not to mention the name of the town. The story begins, for instance, 'We had been talking of the Georgian glories of our old-fashioned watering-place...' And similarly, though the story is in his overtly historical mode, it is thoroughly integrated into Wessex, as, for example in the following:

> Thus she held self-communion in her seat in the coach, passing through Casterbridge, and Shottsford, and on to the White Hart at Melchester, at which place the whole fabric of her recent intentions crumbled down.

'The Duke's Reappearance' goes even further back, to the Monmouth rebellion at the end of the seventeenth century, and was overtly a tradition of Hardy's mother's family, since he eventually decided to use the correct surnames, Swetman and Childs (though in the manuscript of the story the first was Wedman). Nevertheless (and inevitably) he also uses the Wessex name for Melbury Osmond – King's Hintock.

The Well-Beloved
Osgood: Volume XVII, Preface: January 1897, Illustration: The Isle.
Wessex: Volume XIII in Romances and Fantasies, Preface: August 1912. Illustration: The Isle of Slingers.

The preface begins with a description of Portland that comes direct from new Wessex:

The Isle

> The peninsula carved by Time out of a single stone, whereon most of the following scenes are laid, has been for centuries immemorial the home of a curious and almost distinctive [**and well-nigh distinct W**] people, cherishing strange beliefs and singular customs, now for the most part obsolescent.

The long view of time, from the geologic past closing up through many centuries to the present, the strange beliefs and singular customs that Hardy is here rescuing from oblivion, and the fascination with a place of distinct and individual qualities, are all quintessential. Later on Hardy presents the place again:

> the rocky coign of England here depicted – overlooking the great Channel Highway with all its suggestiveness, and standing out so far into mid-sea that touches of the Gulf Stream soften the air till February

And gives an example of obsolescent local practice – in the buying and selling of houses:

> These transactions, by the way, are carried out and covenanted, or were till lately, in the parish church, in the face of the congregation, such being the ancient custom of the Isle.[3]

The transformation of *The Pursuit of the Well-Beloved* into *The Well-Beloved* has been much written about, and details can be found in a number of places.[4] This justifies a minimalist treatment here, though the record would be skewed without including on the website some of the relevant material. In general terms, it is the well-beloved aspect of the novel that gets altered; the several aspects of Wessex significant in the novel are rather augmented and intensified. There are virtually no relevant changes in the Wessex edition.

So for instance the opening of the novel in the first edition relates to a passage in the second chapter of the serial, which, it will be remembered, read:

> the steep roadway which led from the village of Slopeway Well to the summit of the rocky peninsula, called an island; that juts out like the head of a flamingo into the English Channel, and is connected with the mainland of Wessex by a long, thin beach of pebbles, representing the neck of the bird.

In the Osgood edition this becomes:

> the steep road which leads through the sea-skirted townlet definable as the Street of Wells, and forms a pass into that Gibraltar of Wessex, the singular peninsula once an island, and still called such, that stretches out

like the head of a bird into the English Channel. It is connected with the mainland by a long thin neck of pebbles 'cast up by rages of the se,' and unparalleled in its kind in Europe. (I.I)

It is evident that Hardy had reflected on the role he required the island to play in his narrative; it is more exceptional than in the serial, absolutely unique in certain respects, while the quotation from Leland adds a characteristic historical dimension, and (with the description of the Street of Wells as 'sea-skirted') gives some hint of the intimate relation between land and sea freshly developed in this version.

The wayfarer reflects on what he sees as he walks:

What had seemed natural [**seemed usual** O] in the isle when he left it now [**he lived there always** O] looked quaint and odd amid these [**odd after his** O] later impressions. The [**More than ever the spot seemed what it was said once to have been, the ancient Vindilia Island, and the Home of the Slingers. The towering rock, the** O] houses above houses, one man's doorstep rising behind his neighbour's chimney, the gardens hung up by one hedge [**one edge** O] to the sky, [**sky, the vegetables growing on apparently almost vertical planes,** O] the unity of the whole island as a solid and single block of stone [**of limestone** O] four miles long, were no longer familiar and commonplace ideas. All now stood dazzlingly clean [**dazzlingly unique** O] and white against the blue [**the tinted** O] sea, the sun flashing on the stratified façades of rock – [**sea, and the sun flashed on infinitely stratified walls of oolite,** O]
      The melancholy ruins
   Of cancelled cycles.... Prodigious shapes
   Huddled in grey annihilation. [**cycles,...**
With a distinctiveness that called the eyes to it as strongly as any spectacle he had beheld afar. O] (I.I)

Again the special nature of the isle is stressed, and its long history, the bareness of its rocky unity. Hardy for once, it is evident, was doing the rewriting at length necessary to achieve more fully his vision of a place. Portland, as a result of a string of similar changes, becomes vividly like Egdon, or Casterbridge, or the Hintock woodlands – a circumscribed environment with its own intensely interesting individuality.[5]

Hardy had always felt that paganism was just beneath the surface of places and people all over Wessex, and in this respect also the Isle becomes like Egdon. This, for example, is a fragment of a substantial addition in Part I Chapter 2:

The church had slipped down with the rest of the cliff, and had long been a ruin. It seemed to say that in this last local stronghold of the

Pagan divinities, where Pagan customs lingered yet, Christianity had established itself precariously at best.

Hardy also makes the well-beloved herself a product of Jocelyn's heredity and environment.[6] Such changes are Hardy's attempt to provide a basis in historical reality for the idealistic notions of his hero; at the same time he is able to place cultural history and environment in a far richer relationship – a project at the heart of Wessex.

It is necessary at this point to set aside the chronological study of Hardy's changing vision of Wessex in order to complete the examination of his prose before turning to his poetry. He published three more stories before giving up fiction for good. 'The Grave by the Handpost' was a Christmas story in 1897, and (circling back at the end of his career in prose to his beginnings) he made use again of carol singing by a parish choir – this time of Chalk-Newton – whose members, unsurprisingly, are compared to their detriment with the Mellstock players; indeed the source of the story is 'the testimony of William Dewy of Mellstock, Michael Mail, and others'. The opening sentence of the narrative concludes with a suggestion, for the first time, that the kind of story that has been central to Wessex from the beginning may, in the changing spirit of the *fin-de-siècle*, be no longer relevant or justifiable: 'it may seem superfluous, at this date, to disinter more memories of village history...' and though, of course, he goes on to do so, here may be another reason for the petering out of Hardy's fiction in these last short stories. It is possible that this doubt surfaced in his mind as a result of the long process of revisiting his work that he had just concluded, and another phrase in the story shows the effect of the Osgood edition:

> the lonely monotonous old highway known as Long Ash Lane, which runs, straight as a surveyor's line, many miles north and south of this spot, and has often been mentioned in these narratives.

'These narratives.' Hardy confidently assumes that his reader will be familiar with his whole work, that it is one work almost, made up of a series of stories all linked together along Long Ash Lane, as it were.

'A Changed Man' came out in the spring of 1900. It is essentially a story of Casterbridge, though occasionally the action moves outside Casterbridge and Durnover, to Fountall, Ivell and Mellstock, as well as to Creston (which, it will be remembered, had been until lately Weymouth, as far as *Desperate Remedies* was concerned, but was now Preston):

> She suggested a village by the sea, near Budmouth Regis, and lodgings were obtained for her at Creston, a spot divided from the Casterbridge valley by a high ridge that gave it quite another atmosphere, though it lay no more than six miles off. (V)

Hardy's last published piece of fiction was 'Enter a Dragoon'. It is fitting that it should take place in a cottage much like that Hardy was born in:

> Some of the thatch was brown and rotten as the gills of old mushrooms, had, indeed, been removed before I walked over the building. Seeing that it was only a very small house – which is usually called a 'cottage-residence' – situated in a remote hamlet, and that it was not much more than a hundred years old, if so much...
> It stood at the top of a garden stretching down to the lane or street that ran through a hermit-group of dwellings in Mellstock parish. From a green gate at the lower entrance, over which the thorn hedge had been shaped to an arch by constant clippings, a gravel path ascended between the box edges of once trim raspberry, strawberry, and vegetable plots, towards the front door. This was in colour an ancient and bleached green that could be rubbed off with the finger, and it bore a small long-featured brass knocker covered with verdigris in its crevices.

There are a couple of connections with other narratives, both to do with drink. When the dragoon enters he brings with him 'a nine gallon cask o' "Three Mariner" beer', (ch III) and when some restorative is required, 'a drop o' that Schiedam of old Owlett's, that's under stairs' (ch IV) is suggested. The central character Selina Paddock goes away from Mellstock to open a small shop, and it seems that Maiden Newton was on Hardy's mind during these last years of fiction, for it is there she goes.

These three stories and most of the others that Hardy had left uncollected were finally brought together in 1913, in a volume he called:

A Changed Man
The Waiting Supper and Other Tales
Concluding with The Romantic Adventures of A Milkmaid
First Edition uniform with Osgood Edition, given Volume XVIII, Preface: August 1913. Illustration: The Castle of Mai-Dun (the same photograph also used in the Wessex edition).
Wessex Edition: Volume XVIII, Preface: August 1913, Photograph: The Castle of Mai-Dun.

Most of the stories were revised to a greater or lesser degree.

A Changed Man

For this story Hardy made three alterations to the topography of Casterbridge, and one to the imaginative description of the London road's progress eastward.[7]

The Waiting Supper

The environment of this story is considerably altered. The river Swenn becomes the Froom throughout, and Swenn-Everard house is changed to Froom-Everard; Hardy revised a fragment of the description of it: 'At that time of the century Swenn-Everard House [**Froom-Everard House 13**] had not been altered into a farm-homestead [**altered and enlarged 13**]', transforming the scope of the later reconstruction. Eldhampton Hall also takes its now-established Wessex name Athelhall. Nic Long's 'ordinary farmhouse', unnamed in the magazine, is called Elsenford Farm, the distance from it to Athelhall is five, not eleven miles (though even then, if the distance is to be taken seriously, it is hard to imagine exactly where his house might be), and it is no longer in the same parish as Froom-Everard, but in a neighbouring one. Since Nic crosses the Froom to get from Christine's house to his own, this is essential for the accuracy at the heart of the new Wessex. On the other hand, though, the new parish is, like the house, called Elsenford; the name does not echo any Dorset place, which suggests that Hardy did not wish to intrude upon Mellstock or Weatherbury, which are the parishes the other side of the Froom from Froom-Everard, and, unusually at this late stage, settled for some imaginative geography.

It must have been somewhat surprising to Hardy to find in a story he wrote in 1887 that Salisbury was named for itself, especially since it was in combination with a respectable Wessex name:

> At daybreak he stood on the hill above Shottsford Forum, and awaited a coach which passed about this time along that highway towards Salisbury [**towards Melchester 13**] and London. (67)

This was Nic leaving home. When he returns years later, he

> arrived at Troyton Inn, an isolated tavern [**at Roy-Town, a roadside hamlet 13**] on the old western turnpike road, not five miles from Swenn-Everard [**from Froom-Everard, and put up at the Buck's Head, an isolated inn at that spot 13**]....
> Troyton Inn [**The Buck's Head 13**] was a somewhat unusual place for a man of this sort to choose as a house of sojourn [**sojourn in preference to some Casterbridge inn four miles further on 13**] (ch VI).

The revisions are in line with those to *Far From the Madding Crowd*, and it is the first time that the neighbouring market town in the story has been named. But there remains a puzzle, for the distance of four miles or so between Froom-Everard and Roy-Town makes the identification of the former with any Dorset house rather difficult. Nic visits Christine at Froom-Everard from Casterbridge, and Hardy has to change the direction that had led Lucy to think of the market town as Anglebury earlier. He 'walks along the south side of the valley to visit her,' and looks at 'the well-watered meads on the right [**the left 13**] hand'.

In one final detail the name of the rector of Froom-Everard's parish is changed from Eastman to Bealand, though why it should be is unknown.

The Grave by the Handpost

There are two changes to be noted; the first is to the description of Long Ash Lane, 'which runs, straight as a surveyor's line, many miles north and south of this spot, [**spot, on the foundation of a Roman road 13**]' and the second is what might be thought an unfortunate removal of dialect from the speech of Ezra Cattstock the sexton, made not in the first edition of *A Changed Man*, but in the Wessex Edition version published a year later:

> 'Well, sir; I've made inquiration o' the Sidlinch men that buried en [**made inquiry of a Sidlinch woman as to his burial 14**], and what I thought is [**thought seems 14**] true. They buried en wi' a new six-foot hurdle-saul drough's body, from the sheep-pen up in North Ewelease....'[8]

What the Shepherd Saw

The location of the story is moved some forty miles north-east as the crow flies from the downs in the region of Pentridge to those about Marlborough (the change of name of a character from Pentridge to Ogbourne makes this certain – there are three Ogbourne villages north of Marlborough). Thus the opening description:

> The spot was called Lambing Corner, and it was a sheltered portion of that wide expanse of rough pasture-land known as Verncombe Down, which you cross in its lower levels when following the turnpike-road from Casterbridge eastward, before you come to Melchester [**as Marlbury Downs, which you directly traverse when following the turnpike-road across Mid-Wessex from London, through Aldbrickham, in the direction of Bath and Bristol 13**].

The big house involved is altered from Verncombe Towers to Shakeforest Towers, and what was in the magazine called the Ringdon road – intending Ringwood, as Martin Ray suggests in his *Thomas Hardy: A Textual Study of the Short Stories* (Aldershot: Ashgate, 1997; p. 306) – becomes simply the great western road in the first edition.

It is perhaps not surprising that a story in which a character is made to swear on a trilithon known as the Devil's Door that he will not tell a secret, and in which a character walks outdoors in his sleep, should be removed from what had since become a significant site of *Tess of the d'Urbervilles*.

A Mere Interlude

It is, though, slightly surprising that Hardy decided to try to bring this story into Wessex. Perhaps it was because of the interest in North Cornwall revitalized by his visit in March of 1913 after the death of his first wife, and by the poems that came out of it. In any case the Scilly Isles become 'the Isles of Lyonnesse beyond Off-Wessex', Devonshire becomes Lower Wessex, the school Baptista teaches at is near Tor-upon-Sea rather than Exeter, Hugh Town on St Mary's Island is Giant's Town on St Maria's Island, Penzance becomes Pen-zephyr, Truro is Trufal, and Redruth is Redrutin. However, in keeping with the new Wessex plan, St Michael's Mount keeps its Cornish name, as (for some unfathomable reason) do Mousehole and Falmouth. This is almost absurdly mechanical, though the idea of bringing to life Isles of Lyonesse must have appealed to Hardy's romantic streak, and he will have been pleased at his coinage alluding to Redruth's primary claim to fame – its tin-mining.

In other respects there are no relevant revisions, though it is worth noting in passing that the map attached to the Wessex Edition was altered to reflect these new names, and those he included in the following story (see p. 162).

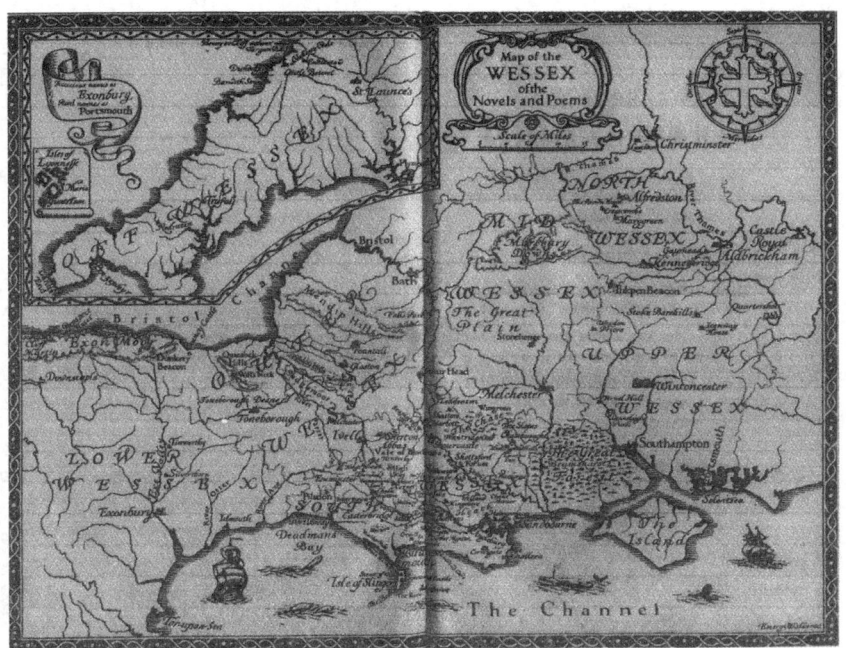

The Romantic Adventures of a Milkmaid

Like 'What the Shepherd Saw', the last story in *A Changed Man* is shifted wholesale from one county to another, and it has been accepted since Richard Little Purdy made the suggestion in *Thomas Hardy: A Bibliographical Study* (p. 49), that Hardy thought two longish narratives about dairymaids in the Frome Valley were one too many. I have argued elsewhere that Hardy also probably decided that moving the tale to a district with no existing Wessex associations was a good idea, in that such a move would require considerably less rewriting than an attempt to integrate it with the other narratives that crowd around the Frome.[9]

Thus the Swenn becomes the Exe rather than the Froom, Stickleford becomes Silverthorn (which might be a combination of Thorverton and Little Silver, villages to the north of Exeter), the ball is held at Lord Toneborough's rather than Lord Blakemore's; the review is at Exonbury rather than Casterbridge, and as a consequence the place is called a city rather than a town, and has a cathedral. The Baron's yacht is moored at Idmouth rather than the unnamed cove of the *Graphic*, and the 'semi-circular cove between rocks' becomes an 'inlet of the sea' (XVII). Budmouth once becomes Tivworthy (to which a musician is seeking a short cut [X]), and once Plymouth (where a sailor's widow finds another husband [XVII]). The anticipated route of elopement 'through Melchester to London' is extended to 'through Sherton-Abbas and Melchester to London' (XVII). Anglebury disappears, and Lower Wessex is added at the end of the story for Stickleford.

Other names, however – of the houses and of Chillington Wood – are unchanged, as are all the passages descriptive of the scenery; which, as with the reorganization of the Hintocks in *The Woodlanders* (see above pp. 137–8), raises what is almost a moral question about the propriety of such relocating without rewriting. Margery Tucker, the milkmaid in question, is described thus in the first chapter:

> Her face was of the hereditary type among families down in these parts; sweet in expression, perfect in hue, and somewhat irregular in feature. Her eyes were of a liquid brown.

When you change 'these parts' from Dorset to Devon do you do an injustice to a description such as this, or can it reasonably be said that by 'these parts' Hardy intended all of Wessex anyway? He was at least sufficiently attentive to the underlying structure of the new location to make this change to the site of Jim's kiln: 'It was at the end of a short ravine in the lower chalk [**in a limestone 13**] formation, and all around was an open hilly down or coomb [**down 13**]' (VII); and he also paid attention to Jim's speech, though whether he had heard something specific to the region around Exeter is unclear:

how tired you do [**you dew** 13] look ... You've walked too [**walked tew** 13] far

What do [**What dew** 13] that bit of incivility mean

You [*Yew* 13] don't expect to have such things (all in ch VI)

There was also one final change, this time to Margery's speech: 'I don't like standing here in this mean [**this slummocky** 13] crowd' (ch XVI).

There were no relevant alterations to '**Alicia's Diary**', '**A Tryst at an Ancient Earthwork**', '**A Committee-Man of the "Terror,"**' '**Master John Horsleigh, Knight**', or '**The Duke's Reappearance**'.

This is the end of the prose, though it should be remembered that Hardy made a handful of revisions to later editions, the American Autograph of 1915, the English Mellstock of 1919–20, and for reprints of one or two texts in the Wessex Edition at about the same date. None, however, raises particular Wessex issues. It is now time to turn back to the poetry, which will be treated somewhat differently.

8
The Poetry

Note: The texts of the poems discussed but not reproduced here will be found on the website.

Hardy had been writing poetry again at least since the beginning of the 1890s, and his first collection of verse was published in 1898. It is, however, with a poem not included in *Wessex Poems*, that I want to begin this chapter.

Wessex Heights

(1896)

There are some heights in Wessex, shaped as if by a kindly hand
For thinking, dreaming, dying on, and at crises when I stand,
Say, on Ingpen Beacon eastward, or on Wylls-Neck westwardly,
I seem where I was before my birth, and after death may be.

In the lowlands I have no comrade, not even the lone man's friend –
Her who suffereth long and is kind; accepts what he is too weak to mend:
Down there they are dubious and askance; there nobody thinks as I,
But mind-chains do not clank where one's next neighbour is the sky.

In the towns I am tracked by phantoms having weird detective ways –
Shadows of beings who fellowed with myself of earlier days:
They hang about at places, and they say harsh heavy things –
Men with a frigid sneer, and women with tart disparagings.

Down there I seem to be false to myself, my simple self that was,
And is not now, and I see him watching, wondering what crass cause
Can have merged him into such a strange continuator as this,
Who yet has something in common with himself, my chrysalis.

I cannot go to the great grey Plain; there's a figure against the moon,
Nobody sees it but I, and it makes my breast beat out of tune;

> I cannot go to the tall-spired town, being barred by the forms now passed
> For everybody but me, in whose long vision they stand there fast.
>
> There's a ghost at Yell'ham Bottom chiding loud at the fall of the night,
> There's a ghost in Froom-side Vale, thin lipped and vague, in a shroud
>   of white,
> There is one in the railway-train whenever I do not want it near,
> I see its profile against the pane, saying what I would not hear.
>
> As for one rare fair woman, I am now but a thought of hers,
> I enter her mind and another thought succeeds me that she prefers;
> Yet my love for her in its fulness she herself even did not know;
> Well, time cures hearts of tenderness, and now I can let her go.
>
> So I am found on Ingpen Beacon, or on Wylls-Neck to the west,
> Or else on homely Bulbarrow, or little Pilsdon Crest,
> Where men have never cared to haunt, nor women have walked with me,
> And ghosts then keep their distance; and I know some liberty. (ll.25–7)

'Wessex Heights' was written, according to the date on the manuscript, in December 1896, and is thus a product of the same year that Hardy finished revising his fiction for the Osgood edition, and was in the process of turning 'The Portrait of the Well-Beloved' into *The Well-Beloved*. This work forced him to confront his distaste for two of what he saw as essential requirements in writing novels. The first was to deal in a naturalistic way with his world, the world below the heights one might say, which meant that he had to shape plots and characters with a level of probability that had begun to go against the grain of his temperament – *Jude the Obscure* and *The Well-Beloved* suggest how irksome the realism of the Victorian novel was becoming to him. The second was the need always to keep in mind his paying audience; this meant the maintenance of the dual- or multi-voiced narrator which is a pervasive characteristic of all his fiction, one voice lecturing to an urban middle-class readership, another delighting in the moment by moment intensity of experience of character or environment. What was more, the reviews of *Jude the Obscure* had reminded him that in his novels he had to abide by the governing conventions of that same group or to accept the consequent rattle of hostile criticism.[1] Hardy's second wife Florence wrote to her friend Lady Hoare at Stourhead: '"Wessex Heights" will *always* wring my heart, for I know when it was written, a little while after the publication of "Jude", when he was so cruelly treated.'[2] At some time around the turn of the century Hardy decided he would write no more novels; there is no knowing exactly when, but 'Wessex Heights' can be read to imply such a desire, if not such a resolve.

On the heights he is alone, there is no audience, and he does not have to take into account any generally held opinion or convention. He possesses there for a time liberty; freedom from mind-chains, freedom to think, to dream. His spirit, he feels, haunted these heights before it was embodied, and might do so again after the dissolution of the flesh. The heights are places where poetry can be written, in contrast to the mess of the contingent world below that had nourished the novels he had perhaps decided to write no more of. Such a thought would be a fragment of an idealist notion of poetic creation; but what distinguishes Hardy's poetry from his fiction more clearly than anything else is that the audience he writes to please is made up of one – himself. He was doubtless glad that others would buy, read, and delight in his poetry, and he was careful to explain and justify his work; but the money made from the last controversial fictions, and then from the first sales of the collected edition, meant that an audience for his verse was not a financial necessity. He could please himself. At the same time, though, 'Wessex Heights' shows that the material from which his verse will derive will often be the trains and the cities and the streets and the streams and woods and the human spirits embodying the past down there in the lowlands. Freed from the need to please that world, or to represent in a naturalistic way the complexities of its passions and emotions, he could observe, even participate, and then retire to the heights, and report unconditionally what he found in his mind of his experience.[3]

The poem also springs from his anxieties about Wessex. In the preface to *Far From the Madding Crowd* he had begged his readers to set aside the fact that Wessex had become a region of Victorian England, a place to write to the newspapers from, but he was well aware that such a plea was futile. By 1896 readers were making the one-for-one switch between Casterbridge and Dorchester without thinking about it very much, and there was no way he could prevent them, and with the cultural-historian part of his creative impulse he made it easier for them. As a direct consequence of the new Wessex plan, outlined in the prefaces to *Tess of the d'Urbervilles* and *Far From the Madding Crowd* and implemented in the revisions for the collected edition, Ingpen Beacon, Wylls-Neck, Bulbarrow and Pilsdon Pen, are simultaneously Wessex and English heights, or rather, they are Wessex-in-fiction heights and they are Wessex-in-England heights. So when Hardy called his poem 'Wessex Heights', when he wrote 'There are some heights in Wessex...' he might have meant Wessex-in-fiction or Wessex-in-England, or both. The poem that follows is purely autobiographical, and the only hint of fiction is in the *Tess*-associations of the Froom Valley (though since rivers as well as hills were governed by new Wessex principles, it is not a very persuasive hint). The implication, therefore, is that for the space of the poem the heights are in Wessex-as-England alone; and such a conclusion might be pushed further to suggest that for this same space at least Hardy, weary of the conflict within himself between his compulsion to bring Wessex as close as possible to England, and the impulse to preserve the integrity of his imagined Wessex, is giving up the latter. And if Hardy does also believe that the heights are places poetry might be written, then it should also follow that the poems he imagines being created there will have nothing to do with fictional Wessex.

But Hardy did not collect 'Wessex Heights' in *Wessex Poems*. This was perhaps in part because he had lied in the last line of the penultimate verse: 'Well, time cures hearts of tenderness, and now I can let her go.' Almost certainly it was in part because he was not yet confident (or thick-skinned) enough to bare his soul so intimately in a poem that would inevitably be read as personal confession. But also it was because the poem had not yet found its moment in Hardy's creative life. It was a vivid, perhaps too vivid an evocation of a perception that in 1898 he recognized as transient – important, but not the whole story. He had perhaps decided no longer to make the compromises necessary to write the high Victorian novel, but he was not yet interested in isolating himself and his work from the imagined world of Wessex. It had only just reached its fully achieved state, and he was enjoying its currency; and for the time being Wessex-in-fiction flourished in his poetry.

When Hardy decided to call his first volume of verse *Wessex Poems* he was doing a number of things: trading on the name he had more or less copyrighted in the collected edition; acknowledging that there were many poems in the volume that were thoroughly in harmony with his fiction – including some that derived directly from it; and he was also – intentionally or otherwise – making a compact with the reader that there would not be a disjunction in the change of genres, that they would feel at home in the verse. In such a volume 'Wessex Heights' would have been a discordant note, though there are many poems in it that exist because of the freedoms that Hardy claims to find on the heights. 'The Impercipient' (I.87) is a good example. The thought that drives most of the poem – that the narrator wishes he could have the comforting faith of those he sees about him at a cathedral service – was not then, and is not now, Hardy's alone; but it was his profoundly. It is the last verse in particular that fills the poem with his own personality. There, through the painful image of his spiritual self as a bird shorn of its wings, longing to fly, but unable to do so, he refutes the notion that he is, as reviewers of *Jude the Obscure* suggested, an atheist, a preacher against belief in the divine power that permeates the world. As the earlier part of the poem makes clear, he envies rather than despises those soaring in the air above him: he would believe if he could.

When, in *Jude the Obscure*, he had also wished to express some of his most deeply felt convictions, he was constrained by ideas about realism and the role of the narrator. He was sufficiently aware of the way he was subverting these ideas to assert in the novel that an author could not be responsible for the views of his characters, but the assertion quite fails to convince because the narrative voice so often anticipates or echoes with authority the views and actions of the characters, and it all speaks Hardy.[4] But no reader's feathers are ruffled by reading such speculations in a poem. And though 'The Impercipient' is apparently universal and placeless, Hardy linked it to Wessex by providing an illustration of the interior of the cathedral of the poem's subtitle – though the readers who recognized the building would have had to make up their own minds whether it was Salisbury or Melchester.

Representative in a different way is 'Valenciennes', which brings into play several aspects of Wessex; first of all it is a poem in Dorset dialect, and then it is voiced for a character in *The Trumpet-Major*, Corporal Tullidge of the silver plate in his head – indeed the poem explains how he came by it – he had his head split open by a shell, and then joined together by field surgeons 'wi' a zilver clamp.' The poem begins with his account of the siege of the town where it happened:

> Such snocks and slats, since war began
> Never knew raw recruit or veteràn:
> Stone-deaf therence went many a man
> Who served at Valencieën. (I.25)

Tullidge too, it will be recalled, was one of those who was deafened for life by the roar of the guns. His reminiscences end:

> Well: Heaven wi' its jasper halls
> Is now the on'y Town I care to be in....
> Good Lord, if Nick should bomb the walls
> As we did Valencieën!

Thus Tullidge is given a life and a distinctive ironic voice beyond the novel, and in keeping with the preface to the Osgood edition of *The Trumpet-Major*, the poem is linked to the realities on which Hardy based his fiction, through its dedication: 'IN MEMORY OF S.C. (PENSIONER). DIED 184-'.

'The Alarm' more clearly embodies the new sense of imagined Wessex as explicitly sharing the same space as England. The poem is dedicated to the memory 'of one of the writer's family who was a volunteer during the war with Napoleon' – his paternal grandfather, as Purdy points out (*Bibliographical Study* p. 100), but before that there is the note 'See "The Trumpet-Major"'. The opening describes Hardy's birthplace:

> In a ferny byway
> Near the great South-Wessex Highway,
> A homestead raised its breakfast-smoke aloft;
> The dew-damps still lay steamless, for the sun had made no sky-way,
> And twilight cloaked the croft. (I.46)

The volunteer sees that the alarm-beacon nearby has been burning, and debates whether to go forward to the coast or back to his wife, whom he has assured Bonaparte will not invade. Eventually he goes south to the coast, learns the alarm was false, and returns home. We are to suppose, I think, that this is a recreation of something one of his parents told him. But the names of places, both those the volunteer passes, and those he directs his wife to seek in case of danger, are Wessex names. The poem also develops *The Trumpet-Major* by offering a different version from that in the novel of the response to the spread of news in Wessex that Boney and his army had arrived.[5]

It is in fact a feature of Hardy's poetry that he gives, from time to time, extended existence to characters and sometimes moments from his novels, expanding the pattern of Wessex as a continuous imagined world. It has been a question of debate, particularly among Hardy's biographers, the degree to which all of Hardy's characters were based on personal knowledge or on first-hand accounts he had heard; but certainly those who turn up most frequently in his poetry were those familiar to him – the members of the Mellstock band of players and singers. The earliest such poem, 'Friends Beyond', is a graveyard poem, which begins:

William Dewy, Tranter Reuben, Farmer Ledlow late at plough,
    Robert's kin, and John's and Ned's,
And the Squire, and Lady Susan, lie in Mellstock churchyard now! (I.78)

If we take Robert to be Robert Penny, John to be John Woodward and Ned to be Ned Hipcroft of 'The Fiddler of the Reels', then it is only the gentry who are unaccounted for in either *Under the Greenwood Tree* or the story. All of 'that group of local hearts and heads' are dead now, but their spirits murmur triumphantly to the narrator of the freedom from care that they experience in death. Two successive poems in *Time's Laughingstocks* also recall the quire – 'The Rash Bride' and 'The Dead Quire'. (I.306, 310). The first is the story of a love-suicide on their Christmas-eve carolling, while in the second the descendants of the quire, carousing irreligiously in an inn, hear them sing and play 'While shepherds watched their flocks' as the clock strikes to usher in Christmas day. The 'livers in levity' are drawn to follow the disembodied sound by the embowered path along the Froom, till they reach Mellstock churchyard and the quire-members' graves, when 'it smalled, and died away'. As a consequence, it is said, none of the revellers 'sat in tavern more'. Thus Hardy begins to exorcize his feeling that in *Under the Greenwood Tree* he had treated the quire with too much levity himself.

The first person narrator of 'In a Wood: From *The Woodlanders'* speaks in the urbane narrative voice that has a share in the conduct of the novel; it is the voice of one who, reaching (as it were) the Wye above Tintern Abbey, quite fails to find the hoped-for restoration in nature. Rather, he takes the agony he intuits in the deadly competition amongst the trees for survival to one of its logical conclusions:

> Since, then, no grace I find
> Taught me of trees,
> Turn I back to my kind,
> Worthy as these.
> There at least smiles abound,
> There discourse trills around,
> There, now and then, are found
> Life-loyalties. (I.84)

This embodies Hardy's perennial sense that the wear on a threshold was more to him than any manifestation of nature (though we have plenty of evidence that he was deeply moved by such shows), and though the consolations offered by his own kind are superficial or severely limited, the poem does end on 'Life-loyalties' – a lesson perhaps to some readers for whom Wessex means first of all a series of memorable landscapes.

Such elaborations of moments in novels are made quite overtly in Hardy's first three collections: 'The Pine Planters' (I.328) in *Time's Laughingstocks* is subtitled '(Marty South's Reverie)', and thus also derives directly from *The Woodlanders*, so directly indeed that it seems like a versification of a few sentences from the novel – which raises the question why Hardy thought it worthwhile to rewrite what had already had its day.[6] There are at least three answers in this instance; one is that the first part of the poem, by isolating a moment in the pain of Marty's love for Giles, forces readers to focus their whole attention on what there is only intermittently room for in the novel; a second is that verse seems particularly appropriate to the intensity of Marty's feeling; and a third is that the second part of the poem makes a connection with *Tess of the d'Urbervilles*: Marty, struck by the sighing of the saplings she and Giles are planting, sighing that begins as soon as they are upright and never ceases until they die, fills them with her consciousness, imagining that each will grieve

> ... that never
> Kind Fate decreed
> It should for ever
> Remain a seed

This thought is an echo of the line 'I'd have my life unbe' from 'Tess's Lament' in Hardy's second collection *Poems of the Past and the Present* (1902), and our attention is drawn to similarities in the sensibilities of the two characters that are hard to see amidst the rush of detail of the novels. On the other hand, while Marty's voice in the poem seems in harmony with that in the novel, the same is not quite true of Tess in her 'Lament'.

It seems perhaps that Hardy has imagined her soliloquy being spoken in the plantation where she encounters the dying pheasants:

> I would that folk forgot me quite,
>   Forgot me quite!
> I would that I could shrink from sight,
>   And no more see the sun.
> Would it were time to say farewell,
> To claim my nook, to need my knell,
> Time for them all to stand and tell
>   Of [O' W] my day's work as done. (I.216)

This is how the moment comes in the narrative voice of *Tess of the d'Urbervilles*:

> If all were only vanity who would mind it? All was, alas, worse than vanity – injustice, punishment, exaction, death. The wife of Angel Clare put her hand to her brow, and felt its curve, and the edges of her eye-sockets perceptible under the soft skin, and thought as she did so that a time would come when that bone would be bare. 'I wish it were now,' she said. (XLI)

Though the single sentence she utters here is in keeping with the poem, there is nothing in the 'Lament' of a sense of injustice; the Tess of the poem seems weaker, more self-pitying. It is a cry of despair more than a lament – beginning with her desire for death and ending with the wish to have her life 'unbe'. She reimagines her time at Talbothays and takes upon herself all responsibility for the destruction of her marriage: 'I must take my Cross on me/For wronging him awhile.' In the novel, Tess's only extended soliloquy after Angel abandons her is the one half-overheard by Mrs Brooks after Tess has sent Angel away from The Herons at Sandbourne, the anguished outpouring that Alec ridicules, thus provoking Tess to a gesture even more bloody than her earlier blow to his face with a leather gauntlet. 'Tess's Lament' has none of that strength either. So why did Hardy write it? Perhaps because he felt that he had not sufficiently evoked Tess's misery after Angel had abandoned her; perhaps because he felt he had not made clear enough her sense of her own guilt – though if so he underestimated his achievement in that respect; perhaps because he wanted to let her speak for herself. But perhaps also because this more ordinary girl is closer to his original conception of Tess, hidden in the earliest leaves of the novel's manuscript, a conception that got overlaid by later arguments about her purity and her ancestry which required her to be special, even unique.[7]

The immediately previous poem in *Poems of the Past and the Present* is called 'The Lost Pyx', and is a retelling of a legend regarding the monument Cross-in-Hand (in the poem Hardy calls it Cross-and-Hand) that is a significant presence in *Tess of the d'Urbervilles*. The narrator there talks of it without elaboration as a boundary stone or the base of a cross, and Alec d'Urberville, having heard the latter version, makes Tess swear on it not to tempt him. After they part Tess hears a different account:

> Cross – no; 'twer not a cross. 'Tis a thing of ill-omen, miss. It was put up in wuld times by the relations of a malefactor who was tortured there by nailing his hand to a post, and afterwards hung. The bones lie underneath. They say he sold his soul to the devil, and that he walks at times. (XLV)

And this, the last we hear of it, is what we remember. The new story comes closer to justifying Alec's confidence. Though not exactly a Holy Cross, it was, according to this legend, placed there to mark a miracle that happened on the spot. Hardy redressing the balance, perhaps? Did he hope that we might think that, after all, the act that Tess was made to perform – this act among many – was not of such ill-omen? Does the new legend become a part of the reading experience of *Tess of the d'Urbervilles*? Does 'Tess's Lament?'

In *Poems of the Past and the Present* also there is 'The Well-Beloved', whose connection with the eponymous novel is to isolate its underlying idea. A man walking to meet his bride encounters a figure on the way, who convinces him that she is his ideal of love, his well-beloved, who can fill or withdraw from ordinary women at will. When he meets his bride at the end of the poem

> Her look was pinched and thin,
> As if her soul had shrunk and died,
> And left a waste within. (I.170)

And so, by implication, it will be with all who share the man's experience – and so by implication it was for Pierston. In this instance the poem provides, by repeating the conception, without any need for even minimal realist probability, a reinforcement for the novel's central theme. This poem is interesting also because it exists, like many of Hardy's poems, in multiple versions, and some of the variants (including changes of location between Budmouth and Kingsbere) alter the effect of the poem in subtle but significant ways.[8]

Before leaving *Poems of the Past and the Present*, there is a little sequence of wryly humorous pieces that reflect that side of Hardy's understanding of Wessex character, one of which is the often-anthologized 'The Ruined Maid' (I.197); another is 'The Milkmaid', in which Hardy seems gently to mock the intensity with which he had interconnected milkmaid Tess Durbeyfield with her environment. The poem's narrator is omniscient, but pretends for a moment to be an alien urbane observer looking for 'the peace of life', which he finds embodied by a milkmaid milking a cow amid the 'flowery river-ooze'. He watches, but cannot hear, the maid speaking to herself, and jumps to the conclusion that she must be expressing

> ... her sense of Nature's scenery,
> Of whose life, sentiment,
> And essence, very part itself is she. (I.195)

As Hardy himself said in *Tess of the d'Urbervilles* 'a field-woman is a portion of the field; she has somehow lost her own margin, imbibed the essence of her surrounding, and assimilated herself with it' (XIV), and in the same novel Angel, uneducated as yet by experience, sees Tess the milkmaid as a 'daughter of Nature' (XVIII). The maid seems to be pained, sheds a tear, and the observer wonders if it is the passing railway train that 'offends her country ear'. Having thus nicely set things up Hardy undercuts his own seriousness by telling us that what in fact moves Phyllis so is the longing for a new dress to stun Fred with, and so cut out her rival for his affection. Anti-pastoral, one might say – Fred, not Corydon. The poem certainly owes something to William Barnes, but when Hardy writes pastoral, or anti-pastoral, there is the whole sequence of his antecedent novels to provide for the poem an expansive context.

Hardy spent most of the first decade of the twentieth century working on his Napoleonic drama *The Dynasts*, which contains, as is well known, a number of Wessex scenes. It is hardly surprising that fragments of *The Trumpet-Major* are reproduced or echoed in the play, but there are also details recalling other fictions. It is not just that Hardy always felt that his epic should have a grounding in the Wessex people whose stories first fascinated him with the politics and characters of the wars, but that it should also link at places into already published fragments of the narrative of Wessex; and it does add an extra element of interest to, say, *The Mayor of Casterbridge* and *The Return of the Native* to know that Solomon Longways and Grandfer Cantle were there when they burned the effigy of Boney on Durnover Green (V.161), or to hear told another of Bob Loveday's stories. (IV.146)

The Dynasts, too, is the right place to remember that Hardy had discovered during the twenty-five year process of writing his fiction that Wessex meant a structure of thought as well as a place and a history. Moreover, it was his own pattern of mind, where places and history were (he gradually came to realize) only his own to the degree that he selected or omitted detail. Foremost amongst the complexities of the pattern of thoughts and beliefs that governs Wessex is a shifting theory about concepts like fate or destiny, ideas about how things happen in the world. The meta drama of *The Dynasts* is another and more systematic attempt to understand these issues; and it is fascinating to watch Napoleon behaving through the play in this respect very much as Michael Henchard in *The Mayor of Casterbridge*.

With his drama completed, Hardy brought out in 1909 his third collection of verse, *Time's Laughingstocks*, which included 'A Trampwoman's Tragedy' (I.243). He thought very highly of the poem and it is clear enough why he did so. It is a well-made story that ends in a hanging and a ghost, which he has shaped in traditional ballad-form with ballad spareness, and it is, like

Tess of the d'Urbervilles, a narrative of continual travel across Wessex, evoked in significant details of places that had memories for Hardy (some vouched for by the abundant notes, which, like those in the Wessex edition of some novels, also point out for readers why they will not now find what he describes).[9] The poem with its notes shows there is still accommodation in Hardy's imagination between Wessex-as-fiction and Wessex-as-England, as do 'A Sunday Morning Tragedy' (I.250) and 'The Revisitation' (I.237), both of which share some of the same characteristics – the kind of work that kept 'Wessex Heights' at bay. And *Time's Laughingstocks* also includes the group of eighteen poems called 'A Set of Country Songs', which taken together reveal the delighted range that Hardy can command in lyrics that mediate between the imagined and the remembered, between the fiction and the life. The sequence begins with 'Let Me Enjoy', that catches a positive-stoical phase of the Wessex world view, to be sung in a minor key:

> Let me enjoy the earth no less
> Because the all-enacting Might
> That fashioned forth its loveliness
> Hath other aims than my delight. (I.290)

And there follow the seven fragments of experience 'At Casterbridge Fair,' opening appropriately with 'The Ballad-Singer':

> Sing, Ballad-singer, raise a hearty tune;
> Make me forget that there was ever a one
> I walked with in the meek light of the moon
>   When the day's work was done.
>
> Rhyme, Ballad-rhymer, start a country song;
> Make me forget that she whom I loved well
> Swore she would love me dearly, love me long,
>   Then – what I cannot tell!
>
> Sing, Ballad-singer, from your little book;
> Make me forget those heart-breaks, achings, fears;
> Make me forget her name, her sweet sweet look -
>   Make me forget her tears.

The vocabulary is simple, the state of mind commonplace, but the emotion generated is powerful and complex. Hardy often uses repetition-with-variation to stunning effect, and his command over form is well known – here in particular the shorter last line carries much weight. But the poem's interaction with Hardy's own ballads in the same volume, like 'A Trampwoman's Tragedy', undercuts both the speaker's melancholy and his anticipation of relief.

We may well think that a singer of such ballads is hardly likely to provide material for the forgetting of love-pains.

This, one might say, is a poem of Wessex-in-England, but in what follows Hardy evokes also the fictional Wessex, in 'Former Beauties', say, or 'After the Club-Danc'. Indeed the narrator of the latter expresses a related but slightly different response from Tess's to sexual experience out of wedlock:

> The roadside elms pass by me,-
> Why do I sink with shame
> When the birds a-perch there eye me?
> They, too, have done the same!

She recognizes, as Tess cannot, her identity in this respect with wild nature, and she questions the imposed social shame; but still she feels it just as intensely. By contrast 'The Dark-Eyed Gentleman' (which immediately follows the 'At Casterbridge Fair' poems) and 'Julie-Jane' both visit this same sexual situation, and in both the consequence is joy and not sorrow; for one her son is her 'comrade and friend' (I.296), for Julie-Jane her child is indeed only a matter of nature, not to be regretted (I.298).

'The Fiddler', too, which harmonizes so well with 'The Ballad-Singer', interacts with the Wessex of Hardy's fiction:

> The fiddler knows what's brewing
>   To the lilt of his lyric wiles:
> The fiddler knows what rueing
>   Will come of this night's smiles!
>
> He sees couples join them for dancing,
>   And afterwards joining for life,
> He sees them pay high for their prancing
>   By a welter of wedded strife.
>
> He twangs: 'Music hails from the devil,
>   Though vaunted to come from heaven,
> For it makes people do at a revel
>   What multiplies sins by seven.
>
> 'There's many a heart now mangled,
>   And waiting its time to go,
> Whose tendrils were first entangled
>   By my sweet viol and bow!' (I.300–301)

This is the dark, Mop Ollamoor aspect of traditional music, essential to set against the good-natured dance and church music associations that predominate in Hardy's work – this fiddler was probably playing at the Casterbridge Club-dance.

It is only the last poem in the set, 'The Homecoming', that moves beyond song back to the ballad, a modern ballad rather than a traditional one, in which the refrain reunites the sequence explicitly with both South Wessex and Dorset – Toller Down, Whitesheet Hill, Benvill Lane, Crimmercrock Lane.[10]

Hardy sent his fourth collection *Satires of Circumstance* to Macmillan on 10 August 1914, six days after the outbreak of war, and at last he chose to include 'Wessex Heights' – indeed at first he intended it to open the book, though he changed his mind before submitting the manuscript. Why now? Perhaps because his wife had died in 1912; but if he did feel free to publish the poem because of Emma's death, at the same time he would have read it in a new light through his experience of labouring once again, in the same year, at the topographical and historical details of Wessex for his new revised edition. He had reached the final stage in his attempt to ensure that Wessex and England coincided as far as possible, and he had felt he had to apologize to his readers when they did not. Now this was all over, and he could let Wessex-as-fiction rest. In this new context the publication of 'Wessex Heights' marked a reaction against the idea of an imagined Wessex, a rejection for his future writing of the dream-world element implicit in his use of the name.

The poem that replaced 'Wessex Heights' at the beginning of the volume is interesting when read in this light. 'In Front of the Landscape' begins:

> Plunging and labouring on in a tide of visions,
>   Dolorous and dear,
> Forward I pushed my way as amid waste waters (II.7)

Life in the lowlands below the heights is once again arduous, and painful too, if the clotted and sometimes desperate diction is any guide, and since Emma's death it is even less terrestrial, for the landscape visible to others –

> Ancient chalk-pit, milestone, rills in the grass-flat
>   Stroked by the light,
> Seemed but a ghost-like gauze

to the narrator – though because of the characteristically Hardyan double-vision, a man observing himself observing himself, the grass-rills are there for the reader with sharp particularity. The narrator within the poem, however, only sees 'ghosts avenging their slights by my bypast/Body-borne eyes'. No wonder 'Wessex Heights' seemed now an essential poem. Hardy's verse, so full of ghosts of people (particularly Emma) and actions for this and the next two collections, certainly seems to suggest that he found it hard to evade such a complex of visions.[11]

The most celebrated poems in the collection are those Hardy wrote after Emma's death, brought together as 'Poems of 1912–13'. They begin in Max Gate and Mellstock and move to Cornwall, which for this purpose he calls Lyonnesse rather than Off-Wessex (as it was on the revised version of the map at the end of *A Changed Man* in the Wessex edition, also published in 1914 – see above p. 162). In this sequence of elegiac poems, the pattern is that names already existing in Wessex forms from the revisions to *A Pair of Blue Eyes*, Castle Boterel and St Launce's, are kept thus, but no new Wessex names are invented; it had been less than a year since he had worked his way through the novel, revisualizing the scenes of his early passion, but his wife had been alive then, and the feelings with which he read the novel of almost forty years earlier were very different in intensity, if not in kind, from those under the influence of which he wrote the poems. And yet in that marvellous poem 'Beeny Cliff' Hardy borrows images from a passage in his preface to the novel. Compare:

The ghostly birds, the pall-like sea, the frothy wind, the eternal soliloquy of the waters, the bloom of dark purple cast that seems to exhale from the shoreward precipices....

with:

The pale mews plained below us, and the waves seemed...
   ...engrossed in saying their ceaseless babbling say...

...the Atlantic dyed its levels with a dull misfeatured stain,
And then the sun burst out again, and purples prinked the main. (II.62)

So that in addition to all that has been written of these poems of genius it is possible to suggest through names and allusion that Hardy's guilt and grief and passionate intensity are part of Wessex as well as part of universal human experience – or that Hardy was still interested to make clear that the Wessex experience is universal.

Within its web of memory *Satires of Circumstance* does also contain some poems that follow the pattern already established in relation to fictional Wessex: 'The Moth-Signal', with its subtitle '(on Egdon Heath)' (II.111) refocusses a detail from *The Return of the Native*. In the novel, when Wildeve sends his moth through the open window of Clym and Eustacia's living room, Eustacia's attempt to respond to his signal is circumvented by Diggory Venn, and the meeting does not occur (IV.iv). If read in relation to the novel, the poem makes explicit that Damon and Eustacia have been lovers, something Hardy could not make clear in 1878. It also, disconcertingly enough, continues the Heath's manipulation of time by concluding with the grinning comment of an Ancient Briton buried in a nearby tumulus: 'So, hearts are thwartly smitten/In these days as in mine!'

It is likewise impossible to come to the end of the last astonishing verse of 'Channel Firing':

> Again the guns disturbed the hour,
> Roaring their readiness to avenge,
> As far inland as Stourton Tower,
> And Camelot, and starlit Stonehenge (II.9)

without seeing Tess as well as the calmly brutal present and the remotely brutal pagan past.[12] But it is possible to sense another tendency beginning. Take 'The Recalcitrants', for example (II.107). Only modern Hardy scholars could be aware that this was the title that Hardy wanted too late to give to the serialization of what ultimately became *Jude the Obscure*.[13] It is likely though that some earlier readers would anyway have made the connection between the pair in the poem and Jude Fawley and Sue Bridehead, and once the connection *is* made, the poem gives a fresh understanding of the way they view their relationship together and respond to the hostility of the world at large. An immediate question is whether Sue or Jude speaks in the poem, and the difficulty in deciding is perhaps some support to the narrative voice of the novel that claims the two thought so far alike as almost to be twins. What the poem proposes is travel to a place with a different culture, where they can live 'natural lives' without incurring judgement or condemnation for transgressing empty social laws, and where they feel no pressure to justify themselves. The poem ends, 'Well, let us away', and we might be hopeful for them, but for the whole weight of *Jude the Obscure* that is against their escape. But what is most striking in the context of earlier poems that are intimately related to fictional Wessex, is that Hardy offers no indication to the reader that the poem has anything to do with *Jude the Obscure*.

In fact Wessex names and indications of Wessex associations almost disappear from Hardy's next two volumes, *Moments of Vision* (1917) and *Late Lyrics and Earlier* (1922), a state of things predicated by the presence of 'Wessex Heights' in *Satires of Circumstance*. The three names that do survive in *Moments of Vision* are quite predictable: Mellstock, Casterbridge and Egdon. There is the transparently autobiographical 'Afternoon Service at Mellstock' (II.161); the parish name Stinsford was almost unavailable to him. In 'Old Excursions' (II.269), Hardy uses Casterbridge alongside several English names (some with existing Wessex versions), so that it is proposed to go to Casterbridge by way of Yell'ham Hill. Perhaps the Wessex name was too deeply ingrained – as too was the Egdon in 'Before Marching and After' (II.297), a poem written in memory of a relative who was killed in the war – the war which may well have helped to turn Hardy's mind against the dwindling fantasy of his fictional region. In the preface to *Late Lyrics*, written well after the war ended, he wrote of the onset of a new dark age, but even as *Satires of Circumstance* was being published in August 1914 he was already writing in despair of civilization to friends. Wessex must have seemed too cosily comfortable and even too innocent for the times.

There are in *Moments of Vision* still one or two poems that expand the novels, but Hardy's weariness with fictional Wessex, or his abandonment of it, means that, following 'The Recalcitrants', he gives no sign to the reader that the poem and novel are connected. The most obvious instance is 'Midnight on the Great Western' (II.262). To anyone who has read *Jude the Obscure*, the 'journeying boy' is at once young Jude Fawley, 'Little Father Time', on his way to find his father, and indeed the physical description coincides in many particulars with the account in the novel. The time in the novel is a few hours earlier, and there is no sense in the poem that the boy's eyes are 'frightened', but the carriage is third class, the key round his neck reflects the lamplight, in both his ticket is passively stuck in his hatband. The identity seems unmistakable. In the novel: 'His eyes remained mostly fixed on the back of the seat opposite, and never turned to the window even when a station was reached and called'(V.iii). In the poem his form and face are 'listless', which adjective does not damage the resemblance. But the remainder of the account in the poem moves differently from that in the novel. The underlying difference between the two is in the personal speculative tone of the narrator of the poem – clearly one of those in the compartment with the boy – when compared with the omniscience of the novel's narrator, who penetrates confidently 'through crevices' to an alien spirit, an age-old Divinity, forced unwillingly to inhabit the boy's body, judging the past and judging the other occupants of the carriage with melancholy but divine vision. For the narrator of the poem the boy sees nothing of his 'companions', but is 'Bewrapt past knowing to what he was going,/Or whence he came.' The poem's narrator wonders about the boy's past, but only in a general way, seeking some explanation for the boy's self-possession, his indifference to the incidents of travel, the lack of any sign of the anxiety that might have been expected in one so young travelling alone at so late an hour. The final verse of the poem moves the speculation into a field similar to that in the novel, but yet quite different in effect. It is the boy himself, his soul, rather than some captive god, that seems perhaps to be judging this 'region of sin' to which he does not belong. What was portentous, almost melodramatic in the novel, is more clearly in the poem an engaging, characteristic, but improbable speculation of the narrator's mind. As with other poems that revisit novels, it seems that Hardy wished to work again with something he had not quite done justice to. Young Jude Fawley had no place in a naturalistic novel, was a fitter subject for a poem, and though there is no evidence to support this idea, it seems likely that in the poem Hardy went back to the encounter that had sparked in his imagination the concept of Little Father Time, and offered it again to his readers in a shape that expressed more accurately his thought at the time.

In a slightly different way the same point can be made about 'The Choirmaster's Burial' (II.284), a brief story that in an earlier volume would have been prefaced by 'An Experience of the Mellstock Quire' or some such note, and which ends with a couplet indicating that the tale was told by 'the tenor man' – who would earlier have been identified as Michael Mail.

It is, though, not just the negative evidence of absence that can be brought to bear; there was also deliberate erasure. In 'Great Things', one of the best known poems in *Moments of Vision*, the first verse originally began:

> Sweet cyder is a great thing
> A great thing to me,
> Vamping down to Budmouth town
> By Ridgeway thirstily...

This was in the manuscript; but, as everyone knows, it now goes:

> Sweet cyder is a great thing
> A great thing to me,
> Spinning down to Weymouth town
> By Ridgeway thirstily... (II.214)

The last of the little sequence of three Sturminster Newton poems in the same volume was called in the manuscript 'On Stourcastle Foot-bridge', but was published as 'On Sturminster Foot-Bridge' (II.225). The rest of the poems in the collection follow these moves away from Wessex, so that we are firmly in England – in Bournemouth, Swanage, Bockhampton, Wimborne, Kingston-Maurward, and even Boscastle.

There are also poems in *Moments of Vision* that have to do with fictional Wessex, not as a place, but as a way of thinking, of understanding life (and death). When Hardy writes idiosyncratically about time in 'In a Museum' (II.163), or fate in 'At the Word "Farewell"' (II.164) or 'The Blow' (II.218), or the interfusion of all living things in 'The Wind Blew Words' (II.181), he is, for anyone who cares, further filling the frame of fictional Wessex. But he has no room, or no heart, at present, for the day-to-day existence of that place.

Much the same could be written of *Late Lyrics and Earlier*. 'The Sailor's Mother' (II.442) does have as footnote '(From "To Please His Wife")', but, though 'The Two Wives' (II.418) is a variant on the central episode in 'Fellow-Townsmen', there is no note of the connection (though Hynes points it out, II.518). It is no coincidence that 'Mismet' (II.381) is placed directly after 'The Child and the Sage', for both dramatize significant fragments from the narrator's world-questioning in *Tess of the d'Urbervilles*, though there is no indication of this. When 'By Henstridge Cross at the Year's End' (II.402) was first published, in the *Fortnightly Review*, it was called 'By Mellstock Cross at the Year's End'. The poem, like so many of Hardy's at this stage, raises ghosts; here each is introduced by the question Why go east (or north, or west or south) of the cross; some of the spirits are clearly personal – Emma comes from the west, for instance. The removal of Wessex-as-fiction here means also a radical change of place, and there arises again the almost moral question associated with Hardy's 1913 removal of 'The Romantic Adventures of a Milkmaid' from the Frome Valley to that of the Exe without redescribing the environment. The change of place makes untenable to a modern reader familiar with Hardy's biography the idea that the road north leads past 'fiefs of my forefolk yeomen'. Did any reader know this in 1922? Would Hardy have cared if they did?

One poem in particular illuminates the tricky position Hardy found himself in, deliberately trying to diminish the effect of forty years of generating Wessex, but bound by it at the same time. It is called 'The Country Wedding (A Fiddler's Story)' (II.427), a title that for a reader of Hardy's fiction speaks directly of fictional Wessex. And, indeed, the first three verses are of a piece with, say, *Under the Greenwood Tree*, or the other poems of the Mellstock Quire; but suddenly in the fourth, for those who know or care to find out, there are Puddletown street names in the poem, and we see that we are dealing with Dorset, not Wessex. Tryphena Sparks lived by Mill-tail shallow, and so Hardy may have had a family marriage in mind – the poem may even be autobiography.[14] But the next verse contains more surprises:

> I bowed the treble before her father,
> Michael the tenor in front of the lady,
> The bass-viol Reub – and right well played he! –
> The serpent Jim; ay to church and back.

At first glance this seems to revert to *Under the Greenwood Tree*; Michael Mail and Reuben Dewy must be the first players named; but then we recall that there was no serpent-player in the Mellstock band, and that old William Dewy, not Reuben, played the cello, and the mind begins accommodating the discrepancies with the known Wessex world. Perhaps this is the band at a later date, William being dead and the strings only rule broken; perhaps it is a combination of the Mellstock and Weatherbury bands... but the place is Puddletown, not Weatherbury. And who is then the narrator of the poem? Dick Dewy? Some version of Hardy? Is it biography, autobiography or fiction? These questions are beside the point of the poem, which carries on to describe the wedding, and to remember, years later, the bride's death day. The poem, it might be said, is burdened by its Wessex associations rather than enriched by them – or perhaps, as well as enriched by them. Hardy wants to write of the memory world of his own experience for his own satisfaction, but (assuming for the moment that the names *were* those of members of the Puddletown band at some epoch) it is hard to both reflect reality as he wishes, and evade fictional Wessex and its imperatives.

Life's Little Ironies, like *Moments of Vision*, is saturated with memories of Emma, but a handful of other poems have features of fictional Wessex interest. A small and mostly unread poem, 'Sacred to the Memory' is an elegy for his sister Mary:

> That 'Sacred to the Memory'
> Is clearly carven there I own,
> And all may think that on the stone
> The words have been inscribed by me
> In bare conventionality.
> They know not and will never know
> That my full script is not confined
> To that stone space, but stands deep lined
> Upon the landscape high and low
> Wherein she made such worthy show. (II.452)

This expresses in a simple way a perception of Hardy's that has informed Wessex from the moment of its inception, the idea that the relationship between a person and a landscape is intimate and lasting. What is different here is that Hardy surviving says he has inscribed his dead sister's name deep in her familiar landscape, with the sense that she will thereby live in the hills and valleys; but live for him alone, for how could anyone else perceive this interconnection. But he has written the poem, and published it, so we all know what he has done, and now, if we exercise our imaginations, we can share his perception, or at least find analogies in our own experience, and see the landscape, or at least some landscape, differently.

When you get to *Human Shows* (1925) everything changes again. It is remarkable to be able to say of a writer in his eighties that he seems refreshed, but it is the case, for Hardy has come through to a delighted belief in the range of imaginative possibilities inherent in a Wessex in which the fictional and the now thoroughly established English aspects of the word combine once more.[15] There is a large number of poems that might be chosen as representative of this – 'A Last Journey' (III.25), for instance, or 'Winter Night in Woodland' (III.44), 'The Paphian Ball' (III.137) or 'The Sheep-Boy' (III.109); but I have chosen 'Life and Death at Sunrise' that has the subtitle 'Near Dogbury Gate, 1867'.

> The hills uncap their tops
> Of woodland, pasture, copse,
> And look on the layers of mist
> At their foot that still persist:
> They are like awakened sleepers on one elbow lifted,
> Who gaze around to learn if things during night have shifted.

> A waggon creaks up from the fog
> With a laboured leisurely jog;
> Then a horseman from off the hill-tip
> Comes clapping down into the dip;
> While woodlarks, finches, sparrows, try to entune at one time,
> And cocks and hens and cows and bulls take up the chime.
>
> With a shouldered basket and flagon
> A man meets the one in the waggon,
> And both the men halt of long use,
> 'Well,' the waggoner says, 'what's the news?'
> '-'Tis a boy this time. You've just met the doctor trotting back.
> She's doing very well. And we think we shall call him "Jack".
>
> 'And what have you got covered there?'
> He nods to the waggon and mare.
> 'Oh, a coffin for old John Thinn:
> We are just going to put him in.'
> ' – So he's gone at last. He always had a good constitution.'
> ' – He was ninety-odd. He could call up the French Revolution.' (III.40)

The title invites a reader to expect one of Hardy's little period melodramas – a duel perhaps; but that is only his joke. In fact the poem reproduces some of the central elements of fictional Wessex. The landscape is alive with significance, though on the whole it is only the narrator who sees it. The range of characters, doctor to labourer, is characteristic of Wessex, though they seem at first of less significance than the dawn-chorus of birds or the hills freed of mist. But then the brief exchange between waggoner and labourer places the environment in a different perspective. Though man may appear as a brief-lived intruder to the Wessex hills, his voice will endure, along with those of the finches or the larks – Hardy does not subscribe to the 'Ode to a Nightingale' or 'Wild Swans at Coole' comparison of the shortness of man's life and the apparent immortality of individually indistinguishable birds.[16] Moreover, man alone has the speech and memory that permit him to leave, for better or ill, a permanent mark on the permanent hills – so far as anything is permanent. Such a handing-off from death to birth as this poem celebrates is enacted a million times each day, and the whole of human history is symbolized in the French Revolution. But Hardy was also looking back almost sixty years from the vantage point of 1925, when the poem was published, on a fragment of passed community. The doctor in 1925 would perhaps have buzzed down the hill in his small Austin, and the labourer probably would have cycled to work.

There are many poems in *Human Shows* that exist purely or primarily for the sake of a moment observed – there are more moments of vision than in

Moments of Vision (though, to be fair, it is inward not external vision that Hardy had in mind in naming the earlier volume). We are given again fragments of the ordinary life in Wessex that is also Dorset. Hardy says in these pieces: 'Things were so then to my eye, and are valuable because they were so. Valuable too, of course for some quality in them worth preserving, but you may not feel so, dear reader, and quite frankly, I couldn't care less. I do not mean that they are verse equivalents of snapshots, though; language is not transparent, and poetry even less so than other forms of communication.' Here is 'Ice on the Highway':

> Seven buxom women abreast, and arm in arm,
>   Trudge down the hill, tip-toed,
>   And breathing warm;
> They must perforce trudge thus, to keep upright
>   On the glassy ice-bound road,
> And they must get to market whether or no,
>   Provisions running low
>   With the nearing of Saturday night,
> While the lumbering van wherein they mostly ride
>   Can nowise go:
> Yet loud their laughing as they stagger and slide!
>   Yell'ham Hill. (III.45)

The only reason for writing or for reading this poem is delight in the moment; the long and difficult walk of the women to market ('trudge' doubled), compensated for by their companionship and high spirits. The placing of the moment on Yellowham Hill means they have three miles and more to walk to Dorchester, and it also means that if readers care to look the name up in a gazetteer they can know this too. This is a characteristic Wessex poem, even though the incident might have been observed anywhere. It is so because of the observing eye and recording hand that thought such an apparently commonplace and trivial moment worth shaping and offering to the public: this, even in 1925, is how it is for some of us, despite motors and railways. Wessex in *Human Shows* is a story-told place, as in 'Life and Death at Sunrise', and it records, like 'Shortening Days at the Homestead' (III.133), the interpenetration of man and nature; it is the reminiscence of the novel-established territory found in 'Winter Night in Woodland', and it is, as ever, a philosophical enquiry of nature and/or fate and/or the immanent will about the reason man is on the world and the possibility of change in the future, like 'Discouragement' (III.155), but above all it is a state of mind in which ordinary incidents like that recorded in 'Ice on the Highway' have transcendent value; such poems make reading the collection an exhilarating experience.

In *Winter Words* Hardy maintains this rediscovery of a Wessex that combines the present place with the fifty years of fiction. 'The Third Kissing-Gate'

(III.246), for instance, is a skilful trivial little poem, but it gains a depth of association by setting the action on the way between town (which becomes at once Casterbridge) and Mellstock. Hardy has earned the right to the value attaching to the name by long imaginative labour. It would be wrong to give the impression, though, that the volume is full of such poems; it is not. But there are more poems like 'The Second Visit'

> Clack, clack, clack, went the mill-wheel as I came,
> And she was on the bridge with the thin hand-rail,
> And the miller at the door, and the ducks at mill-tail;
> I come again years after, and all there seems the same.
>
> And so indeed it is: the apple-tree'd old house,
> And the deep mill pond, and the wet wheel clacking,
> And a woman on the bridge, and white ducks quacking,
> And the miller at the door, powdered pale from boots to brows.
>
> But it's not the same miller whom long ago I knew,
> Nor are they the same apples, nor the same drops that dash
> Over the wet wheel, not the ducks below that splash,
> Nor the woman who to fond plaints replied, 'You know I do!' (III.232)

It is hardly profound, even trite; it is blatantly repetitive (though Hardy's skill in making multiple satisfying variations on the same pattern of images is unmatched by any other writer I know); and if he had not already written fourteen novels, forty odd stories, a play or two, and nine hundred or so poems, and if Wessex and Dorset had not been so intertwined and foregrounded and backgrounded therein by now, a reader would think nothing of it. Perhaps a casual reader who knows nothing of Hardy or his Wessex would even now pass it over as inconsequential. But to one who has worked through the fiction and the poems to the end in *Winter Words*, who has been entranced by the growth of Hardy's command over Wessex, the poem prompts a long backward look. The miller and his active wheel are in the past altogether for us, and must have been rare enough in 1928 when the book was published, though the bridge may still be there, wherever it was, and the ducks certainly are, if the race has not been diverted or dammed or put in a pipe under a road; and there will always be women saying 'You know I do.' All this is of Wessex; the disappearing rural technology and the disappearing rural environment recorded, though here recorded as if, within cyclical change, they were eternal; the human emotion that is permanent recorded also – or especially, since it is with that the poem ends. It is part of the sum of Wessex, like a paragraph or two of a novel, an insight put down in passing. So it is with many other poems here. 'An Unkindly May' comes to mind – just a piece of the weather-description that Hardy does so well (and quite frequently in *Human Shows* and *Winter Words*), but the account has two lines of preface:

> A shepherd stands by a gate in a white smock-frock:
> He holds the gate ajar, intently counting his flock.

Then Hardy talks for twelve lines of the 'sour spring wind' and its effects:

> The buds have tried to open, but quite failing
> Have pinched themselves together in their quailing.

However, at the end

> That shepherd still stands in that white smock-frock,
> Unnoting all things save the counting his flock. (III.174)

And the whole poem is not just an evocation of a scene and a mood of late spring, but of *Far From the Madding Crowd* and 'The Three Strangers'.

Hardy's own ghost still haunts with resentment all those who write books about his whole work and give short shrift to his poetry. My only hope is that he will understand that what I've been trying to show is how he developed Wessex, and that his poetry was all published after Wessex had become what it is. Poems develop Wessex and its inhabitants in different and interesting ways, but what the study of his verse shows most clearly is that the work he felt constrained to do for the 1912 revision brought sharply home to him how far Wessex had escaped his control. He felt for a while that he ought to face this reality, and detach his poetry from all that Wessex-as-fiction had become in his own and others' hands – though, like heights in Wessex, standing above the misted lowlands but nevertheless inescapably in Wessex, he could not even then escape the last links of Mellstock and Egdon and Casterbridge, places where by long use he was still a child.

It is impossible to know what part his wife's death had in such a decision – certainly her ghostly presence tends to crowd others off the stage for ten years and more – or how far his despair of humanity in response to the war changed his feelings about Wessex. But their power faded somewhat with time, and allowed room for a resurgence of interest in the ordinary life of his region. He felt the need to show that fictional Wessex was not out of date, that noticing human things was still a part of his experience of life. 'Afterwards' (II.308) is a wonderful poem, but it could only have appeared in *Moments of Vision* or *Late Lyrics and Earlier*, for though Hardy wonders how men and women will remember him, he is not interested that they should do so for his attention to fragments of human nature.

One last poem shows how far Hardy has taken his new version of Wessex in his last volumes:

Nobody Comes

Tree-leaves labour up and down,
    And through them the fainting light
    Succumbs to the crawl of night.
Outside in the road the telegraph wire
    To the town from the darkening land
Intones to travellers like a spectral lyre
    Swept by a spectral hand.

A car comes up, with lamps full-glare,
    That flash upon a tree:
    It has nothing to do with me,
And whangs along in a world of its own,
    Leaving a blacker air;
And mute by the gate I stand again alone,
    And nobody pulls up there.

            9 October, 1924. (III.55)

The telegraph wire is old hat, a feature of the new world of *A Laodicean*, though the lyre it is likened to only goes back as far as 'The Darkling Thrush'. The motor car, however, is something different. Fictional Wessex had been preoccupied with the obsolescence of the ancient pattern of roads in face of the devouring railway, and Hardy nowhere addressed what by the 1920s was the beginning of a revitalization of roadside communities by the car. But here it is, a momentary alienating presence in the night. The poem is autobiographical, Hardy examining his own distress, his own loneliness; but because nobody had paid a call on the visitor to Weatherbury who saw only Mr Boldwood driving obliviously past, because nobody came for Phyllis Grove in Overcombe, because whenever a leaf fell Clym Yeobright thought Eustacia had come back to him, it is also a Wessex poem; because of all the significant journeying in *Desperate Remedies* and *Tess of the d'Urbervilles* and *Jude the Obscure* and 'My Cicely' and 'The Trampwoman's Tragedy' and so on and so on, Wessex also has the motor car.

Hardy did not live to see the publication of *Winter Words*; he has not been dead for three quarters of a century yet. But how is it possible to doubt that his work will endure with Chaucer's and Shakespeare's and Pope's as essential to any experience of English literature?

There follow four chapters that examine aspects of Hardy's representation of Wessex that are of interest in all his work: drink, noises, dialect and railways. Other topics might also have been chosen: fate, work, class, town and country; the materials on which these accounts might be based, including the essential revisions, will be found in the general entries for each novel on the website.

9
Cider, Mead and Ale

It is commonplace in writing on the Victorian rural working classes that heavy drinking was a favourite, sometimes the only, release from the perpetually painful realities of a poor and arduous life, and what was true in Dorset in this respect is certainly true in Wessex. The full evidence can be found on the website. Throughout his fiction and his poetry Hardy celebrates the social pleasures of drinking, from the first chapters of *Under the Greenwood Tree* to 'Great Things', and at different times he writes with affection about cider-making and the rich varieties of cider, about the glory of Dorchester strong beer, about the delight of tasting old mead. But everyone can also call to mind Joseph Poorgrass failing to get Fanny Robin's body to the churchyard in time for it to be buried, Michael Henchard selling his wife under the influence of rum-laced furmity, Arabella Cartlett's vile administration of a carefully designed mixture of drinks that gets Jude Fawley to the state in which he will marry her again. The position in Wessex then seems to be the fairly conventional one, that moderate consumption of alcohol amongst friends can be delightful, but that excess leads to miseries. In fact, though, the issue is more complicated.

An exchange in *Far From the Madding Crowd* between Jan Coggan and Mark Clark, urging Joseph Poorgrass to stay longer at the inn seems to propose some ambiguity:

> 'Of course, you'll have another drop. A man's twice the man afterwards. You feel so warm and glorious, and you whop and slap at your work without any trouble, and everything goes on like sticks a-breaking. Too much liquor is bad, and leads us to that horned man in the smoky house; but, after all, many people haven't the gift of enjoying a soak, and since we be highly favoured with a power that way we should make the most o't.'
>
> 'True,' said Mark Clark. ''Tis a talent the Lord has mercifully bestowed upon us, and we ought not to neglect it. But, what with the parsons and

clerks and school-people and serious tea-parties, the merry old ways of good life have gone to the dogs – upon my carcase they have! (vII cXII)

Here is the thought that alcoholic anaesthesia helps the labourer to perform his arduous and repetitive labour with less pain. But more, it is in Weatherbury as in Mellstock, that modern vicars and teachers (and novelists?) seem bent on altering a traditional Wessex pattern of life held to be valuable by those who live it. And though Gabriel Oak roundly chastises the topers, though as a consequence of Poorgrass's overindulgence Fanny Robin cannot be buried, and Bathsheba finds out the truth about her baby, it is also true, as the narrator points out, that she would have discovered it sooner or later, and it was better for her eventual peace of mind to know the truth sooner rather than later. So one might argue that drunkenness proved a blessing as well as a talent. However, as far as *Far From the Madding Crowd* is concerned, the drunken 'debauch' that Troy induces at the harvest home has already more than compensated for such an uncertain conclusion. The action of *The Mayor of Casterbridge* might then be thought to seal the matter unambiguously; but not so; for in *Tess of the d'Urbervilles* Hardy poses the full dilemma of alcoholic consumption in Wessex.

At the outset Parson Tringham tells John Durbeyfield, with a touch of contempt, that he has had already had more than enough to drink. When Sir John, now singing drunk, drives past the club-walking women, they laugh, saying to Tess that her father has his 'market-nitch', at which Tess gets upset.

When Tess gets home from the dancing, it is to find that her father, not satisfied with the level of inebriation he has reached, has gone to an alehouse, 'to get up his strength' for the journey he has to take in a few hours time. When her mother tells Tess this, she begins 'Now don't you be bursting out angry'. Which is just what Tess does: 'O my God! Go to a public-house to get up his strength! And you as well agreed as he, mother!' Joan denies approving of her husband's visit to Rolliver's, but Tess understands, as well as we do, what it means when she finds her mother determined to go to 'fetch' her husband.

From these early details, it would seem that Hardy was using Tess to express his indignation at the way the Durbeyfield parents evidently drink away their children's futures. But almost immediately the narrator (or I should say, one of the narrators) describes why Joan Durbeyfield is so keen to go to the pub:

This going to hunt up her shiftless husband at the inn was one of Mrs. Durbeyfield's still extant enjoyments in the muck and muddle of rearing children. To discover him at Rolliver's, to sit there for an hour or two by his side and dismiss all thought and care of the children during the interval, made her happy. A sort of halo, an occidental glow, came over life then. (III)

The 'muck and muddle of rearing children' is hard work, akin to anything the field-worker, or for that matter, the higgler, might perform, and Hardy recognizes it as such, and recognizes once again that all such unremitting labour requires intense passages of relief if it is to be borne. Drinking is one such release, by which troubles temporarily vanish in a rosy glow, pains melt away, ordinary life becomes delightful to contemplate; and her husband becomes a lover again. But at the same time, the glow is in the west, a sunset glow, that will not last long before the night sets in; and her husband is still John Durbeyfield with all his 'defects of character'. So we see the situation both from the inside and the outside at once, both as Joan experiences it and as a dispassionate observer would regard it. Hardy uses the words 'realities' and 'ideal' later in the passage, and there lies within them an implication that some such vehicle as alcohol is necessary for most of us to be able to reach to the ideal that lurks behind or within the real. And moreover, such a reaching out to the ideal is a basic human desire, for Joan is by no means alone. In the next chapter the narrator talks of 'nearly a dozen persons' at Rolliver's, 'all seeking beatitude'. There is some irony in the last word perhaps – but how strong? Certainly not strong enough to be unmistakable. A little later we see that 'their souls expanded beyond their skins' and in the process the room itself that had been rather a sordid place in which to enjoy the pleasures of drink – with its gaunt bedstead, and its night stool – this room becomes rich and strange for them, and through them, for us:[1]

> the shawl hanging at the window took upon itself the richness of tapestry; the brass handles of the chest of drawers were as golden knockers; and the carved bed-posts seemed to have some kinship with the magnificent pillars of Solomon's temple. (IV)

As soon as Tess appears in this newly transfigured room, it is as if everything in it reverts to its commonplace state; her parents get up and leave without Tess having to utter a word; but again the way in which this is conveyed is worth looking at:

> Even to her mother's gaze the girl's young features looked sadly out of place amid the alcoholic vapours which floated here as no unsuitable medium for wrinkled [**for wrinkling MS**] middle-age; and hardly was a reproachful flash from Tess's dark eyes needed to make her father and mother rise from their seats, hastily finish their ale, and descend the stairs behind her... (IV)

We have to note that the narrator by no means condemns the alcoholic vapours as Tess does – they are an appropriate context for 'wrinkling middle age', he says, and this is in spite of both the immediate and the secondary sequel – the grotesqueness of Durbeyfield's drunken walk home, and the pain of Tess's journey with the hives.[2]

So the question is posed: what does Hardy intend that we should make of this apparent contradiction of moral intent with regard to drunkenness? There is enough material, perhaps, in these first four chapters to furnish a response; however, Chapter 10 also takes up the theme. Here's the opening in the first edition version (without any of the revisions):

> Every village has its idiosyncracy, its constitution, its own code of morality. The levity of some of the younger women in and about Trantridge was marked, and was perhaps symptomatic of the choice spirit who ruled The Slopes in that vicinity. The place had also a more abiding defect; it drank hard. The staple conversation on the farms around was on the uselessness of saving money; and smockfrocked arithmeticians, leaning on their ploughs or hoes, would enter into calculations of great nicety to prove that parish relief was a fuller provision for a man in his old age than any which could result from savings out of their wages during a whole lifetime.
>
> The chief pleasure of these philosophers lay in going every Saturday night, when work was done, to Chaseborough, a decayed market-town two or three miles distant; and, returning in the small hours of the next morning, to spend Sunday in sleeping off the dyspeptic effects of the curious compounds sold to them as beer by the monopolizers of the once independent inns.

The moral code of Trantridge, in this account, encompasses sexual freedom and contempt for financial providence, as well as dependence upon alcohol – a litany of everything (if, perhaps, stupidity were added to it) that the average metropolitan man of the middle-class would have thought about the rural working-class. There is no doubt, at least, in the narrator's attitude here to the dependence upon drink: it is an 'abiding defect'. It is not surprising that the place they go to drink is called a 'decayed' market town, to which the narrative soon takes Tess and the reader.

The account of the dance in the hay-trusser's barn there (which only appears in the manuscript and the Wessex edition) could be the subject of its own chapter-length piece of exegesis, and it is worth pointing out in passing, that dancing is another activity which can, and in Hardy very often does, suspend inconvenient realities, and bring together a man and a woman in harmony and ecstasy who might otherwise never have found the spark of the passionate ideal in each other – though that is not the case here. In all respects *this* dance is a perverse one, and Tess's refusal to join it, is of a piece with her antipathy to alcohol.[3]

She is, however, nervous of going home late at night alone, so she waits for the dancers, and returns with them, as we see, across the fields to Trantridge.

> Tess soon perceived as she walked in the flock, sometimes with this one, sometimes with that, that the fresh night air was producing staggerings and serpentine courses among the men who had partaken too freely; some of the more careless women also were wandering in their gait...

So far the group is seen through Tess's consciousness, and we are reminded of John Durbeyfield's diagonal walk home from Rolliver's. But in the middle of the paragraph the point of view shifts to an omniscient narrator:

> Yet however terrestrial and lumpy their appearance just now to the mean unglamoured eye, to themselves the case was different.

Now, the unavoidable implication of this sentence is that Tess's is the 'mean unglamoured eye' – the dark eye that has hardly to flash before her mother and father rise to quit Rolliver's. Again there may be irony in those adjectives, and in any case to be 'unglamoured' is mostly felt to be a virtue, but such irony as there is, seems to melt in the face of the rhetoric in the following account, of how those high on alcohol viewed themselves:

> They followed the road with a knowledge [a sense MS; a sensation O] that they were soaring along in a supporting medium, possessed of original and profound thoughts, themselves and surrounding nature forming an organism of which all the parts harmoniously and joyously interpenetrated each other. They were as sublime as the moon and stars above them, and the moon and stars were as ardent as they.

Most of Hardy's readers will have some experience of the effects of alcohol, but how many would be able to find such glory in the state? Should this description not evoke, at least in those of a certain age, memories of Timothy O'Leary and Jim Morrison and 'Lucy in the Sky with Diamonds'?

What is especially telling in this description, though, is the sense the exalted ones have of the interpenetration between themselves and nature in a single organism. This is one of the fundamental themes of Hardy's fiction in general, and of *Tess* in particular – that what is pathetic fallacy in other writers is intensified to a way of seeing in Hardy, in Wessex. That when life is at its best or its worst, there is harmony, interinvolvement, between man and the environment. This is a perception that none of those who experience it in this instance could possibly have had without the stimulus (or the suppressant) of alcohol. It is in particular this assertion of one of Hardy's fundamental ideas about the world, that makes it very difficult to dismiss the dream as illusion, but the tone of the whole passage is seductively hard to resist. The paragraph that follows, returning to Tess again, by contrast reinforces the impression of meanness of vision, however justified her sentiment:

Tess, however, had undergone such painful experiences in this kind in her father's house, that the discovery of their condition spoilt the pleasure she was beginning to feel in the moonlight journey.

She is excluded from something marvellous, though we can sympathize with her pain.

There follows another wonderful scene in which one of the drunken women, jealous of the attention Tess has been getting from Alec, strips off her bodice in the moonlight and offers to fight Tess; and again Tess's angry reply to this display of luminous and beautiful limbs, despite the justice that lies behind it, stresses her exclusion:

> Indeed, then, I shall not fight!' said the latter majestically; 'and if I had known you was of that sort, I wouldn't have so let myself down as to come with such a whorage as this is!

Tess escapes the fight on the back of Alec d'Urberville's convenient horse, and the others resume their journey:

> then these children of the open air, whom even excess of alcohol could scarce injure permanently, betook themselves to the field-path; and as they went there moved onward with them, around the shadow of each one's head, an opalized circle of glory, formed by the moon's rays upon the glistening sheet of dew. Each pedestrian could see no halo but his or her own, which never deserted the head-shadow whatever its vulgar unsteadiness might be; but adhered to it, and persistently beautified it; till the erratic motions seemed an inherent part of the irradiation, and the fumes of their breathing a component of the night's mist; and the spirit of the scene, and of the moonlight, and of Nature, seemed harmoniously to mingle with the spirit of wine.[4]

And the chapter ends. Again the language is rich and the interpenetration of the individuals with their environment is confirmed. However, in that final 'seemed' there is perhaps a hint of qualification.

So, to come to the question again: what does the novel expect us to think on the question of alcohol?

I think the answer to the question leads to the heart of one of the distinguishing characteristics of Hardy as a writer. The answer depends upon whom you choose to trust, or to put it without a moral overtone, whose view you choose to give authority to. There are three options, I think: two are clear enough; you can authorize Tess's position, which presents irrefutable evidence of the damage done by alcoholic dependence, or you can authorize the narrator's accounts, which overwhelm the practical misery caused through the power of the delighted magical insights into the nature of the world that alcohol releases. The positions are diametrically opposed, and both heroine and narrator have persuasive voices. How to choose? Do you choose the view that comes closest to your pre-existing opinions? Do you cast about looking for that decisive detail that will shift the balance one way or the other? Do you... But it might be best to do none of these. It is profitable to draw back from the immediacies of the text, and consider Hardy's creating mind. It is clear, once you do, not only that it is capable of holding *both* positions, but what is more remarkable, that it is capable of holding them simultaneously. What other novelist can *at the same time* condemn and glorify in this way? Once you recognize this as the effect aimed at, then you understand you are not being asked to choose between competing views, but rather you are being directed, in this respect as in very many others, to be encompassing, to be inclusive not exclusive, to be comprehensive and not selective. Other great novelists help you to see various fragments of the world in the space of their novels. But none, I think, enables you to see all sides of such a fragment simultaneously. You do not take sides, you are not told what to think; you are forced to perform the work of inclusiveness as you experience the text.[5]

10
Sounds

I had intended this to be a full-scale chapter, but fortunately much of what I would have wished to talk about has been discussed already by Michael Irwin in an excellent chapter of his *Reading Hardy's Landscapes* (published by Macmillan as I was preparing to submit my copy), entitled 'Noises in Hardy's Novels' (pp. 37–61). So, instead, this seems a good opportunity to reinforce the points Irwin makes by providing further examples with a minimum of commentary, and a more taxonomic organization.

It will be understood, in the light of the theme of this book, that it is one of the more remarkable aspects of Hardy's evocations of sounds throughout his work, that once written they were almost never revised; there are a few exceptions, which will be noted as they come, but in this aspect of his art he was at once secure. Perhaps he trusted his ear even more than he trusted his eye, and the words to shape his perception came more easily. However it was, we, as tourists in Hardy's virtual country, are made to hear things with a startlingly heightened awareness. Sometimes they seem at the edge of possibility:

> No sign of any other comer greeted her ear, the only perceptible sounds being the tiny cracklings of the dead leaves, which, like a feather bed, had not yet done rising to their normal level where indented by the pressure of her husband's receding footsteps. (*The Woodlanders*: vIII cX)

Perhaps, though, that is because such silence hardly exists in the populated parts of the world any more, even in the country – the kind of underlying silence against which many of Hardy's most acutely perceived sounds are audible. The narrator of 'The Melancholy Hussar' (a story, it will be remembered, that takes place at the beginning of the nineteenth century) makes this point. The heroine in her isolated village longs for someone to come:

> When a noise like the brushing skirt of a visitor was heard on the doorstep, it proved to be a scudding leaf; when a carriage seemed to be nearing the

door, it was her father grinding his sickle on the stone in the garden for his favourite relaxation of trimming the box-tree borders to the plots. A sound like luggage thrown down from the coach was a gun far away at sea... (I)

Though it is his purpose almost universally to educate the visitor to Wessex to listen attentively and to hear accurately, Hardy also knows how easily a strong emotion can lead the brain to misinterpret sensory experience. His narrator, who is the oral storyteller that Hardy imagines for some of his shorter narratives, comments: 'There is no such solitude in country places now as there was in those old days.' This silence, guarded by this solitude, is what allows Phyllis to make her wilful interpretations. At the very beginning of the story – one of the best openings Hardy wrote – the narrator also hears sounds that some may think are not there:

> Here stretch the downs, high and breezy and green... At night when I walk across the lonely place, it is impossible to avoid hearing, amid the scourings of the wind over the grass-bents and thistles, the old trumpet and bugle calls, the rattle of the halters; to help seeing rows of spectral tents and the *impedimenta* of the soldiery. From within the canvases come guttural syllables of foreign tongues... (I)

Irwin notes a similar piece of sympathetic hearing in another first-person narrative, 'Tryst at an Ancient Earthwork' (59), a passage which articulates more openly what is implied here, Hardy's growing belief that many places, perhaps all places, are impregnated with the retrievable record of events that took place there, an idea of which the classic expression is his poem 'At Castle Boterel'.

But these misinterpretations and retrievals of sounds are exceptional, and it was silence I was considering, in this note on noises. Here is another example, this time from *A Pair of Blue Eyes*:

> The faint sounds heard only accented [**accentuated O**] the silence. The rising and falling of the sea, far away along the coast, was the most important. A minor sound was the scurr of a distant night-hawk. Among the minutest where all were minute were the light settlement of gossamer fragments floating in the air, a toad humbly labouring along through the grass near the entrance, the crackle of a dead leaf which a worm was endeavouring to pull into the earth, a waft of air, getting nearer and nearer, and expiring at his feet under the burden of a winged seed.
>
> Among all these soft sounds came not the only soft sound he cared to hear – the footfall of Elfride. (vII cXI)

The silence is the dominant presence, and through it come the slightest of noises. Like Phyllis Grove, Stephen Smith is listening anxiously, intently;

but though he makes no mistakes, is it possible that the most acute human ear could distinguish and identify the settlement of gossamer fragments, or the worm's activity in the soil? It is the silence, such as we do not hear nowadays, that is so intense that it might permit the infinitesimal disturbance of it to be audible. In this particular instance it seems most probable that the remote murmur of the sea would have drowned out the gossamer thread – but Stephen really might have heard, against such silence, the worm's leaf and the toad's progress, and even the faint whirring of the sycamore seed as it spun before him.

It is against this background of silence that some of Hardy's most vivid evocations of a scene through sound are made:

> The breeze had gone down, and the rustle of their feet, and tones of their speech, echoed with an alert rebound from every post, boundary-stone, and ancient wall they passed, even where the distance of the echo's origin was less than a few yards. Beyond their own slight noises nothing was to be heard, save the occasional howl [**occasional bark** O] of foxes in the direction of Yalbury Wood, or the brush of a rabbit among the grass now and then, as it scampered out of their way. (I.iv)

This frosty night walk through Mellstock is from *Under the Greenwood Tree*; the noises here are sharp, crisply defined, echoed – a bark suits this atmosphere so much better than a howl. It is remarkable how the sounds do all the work needed for a satisfying imaginative recreation of the scene by the reader.

There are several occasions when people hear from their windows at night, through the prevailing silence, a solitary traveller on a nearby road:

> The window was open. On this quiet, late summer evening, whatever sound arose in so secluded a district – the chirp of a bird, a call from a voice, the turning of a wheel – extended over bush and tree to unwonted distances. Very few sounds did arise. But as Grace invisibly breathed in the brown glooms of the chamber, the small remote noise of light wheels came into her, accompanied by the trot of a horse on the turnpike road. There seemed to be a sudden hitch or pause in the progress of the vehicle, which was what first drew her attention to it. She knew the point whence the sound proceeded – the hill-top over which travellers passed on their way hitherward from Sherton Abbas – the place at which she had emerged from the wood with Mrs. Charmond. Grace slid along the floor, and bent her head over the window-sill, listening with open lips....
>
> The accident, such as it had been, was soon remedied, and the carriage could be heard descending the hill on the Hintock side, soon to turn into the lane leading out of the highway, and then into the 'drong' which led out of the lane to the house where she was. (*The Woodlanders*: vIII cVII)

As we follow with Grace Fitzpiers' ear the progress of the vehicle through the neighbourhood, we imagine the sounds of different surfaces, of straights and turns. Michael Henchard ironically recognizes the sound of the gig driven by Donald Farfrae:

> At first nothing, beyond his own heart-throbs, was to be heard but the slow wind making its moan among the masses of spruce and larch which clothed the heights on either hand; but presently there came the sound of light wheels whetting their felloes against the newly stoned patches of road, accompanied by the distant glimmer of lights.
> He knew it was Farfrae's gig [**gig descending the hill O**], from an indescribable personality in its noise, the vehicle having been his own till bought by the Scotchman at the sale of his effects. (*The Mayor of Casterbridge*: vII cXVII)

All of these have been night-time passages, when the eyes depend upon the ears. Fog, though, can produce the same effect, as in *Far From the Madding Crowd*:

> The air was as an eye suddenly struck blind...The trees stood in an attitude of intentness, as if they waited longingly for a wind to come and rock them. A startling quiet overhung all surrounding thing – so completely, that the crunching of the waggon-wheels was as a great noise, and small rustles, which had never obtained a hearing except by night, were distinctly individualized. (vII cXII)

The trees are fellows of those in *The Woodlanders*. And in 'The Romantic Adventures of a Milkmaid':

> The noises that ascended through the pallid coverlid were perturbed lowings, mingled with human voices in sharps and flats, and the bark of a dog. These, followed by the slamming of a gate, explained as well as eyesight could have done, to any inhabitant of the district, that Dairyman Tucker's under-milker was driving the cows from the meads into the stalls. (I)

As visitors for the length of a book to Wessex, it is above all in the discrimination of sounds that we are educated by our sole guide. The opening to *Under the Greenwood Tree* is a celebrated example, but this from *Desperate Remedies* is also representative:

> The rain now came down heavily, but they pursued their path with alacrity, the produce of the several fields between which the lane wended

its way being indicated by the peculiar character of the sound emitted by the falling drops. Sometimes a soaking hiss proclaimed that they were passing by a pasture, then a patter would show that the rain fell upon some large-leafed root crop, then a paddling plash announced the naked arable, the low sound of the wind in their ears rising and falling with each pace they took. (vIII cIV.i)

London, though, also has its noises, and the most striking passage recording them comes from *The Well-Beloved*, as Hardy draws the city into relationship with Portland, through the perennial underlying noise heard there, especially in the 1897 Osgood version. In doing so he elaborates on the perception that Pearston/Pierston's life in one place is in the end inseparable from his life in the other:

From the whole scene proceeded a ground rumble, miles in extent, upon which individual rattles, voices, a tin whistle, the bark of a dog, rode like bubbles on a sea. The whole noise impressed him with the sense that no one in its enormous mass ever required rest. (II.xi)

Irwin points out thematic effects achieved by Hardy through sound, but there is one he does not have room for in his argument. *The Mayor of Casterbridge* is instinct with class-distinctions, not to say class-hostility, and it is characteristic that Hardy can hear such difference as well as see it:

Field labourers and their wives and children trooped in from the villages for their weekly shopping, and instead of a rattle of wheels and a tramp of horses ruling the sounds as earlier, there was nothing but the shuffle of many feet. (vII cI)

Finally, I should like to take slight issue with Irwin over what seems a significant detail. In discussing the relationship between human and natural noises Irwin begins with this passage from Hardy's last-completed novel:

The sea moaned – more than moaned – among the boulders below the ruins, a throe of its tide being timed to regular intervals. These sounds were accompanied by an equally periodic moan from the interior of the cottage chamber; so that the articulate heave of water and the articulate heave of life seemed but differing utterances of the self same troubled terrestrial Being – which in one sense they were.
  ...then back again, as he waited there between the travail of the sea without, and the travail of the woman within. Soon an infant's wail of the very feeblest was also audible in the house. (*The Well-Beloved* II.xiii)

and comments 'The sea and the woman are seen as involuntarily expressing, in their different ways, the energies of a single life-force' (47). The argument proceeds for a couple of pages, and reaches the famous passage in *The Return of the Native* in which Hardy's narrator describes the noises of the Heath, ending with the scouring of the heath-bells and Eustacia's long-drawn out sigh, which, the narrator says, 'was but as another phrase of the same discourse as theirs'. At this point Irwin's comment is:

> The girl, the Heath and the breeze would seem to share a common melancholy. But her sigh is surely different in kind from the sounds of Nature as is Oak's flute-playing: the sadness is consciously experienced and rationally explicable. (50)

These two moments when human noise and Nature's noise are brought together in harmony by the narrator seem to me to express the same thought, except that in the later novel Hardy has already let go of many of his obligations to realism, and is able confidently to invoke a 'Being' that is capable of being troubled, and is responsible for both the sea's trouble and the woman's travail. The wind off the landscape and vegetation of Egdon is only another manifestation of the proper anxieties of this Being, (who is given fuller life in many of Hardy's poems, particularly in *Poems from the Past and the Present*), and Eustacia's sigh is as involuntary as the second Avice's cries in labour. Irwin's commentary on the passage from *The Return of the Native* is true from a certain point of view; but I do not believe that is in this instance Hardy's point of view. He alludes to Gabriel's flute-playing:

> The thin grasses, more or less coating the hill, were touched by the wind in breezes of differing powers and almost of differing natures – one rubbing the blades heavily, another raking them piercingly, another brushing them like a soft broom. The instinctive act of human-kind was to stand and listen, and learn how the trees on the right and the trees on the left wailed or chaunted to each other in the regular antiphonies of a cathedral choir; how hedges and other shapes to leeward then caught the note, lowering it to the tenderest sob; and how the hurrying gust then plunged into the south to be heard no more....
>
> Suddenly an unexpected series of sounds began to be heard in this place up against the sky. They had a clearness which was to be found nowhere in the wind, and a sequence which was to be found nowhere in nature. They were the notes of Farmer Oak's flute. (*Far From the Madding Crowd*: vI cII)

The essential difference between Eustacia's sigh and Gabriel's flute-playing is that his noise is a self-consciously arranged series of sounds deliberately produced – that it is an artifact – that it is indeed a manifestation of the consciousness that distinguishes humans from the rest of nature. Irwin goes on to consider the question of music and of aeolian harps in this context.

Near the beginning of his chapter Irwin writes: 'Hardy was exceptional, even among Victorian novelists, for the intensity with which he could imagine a scene, whether an indoor or an outdoor one, having it as vividly present to his ears as his eyes' (40) – and with this I wholeheartedly agree; it is one of the reasons why Wessex is still so alive for readers today.

11
The Languages of Wessex

The languages of Wessex are properly those which Hardy used to convey the concept in all its various forms to his readers. However, this is not the place to begin an investigation of the Englishes Hardy's successive narrators employ, and the focus here will be on 'the Wessex tongue', as one of them calls it in *Jude the Obscure*. Nevertheless, it is worth at least drawing initial attention to the contrasts that everyone feels between the native speakers of Wessex and the literary dialects of those narrators who present them – a contrast that is in itself part of that country–city divide which is a driving force behind the creation and continuing development of Wessex.[1]

The Hand of Ethelberta has become of recent years an important site of fresh critical interest in Hardy's work, and its opening pages provide good material for such a brief investigation:

> she emerged into the summer-evening light with that diamond-and-sceptre bearing – many people for reasons of heredity discovering such graces only in those whose vestibules are lined with ancestral mail, forgetting that a bear may be taught to dance. While this air of hers lasted, even the inanimate objects in the street appeared to know that she was there; but from a way she had of carelessly overthrowing her dignity by versatile moods, one could not calculate upon its presence to a certainty when she was round corners or in little lanes which demanded no repression of animal spirits.

This is Ethelberta Petherwin, the daughter of a butler, but married into the gentry. And the language used to describe her bears out this complexity of social situation. 'Diamond-and-sceptre bearing' functions brilliantly as a compressed expression of her determined superiority to the provincial town she finds herself in; on the other hand the carefully calculated colloquial vulgarity of 'a bear may be taught to dance' works to undercut the implications of 'ancestral mail' and 'vestibule'. Similarly it is characteristic of Hardy's imagination that he should conceive of the buildings and pavements and lamps and so on revealing their awareness of Ethelberta's presence, but it is characteristic also of this stage in his career that he should present the conception in formal abstract terms – 'the inanimate objects in the street' – rather than detailing them, as he might have done later when he was in command of more flexible versions of the formal late-Victorian literary dialect. But then the dignity even of 'versatile moods' is overthrown by the commonplace skipping 'round corners or in little lanes', full of the relief from being on show, from acting a role, places where a lively girl might act naturally, an effect which the alliteration in 'little lanes' helps materially to bring about. This is carefully considered prose; and no less carefully calculated is the shock administered to an unsuspecting standard-English-speaking reader in the next paragraph:

> Well to be sure!... We should freeze in our beds if 'twere not for the sun, and, dang me! if she isn't a pretty piece. A man could make a meal between them eyes and chin – eh, hostler? Odd nation dang my old sides if he couldn't!

This is not 'the Wessex tongue', particularly, though it is certainly rural and non-standard; but it is full of that energy of expression which Hardy habitually associates with dialect speakers. The academic studies of Hardy's dialect have mostly stopped short of considering the phrase-making richness that Hardy brings to his representation of local speech, of which this is as good an example as any. But the reader has to be pretty flexible, for this lively speech is followed by:

> His remarks had been addressed to a rickety person, wearing a waistcoat of that preternatural length from the top to the bottom button which prevails among men who have to do with horses.

This has an uncomfortably knowing, jocular tone, which is only slightly ameliorated by the unusual 'rickety', and which is also often found in Hardy's earlier novels, less commonly in the later.

Towards the end of this first chapter Ethelberta runs across some heathland trying to keep in view the attempt of a duck to escape from a buzzard. During this chase, Hardy makes, in a characteristically close-focussed way, an observation about how her footprints appeared on the ground she covered, but here again, it is the language he uses that I want to draw attention to. It begins with another of those rather falsely jocular details, but soon gathers imaginative intensity:

> being a woman slightly heavier than gossamer, her patent heels punched little D's in the soil with unerring accuracy whenever it was bare, crippled

the heather-twigs where it was not, and sucked the swampy places with a sound of quick kisses.

Who else would risk the 'little D's', given life by 'punched'; who else would think of the casual pain inflicted on the heather-stalks? But it is in 'and sucked the swampy places with a sound of quick kisses' that Hardy shows his skill: the alliteration and internal rhyme draw attention to the kisses, and thus provide the reader with an unconsciously registered introduction to her imminent meeting with her former lover Christopher Julian. No reader could notice the connection at first reading, but it is none the less there, and that Hardy deliberately planned for it is rendered more likely by the similar use of a kiss – of a grapnel on well water – at the first daylight meeting between Clym and Eustacia in his next novel *The Return of the Native*. (III.iii)

It is too much of a generalization to say that Hardy works best in his fiction when in his narrative dialects he uses predominately simple, common words, but it is certainly possible to pile up a convincing mass of evidence along the lines of this tiny sample I have offered. Finally, *The Hand of Ethelberta* offers a relatively rare opportunity to look at Hardy's representation of the dialect of Society with a capital S. Here is another brief sample; two ladies are discussing Ethelberta:

'She has apparently a very good prospect.'
'Yes; and it is through her being of that curious undefined character which interprets itself to each admirer as whatever he would like to have it. Old men like her because she is so girlish; youths because she is womanly; wicked men because she is good in their eyes; good men because she is wicked in theirs.'
'She must be a very anomalous sort of woman, at that rate.'
'Yes. Like the British Constitution, she owes her success in practice to her inconsistencies in principle.'
'These poems must have set her up. She appears to be quite the correct spectacle. Happy Mrs. Petherwin!' (X)

If Hardy ever wrote, in the words of the Athenaeum critic of *The Return of the Native*, dialogue in a language that was or is never spoken, this is it; though the internal rhyme that he cannot resist, in 'correct spectacle', is thoroughly engaging. 'Spectacle' is such an improbable word in the context that Hardy is mischievous in using it, and indeed the whole succession of artificialities masquerading as speech makes clear – too clear – his satiric intent.[2]

It is, though, essentially the Wessex dialect that is the focus here – the grammar and the vocabulary. In this, William Barnes was the authority. As an introduction to his *Poems of Rural Life in the Dorset Dialect* (first published in 1844) he had written a thorough 'Dissertation on the Dorset Dialect', and as an appendix he included a substantial glossary, both of which were revised until a fifth edition appeared in 1866. If Hardy knew the book before he began to write, then he would have found in it, laid out in systematic fashion, analysis of the language he heard about him every day, and had most likely been accustomed to hear his mother denigrate as a barrier to social advancement. He would have read these aggressive claims, and seen them substantiated in what followed:

> The Dorset dialect is a broad and bold shape of the English language, as the Doric was of the Greek. It is rich in humour, strong in raillery and hyperbole; and, altogether, as fit a vehicle of rustic feeling and thought, as the Doric as found in the *Idyllia* of Theocritus.
> Some people, who may have been taught to consider it as having originated from corruption of the written English, may not be prepared to hear that it is not only a separate offspring from the Anglo-Saxon tongue, but purer, and in some cases richer, than the dialect which is chosen as the national speech; purer inasmuch as it retains many words of Saxon origin, for which the English substitutes others of Latin, Greek, or French derivation; and richer, inasmuch as it has distinctive words for many things which book-English can hardly distinguish but by periphrasis...
> (Second Edition, London: John Russell Smith, 1847, pp. 15–16)

As a young man Hardy knew Barnes, and it may have been that in conversation with him in his teens Hardy was made aware of the purity and richness of the local language, and of its ancient origins in Wessex. But whether through speech or writing, it seems most likely that Hardy would have experienced the passion of Barnes's ideas by the time he began to write *Desperate Remedies*. Certainly his practice in that novel is more often close to Barnes' than in any that came after. Here is a specimen of dialogue from the first edition, including the changes made by subsequent revision (**WD**= Ward and Downey one-volume edition 1889, **O** = Osgood, **W** = Wessex):

> 'Our friend here pulled proper well – that 'a did – seën [**seeing O**] he's but a stranger,' said Clerk Crickett, who had just resigned the second rope, and addressing the man in the black coat.
> ''A did:' said the rest.
> 'I enjoyed it much,' said the man, modestly.
> 'What we should ha' done 'ithout ye [**without you O**], words can't tell. The man that d'belong [**belongs W**] by rights to that there bell is ill o' two gallons o' wold [**old W**] cider.'
> 'And now so's,' remarked the fifth ringer, as pertaining to the last allusion, 'we'll finish this drop o' metheglin and cider, and every man home-along straight as a line.'
> 'Wi' [**With W**] all my heart,' Clerk Crickett replied. 'And the Lord send if I ha'n't done my duty by Master Teddy Springrove – that I have so.'

'And the rest o' [**of W**] us,' they said, as the cup was handed round.

'Ay, ay – in ringen – but I was spaken in a spiritual sense o' this mornen's business o' mine up by the chancel rails there. 'Twas very convenient to lug her here and marry her instead o' do'en [**doen WD**] it at that twopenny-halfpenny town o' Cres'n [**Budm'th O**]. Very convenient.' (vIII epilogue)

Most of what Hardy records here as deviation from standard English or 'book English' as Barnes calls it, is documented in Barnes' 'dissertation', to which the reader is referred. It is evident that in this pre-Wessex novel, the local dialect conforms with the Dorset dialect, to the degree that the two may be taken as identical. In the above example it will be seen that the revisions return some of the Dorset to English, though only the word with the en ending that required a dieresis is altered. Contrast this with a passage somewhat earlier:

Now you'll hardly believe me, neighbour, but this little scene in front of us d'make [**makes WD**] me feel less anxious about pushen [**pushing WD**] on wi' that threshen [**threshing WD**] and winnowen [**winnowing WD**] next week, that I was speaken [**speaking WD**] about. Why should we not stand still, says I to myself, and fling a quiet eye upon the Whys and the Wherefores, before the end of [**o' O**] it all, and we d'go [**go WD**] down into the moulderen [**mouldering WD**] place, and are forgotten?'

"Tis a feelen [**feeling WD**] that will come. But 'twont bear looken [**looking WD**] into. There's a backward [**back'ard O**] current in the world, and we must do our utmost to advance in order just to bide where we be. But, Baker, they are turnen [**turning WD**] in here with the coffin, look. (vIII cVIII.i)

Here Hardy decided to eliminate the en endings for the 1889 edition as well as twice removing the abbreviated auxiliary verb 'd" (Barnes transcribes this as 'da', saying that verbs are frequently conjugated thus in Dorset [p. 39]). Why he let the previous dialogue alone, it is impossible to say; but there is inconsistency in his practice for the Osgood, McIlvaine revision also. In the first-quoted passage it is in Osgood that the auxiliary 'd" is removed, and ''ithout ye' standardized to 'without you', but here during the same process of revision Hardy altered 'of' to 'o'' and 'backward' to 'back'ard'. Later on during the same discussion it was not until Osgood that Hardy noticed how far he had been enticed by the philosophical content of Farmer Springrove's thought, to allow him to wander into book English:

'A very plain box for the poor soul – just the rough elm, you see.' The corner of the cloth had blown aside.

'Yes, for a very poor man. Well, death's all the less insult to him. I have often thought how far the richer class sink into insignificance beside the poor on extreme occasions [**poor at last pinches O**] like this. Perhaps the greatest of all the reconcilers of a thoughtful mind to poverty – and I speak from experience – is the grand quietness [**grand quiet** O] it possesses [**it fills** O] him with when the uncertainty of his life shows itself more vividly [**more** O] than usual.'

Really the changes do no more than gesture at a return to rural speech by eliminating one or two of the improbable phrases; 'sink into insignificance' and 'the reconcilers of a thoughtful mind to poverty' still remain.[3]

In several novels Hardy represents the dialects of other regions, and they will be noted as they come; in *Desperate Remedies* there is a nice brief example of a Dorset speaker attempting to imitate an RP speaker: '...this time she said, in a very particular ladylike tone, "Roobert, gaow with the pony-kerriage"' (vI cV.i). Farmer Springrove's man Gad Weedy says of Cytherea Graye: 'I could tell by the tongue o' her that she didn't take her degrees in our country' (vI cVIII.iii), and there are places to be mentioned in other narratives where people are similarly distinguished by their dialects.

Dorset speakers in *Desperate Remedies* have relatively little place in the action, but in *Under the Greenwood Tree* everyone except the vicar, Farmer Shiner and Fancy Day speaks the dialect to a greater or lesser degree. In *Desperate Remedies* the grammar and the pronunciation had been Dorset, but there was relatively little that was lexically unique to the region; this changes in *Under the Greenwood Tree*: 'If so be I hadn't been as scatter-brained and thirtingill as a chiel, I should have called at the schoolhouse wi' a boot as I cam up-along' (I.iii). This is Mr Penny, who a little later draws a last from his pocket: 'Yes, a very quaint humorous [**very queer natered** O; **very queer natured** W] last it is now, 'a b'lieve', where we can see repeated in small the kind of revisions examined at greater length in considering *Desperate Remedies*. To begin to understand why critics took Hardy to task for writing unintelligible dialogue there is this from Reuben Dewy's father, talking to Geoffrey Day:

'What wi' one thing, and what wi' 'tother, he's all in a mope, as m't [**as might** W] be said. Don't seem the feller 'a [**he** W] used to. Ay, 'a will sit studding and thinking as if 'a were going to turn chapel-member, and then 'a don't do nothing but traypsing and wambling about. Used to be such a chatty feller, too, Dick did; and now 'a don't spak [**speak** W] at all. But won't ye stap [**step** W] inside? Reuben will be home soon, 'a b'lieve. (IV.iv)

A standard English speaker might be grateful that Hardy used the 'ing' ending for participles. Perhaps 'traypsing and wambling' are difficult, but their general sense is clear enough; otherwise there is nothing by itself that would warrant the use of 'unintelligible', but the cumulative effect is very alien indeed from the majority of Hardy's upper-middle-class readership.

It is part of one of the themes of Wessex that each generation in his novels speaks less dialect than the one that came before it. Here Dick Dewy the tranter's son uses somewhat less dialect than his father, while Fancy Day, having been trained as a schoolteacher, has none at all, though her father and Reuben Dewy meet on equal terms in this respect, even though, by the Wessex edition, Day is a man of much responsibility.

Mrs Dewy is continually sniping at her husband, and his pronunciation is only one of many targets:

> And did you ever hear too – just now at supper-time – talking about 'taties' with Michael in such a labourer's way. Well, 'tis what I was never brought up to! With our family 'twas never less than 'taters,' and very often 'pertatoes' outright; mother was so particular and nice with us girls: there was no family in the parish that kept theirselves up more than we. (I.viii)

She is making real class distinctions here, and making it clear that a way of speaking marks the speaker socially; only Day's trapper Enoch in the novel would think of himself as a labourer, though evidently Reuben Dewy had picked up bad habits. The others were craftsmen and small businessmen and their wives – independent men and women; though it is never quite clear what Michael Mail does. But of course there is another level of irony working between the narrator and his readership here, for Mrs Dewy's speech – even her family-best way of pronouncing 'potatoes' – marks her just as vividly as socially inferior to Hardy's audience, and they are invited to find her pretentiousness comic.

With *A Pair of Blue Eyes* Hardy faced a potential problem, since the dialect speakers of this novel were not of Dorset, but of Cornwall, and though he had been visiting that county for two or three years, he had not grown up hearing the language every day, or speaking it. He solved the problem by not distinguishing between the two counties. The workfolk use much the same locutions as we are already familiar with from the earlier two novels – here is a brief example:

> 'I seed her, poor soul,' said a labourer from behind some removed coffins, 'only but last Valentine's-day of all the world. 'A was arm in crook wi' my lord. I says to myself, "You be ticketed Churchyard, my noble lady, although you don't dream on't."' (vII cXIII)

Though in general there is not a lot of revision to dialect in this novel, the pattern is similar to the others, in that in Osgood Hardy tended to add a little and in Wessex to remove some. The one striking exception to this pattern is in Volume III Chapter IX, in which Stephen Smith's parents gain reflected status from his success as an architect in India; their speech is altered to reflect their new position, though whether Hardy intended readers to think that because they were more highly thought of they suddenly began to speak a more standard English is doubtful. Most of this alteration away from dialect forms is done in 1895, and is the more significant because it goes against the general trend for that edition. It is part of another pattern that holds throughout Hardy's fiction, that of gentrification, by which in successive revisions from the manuscript onwards certain characters – occasionally, as in *The Return of the Native*, all the protagonists – are elevated in social rank. We have already met this in Keeper Day of *Under the Greenwood Tree*. It is hard to know why Hardy did this; in part it seems to be a response to criticisms from some editors and reviewers that if he succeeded as a novelist it was in spite of having no characters of a class and education (and thus with concerns and values) to be of intrinsic interest to most readers. Depending upon your point of view, this gentrification might be called a failure of nerve, or a shrewd marketing ploy. In *Far From the Madding Crowd* Troy's noble ancestry was added late, and augmented later still, while Oak at first was just a shepherd, though the signs of his origins are mostly hidden in fragments of the manuscript – indeed when he first appears as the fledgling sheep-farmer in freshly written manuscript pages he has almost no dialect in his speech at all. The first hint had to be added as a revision in the manuscript (Hardy made this particular revision intermittently throughout every text in the Wessex edition):

> 'How can I thank ye [**you MS deleted**; 'ee W],' he said at last gratefully... (vI cIII)

Another speech shows clearly how Hardy's thoughts worked with Oak over the long period from 1874 to 1901:

> 'Because I am open enough to own what every man in my position [**my shoes O**] would have [**ha' MS**] thought of, you make your colours come up your face, and get crabbed with me. That about your [**about you W**] not being good enough for me is nonsense. You speak like a lady – all the parish notice it, and your uncle at Weatherbury is, I have heard [**heerd O**], a large farmer – much larger than ever I shall be. May [**Mid O1 only**] I call in the evening, or will you walk along with me on [**me o' O**] Sundays?' (vI cIV)

In revising proof for *Cornhill*, Hardy even felt that the mild indicator of local pronunciation 'ha'' was too extreme for Oak, but by 1895 he had changed his mind, and added a different Wessex formation, this time a grammatical distinction, in that the verb to hear in Dorset dialect is weak, so that the past tense is sounded as Osgood spells it. The paperback alteration is also to the Dorset form of the auxiliary verb. By the time of this revision in 1901 the speech has at least hints that Oak is a dialect speaker, or that he retains part of his dialect heritage.

When the editor of *Cornhill*, Leslie Stephen, read the last-but-one episode of the novel in proof he wrote to Hardy 'it seemed to me in one or two cases that your rustics – specially Oak – speak rather too good English towards the end. They seem to drop the dialect a little. But of this you are the best judge.' (Bibliographical study p. 339) This is very strange, for Oak speaks almost perfect standard English throughout his residence on the Everdene farm:

> 'You can bring up some reed-sheaves to me, one by one, ma'am; if you are not afraid to come up the ladder in the dark,' said Gabriel. 'Every moment is precious now, and that would save a good deal of time. It is not very dark when the lightning has been gone a bit.' (vII cVII)

The most dialect he rises to is a very occasional 'bain't' or 'ye'. Hardy was well aware of the distinction he was drawing through speech between shepherd Oak and the other labourers, but he was so responsive to Stephen's criticisms that when he got the proofs of the last two episodes himself, he set about making changes:

> I hope that nothing so dreadful hangs on [**dreadful attaches MS**] to it as you fancy. His natural manner has always been dark and strange, you know. But since the case is so sad and odd-like [**and peculiar MS**], why don't ye give the conditional promise? I think I would.'... (vII cXXI)

The effect is to change Oak anomalously from a standard-English speaker to one partly educated out of the dialect, but still rooted within it.

There is otherwise nothing specially noteworthy about the handling of dialect in *Far From the Madding Crowd*, but the case is quite otherwise in *The Hand of Ethelberta*. This is the novel above all others in which Hardy is alert to class-distinctions of all sorts, and as we have seen already the degree of the use of dialect is, amongst other things, a marker of class. The tone is set for the novel by the dialogue between an ostler and the milkman in the first chapter that has already been quoted. Later on Ethelberta moves most of her family to a big house in London, where they act as her servants. Gwendolen, who is the cook, finds out that they do not speak the same language in town:

> Well, as I was a-coming home-along I thought, 'Please the Lord I'll have some chippols for supper just for a plane trate,' and I went round to the late greengrocer's for 'em; and do you know they sweared me down that they hadn't got such things as chippols in the shop, and had never heard of 'em in their lives....

Most readers would side with the greengrocer, and the sequel is: '"They call them young onions here," said Ethelberta quietly; "you must always remember that"' (XXV) – demonstrating the lexical richness of all dialects in general and the Wessex dialect in particular. Young Joey Chickerel, who is a footman in Ethelberta's establishment, is better at acquiring the London note; here he talks with his sister Picotee:

> 'Does Mr. Julian come to see her very often?' said she.
> 'Oh, yes – he's always a-coming – a regular bore to me.'
> 'A regular what?'
> 'Bore! – Ah, I forgot, you don't know our town words.' (XX)

In fact Joey has both Wessex and London in his first brief speech here. A little later Joey and Picotee have another conversation:

> ''Tis yer ignorance of town life that makes it seem a good deal to ye.'
> 'You can't make much boast about town life; for you haven't left off talking just as they do down in Wessex.'
> 'Well, I own to that – what's fair is fair, and 'tis a true charge; but if I talk the Wessex way 'tisn't for want of knowing better; 'tis because my staunch nater makes me bide faithful to our old ancient institutions....' (XX)

Wessex, it seems, is more resistant to urban influences than might be expected.

The long third chapter of *The Return of the Native*, in which the heath-dwellers discuss affairs around the November-the-fifth bonfire, has the most intense concentration of dialect speech yet in a Hardy novel, and in particular of Wessex words probably unfamiliar to Hardy's readership. It begins with the deliberate insertion in a manuscript revision of a dialect word and its gloss:

> With a speäker, or stake, [**With a hedge-stake, MS1**] he tossed the outlying scraps of fuel into the conflagration (I.iii)

And there follows in the same chapter a sequence of similar words:

> 'A fair stave, Grandfer Cantle; but I am afeard 'tis too much for the mouldy weasand of such a old man as you,'
>
> neither vell nor mark have been seen of 'em since
>
> '...I saw [**seed MS, B; zid O**] myself as the next poor stunpoll [**next fool MS1**] to get into the same mess [**puxy MS**].... Ah – well, what a day 'twas!'

This last is an interesting brief passage; there will be more to say of the versions of 'saw' later, but there are also opposing impulses at work; in the manuscript Hardy wanted as much dialect as he could manage, but gradually it is eroded in revision for the serial and for the first edition – then partially reinstated in 1895.[4]

Such a display of the resources of the Wessex language may well have provoked some readers to irritation at being forced to puzzle through unfamiliar words in an English novel, and it brought this response from the critic of the *Athenaeum*: 'People talk as no people ever talked before, or perhaps we should rather say as no people ever talk now.' This review (23 November 1878) stimulated Hardy to respond for once in a letter to the same journal, published a week later:

> An author may be said fairly to convey the spirit of intelligent peasant talk if he retains the idiom, compass and characteristic expressions, although he may not encumber the page with obsolete pronunciations of the purely English words, and with the mispronunciation of those derived from Latin and Greek. In the printing of standard speech hardly any phonetic principle at all is observed; and if a writer attempts to exhibit on paper the precise accents of a rustic speaker he disturbs the proper balance of true representation by unduly insisting upon the grotesque element; thus directing attention to a point of inferior interest, and diverting it from the speaker's meaning, which is by far the chief concern where the aim is to depict the men and their natures rather than their dialect forms. *Thomas Hardy's Personal Writings*, (ed.) H. Orel (London: Macmillan, 1967), p. 91.

In fact this ambiguous statement (evidently far from William Barnes's practice in his poems in the Dorset dialect) does not really address the point made by the *Athenaeum* reviewer, who had continued:

> The language of his peasants may be Elizabethan, but it can hardly be Victorian. Such phrases as 'being a man of mournfullest make, I was scared a little,' or 'he always had his great indignation ready against anything underhand,' are surprising in the mouth of a modern rustic.

There is no attack on the dialect element in their speech here, but his point is rather that their language is pitched 'too high' (as he later avers), apparently considering that Shakespearean workfolk were capable of more in such a line. That his rural working class expressed ideas of too great a sophistication for credibility was a common criticism of Hardy's novels throughout his career. But why Hardy should choose to misinterpret the comment is unclear, though there is certain amount of evidence that he had considered the issue his letter addresses a few weeks earlier, in reading through the proofs for the first edition of *The Return of the Native*.

In the Wessex dialect many verbs that are strong in English remain weak, and he revised a number of such Wessex past tenses (though some remain), perhaps thinking that they added no particular richness to speech, while distracting a reader by their oddness:

> 'Yes, I knew [**knowed MS; know'd B**] of such a man,' he said. (I.iii)
>
> 'No, that's true. But 'tis a melancholy thing, and my blood ran [**runned MS; runn'd B**] cold when you spoke, for I felt [**feeled; MS feel'd B**] there were two poor fellows [**fellers MS, B**] where I had thought only one. (I.iii)
>
> 'Twas a little boy that saw [**seed MS, B; zid O**] it. (I.iii)
>
> 'Surely, surely that's never the same man that I seed [**zid O; saw W**] handling the clarinet so masterly by now!' (I.v)
>
> But I saw [**zeed O**] her the morning of the same day (V.ii)

The case of the Wessex equivalent of 'saw' is interesting, as the last three examples show. Hardy was inconsistent throughout the novel's many layers of revision, in several different ways. Inconsistency is not a weakness. Hardy was under no obligation to do anything other than present what seemed to him right in a particular instance at a particular time; so when at least one instance of 'seed' was permitted to remain in the first edition, when he wavered in the Osgood edition between 'zid' and 'zeed', and that occasionally in 1912 he felt he had to revert to standard English, it only shows that a range of possibilities was available on Egdon and he had to decide amongst them each time the word came up in the speech of a character who might be supposed to speak the dialect to some degree. Similar variety of form can be found in most of his novels.

At the beginning of *The Trumpet-Major* Hardy explains how Mrs Garland, who thinks of herself as a gentlewoman, and her daughter Anne, come to share the mill-house at Overcombe with Miller Loveday – and considers some of the consequences:

> Those who have lived in remote places where there is what is called no society will comprehend the gradual levelling of distinctions that went on, in this case at some sacrifice of gentility on the part of one household. The widow was sometimes sorry to find with what readiness Anne caught up some dialect-word or accent from the miller and his friends... (I)

In fact in the first part of the manuscript of the novel Anne speaks quite a lot of dialect, which mostly gets erased for the serialization in *Good Words*, as if the dialect were indeed a plague. Festus Derriman also speaks rather more standard English in the serial than in the manuscript, but his speech is still full of what Hardy's reviewers probably thought of as linguistic eccentricities: for instance, he calls his miserly uncle a 'scram, blue-vinnied gallicrow' (IX), and 'a regular sniche one' (VI), to which last his uncle's man Cripplestraw responds mockingly:

> Gentlefolks shouldn't talk so. And an officer, Mr. Derriman! 'Tis the duty of all calvery gentlemen to bear in mind that their blood is a knowed thing in the country, and not to speak ill o't.

There were also two systematic proof-changes to the language of the manuscript that are of passing interest. One is the cancellation in the *Good Words* proofs of anything that might possibly be construed as swearing in Festus Derriman's speech – hence 'Gad, it is though' becomes 'But it is, though' (XXV); all his nicely extended 'Daam's' are excluded also, as when 'Daam me – why – 'tis Uncle Benjy!...Nunc, why how the devil's this?' becomes 'Scrounch it – why – it is Uncle Benjy!...Nunc, why how's this?' (IX. This speech was returned to its manuscript form in the first edition.) The bowdlerization was evidently undertaken at the insistence of the editor of *Good Words*, a religious gentleman of a dissenting persuasion.

The other kind of change came when, part way through the composition of the novel Hardy had the idea of getting his naval Loveday brother to use nautical language whenever possible. Unfortunately there was already a fair amount of Bob's speech in manuscript pages already sent to the printer, so Hardy had to make appropriate changes on the proofs as they came; 'she's living here' became in *Good Words* 'she's signed articles and got a berth here' (XIX), or 'I can go away that day' became 'I can sheer off that day' (XX). The most striking instance of addition of this special nautical dialect is when 'an angel of light' becomes 'a mermaiden of light' (XXXVIII) – which might be thought to be taking an interesting idea a little far.

In the stories that Hardy began writing about this time, and carried on writing after he had in his own mind given up on novels, there is not enough space for much richness of dialect to be worth a note, given Hardy's published ideas as to the proper approach to its representation; but there are a few isolated details that help to build the picture of the Wessex language. A character, for example, in 'The Three Strangers' is placed by his accent and perhaps vocabulary. Mrs Fennel asks the first stranger:

> 'One of hereabouts?' she inquired.
> 'Not quite that – further up the country.'
> 'I thought so. And so be I; and by your tongue you come from my neighbourhood.'
> 'But you would hardly have heard of me' he said quickly. 'My time would be long before yours ma'am, you see.'

Hardy makes no attempt to represent such fine distinctions, but he lets us know that he is well aware of them, and implies that he too would be able to distinguish between a native of Dorchester and a native of Wareham or Blandford. Wessex speech has a linguistic base, an established grammar, but there are local words and local accents that make distinct pocket after pocket of villages – or there were, before the erosive effect of the railways and national schools began to be felt by the 1870s and 80s – though in *Tess of the d'Urbervilles* the narrator notes:

> Even the character and accent of the two peoples had shades of difference, despite the amalgamating effects of a roundabout railway; so that though less than twenty miles from the place of her sojourn at Trantridge, her native village had seemed a far-away spot. (XII)

'Fellow-Townsmen' is notable for being the first fiction of Hardy's that has no dialect in it at all, and there is not very much in *A Laodicean* either, which, considering the main characters and the plot, is hardly surprising. What there is, mainly on the tongue of the landlord of the inn at Sleeping-Green, was, until the Osgood edition moved the site of the novel from somewhere in the region of Corfe Castle in Dorset to Dunster in Somerset, not particularly emphatic. But by 1896 this had changed quite dramatically. Here is an example:

> 'I have often noticed,' observed the landlord, 'that folks [**volks O**] who have come to grief, and quite failed, have the rules how to succeed in life more at their fingers' [**vingers' O**] ends than folks [**volks O**] who have succeeded.... He was the star, as I may say [**zay O only**], of fashion [**of good company 1v**] forty years ago. I remember him in the height of his splendour [**jinks 1v**], as I used to see [**zee O only**] him when I was a very little boy, and think how great and wonderful he was. I can seem to see [**zee O only**] now the exact style of his clothes ... and his handsome [**his jonnick O**] face, as white as his clothes with keeping late hours. There was nothing black about him but his hair and his eyes – he wore no beard at that time – and they were black indeed [**black as slooes O**].' (I.v)

The dialect pattern in such speeches is different from any found elsewhere. It is quite unusual for so much material to be changed in the one-volume edition of a Hardy novel – indeed in *The Trumpet-Major* he gave up revising altogether less than a quarter of the way through the book. As far as the Osgood edition changes are concerned, the heavier emphasis than usual on the initial 'z' suggests that Hardy was trying in a small way to suggest Somerset, where this feature of pronunciation was even more marked than in Dorset. But he was always suspicious of this method of indicating dialect, and in 1912 they all get eliminated. The reason for this is not far to seek – as far as the introduction that Hardy wrote to his selection from the poems of William Barnes in 1908, in fact:

> For some reason, or none, many persons suppose that when anything is penned in the tongue of the countryside, the primary intent is burlesque or ridicule, and this especially if the speech be one in which the sibilant has the rough sound, and is expressed by Z. Indeed scores of thriving storytellers and dramatists seem to believe that by transmitting the flattest conversations into a dialect that never existed, and making the talkers say 'be' where they would really say 'is', a Falstaffian richness is at once imparted to its qualities.

He may well have decided that he looked in this speech, and in the few others like it in *A Laodicean*, to be in danger of falling under the lash of his own bitter criticism.

As *A Laodicean* was drawing to a close in *Harpers*, Hardy read in the *Spectator* a review of Volume VII of *Papers of the Manchester Literary Club* (15 October 1881). Included in the collection was an essay on George Eliot's handling of dialect, and the *Spectator* reviewer, in approving of Eliot's practice, berated Hardy, along with George Macdonald, 'whose thorough knowledge of the dialectal peculiarities of certain districts has tempted them to write whole conversations which are, to the ordinary reader, nothing but a series of linguistic puzzles'. Hardy at once responded; his initial point is substantially the same as he had made three years earlier, but a subsequent note of regret is new – or at least newly made public:

> It must of course always be a matter for regret that in order to be understood, writers should be obliged thus slightingly to treat varieties of English which are intrinsically as genuine, grammatical and worthy of the royal title as the all-prevailing competitor which bears it... *Personal Writings* (pp. 92–3)

Given that one reader at least thought that he was already creating 'linguistic puzzles' with his dialect speech as it stood, it is hardly surprising that Hardy should reject the representation of full Wessex in his novels on the grounds that it would only be understood by a tiny minority of his readers – however highly he valued it and desired its preservation. However, in the novel he was beginning to write, *Two on a Tower*, Hardy took some pains to introduce in the relatively few exchanges amongst working people a rather high density of dialectal individuality – particularly in the speech of Amos (or rather Haymoss) Fry:

> 'Yes, my lady,' said Haymoss; 'a homely barley driller, born under the very eavesdroppings [the eaves O] of your ladyship's smallest [**ladyship's** O] out-buildings, in a manner of speaking, – though your ladyship was neither born nor 'tempted at that time.' (vI cI)

It is unusual for Hardy to feel he had to cancel any idiosyncracy of speech in the Osgood edition. This passage and others like it come from the opening of the novel, and it may be that the correspondence with the *Spectator* stimulated him to a little more aggression on the side of Wessex speech. Another fragment shows that he was aware that his critics might have had a point on occasion about the kind of language his workfolk use:

> 'Did ye bring along the flagon, Haymoss? Then we'll sit down inside's boarden house [**inside his little board-house** O] here and wait. He'll come afore bed-time. Why, his spy-glass will stretch out that there comet as long as Welland Lane!'
> 'I'd as soon miss the great peep-show that comes every year to Greenhill Fair as a sight of such a immortal spectacle as this!' said Amos Fry.
> '"Immortal spectacle," – where did ye get that choice morsel [**mossel** O], Haymoss?' inquired Sammy Blore. 'Well, well, the Lord save good scholars – and take jist [**just** O] a bit o' care of them that bain't!' (vI cXIII)

Again Hardy altered a good Wessex formation in the adjective 'boarden', perhaps because he thought some standard-English readers might mistake it for 'boarding'; but it is Blore's comment on 'immortal spectacle' that is particularly striking – attempting to draw the sting from the next round of hostile reviewers.

The group of workfolk comment on the state of affairs at the end of this novel as they do in others; the difference in *Two on a Tower* is that Hardy is more alert to the possibilities of dialect words. Despite the fact that the narrative for the most part passes them by, despite the fact that many readers might take them for decorative irrelevancies, Hardy is asserting their significance as representatives of the men and women whose connection with the land of Wessex is the most intimate of all, and whose speech demonstrates their independence of the world of economic and social power from which Lady Constantine comes and to which Swithin aspires. Hardy does almost write deliberate linguistic puzzles for that class in these final pages. This is Hezzy Biles:

> 'Well, Mr. San Cleeve,' Hezzy replied, 'when you've said that a few stripling boys and maidens have busted into blooth, and a few married women have plimmed and chimped (my lady among 'em), why, you've said anighst all, Mr. San Cleeve.' (vIII cXII)

When Hardy returned with his wife to Dorchester he renewed his acquaintance with William Barnes, and it may not be too much to suggest that a new tone and a new richness in the language of the working people of Casterbridge owes something to the refreshing commitment of the older poet to the Dorset dialect; but also he did not lose the combativeness implied in what we have just seen from *Two on a Tower*. Barnes wrote in his dissertation on the Dorset dialect that it 'is rich in humour, strong in raillery and hyperbole', and the talk at the King of Prussia or Peter's Finger bears this out more vividly that in any of Hardy's novels to date – particularly where raillery is concerned. It would be good to give a substantial quotation here, for this is exactly what most of those university-educated critics objected to, who did not believe that Wessex 'boors' or 'clowns' had command of so fertile a vocabulary as Hardy gave them; but here is a fragment of the dialogue about Michael Henchard's marriage to Susan Newson (the whole is in **wsLanguage**):

> '... do ye mind?'
> 'I do, hee-hee, I do!' said Christopher Coney.
> And well do I – for I was getting up husband-high at that time – one-half girl, and t'other half woman, as one may say.- And canst mind' – she prodded Solomon's shoulder with her finger-tip while her eyes twinkled between the crevices of their lids – 'canst mind the sherry-wine, and the silver [**zilver** O] snuffers, and how Joan Dummett was took bad when we were coming home, and Jack Griggs was forced to carry [**carr' MS**] her through the mud; and how 'a let her fall in Dairyman Sweetapple's cow-barton, and we had to clane her gown wi' grass – never such a mess as 'a were in?'
> Ay – that I do – hee-hee – such doggery as there was in them ancient days to be sure! Ah, the miles I used to walk then; and now I can hardly step over a furrow! (vI cXIII)

The rhythm and the liveliness of the discussion are what strike the reader most forcibly, despite occasional moments of impenetrability for a standard speaker. Hardy has learned how to be more flexible since *Far From the Madding Crowd*.

Michael Henchard uses the dialect to a degree, though Hardy probably gives him less dialectal forms than he imagined him using, because he is the central character. It is psychologically acute that when he wishes to hurt Elizabeth-Jane because she is not after all his daughter, he uses language, that ready marker of class. He has risen in spite of his tongue, but he is well aware that he is an anomaly as mayor of the town, as chief merchant; his social position demands a different language, and once he cannot love Elizabeth, he cannot condone her dialect. She reforms her speech, but occasionally relapses (**G** indicates readings in the *Graphic*):

> 'Well, where have you been?' he said to her, with off-hand laconism.
> 'I've been strolling in the Walks and churchyard, father, till I feel quite leery.' She clapped her hand to her mouth, but too late.

This was just enough to incense Henchard after the other crosses of the day. 'I *won't* have you talk like that!' he thundered. [**thundered – 'the lowest in the town don't use such words.'** G]. '"Leery," indeed. [*omit* **"Leery," indeed.** G] One would think you worked upon a farm. One day I learn that you lend a hand in public-houses. Then I hear you ['**ee** G] talk like a clodhopper. I'm burned, if it goes on, this house can't hold us two.' (vI cXX)

The manuscript is missing here, so the *Graphic* version is the earliest we have; the first edition perhaps changed "ee' to 'you' in order to make the contrast with Elizabeth a little stronger, but at the same time it blunts the irony that underlies Henchard's criticism. When, in the same chapter, Elizabeth-Jane goes to stay with Lucetta Le Sueur, she learns that another attitude is possible:

'I am no accomplished person. And a companion to *you*, dear madam, [*you* 1vol] must be that.'
'Oh, not necessarily.'
'Not? But I can't help using rural words [**Not? – will it do if one can't** [***can't kerp and MS2***] **talk** [*G* misreads the MS2 addition as *if one can't help talking*] **the up-country way? It makes me sorry, but I can't help using work-folk words MS1, HW**] sometimes, when I don't mean to.'
'Never mind. I shall like to know them.' [**the whole passage added in MS**] (1.262)

The reader might feel that attitude to the dialect in both instances is only a manifestation of an underlying emotional response to Elizabeth-Jane herself; but at the same time Lucetta, with her new financial security and the independence that comes with it, can afford to treat the dialect as a quaint and interesting manifestation of difference, whereas Henchard has to deal with it everyday in the marketplace, and cannot but recognize its social significance. Farfrae, of course, has his own regional voice, but as it is alien to Wessex it is no barrier to him.

When (as rarely in this novel) a farm-labourer speaks, it is in thorough Wessex from the start, and Hardy only finds a minor element of accent to change in 1895: 'If ye'd been minding your business instead of zwailing along in such a gawkhammer way, you would have seed [**zeed** O] me!' (vII cIV). A critical reader might, however, wonder why 'your' is not 'yer', 'of' is not 'o'' and 'you would have' is not 'you'd ha''. Hardy had already responded to this kind of criticism in his public letters on the matter, but not everyone was prepared to accept that 'scrupulously preserving the local idiom, together with the words which have no synonym among those in general use, while printing in the ordinary way most of those local expressions which are but a modified articulation of words in use elsewhere' was a satisfactory compromise. The reviewer of *The Mayor of Casterbridge* in the *Athenaeum* (29 May 1886) wrote:

> The language of the peasants again is a point on which we have an old quarrel with Mr. Hardy. It is neither one thing nor the other – neither dialect exactly reproduced nor a thorough rendering into educated English.... this is perhaps too long a question to be entered into here; only Mr. Hardy may take our word for it that his method diminishes the reader's satisfaction.

Hardy was not brought to change his approach in *The Woodlanders*; here is a representative speech from one of Melbury's workmen:

> What maggot has the gaffer got in his head now?' said Tangs the elder. 'Sommit to do with that chiel of his! When you've got a maid of yer own, John Upjohn, that costs ye ['**ee W**] what she costs him, that will take the squeak out of your Sunday shoes, John! (vII cVI)

The language is picturesque, but not fully dialect; one might pick out 'gaffer', 'Sommit', 'chiel', 'yer', 'ye/'ee', which are perhaps enough to suggest Wessex. Robert Creedle, Marty South and other workfolk speak in the same way. Reviewing *The Woodlanders* in the *Saturday Review* (2 April 1887), Edmund Gosse carries on the *Athenaeum* reviewer's criticism of Hardy's method:

> although we know the Dorsetshire man too well not to be aware that Mr. Hardy holds the secret of his speech, and perfectly well understands what he is doing in reproducing his idiom, we yet think that the novelist is a little inconsistent in his standard of conversation. It appears to us that he vacillates between giving an exact facsimile of the village talk and... putting pure town talk into the lips of [his] peasants.

The point is not that Hardy's announced practice is wrong in itself, but that he does not follow it carefully enough. There are very many speeches that readers accept as being wholly spoken in dialect, even though there are only occasional divergences from standard English on the page; the problem is that Hardy includes sentences or phrases in some of these speeches that many readers feel can by no stretch of the sympathetic imagination be thought of as belonging appropriately to the speaker. Gosse gives as example a sentence from Grammer Oliver's account of selling her brain to Fitzpiers:

> 'Ay, one can joke when one is well, even in old age; *but in sickness one's gaiety falters*; and that which seemed small looks large, and the grim far-off seems near.' This, surely, strikes a false note, especially the words we

have italicised, than which nothing less in keeping with poor old Grammer's habits of mind or speech could well be conceived.

This analysis is more thoughtful than many, and is hard to refute, if naturalism is the criterion used. Hardy seems at such moments to have melded himself with his character, so that a perception she might have or an emotion she might experience, but does not have the education, the vocabulary, or the habit of thought to bring to words, he puts into words for her. This certainly is not realism, but it does embody Hardy's belief that all people are capable of sophisticated inward responses to complicated issues, however unused they may be to expressing them; he understands that Grammer Oliver *felt* this, even though she could not have generalized her feeling so, or at all.

Grammer Oliver's speech is the site of a different kind of interest also. Hardy gives her Wessex forms that he has used nowhere else, but which are attested to in Barnes's 'Dissertation' and in his poems.

> "'Ch will [**I will MS-A1**; '**Ch woll W**] not have him,' said Grammer Oliver...
> 'Can't abear it!...
> 'The ten pounds he [**er W**] offered me for my head...'Ch have been going to ask him again to let me off, but I hadn't the face....
> "'Ch have done it once already, miss. But he laughed cruel-like....' (vII cI)

The novel takes place in the Vale of Blackmore, the location also of Barnes's poems, and whether Hardy's usage was stimulated by his renewed conversations with Barnes, or whether he was going by his mother's pronunciation of the first person singular pronoun, is unclear. It is particularly unusual that Hardy should make positive dialectal revisions for the Wessex edition, which suggests again that for him Grammer Oliver's speech was more than usually authentic in its transcription.

Gosse would have been happier by the end of the novel, when, after Melbury's search party has walked all the way to Sherton only to find Grace willingly in Fitzpiers's company, the hollow-turner speaks with hardly any standard English:

> 'Well,...here be we six [**seven O**] mile from home, and night-time, and not a hoss or four-footed creeping thing to our name. I say, we'll have a mossel and a drop o' summat to strengthen our nerves afore we vamp all the way back again? My throat's as dry as a kex. What d'ye say so's?' (vIII cXV)

Between *The Woodlanders* and *Tess of the d'Urbervilles* Hardy wrote another group of short stories, and there are one or two points of interest in them.

After the particularity of Grammer Oliver's speech, it is interesting to note this from 'A Tragedy of Two Ambitions':

> 'Dammy, the mis'ess! Your step-mother! Didn't you know I'd married? She helped me home one night, and we came to terms, and struck the bargain. Didn't we Selinar?'
> 'Oi, by the great Lord an' we did!' simpered the lady.

The story is set in what becomes Outer Wessex, or Somerset (like *A Laodicean*); the form 'Oi' for 'Ay' is unique to this story, and seems to represent Hardy's attempt to reproduce a sound he thought of as peculiar to eastern Somerset – he had lived in Yeovil for a few months in 1876.

In 'The Waiting Supper' there is a member of the landowning gentry who uses the dialect. Squire Everard's voice, the narrator says, was strongly toned with the local accent, so that he said 'draïns' and 'geäts'. He also says 'vew' for 'few', 'gwine' for 'going', 'wool' for 'will', 'taant' for 'taunt', and 'oone' for 'one'; but it is entirely a matter of pronunciation – in which Hardy contrasts him ironically with Nic Long, the farmer whose suit for his daughter's hand the squire rejects because he is 'oone of our parish people', but who speaks perfect standard English. Hardy admired *Tom Jones*, and it is possible at least that he took authority for the language of these eighteenth or early nineteenth century country gentlemen from Fielding's Squire Western.

As almost every commentator on the novel has noticed, it is one of the features of *Tess of the d'Urbervilles* that the heroine is double-tongued – that she speaks both Wessex and standard English as the occasion demands – and that this comes from the mixture of her nurture at home and her education at a national school. Hardy contrasts her speech pattern with that of her mother, but found it difficult to make up his mind about either:

> Mrs Durbeyfield still habitually spoke [**Durbeyfield spoke MS1; Durbeyfield still spoke portions of MS2; Durbeyfield habitually spoke 1v**] the dialect; her daughter, who had passed the Sixth Standard in the National School under a London-trained mistress, used it only when excited by joy, surprise, or grief [**mistress, spoke two languages; the dialect at home, more or less; ordinary English abroad and to persons of quality 1v**]. (III)

In the manuscript at first Joan Durbeyfield simply 'spoke the dialect', which Hardy then altered to 'still spoke portions of the dialect', suggesting that she too is becoming educated out of it – perhaps by the example of Tess. When revising proof for the serial Hardy went back to his original idea, though retaining 'still', which he was careful enough to remove in 1892, since it gave the impression that she was an exception in her generation. As far as Tess is concerned, the first edition and the one-volume edition offer quite different accounts. Neither reflects wholly the language that Hardy in fact gives her, but on the whole the former seems to be more accurate – perhaps in part because it leaves room for the reader to interpret her mood. Her speech immediately following offers an ambiguous example:

> 'Had it anything to do with father's making such a mommet [**show MS1**] of himself in the [**thik O**] carriage this afternoon?-Why did he ['**er 1v**]? I felt inclined to sink into the ground with shame!'

As it stood at the manuscript's first inscription there was no dialect at all (unless you count 'I felt inclined to'), which, since she is at home and since the last sentence seems to imply some shade of grief, seems wrong by either of Hardy's criteria. After three separate stages of revision the speech reaches, or somewhat exceeds the level of dialect individuality that Hardy was accustomed to use for his dialect speakers. If her speech is traced through the novel, it will be found that on the whole she speaks more standard English than might be expected, though in part this can be attributed to Angel's powerful influence with her.[5]

Talbothays and its milkmaids have themselves a profound affect on Angel, and there is a brief fragment of dialogue that shows that even some of the vocabulary has rubbed off on him:

> '...that mead was a drop of pretty tipple.'
> 'A what?' said Cuthbert and Felix both.
> 'Oh – 'tis an expression they use down at Talbothays,' replied Angel blushing. (XXV)

In *The Well-Beloved* Hardy tunes his ear to the Portland accent:

> Lord, sir' broke in Mrs. Kibbs, 'I should be afeard o' my life to tine my eyes among these here kimberlins at night-time; and even by day, if so be I venture into the streets, I nowhen forget how many turnings to the right and to the left 'tis to get back to Ike's [**to Job's O**] vessel – do I, Ike [**I, Job O**]. (II.v)

But the most striking of his experiments is his first and only attempt at Irish:

> ...O, yes, sending messages down the spakin'-tube which were like madness itself, and ordering us this and that, till we would take no notice at all.... Shure, if ye'd written, saur, I'd ha' got the place ready, [**ready, ye being out of a man, too, O**] though it's not me duty at all! (II.xi)

It is part of the move of *Jude the Obscure* beyond traditional Wessex that though Jude is surrounded by dialect speakers at almost every stage of his life, he speaks almost none himself. As a child he invites the rooks to eat the seed he is supposed to protect in these terms:

> Poor little dears!... You *shall* have some dinner – you shall! There is enough for us all. Farmer Troutham can afford to let you have some. Eat, then, my dear little birdies, and make a good meal! (I.ii)

The farmer overhears him, beats him, and sends him away. In the speech in which he reports this result to his aunt there is more local speech than we hear in his voice again:

> Mr Troutham have turned me away, because I let the rooks have a few peckings of corn. And there's my wages – the last I shall ever hae!

We know little about his education, but it seems safe to say that Jude marks a further stage in the process begun by Tess Durbeyfield towards standard speech. Older characters like Jude's Aunt Druisilla and Mrs Edlin, relatively uneducated contemporaries like his wife Arabella, and incidental people throughout Wessex do have a varied and sometimes rich local speech; Hardy makes sure we do not miss the fact that Phillotson and his friend Gillingham, when alone together, revert to some of the Wessex vocabulary of their youth. Sue and Jude, though, have no trace of either accent or dialect in their life together, and so it seems strange to hear Jude's much travelled son speak:

> 'Yes, I do. You be the woman I thought wer my mother for a bit, till I found you wasn't,' replied Father Time, who had learned to use the Wessex tongue quite naturally by now. (V.vii)

Is this facility the product of education also? It can hardly be as a consequence of hearing his parents speak.

Hardy never quite followed his friend William Barnes down the road of a Dorset dialect poetry. The nearest he came was in the poem now known as 'The Bride-Night Fire', which has a history relevant to an understanding of the development in Hardy's thinking about dialect (and about Wessex). The poem was first published in the *Gentleman's Magazine* in 1875. There are literally hundreds of differences between the version we now read and the one first published, and these differences involve a massive restoration of dialect.

In 1875 the poem had the subtitle 'A Wessex Ballad' (a very early assertion of the name), but was only marginally local in its spelling and vocabulary. Hardy at that time clearly did not have the courage to offer, or the editor of the magazine to accept, a poem in dialect. In 1894 the poet and critic Lionel Johnson wrote one of the first critical studies of Hardy, *The Art of Thomas Hardy*, and in it was included a version of 'The Bride-Night Fire' in which Hardy had (the implication was) reinstated the readings that he had been obliged to omit for the *Gentleman's Magazine*. It is especially interesting that Hardy took the time to offer to Johnson and his publisher Lane this much changed version at this date, just a year before he began the great enterprise of revising all his prose fiction for publication in a collected edition for the first time. And in fact the version in *The Art of Thomas Hardy* has a number of characteristics which do not appear in the version now most commonly read (the *Collected Poems* text). There are, for instance, readings in which Hardy uses William Barnes's favourite method of indicating a lengthened diphthong with a diaeresis, as in line 12, where 'pair' was spelled 'peäir'; he also introduces several further instances of the z for s substitution, as (together with an inflectional difference) in line 27, where 'seen' was 'zeed'; but even more significantly the Johnson version of the poem is the only one which begins the last verse of the poem thus:

> There was skimmity-riding wi' rout, shout and flare,
> In Weatherbury, Drouse, and out Egdon way, ere
>   They had proof of old Sweatley's decay:
> The Mellstock and Yalbury folk stood in a stare
> The tranter had houses and commonage there...

Here the poem stands with greatly enhanced dialect, and explicitly linked into the Wessex scheme of things through the place names, and indirectly through the tranter; and in this it is a perfect precursor of Hardy's revisions for the Osgood edition of his novels.

'The Bride-Night Fire', though, is by way of being one of a very small group of Hardy's poems in which Wessex speech is prominent or significant. Others include 'Valenciennes', 'The Ruined Maid', 'The Curate's Kindness', 'The Pity of It' with its technical linguistics, and 'At the Mill' briefly; it is not surprising that these are in Hardy's earliest and latest volumes of poetry. There is a much larger group of poems voiced for people who might be expected to use dialectal forms, but do not – 'A Trampwoman's Tragedy', 'A Sunday Morning Tragedy', 'The Farm-Woman's Winter', Marty South's 'The Pine-Planters', 'A Last Journey', 'We Field Women', 'In Weatherbury Stocks' are well-known examples. Hardy grants these speakers an inner voice unaffected by local variations in speech, since, returning to the argument that lies behind 'Wessex Heights', in poetry there is no necessity for intrusive verisimilitude.

12
Wessex Rail[1]

It is commonplace to suggest that the introduction of railways transformed all aspects of Victorian life. Hardy was as well aware of this as anyone else. He was seven when the first engine pulled into the new Dorchester station, and he has the narrator of his story 'The Fiddler of the Reels' consider the impact upon ordinary people of the excursion trains that were run three years later from Dorset to London for the Great Exhibition of 1851:

> For South Wessex, the year formed in many ways an extraordinary chronological frontier or transit-line, at which there occurred what one might call a precipice in Time. As in a geological 'fault,' we had presented to us a sudden bringing of ancient and modern into absolute contact, such as probably in no other single year since the Conquest was ever witnessed in this part of the country.

It is certain that none of those who sat in the open carriages for four hours or more, and then visited the Crystal Palace, would return unchanged – the transformative effect of the railways caught in a single experience. But it should be remembered that Hardy wrote the story in 1894, as he was establishing his new idea of Wessex, in which such moments of local historical significance are central. In 1871 when his first novel was published he had not begun to develop this kind of perspective. For him as an aspiring professional, as for most in the middle classes, railway travel was as much an unexamined aspect of life as the penny post; and when he described in 'The Dorsetshire Labourer' the migration of country workfolk to the towns as the tendency of water to flow uphill when forced, it was probably by steam trains that he imagined the human water being propelled. So it was quite unremarkable that *Desperate Remedies* depended for a considerable amount of its complicated plotting upon a railway line and its timetables, nor was it worth any particular comment that Hardy used some of the more spectacular effects created by the machine to illuminate his characters:

A sudden rattle on his right hand caused [Manston] to start from his reverie, and turn in that direction.

There, before him, he saw rise up from among the trees a fountain of sparks and smoke, then a red glare of light coming forward towards him; then a flashing panorama of illuminated oblong pictures; then the old darkness, more impressive than ever....

The disturbance, a well-known one to dwellers by a railway, was caused by the 6.50 down-train passing along a shallow cutting in the midst of the wood immediately below where he stood, the driver having the fire door of the engine open at the minute of going by. (vII cI.ii)

The train's lurid flash across the darkness as if from hell, the sequence of brightly lit windows, is an apt metaphor for Manston's life, and the old darkness returning, for his execution. It is also characteristic of Hardy to undercut the heightened metaphorical vision with precise and prosaic fact.

In *A Pair of Blue Eyes* too railways are of first importance to the plot, and Hardy exploits their potential with engaging relish. Stephen and Elfride elope from the far west to London by train, but while on the journey, and influenced particularly by the gloomy approach to London, Elfride feels she cannot go through with the marriage plan. So on arrival they dash from one platform to another, and make the 8.10 back to Plymouth, Hardy catching the rush of it all. By the time the return journey is over Elfride has changed her mind again, understanding more clearly the power of the social convention by which, for the sake of her reputation, she should have stayed in London and married Stephen there before returning home. Hardy delights in the rapidity and range, and the irony of their flight and return, in the trance-like state induced in Elfride by the haze of the landscape moving past the window. It is another kind of irony that Hardy enjoys at the end of the novel, as the belated and inadequate lovers Stephen Smith and Henry Knight, debate in a westbound train over which of them will finally marry Elfride, a train to which is, unknown to them or to the reader, attached the funeral carriage bearing the body of 'their' Elfride, the now-dead wife of Lord Luxellian. It is only by train that Hardy could have achieved this wry and characteristic climax for his novel.

In *A Laodicean* Hardy comes close to making the railway an active theme in the narrative, and it is likely that he would have succeeded if he had not been taken severely ill before he had written a third of it. Paula Power's father made his fortune as a railway entrepreneur, something she fights hard to forget, delighting in her medieval castle. She explains away her antipathy as a matter of gender to Somerset, who has said (slightly adapting Tennyson's version of Victorian progress in 'Locksley Hall'):

> '...you represent the march of mind – the steamship, and the railway, and the thoughts that shake mankind.'

She weighed his words, and said slowly: 'Ah, yes: you allude to my father. My father was a great man; but I am more and more forgetting his greatness: that kind of greatness is what a woman can never truly enter into. I am less and less his daughter every day that goes by....

'Do you think it a thing more to be proud of that one's father should have made a great tunnel and railway like that, than that one's remote ancestor should have built a great castle like this?' (I.xi)

Hardy seeks to expose the falsity of Paula's generalization about women and great engineering works in several ways, one of which is a description of the entrance to the marvellous tunnel her father (or at least workmen under his control) built – a description that makes it seem as much a site of romance as any castle-keep:

The absurdity of the popular commonplace that science, steam, and travel must always be unromantic and hideous, was proved on the spot. On either slope of the deep cutting, green with long grass, grew drooping young trees of ash, beech, and other flexible varieties, their foliage almost concealing the actual railway which ran along the bottom, its thin steel rails gleaming like silver threads in the depths. The vertical front of the tunnel, faced with brick that had once been red, was now weather-stained, lichened, and mossed over in harmonious hues of rusty-browns, pearly greys, and neutral greens, at the very base appearing a little blue-black spot like a mouse-hole – the tunnel's mouth. (I.xii)

Somerset goes down to inspect the tunnel, 'mentally balancing science against art, the grandeur of this fine piece of construction against that of the castle, and thinking whether Paula's father had not, after all, the best of it'. Hardy's illness meant that he did not have the imaginative energy to continue this idea very intensely, and it peters out in railway trips across Europe, to resurface rather feebly at the end. His reliance upon memories of his foreign travels meant also that the narrative was hardly connected with Wessex, all of which is a pity, for evidence from other novels suggests that he might have made something fine of a story in which the castle and the railway were seriously juxtaposed throughout.

This discussion has taken me to 1881 and it is time to reflect a little on other novels written before *A Laodicean*. Two of them, *Under the Greenwood Tree* and *The Trumpet-Major*, are set before the railways reached Dorset, and so don't come into the reckoning here, but in two others, *Far From the Madding Crowd* and *The Return of the Native*, the action is of a later date, and yet it is in both almost as if the railway did not exist. This is not altogether a conscious exclusion; it is in part because they are both primarily local – no one travels to London. Bathsheba might have sought Troy by rail, except that she leaves on impulse in the middle of the night; Eustacia might have thought of going to Budmouth by train from Casterbridge, except that the whole point of the heath in the first edition was to make it psychologically remote from everywhere else, and Casterbridge doesn't exist. And both novels do have one reference to the railway. In *Far From the Madding Crowd* the narrator describes how Boldwood sees Bathsheba Everdene for the first time after being awakened to her presence by the valentine she sent him:

> Boldwood looked at her – not slily, critically, or understandingly, but blankly at gaze, in the way a reaper looks up at a passing train – as something foreign to his element, and but dimly understood. (vI cXVII)

This sense of the steam engine as alien from the agricultural labourer is exactly what a reader of these two novels might expect, though if the same reader had also encountered *Desperate Remedies* or *The Hand of Ethelberta*, she might have wondered at its universal validity. In *The Return of the Native* the railway surfaces in one of those comments by the narrator that are the seeds of new Wessex:

> Reddlemen of the old school are now but seldom seen. Since the introduction of railways Wessex farmers have managed to do without these somewhat spectral [**these Mephistophelian 1vol**] visitants, and the bright pigment so largely used by shepherds in preparing sheep for the fair is obtained by other routes. (I.ix)

In fact Hardy is very rarely so specific in his novels about the economic and social effects of the railway on Wessex life. What concerns him most is what Dickens and Eliot, Thackeray and Trollope also regretted, the abrupt cessation of travel by coach; but where they mostly regret the circumambient romance, Hardy characteristically is sad for the small communities that served the mail coaches and the stage coaches, the innkeepers and ostlers and grooms, the inns themselves, and the roads too, once thriving arteries and now shrunk to narrow lanes.[2] But, despite these passing references, it is certain that these novels, in marked contrast to those that surround them, have nothing to do with the railways.

The same is nearly true of *The Woodlanders*. It shares a sensibility towards pre-industrial culture with *Far From the Madding Crowd* and *The Return of the Native*, and a similarly small district in which most of the action takes place; but some of what interests Hardy in the narrative requires a good deal more travelling than in the earlier novels, and there is a greater sense that he is having deliberately to exclude the discordant railway. When Melbury and his lawyer go to London, presumably they do so by train, but we never hear how they travelled. Both Mrs Charmond and Edred Fitzpiers go abroad, and again it is pretty much certain that they do so by train, but we are not told. When Fitzpiers courts his estranged wife, he travels frequently from Exbury

(Exonbury in the Osgood edition) to Sherton-Abbas before walking to Little Hintock. The only way this journey would be viable is by rail, but again there is no direct mention of it. In this instance Hardy decided to remove even the indirect suggestion of rail travel from the Wessex edition, and has Fitzpiers staying in Sherton in the first place. Like the earlier novels, though, there is one open reference to railways, and here it does have some plot-significance. It occurs in the last chapter:

> The responses at last given by him to their queries guided them to the building that offered the best accommodation in Sherton – having been enlarged [**been rebuilt O**] contemporaneously with the construction of the railway – namely, the Earl of Wessex Hotel. (vIII cXV)

This is the third time that the hotel has been described, but it is the only occasion on which Hardy indicates its connection with the railway. He gives the information at the end because Grace and Edred are in the hotel preparing to go off to an undetermined future far from the district of the novel, out of Wessex by rail.

So Lucy in 1887 paying particular attention to railways in Hardy's novels was faced with two quite different strands – one represented by *Desperate Remedies* or *A Pair of Blue Eyes*, the other by *Far From the Madding Crowd* or *The Woodlanders*. But, as we know, she was also fascinated by the idea of Wessex, and had been thinking much more intently about what Hardy had being doing with it over his career. She had understood that Wessex is a place where pre-Victorian ways of life survive with more than usual tenacity, and she thought that Hardy shows trains shuttling people back and forward on urgent journeys to not much good, not connecting at all with the life they rush through. Then she said that really the steam train might represent quite well all those new inventions that are changing things in Wessex and everywhere. And finally she wondered if this makes novels that embrace the railway not really Wessex novels at all, or whether Wessex is, despite so many appearances, both ancient and modern. Four years later she came across a passage in *Tess of the d'Urbervilles* that seemed to address her problem. As Tess Durbeyfield and her lover Angel Clare deliver milk to a station, Hardy deliberately brings secluded Wessex and the intrusive railway into juxtaposition:

> They crept along towards a point in the expanse of shade before them at which a feeble light was beginning to assert its presence, a spot where, by day, a fitful white streak of steam at intervals upon the dark green background denoted intermittent moments of contact between their secluded world and modern life. Modern life stretched out its steam feeler to this point three or four times a day, touched the native existences, and quickly withdrew its feeler again, as if what it touched had been uncongenial.

Modern life, some sort of sensitive insect, puts out its steam feeler, wondering if this secluded world is good to walk upon, to mate with, to eat, perhaps; and despite several unsatisfactory experiences a day, keeps on trying, with the persistence of a very determined creature – or a machine. The traditional, the pre-industrial, seems, as in *Under the Greenwood Tree*, to be able to repel the patient predator, for a while at least. The passage continues:

> They reached the feeble light, which came from the smoky lamp of a little railway-station; a poor enough terrestrial star, yet in one sense of more importance to Talbothays Dairy and mankind than the celestial ones to which it stood in such humiliating contrast. The cans of new milk were unladen in the rain, Tess getting a little shelter from a neighbouring holly tree.
>
> Then there was the hissing of a train, which drew up almost silently upon the wet rails, and the milk was rapidly swung can by can into the truck. The light of the engine flashed for a second upon Tess Durbeyfield's figure, motionless under the great holly tree. No object could have looked more foreign to the gleaming cranks and wheels than this unsophisticated girl, with the round bare arms, the rainy face and hair, the suspended attitude of a friendly leopard at pause, the print gown of no date or fashion, and the cotton bonnet drooping on her brow. (XXX)

The metaphor shifts a little: the feeler becomes a snake gliding in with a slight hiss, and is placed next to Tess, when it is transformed again, its disguise stripped away, and it is seen for the machine it is, foreign but yet brilliant. Hardy's description of Tess – defenceless, sad, and above all timeless – is a marvellous counter to 'gleaming cranks and wheels'. So far so clear, but when he sees her with 'the suspended attitude of a friendly leopard at pause' the rather exotic animal metaphor is a connection back to the snake and the feeler, and an attentive reader thus stimulated might recall that only three chapters earlier, when Angel had met Tess with a yawn, he had seen 'the red interior of her mouth as if it had been a snake's'. The common natural imagery is a tenuous bond between girl and machine to balance the apparent alienation. And this thought turns the mind back to the previous paragraph.

In suggesting that the station, and the railway it is there to serve, are of signal importance to Talbothays Dairy in particular and mankind in general, Hardy is doing what he always does – revealing to the reader how easy and essential it is to hold opposing views at the same time, for each has value. Though the railway will ultimately swallow local traditions, language, handcraft industries, hand-and-horse agriculture without the rail link to London, Talbothays Dairy would have gone under in this time of agricultural depression, and Tess Durbeyfield and the other dairymaids would themselves have been on a train to London to who knows what end. So this memorable detail is not as decisive as it might at first appear. [3]

In fact there is a complicated attitude to the railways throughout *Tess of the d'Urbervilles*. Hardy has imagined Tess inhabiting a border-country where the developed late-Victorian world and the remote pre-industrial pattern of Wessex agriculture overlap and intermingle, which means that the presence of railways in modern Wessex cannot be ignored. But Hardy's conception of the character, vividly illuminated against the gleaming cranks, means that he cannot have her travel by train; so he has to design her journeys carefully so that they could not more conveniently have been made that way, and from time to time he makes the point:

> She went through Stourcastle without pausing, and onward to a junction of highways, where she could await a carrier's van that ran to the southwest; for the railways which engirdled this interior tract of country had never yet struck across it. (XVI)

In 'never yet' there is an implication that though the railway did not strike across country then, it soon would. In fact it never has, and is not likely to now, but the phrasing implies that Hardy envisages a Wessex, and an England, so criss-crossed with railway lines that the smallest village on the way between nowhere much and nowhere still less will have its halt. This is why *Tess of the d'Urbervilles* is the essential Wessex novel; it brings the environment and culture of *Far From the Madding Crowd* and *The Return of the Native* that had so consciously had nothing to do with the railway, into contact with their future in new Wessex, and while not embracing the new, the railway, shows that it is now an essential element of life. For embracement, as new Wessex evolved, there is *Jude the Obscure*.

Despite the claims of earlier books, *Jude the Obscure* is Hardy's essential railway novel, because it takes trains on board with the full knowledge of developed Wessex. When Jude went from Melchester to Kennetbridge – that is from Salisbury to Newbury – he had to start 'early in the morning, for it was only by a series of crooked railways that he could get to the town' (III.x). The carriers have vanished, and though Tess would have set out on foot, for Jude the distance is too far to walk in a day, and even so roundabout a journey is cheap enough by rail for a poorish man to make. Hardy shows himself quite clear about the imaginative and the real impact of the railway, and again takes pleasure in showing how many moments in the lives of his characters in this novel are shaped by the mechanics of the railway timetable:

> He would meet her at Alfredston Road, the following evening, Monday, on his way back from Christminster, if she could come by the up train which crossed his down-train at that station. (III.viii)

Or there is the earlier episode in which Sue spends the night away from the Melchester Training College, with all the scandal that entails, because she and Jude underestimate the time it will take them to reach a railway station to catch their return train.

We are given an excellent example of the casual unconcern about distance that the railway provokes when Jude and Arabella get into a train for Aldbrickham at 9.40 pm, just to go off for the night together, and come back to Christminster the next morning (III.viii–ix). And this spur-of-the-moment there and back journey acquires extra significance when the same day Jude and Sue travel in a similar direction:

> He released her hand till they had entered the train,- it seemed the same carriage he had lately got out of with another – where they sat down side by side, Sue between him and the window. He regarded the delicate lines of her profile, and the small, tight, apple-like convexities of her bodice, so different from Arabella's amplitudes. (III.ix)

The superimposition of Sue upon Arabella in the railway carriage, with its erotic notation, becomes a prefiguring of the more potent later superimposition of Sue on Arabella, when she finds herself with Jude in the same room at the inn at Aldbrickham that he and Arabella had shared. But the most powerful of all the images of railway travel is that of 'Little Father Time' on his journey to his father, alone and separate, an isolation seems intensified by the idea of the train as a capsule of folk being drawn at speed by a machine on an invariable route through a landscape with which they have no contact.[4]

Ultimately the significance of railways in the image-structure of the novel is focussed in Sue's idea that the station (not the barn as in *Far From the Madding Crowd* or the cathedral) is the centrally symbolic building of modern civilization.[5] This is an insight that Edward Springrove, the architect in *Desperate Remedies*, or George Somerset, the architect in *A Laodicean*, might also have expressed; and it might be concluded that, seen in this light, Hardy's understanding of Wessex has gone a long road over twenty and more years to reach the point at which he had begun writing in 1870 – that the books he later called Novels of Character and Environment represent a long exploration of the process by which the pre-railway world of his childhood became the rapidly mobility of later Victorian England that is an essential element of *Desperate Remedies* or *A Pair of Blue Eyes*. In fact *Jude the Obscure* itself presents the same process, from Jude walking around his little area of North Wessex, or driving his baker's cart, or walking into Christminster, through his frequent shifting of place, some of which we have seen, to his death. It is not coincidental that the last journey of Hardy's last novel-hero (or anti-hero) should begin with him walking, wet through, from Marygreen to Alfredston, and that it should end with him on a platform at Christminster station, having shivered to death on a steam tramcar and two branches of railway.

13
Conclusion: Politics, Guides and Critics

It was a consequence of the wholehearted acceptance by the world of Wessex-as-England, that Hardy became in 1922 the focus of what might have been in a different time a Wessex nationalist movement. On 18 May of that year Hardy received a letter from a W G Bowman. He wrote of Hardy as 'the gentleman whose life-work has made a Renascence [of Wessex] possible', and went on:

> The immediate object of this letter is to advise you that a monthly magazine devoted to the Wessex Movement is rapidly nearing the publishing point. In brief the objects of the paper are: (A.) To bring the Wessex Movement into the daily life of the People. (B.) To press for a Wessex University. (C.) to make Modern Wessex a sturdily independent Province with a distinct individuality; with its own characteristics; with its own songs, literature, and Art. (DCM H5880)

Hardy replied on 27 May; his only contribution to 'the Wessex Movement' was to complain about the wearing away of place names: 'the preservation of local names – which are so muddled & neglected by the surveyors of the ordnance maps as to be disappearing fast. (To give one instance "Swan-knolls" at Cattistock near here becomes "Sandhills".)' (DCM H5883a)

In response Bowman sent on 2 June a prospectus of a magazine to be called 'Wessex Life' 'devoted to the Wessex Movement of Thomas Hardy'. If Hardy was surprised to hear that there was a Wessex Movement, he must have been astonished at the news that the Movement was his responsibility. His gentle response, transmitted through his second wife Florence was that his name should be omitted because it 'would certainly prejudice some people against' the magazine. The prospectus also included the following points:

1. The success of the Wessex Movement means greater Unity, greater Activity and greater Prosperity.
2. It unites *three and a half million* men and women in a pro-Southern movement.

On the latter of these Hardy commented that south-western would be preferable to Southern, as it would appropriately exclude Kent and Sussex. Millgate notes (*Letters* VI.144) that no copy of the magazine appeared.

In July there was a letter from Francis Macnamara which announced another magazine, to be called 'Wessex Review', and enclosed another prospectus, which does not now survive. Hardy replied again through Florence, a little more irritated: 'The development of a utilitarian Wessex is entirely beyond the scope of his past conceptions and writings, which have been merely of a dreamland roughly resembling and coterminous with the six counties that now cover the old kingdom.' The language is reminiscent of the earlier version of the preface to *Far From the Madding Crowd*, and though the utilitarian Wessex was indeed beyond his early conceptions, by 1913 Wessex in his work was certainly not merely the dreamland he asserts.

Later in the month, Macnamara returned a proof of his prospectus emended in the light of Hardy's comments; it included:

WHERE AND WHAT IS WESSEX?
It is true that the kingdom of Wessex no longer exists, and probably no West Saxons today desire its revival, at least in a political sense: yet there is a certain community of interest in the South-Western counties, with their application to agriculture rather than to trade, their production for home consumption rather than for export.

THE WORD CREATIVE
And into these realities a poet has breathed, a sense of unity is awakened by the imagination of Thomas Hardy, which discovered a world in the district and its people: to give more diverse expression to these the Wessex Review is now founded, in the belief that an advantage beyond the sentimental will accrue, when the race of the old adventurers explore their own country.

Michael Millgate notes (*Letters* VI.150) that three issues of *Wessex Review* appeared.

It is sadly reading too much into these exchanges to imagine that Hardy's correspondents were feeling him out for the role of president of a breakaway state of Wessex, but the economic realities after the First World War, and the attention inevitably paid by government and the newspapers to the industries of the midlands and the north, whose workers were on the verge of striking, or actually did strike, in 1921 and 1922, perhaps contributed to a more or less sudden awareness amongst people in the south-west of England that in his work Hardy had created a viable political entity that might be promoted in a different arena from the literary. Hardy's response to Macnamara shows a clear distaste for this kind of suggestion. The movement for the establishment of a University of Wessex did survive, though, only to founder in the 1930s in squabbles between the colleges at Southampton and Exeter.

And now, thanks to the present government's commitment to devolution, the Wessex Regionalist Party, which has fought elections since 1974, finds itself with a practical role in life. It is attempting, in concert with a Wessex constitutional convention, to persuade central administrators that the counties of Wessex, rather than being split between the preferred but unhistorical South East, South West and West Midlands, should form one of the new English administrative regions, with its own devolved althing.

It was only natural that the production of guidebooks to Wessex should follow hard on the completion of Osgood, McIlvaine's collected edition, but it is a pleasant coincidence that two of the first of any importance, one published in 1902, the other in 1906, both brilliantly illustrated, should represent the distinction that I have made in earlier chapters between Wessex-as-fiction and Wessex-as-England, one called *The Wessex of Thomas Hardy*, the other simply *Wessex*.

The Wessex of Thomas Hardy was a collaboration between Bertram Windle, who wrote, and Edmund New, who drew. Windle first wrote to Hardy in 1896, much as Robertson Nicholl had five years earlier, to ask for some authoritative identifications of Wessex places:

> I have, I think, identified most – at least many of them – but am unable to feel quite sure about others. I do not know whether you wish that all of them should be known, but if you have no objection you would confer a great favour upon me if you would permit me to ask you to solve a few of my difficulties. (DCM H5921)

He did not name the difficulties in the letter. Hardy was in Brussels when he received the letter, and he responded:

> I will with pleasure give you any information that you may require as to the real names of the places described in my Wessex novels. Such information in the Handbook will perhaps relieve me of the many letters I receive on the subject, & perhaps serve to correct the erroneous identifications of places by journalists & others. (Letters II.131)

Hardy appended what he called 'a few rudimentary notes', which must have exceeded Windle's wildest expectations. The resulting book was published by John Lane, in 1902. As the title indicates, the book's shape and its approach to the country are dictated by Hardy's work – it is appropriate that, after three concentrating on Casterbridge, successive chapters deal with routes radiating out from the county-town like those followed by the carriers' waggons. There is continual reference to the relationship between buildings and landscapes and Hardy's versions of them. It is Hardy's created world brought to intense scrutiny, and illustrated with line-drawings that impart the same immediate conviction as those by Macbeth-Raeburn for the Osgood, McIlvaine edition. One other feature is notable; as a tailpiece to the book there is a map of the 'Principal Towns of South Wessex' – a map that is pure Wessex, without any English names.

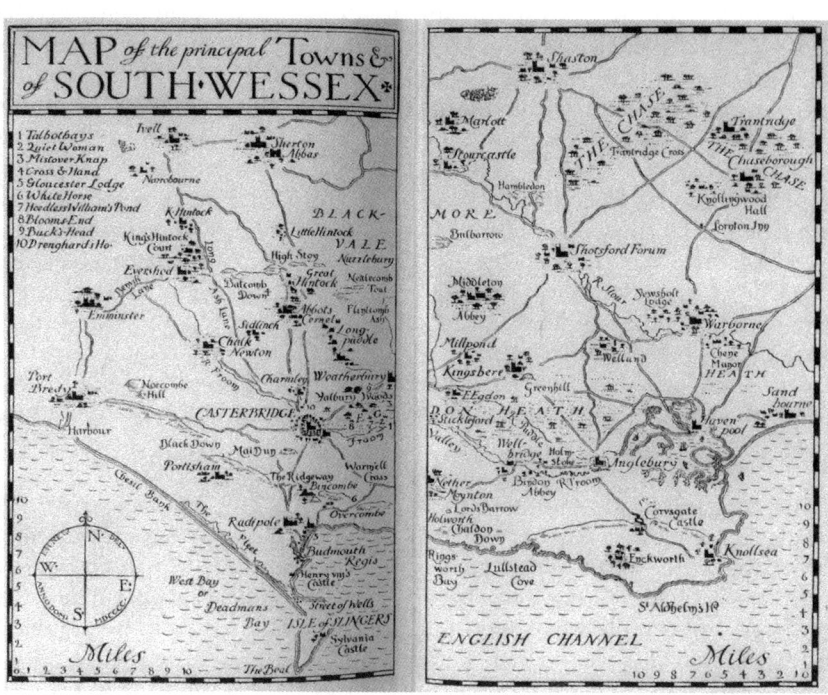

Wessex was also a collaboration, between Clive Holland the journalist and Walter Tyndale, who painted a large number of sensitive watercolours for the book. Holland (his real name was Charles Hankinson) had already published a number of magazine pieces illustrating Hardy's Wessex with photographs. At first (in 1897, *Letters* II.177) Hardy gave him short shrift, perhaps because he thought of Windle as having the prior claim on information, but Holland persisted, and by 1906 he had visited Hardy a couple of times. *Wessex*, however, published in A & C Black's series of colour-illustrated books, draws only to a slight extent on Hardy's work, concentrating instead on the history and culture of the English places in Holland's idea of what constitutes Wessex – more limited than Hardy's. It is only in occasional allusions, captions to many of Tyndale's pictures, and in a final chapter called 'Some lesser towns and villages of Thomas Hardy's Wessex', that Wessex-as-fiction is a presence (but it cannot entirely be excluded). Holland showed Hardy the proofs of the passages that concerned him and his writing, and Hardy suggested some changes (*Letters* III.194–5); Hardy also gave Tyndale some information (*Letters* III.146–7), and it seems that the artist was much more concerned than Holland to make the connections between his work and Wessex-as-fiction.

Hardy came closer to authorizing Hermann Lea's *Thomas Hardy's Wessex* (London: Macmillan, 1913) than any other such book, by allowing it to be published in the same format as the Wessex edition. The history of Hardy's collaboration with Lea is well known.[1] The photographs that fill the book are always of interest (if sometimes only historical), but the text is dull, and was prepared too closely under Hardy's eye so that potential divergences from the proprietor's version of Wessex-as-fiction were muted or suppressed. In that respect the book bears an interesting relationship with Hardy's autobiography published, as all the world knows, after his death and under his wife's name as author. There have followed in the ninety years since very many directories to Hardy's places, but Denys Kay-Robinson's *The Landscape of Thomas Hardy* (Exeter, Webb & Bower, 1984) is the only required reading. It is exhaustive, always plausible, and filled with excellent photographs by Simon McBride; and if all anyone were interested in was the place Wessex as Hardy left it, rather than as he discovered and developed it, then my work would be mostly redundant.

The primary purpose of this book, though, has been to present in a detailed chronological sequence what Hardy did to make Wessex over his long career as a writer, and to shape an argument concerning its evolution out of that mass of material; there has been very little room for engagement with interpreters of completed Wessex, and indeed it was my intention (or at least my hope) that the evidence in the book and on the website should rather provide the basis for further discussion. However there is on the website an annotated bibliography of work on Wessex (both Hardy's and England's) that I have found interesting, and I would also refer the reader to Charles Lock's *Thomas Hardy* in the 'Criticism in Focus' series (New York: St Martin's Press 1992) and to Peter Widdowson's 'critiography' in his *Hardy in History*.

In the introduction I paid homage to (though I did not do justice to) Michael Millgate and Raymond Williams, whose contributions seem to me, in their different ways, to be the foundations of modern discussions of Wessex; but now, at the end, I find that I must address two critical positions that have preyed on my mind since I began writing this book.

The first of these is directly related to the perception that I had to imagine for myself the responses of different kinds of contemporary readers of early

Wessex, readers with different kinds of knowledge and experience. I thought my imagination was up to the task, but in preparing myself to write, one of the pieces I reread was John Barrell's 'Geographies of Hardy's Wessex'. (*Journal of Historical Geography*, 8, 4 [1982] 347–61). He argues a different case, but nevertheless has forced me to reflect whether I could really imagine myself a reader innocent of the long history of Hardy's Wessex. He proposes an epistemological problem with one aspect of Wessex: that the experience of one who has never known an environment beyond her immediate locality (Egdon Heath, Blackmoor Vale) cannot be communicated to anyone whose experience is wider:

> The local geography involves instead a knowledge, and a way of knowing, so intense, so full, so detailed, that it cannot be acquired in more places than one, and cannot be exported from one place to another: it is not knowledge elsewhere. (349)[2]

Barrell argues that each of Hardy's readers is constructed by the narrative as alien from this kind of knowledge, and concludes:

> The invitation the novels extend is that he should stop, observe, penetrate and 'read the secrets' of a place he would usually pass through; but the secrets of the Vale of Blackmoor cannot be 'read', or certainly not by such a reader as this language constructs, one whose knowledge is customarily derived from reading. (356)

I realized that Raymond Williams had part of a response in his chapter 'Wessex and the Border' in *The City and the Country*: Hardy as a child had that kind of local, limited experience (and so still do many children), and, in learning a wider world, he cannot erase, even if he wished, the knowledge of that limited landscape. The second part of the problem, though, is to show how that knowledge can be communicated to the reader, and I saw that here was another way of seeing why Hardy invented and developed, as a matter of necessity, the multiple-voiced narrator that is so striking a feature of any reading of one of his novels. One voice does indeed construct the alienated reader, but the other, amongst other tasks, reenters his childhood experience of a limited and limitless environment, and through the power of recreative imagination gives it life again in his fiction and his poetry, triggering in the responsive reader a knowledge that she too has once, if only as an infant, had this same experience, this same knowledge. When Barrell writes: 'The reader can certainly grasp from *Tess* that there is such a local knowledge, in Hardy's Wessex if not in nineteenth century Dorset; but he can grasp only the notion of its existence, not the knowledge itself', and adds that no reader of wide experience will be able to suspend the knowledge gained through that experience, surely he underestimates the power of the imagination – Hardy's and the reader's. If the novel in part constructs us as alien from this local knowledge, so too it constructs us as sharers of it, tapping our own experience of a room, a house, a garden, a street so big it seemed for a while to be the whole world.

Peter Widdowson has been the most effective exposer of the Wessex of nostalgia, of Hardy as the great retrospective rural pastoralist and tragedian. In *Hardy in History* he works with *The Hand of Ethelberta* and other texts to create an alternative icon, which is a more elaborate and more radical version of Williams's Hardy, disdaining the topographical tourists, sentimental ruin-bibbers, liberal humanists who have produced the Hardy of current popular imagination, amongst whom I have sometimes found myself. I have felt his eye on me during the whole process of conceiving and writing this book. Wessex for him is a site of class-conflict and sexual politics, and I can only hope that I have provided evidence enough to show that indeed it is, as well as very many other things also. Widdowson, I think, might agree that Wessex is a particularly detailed and satisfying way of encountering a complex and unresolvably contradictory world. If you will pardon such tritenesses at the end of a long book, all critics, all readers, see things and elide things and suppress things in all they read, and on reflection recreate what they have read in the light of this interaction between their minds and the text – which is why reading is such a wonderful occupation to do and to observe the consequences of.

Lucy Stowe, the reader I imagined, who entered so fully into Hardy's fictional environment as it grew, has pretty much disappeared from the last few chapters of this book. This is because, as the first collected edition appeared, her responses diminished to mere exclamations, or notations of change – at least until the last volume was published in 1896; and she wrote thereafter no more. The reason for this state of affairs may be found in the carefully thought-out paragraphs that constitute her last interaction with Wessex, written in 1896 after she had worked through Hardy's changes to *Under the Greenwood Tree*:

> So now I know almost everything about Wessex that had bothered me, so now all is made clear for me, even the places where Mr Hardy can't make it clear even by trying ever so; and yet I don't feel as elated as I ought to. I have been puzzling over Mr Hardy's world for twenty years, more, with excitement and delight and frustration. And now I can see where I was wrong and where I was right; but what have I gained from my new knowledge? Every year, every new novel and story, I felt more and more certain that all of his work was founded in places he knew well, that the stories grew out of an intimacy with people and places so strong that he could not, even if he wished, separate himself from them creatively. 'Under the Greenwood Tree' shows this to have been true as much as any of them,

Conclusion: Politics, Guides and Critics 241

more than most. I am sure that if I went to Mr Hardy's birthplace and followed the directions we now have in this revised edition, I could find my way easily enough. I suppose I am worried that, now that the landscape that was known but kept private has become known and made public, the nature of the novels has changed a little, and not for the better. There was a secret hidden from the reader by the writer in the first printing of 'Under the Greenwood Tree'; we might suspect much about his intimacy with what he described, but it remained speculation. This gave for me a quality to the work that I loved, a sense that there was more to it than met the eye, that drove the reader – drove me, at any rate – back to read it again. Now his intimacy is exposed, that incalculable element has gone. It was inevitable, of course, once 'Tess of the d'Urbervilles' became the book of the year – of the decade, probably. Journalists began prodding him, interviewing him; paragraphs of gossip appeared all over the place; maps of Wessex began to be drawn. He was a famous man.

But these revisions don't stem from the increase in publicity, the increase in interest in his places as well as his personality, I think, or not entirely so. When 'Tess of the d'Urbervilles' was published with the division of Wessex into counties, I said something different was going on in Mr Hardy's mind, and the direct consequence of those thoughts is this revision. He has become a teacher (well, he always was, but not so severely) as well as a romancer, a teacher of Wessex, a recorder of its places and sounds and people, so that – in his novels, if not in life – they will survive the new wave of inventions that the magazines tell us will alter everything for ever. So in return for the loss of a little mystery we have gained much fact. I should not regret the bargain. He has not altered the plots, and the characters hardly at all, so one might say that little essential has changed. My whole response to his novels should tell me, does tell me, that this development was part of a process that began with 'Far From the Madding Crowd,' a process whose progress I have taken much pleasure in thinking about. Why should he not take this next step? It was logical, necessary, inevitable. But then I think of the heath of 'The Return of the Native', that I had thought of as a wonderful anomaly, obviously part of Wessex by its shape and tone, but quite apart from the day-to-day life of the county – region I must say now, or province – and now placed precisely on the map of England for good I suppose; there will be guide-books, no doubt.

I have such mixed feelings, and in a way I am most surprised that I feel strongly at all. After all, they are just novels. Its not as if they have anything to do with my life, my children, my garden, is it? Well, of course, my friends think I am fanatical. But I think I shall stop now, here. Something has died, and though I admire what has been born in this edition, it doesn't demand my attention any more.

I have so far immersed myself in the task of imagining how it might have been for a contemporary reader of Hardy's novels fascinated with the sharpness of his eye for places, that I half-believe that I have transcribed these paragraphs rather than created them. My dwelling in Lucy's consciousness on and off over the time of writing this book has brought me to these conclusions. What Lucy is responding to, I have tried to shape in the preceding chapters; she saw that once Wessex was openly superimposed on England, it became altogether different, open to the public, as it were. This is one of the perceptions that drove Hardy to his imaginative retreat on Wessex Heights in the same year that I have imagined Lucy writing her swan-song. Wessex was no longer free for him to do with as he wished; like others before him he had become constrained by his own creation.

I have so far shared Lucy's view that it seems true to say that the tendency of my account of the development of Wessex has been to imply, if not to assert, that Hardy rather spoiled things when he turned local historian. Egdon is experienced more intensely without all the explanatory paraphernalia of the preface, and without all the other novels on its borders – *The Return of the Native* is better read in the version he left in 1878 at the end of the more or less continuous burst of creation across manuscript, serial and first edition; and to a greater or lesser degree this is true of all his fiction before *Tess of the d'Urbervilles*. I have tried to show, here and elsewhere, that there is evidence to support such a view. But among other things, I have learned from Hardy the virtue of being able simultaneously to credit opposites.

I am suddenly reminded, for instance, of the days I spent in Dorchester just after Christmas in 1969, staying at the Antelope (now a mere shopping arcade) and working towards my doctoral dissertation at the Dorset County Museum on the manuscript of *Under the Greenwood Tree*, from which would escape, every time I opened it, a whiff of the study at Max Gate. When my eyes needed a rest I would walk down High East Street, over Swan Bridge, Grey's Bridge, and across the water-meadows to Stinsford, and from there criss-cross in the mud and the frost the whole of Mellstock and Yalbury. At the same time I realized more and more clearly, as I worked further and further into the manuscript, that if Hardy had not made the revisions he did in 1896 and 1912, I would have had no idea of how to find any of the buildings or roads or paths in the novel. But what came as a revelation was that I cared rather deeply about finding them.

It gave me such pleasure to walk beside a branch of the much-divided Frome between Lower Bockhampton and Stinsford church and know that Hardy had imagined the Mellstock choir doing just the same. But he only did so in 1896. In the first edition they crossed an unidentifiable field, and without the revision I should not have been able to experience the exhilarating virtual reality of being inside the novel – quite different, I found, from that of the ordinary recreative acts of reading. Those days were full of similar intense *frissons*, but what I remember most vividly is an impulse like a shock that came as I left Hardy's parents' cottage in Higher Bockhampton at dusk, a mad impulse to run down the lane and across the ewelease as Dick Dewy had done at the opening of *Under the Greenwood Tree*; I had just been thinking that Hardy in his youth must also have run thus on frigid winter evenings, and I was aware, as I ran over the frozen ground, of myself aligned with both character and author, the imagined also the real, the past also the present. But again this lover's lunacy would have been impossible if Hardy hadn't revised the novel in 1912 to tell me where to run. So for reasons that have nothing to do with criticism, but which many readers of Hardy would recognize, I need new Wessex.

Hardy also taught me to use my senses. If he could hear the wind in the heather why hadn't I heard the wind in the chestnut leaves? A landscape worth looking at is not just a pretty picture, but is full of the evidence of the men and women who have shaped it; it is often not even a pretty picture. At the end of an essay on Wessex I wrote a while ago, I tried to give some sense of what being on a Wessex height meant in this way, but I was writing as an exile, and when I returned to Dorset I found that I had got some things wrong. So it seems fitting, in a book that has dealt so much with Hardy's revisions, that I should conclude by doing a bit of revising myself:

> If you sit on a rampart of the iron-age fort on Eggardon Hill, looking south, all that makes Wessex is in your sight: there are buzzards hunting in the valley below, there are bronze-age memories on the hill-top, there is nothing between you and the sky, there are about you all the downland plants and insects in profusion, there beyond is the sea, there to the right is Golden Cap, there between are farms, hedgerows, cattle and furrowed fields, a tractor glinting in the sunlight, other flashes off cars hurrying between Dorchester and Bridport. There are marks of man on the country everywhere, shapes of beauty from west to east, not only transcendent beauty but hand-shaped harmony, in a fair visible pattern, a pattern changed by centuries, but fair in each century. That beauty and that harmony is visible too in a different pattern from the lane that skirts the corn-field and passes the farmhouse, that has been a lane since King Alfred's time, and the one view includes the other. This landscape holds the presence of none of Hardy's famous actions, but Port-Bredy nestles below in its steep defile, and the shepherd's voice from the east hill calling lambing intelligence to his fellow across the town still echoes. Seventy-five years have passed since he finished writing, but nevertheless all you see is within his work, for he has left space for the changes he could not know. I would not have seen or understood any of this if he had not helped me, had not shown me, and left me no choice but to value, the essential Wessex that he knew, transformed in his imagination, and worked out through the sequence of his novels and poems.[3]

Notes

The reference **wsCh1** etc indicates material on the book's website; see p.viii above.

1 The Conception and Birth of Wessex

1. Michael Millgate in *The Oxford Reader's Companion to Hardy* ed Norman Page (Oxford: Oxford University Press, 2000) p. 355.
2. See **wsCh1** for examples.
3. 'Exploiting the *Poor Man*: The Genesis of Hardy's *Desperate Remedies*' in *JEGP* 94:2 (1995) 220–32.
4. For the example of The Three Tranter's Inn, see **wsCh1**.
5. See **wsCh1** for details.
6. See Chapter 11 for a full discussion of dialect.
7. Reviews quoted in this book are taken from Hardy's own scrapbook in the Dorset County Museum.
8. See *Under the Greenwood Tree* ed S Gatrell (Oxford: Oxford University Press, 1985) p. 202 for the earliest versions of Budmouth.
9. Evangeline Smith, the sister of Hardy's friend Bosworth Smith, wrote of Hardy's mother that 'she rather bitterly complained of his not having kept his word to her that he would confine his productions to *London*, and not allow them to penetrate the all-important world of his home'. Michael Rabiger, 'The Hoffman Papers Discovered' *The Thomas Hardy Year Book* 10, p. 49.
10. It is interesting that in these two early examples the power of fate is thoroughly denied.
11. See *Desperate Remedies* vol. III chIV.i.
12. In Wilkinson Sherren: *The Wessex of Romance* (new and revised edn) (London: Francis Griffiths, 1908), there is this (p. 20):

    > Concerning marriage, many were the curious customs observed by Wessex maidens desirous of knowing who their future husbands would be. An even ash leaf having been plucked by the love-lorn girl, it was held alternately in the hand, the glove, and the bosom, the following couplets being recited:
    >
    > > The even ash leaf in my hand,
    > > The first I meet shall be my man
    > >
    > > The even ash leaf in my glove
    > > The first I meet shall be my love.
    > >
    > > The even ash leaf in my bosom,
    > > The first I meet will be my husband.

13. In 1816 a fire destroyed most of the celebrated fair buildings at Makariev, prompting the decision to relocate the fair to Nizhnii-Novgorod, a substantial trading centre some 70 kms upstream on the Volga. The fair operated in its new location from 1817, its duration was extended to a month (15 July to 15 August) in 1822 and by the middle of the nineteenth century an extended site with substantial permanent buildings had been created. Before and after the Crimean War

there was an unprecedented boom in Western publication about the Russian enemy. This unprecedented level of popularity and publication was subsequently sustained by close interest in Tsar Alexander II's reform programme of 1861–74, as Western Europe (rather patronisingly) applauded Russia's shift away from 'Asiatic barbarity' towards 'commitment to European civilisation'. (Information from Professor Raymond Pearson, University of Ulster).

14 The earthwork is so named on nineteenth century Ordnance Survey maps. On modern maps it is called Weatherby Castle.

15 There is another letter in the Dorset County Museum's Hardy archive which gives proof that Lucy was not alone. It is from the novelist Katharine Macquoid; in a postscript she writes: 'My Husband wishes much to know in what County Bathsheba's farm is.' (H4152 Nov 18 1874) He was reading the November number of *Cornhill* as she was writing the letter.

16 The *Saturday Review* made the same point as the *Spectator*, but with heavy sarcasm:

> Ordinary men's notions of the farm labourer of the Southern counties have all been blurred and confused. It has been the habit of an ignorant and unwisely philanthropic age to look upon him as an untaught, unreflecting, badly paid, and badly fed animal, ground down by hard and avaricious farmers, and very little, if at all, raised by intelligence above the brutes and beasts to whom he ministers. These notions are ruthlessly overturned by Mr Hardy's novel. Under his hand Boetians become Athenians in acuteness, Germans in capacity for philosophic speculation, and Parisians in polish.

17 There is no good reason to think that Lulworth appeared under disguise in *The Hand of Ethelberta*.

18 In this matter of disguise, a story that neither Lucy nor any reader in England could have seen is of interest. 'Destiny and a Blue Cloak' was published in the *New York Times* in 1874 and not reprinted during Hardy's life time. Wessex is not mentioned, and in the story Dorset places, Weymouth, Maiden-Newton, Beaminster, Portland, are given their own names. This seems to suggest that it was indeed partly, if not primarily, to prevent embarrassment for his family and friends that he used invented names for all his places in work they were likely to see. It is also interesting that this story provides the first model for a pattern later established in *The Trumpet-Major*: the village at the centre of the action *is* given a fictional name, Cloton. The story will be found in *An Indiscretion* (Oxford World's Classics, 1994) edited by Pamela Dalziel, who assumes that Hardy must have had a Dorset village in mind for Cloton and fixes on Netherbury near Beaminster. It seems to me just as likely that, at this stage in the gestation of Wessex he would have put the fictional village into a blank space on the map.

19 The best study of this aspect of *The Hand of Ethelberta* is in Peter Widdowson's *Hardy in History*, pp. 155–97. For the importance of Wessex dialect in the novel see below pp. 210–11.

2 Variations on the original theme

1 We know now a little more about the map than Lucy did. Hardy wrote to Smith, Elder, the publishers of the first edition:

> I enclose for your inspection a Sketch of the supposed scene in which 'The Return of the Native' is laid – copied from the one I used in writing the story – &

my suggestion is that we place an engraving of it as frontispiece to the first volume. Unity of place is so seldom preserved in novels that a map of the scene of action is as a rule impracticable: but since the present story affords an opportunity of doing so I am of opinion that it would be a desirable novelty, likely to increase a reader's interest. I may add that a critic once remarked to me that nothing could give such reality to a tale as a map of this sort: & I myself have often felt the same thing. (*Letters* I.61 Oct 1 1878)

The critic, as we have already seen (above p. 22) was John Hutton, the earliest of the seekers after reality.

For details of Lucy's investigations into topography, and some details that she was unaware of, see **wsCh2**. Flychett figures in one of Fairway's anecdotes of the past. It is the village to which Thomasin's now-dead father walked on occasion to play the clarinet and the bass-viol in the church (I.v), but, as with Southerton, Flychett could be anywhere. See **wsCh6** for more on Flychett.

The reviewer in the *Daily Telegraph* (3 December 1878), in discussing the map, had not yet caught on to the idea that Hardy's locations are not imaginary:

> The author himself had evidently got the imaginary scene well fixed in his own mind before attempting to convey it to the minds of others; and it is curiously worth notice that he has given a sketch-map of the locality by way of frontispiece, the names of villages and the track of a Roman road being marked thereon, with all the semblance of precise truth.

2   Cresmouth was probably suggested by the Creston that had stood in for Weymouth in *Desperate Remedies*. Another factor in Hardy's reworking of the manuscript was what I have called gentrification, and this also tended to bring Egdon into Wessex (for details see *Hardy the Creator* pp. 39–44). The only other surviving link to earlier novels is a connection to the initial appearance of Wessex in *Far From the Madding Crowd*. Timothy Fairway remembers his wife as a young woman running 'for smocks and gown-pieces at Greenhill Fair' (I.v).
3   The passage was different in both the manuscript and the serial; see **wsCh2**.
4   It is of some interest that in the manuscript the passage ended: 'as we notice now.'
5   'She could show a most reproachful look at times, but it was directed less against human beings than against certain creatures of her mind, the chief of these being Destiny...' (I.vii). Lucy might, however, be mistaken in thinking 'creatures' implies that Eustacia has created them.
6   If Eustacia had had the letter when it was intended she should, it certainly would have prevented her going. If she had got it when Fairway brought it, Hardy felt impelled to add in 1912 for the Wessex edition, it would not have stopped her going:

> But having committed herself to this line of action there was no retreating for bad weather, since Wildeve had been communicated with, and was probably even then waiting for her [**weather. Even the receipt of Clym's letter would not have stopped her now W**]. (V.vii)

7   For a handful of earlier examples, see **wsCh2**.
8   For details see *The Personal Notebooks of Thomas Hardy* ed Richard Taylor (London and Basingstoke: Macmillan, 1978) pp. 115ff.
9   Other new fictional names in the novel are: Pitstock, Springham (both VIII), Duddle Hole, and Muckleford (both IX). All save Springham (a parish adjoining Overcombe) are places where Festus Derriman and his friends have farms. There are as usual

complications and anomalies in Hardy's application of this topography. For details see **wsCh2**.
10 After *The Trumpet-Major* Hardy wrote the story 'The Fellow-Townsmen'. For some interesting Wessex-related details see **wsCh2**.
11 For an account of dialect in the novel see pp. 215–16 below. In June 1881 Hardy and his wife moved to Wimborne in Dorset. Soon afterwards they went on holiday to Scotland, and from this trip came the short story 'Benighted Travellers', which is of interest primarily because the whole of the action appears to take place in a scene from their holiday, far remote from Wessex. For details see **wsCh2**.
12 The railway ran where the eastern part of Cranborne Chase reaches out to the western extensions of the New Forest. There is a similar description in *Tess of the d'Urbervilles*:

> the soft azure landscape of The Chase – a truly venerable tract of forest land, one of the few remaining woodlands in England of undoubted primaeval date, wherein Druidical mistletoe was still found on aged oaks, and where enormous yew-trees, not planted by the hand of man, grew as they had grown when they were pollarded for bows (I.v).

13 I have traced two earlier uses of the word, one in *Desperate Remedies*, the other in *Far From the Madding Crowd*. Details are in **wsCh2**.
14 For an extended analysis of how this works in *Tess of the d'Urbervilles*, see *Proper Study* pp. 100–8.
15 In a final topographical note of some significance, Hardy manages in *Two on a Tower* to find a way to include both Budmouth (where Louis goes for a few days holiday) and Greenhill Fair ('I'd as soon miss the great peep-show that comes every year to Greenhill Fair as a sight of such a immortal spectacle as this!' said Amos Fry. [vI cXIII]) in the narrative. The two places were evidently in some way talismanic for him as guarantees of Wessex, and it is the more striking that the latter does not appear in *A Laodicean*. It is also true, though, that once again neither is a scene of presented action in the novel.

It seems probable that, once finished with the initial inscription of *Two on a Tower*, Hardy first wrote a brief narrative for the Christmas number of *Harper's*, called 'A Tradition of 1804'. For details see **wsCh2**. After this, Hardy turned his attention to the first of a number of significant pieces to be published in the *Graphic*. This was the novella *The Romantic Adventures of a Milkmaid*. The topography of the novel as Hardy developed it in manuscript and serial is complex; details are in **wsCh2**. Amongst the most interesting is that for the first time in his work Hardy names a river, the Swenn, which is evidently a version of the Frome. This was followed by the excellent story 'The Three Strangers.' Once again the narrative has Wessex interest, for which see **wsCh2**.
16 See below chapter 11 for a discussion of the Wessex dialect.
17 See below pp. 48–9 and 85–6 for borrowings from the essay.
18 For more details of this environment see **wsCh2**.

3 The first evolutionary leap

1 It is not coincidental that (as Pamela Dalziel pointed out to me) for the first time the illustrator of the serial version of the novel (Robert Barnes) drew scenes from the reality on which the fictional environment was based.
2 For a complete paragraph and analysis see **wsCh3**; for the whole run of such passages see **wsMayorNotes**.

3 For details see **wsCh3**.
4 Though, if the name is related to the Dorset villages of Long Bredy and Little Bredy a few miles east Bridport, one might propose that Hardy had the wrong river in mind, since the Bredys are on the Bride while Bridport and its harbour at West Bay are on the Brit.

Lucy's acquaintance had already suggested to her that 'Fellow-Townsmen' was set in Bridport, and it is interesting that the story at its climax, when Barnet hears of his wife's death and is flooded with delight, and almost immediately hears that Lucy, the woman he loves, is to be married the same day, destroying all his joy, anticipates directly Henchard's experience with Elizabeth-Jane in this novel. The narrator of the story comments: 'The events that had, as it were, dashed themselves together into one half-hour of this day showed that curious refinement of cruelty in their arrangement which often proceeds from the bosom of the whimsical god at other times known as blind Circumstance,' with its own relevance to *The Mayor of Casterbridge*.

5 There is also a sentence in the novel that in an economical way brings together three of the central Wessex places:

> Farfrae had then said that he would not go towards Budmouth as he had intended – that he was unexpectedly summoned to Weatherbury, and meant to call at Mellstock on his way thither, that place lying but three or four miles out of his course. (vII cXV)

6 For details see **wsCh3**.
7 In *Two on a Tower* Viviette tells Swithin of the Bishop of Melchester: 'I knew him when I was quite a girl, and he held the little living of Puddle-sub-Mixen, near us' (vII cIX). Mixen, of course, is manure heap – and the name was new in the first edition; in the manuscript and the *Atlantic Monthly* it was Puddle-sub-Hedge, with hardly any offensive overtones.
8 It is of considerable interest that in revising for the first collected edition of his work in 1895 Hardy removed the parenthetic 'in their own view', reinforcing the point made here.
9 For a discussion of this, see *Proper Study* pp. 88–96. See also Michael Millgate *Thomas Hardy: A Biography* (Oxford: Oxford University Press, 1982) pp. 248–52 for a more concise account of some of the issues raised in this discussion of *The Mayor of Casterbridge*.
10 This is a district first introduced in 'Interlopers at the Knap'.
11 Full details of Lucy's investigations into the topography of the novel are in **wsCh3**. A valuable article on the same subject is F B Pinion's 'The Country and Period of *The Woodlanders*' (*The Thomas Hardy Yearbook* 2 1971) 46–55.
12 Compare Hardy's poem 'Shortening Days at the Homestead':

> Sparrows spurt from the hedge, whom misgivings appal
> That winter did not leave last year, for ever, after all.

13 Other passages that illustrate the interconnection of trees and people can be found in **wsCh3**, as can examples of woodland work (including notes of important revisions).
14 Relevant details from reviews of the novel will be found in **wsCh3**.
15 For details of witchcraft see **wsCh3**.
16 *Letters* I.171. The letter is here placed at the beginning of 1888, but I have argued elsewhere that a date two years earlier seems more probable.

17 For details of other aspects of *Wessex Tales* and 'The Melancholy Hussar', see **wsCh3**.
18 More details of revision to the story are in **wsCh3**. For Hardy's revision in 1889 to *Desperate Remedies*, a piece of work that echoes in a negative way the development being charted here, see p. 116 below.
19 Details from the stories of Wessex interest are in **wsCh3**; for the textual history of the stories see *Hardy the Creator* pp. 80–96.
20 See wsCh3 for the text of the alterations.

4 Tess of the d'Urbervilles

1 For the full text and variants see **wsCh4**.
2 The narrator shows the relative smallness of the world for most dwellers in Marlott in a different way, when Tess is walking back from The Slopes some weeks after her violation. In the *Graphic* the passage went:

> The ascent was gradual on this side, and the soil and scenery differed much from those within Blakemore Vale. Even the character and accent of the two peoples had shades of difference, so that though less than twenty miles from the place of her sojourn at Trantridge, her native village had seemed a far-away spot. The field-folk shut in there traded northward and westward, travelled, courted, and married northward and westward, thought northward and westward; those on this side mainly directed their energies and attention to the east and south (XII).

3 For revisions to this journey made for the collected editions see below p. 149
4 See David Beaton, *Dorset Maps* (Dovecote Press 2001). For Drayton's lament about the deforestation of Blackmore in *Poly-Olbion* see **wsCh4**.
5 See **wsCh4** for details of her calculations.
6 See **wsCh4** for the full texts of each version, for some consequences of this pattern of revision, and for the history of Stickleford.
7 For the turnpike gate at Marlott see **wsCh4**.
8 When Angel returns from Brazil he retraces Tess's steps in his attempts to find her, thinking she was still at Flintcomb-Ash. The Hintocks are mentioned in this account also:

> Benvill Lane soon stretched before him... In something less than an hour-and-a-half he had skirted the south of the King's Hintock estates and ascended to the untoward solitude of Cross-in-Hand, the unholy stone...Thence he went along the verge of the upland over-hanging the other Hintocks, and turning to the right plunged into the bracing calcareous region of Flintcomb-Ash (LIV)

The phrase 'skirted the south of the King's Hintock estates and' was added to the manuscript, but it must have been done almost immediately, for 'other' in 'the other Hintocks' is not an addition. This is to take account of 'The First Countess of Wessex', and the rest of the Hintocks are to the east of Cross-in-Hand.
9 In fact it might well be said that 'The Dorsetshire Labourer' is one of the springs of *Tess of the d'Urbervilles*. In addition to the borrowing noted above, the two are connected in the well-known house-ridding passage with its attendant commentary on the depopulation of villages (LI); there is also an analogue in the essay to Angel's response to the dairyfolk at Talbothays (XVIII). See **wsCh4** for details.

10 See **wsCh4**.
11 See **wsCh4**. For one fascinating side of an exchange of letters between Hardy and the Earl of Pembroke on the question of pulling down cottages, also see **wsCh4**.
12 Of course it is also the dilemma facing any novelist who wishes to instruct in any way – even if only about human nature, as one must assume almost all novelists do – that a good novel is a 'well-constructed lie' as Penelope Lively puts it in *Passing On* (London: André Deutsch, 1989; p. 65), and that all readers at some time or another realise this. George Eliot and Trollope provide their narrators with a voice of such authority that no reader, however alertly critical, can imagine that they are doing other than telling her what is what. This, I am sure is what Hardy meant when in his one comment on Eliot in the *Life* he calls her not a natural storyteller. He was, I think, probably quite alarmed to find himself facing this problem so acutely, for he did not care for the Victorian solution, and yet he did think there were things he understood better than others, and he wished to impart them.
13 See **wsCh4** for reviews.

5 Handling new Wessex

1 For 'To Please His Wife' of the same period, see **wsCh5**. for a discussion of the manuscript see 'The Early Stages of Hardy's Fiction' *The Thomas Hardy Annual* 2 1984, pp. 3–29 as well as Martin Ray's *Thomas Hardy: A Textual Study of the Short Stories* (Aldershot: Ashgate, 1997), pp. 228–58. Ray's book is an excellent resource.
2 The story also anticipates the importance both of fair-folk and the end-of-century spirit in *Jude the Obscure*. For another Wessex detail see **wsCh5**.
3 See the World's Classics edition, edited by Tom Hetherington (Oxford: Oxford University Press 1986), and particularly Patricia Ingham's Penguin edition of 1997, which is entitled *The Pursuit of the Well-Beloved and The Well-Beloved*.
4 Hardy revised 'hedges to edges' for the book-publication of the novel. Presumably the former was a compositorial error that Hardy didn't catch in proof.
5 For the railway in the story, see below p. 226.
6 For details illuminating aspects of the story see its entry in **wsCh5**.
7 For 'An Imaginative Woman' also see **wsCh5**.
8 Other personal names have Wessex significance: Tess Durbeyfield was Love/Cis/Sue/Rose-Mary Woodrow/Troublefield before she took on the mutated version of d'Urberville, itself a Wessex version of the historical Turberville – and Hardy enhances the historical point by having Retty Priddle a descendant of the Paridelles: 'Why our little Retty Priddle here, you know, is one of the Paridelles-the old family that used to own lots o' the lands out by King's-Hintock now owned by the Earl o' Wessex, afore ever he or his was heard of.' In the first edition Hardy added, immediately before this comment of Dairyman Crick, a further piece of history that is pure Dorset: 'There's the Billetts and the Drenkhards and the Greys and the St Quintins and the Hardys and the Goulds, who used to own the lands for miles down this valley; you could buy 'em all up now for an old song a'most' (XIX). In *The Return of the Native* the Yeobrights were originally the Brittans, as Jude was England once.
9 See the chapter 'Wessex Rail' pp. 226–33 below.
10 For Stoke-Barehills see **wsCh5**.
11 For further details of Shaston and Christminster see **WsCh5**.
12 It is worth noticing in passing that in Phillotson's thoughts, 'artificial' became in the Wessex edition 'cultivated', and 'crude' was added in 'crude loving-kindness' for the same edition.

13 Hardy offered the passage to the journal *The Animal's Friend*, telling the editor he thought it might be useful in exposing the cruelties involved in slaughtering animals for the meat-market. It was accepted and published in December 1895. (*Letters* II.97)

6 The collected editions 1

1. For more details see *Hardy the Creator* pp. 165–75.
2. For details see **wsCh6**.
3. When in the Osgood edition of *Under the Greenwood Tree* Hardy added the detail that nobody was home 'at the Manor', he ought perhaps, in the light of *Desperate Remedies*, to have written 'at Knapwater House' – but he cannot allow the two novels meet.
4. See **wsCh6** for the Preface.
5. See **wsCh6** for details.
6. See **wsCh6** for the Preface.
7. See **wsCh6** for a range of revisions.
8. It is of some interest that in the essay in the *Examiner* Hardy mentions below, and which is discussed on pp. 23–4 above, Kegan Paul wrote: 'advancing civilisation has given the labourer only lucifer-matches and the penny post'.
9. See **wsCh6** for extensive details under these four headings.
10. An example of how this worked is in **wsCh6**.
11. For details see **wsCh6**.
12. For the Preface see **wsCh6**.
13. See **wsCh6** for quotations.
14. See **wsCh6** for full references.
15. A few other changes of Wessex relevance will be found at the end of **wsCh6**.
16. For part of the Preface see **wsCh6**.
17. For details of the transformation from England to Wessex see **wsCh6**.
18. For an analysis of the Piddle Valley in Hardy's revisions see **wsCh6**.
19. See **wsCh6** for details.
20. A full listing is in **wsCh6**.
21. See **wsCh6** for Portesham, for Portland and for the Uniform Edition.
22. For the details, see **wsCh6**.
23. See **wsCh6**.
24. For Hardy's anecdote concerning the making of this illustration see *Life and Work* pp. 284–5.
25. Details may be found in **wsCh6**.
26. Full details of these changes may be found in **wsCh6**.
27. Complete details of these four kinds of change are in **wsCh6**.
28. For the relevant portion of the Osgood preface see **wsCh6**.
29. For the substantial number of further examples see **wsCh6**.
30. To consider the evidence for these transformational effects turn to **wsCh6**.

7 The collected editions 2

1. It seems probable also that for Hardy it was impossible to recognize that the 'fact' he accuses himself of misrelating here is also, as he tells of it, only a memory, and thus itself liable to misrelation. His oral sources are as fact for him, because they are the only remaining direct contact with the past.

2 Details of these changes and those to other stories will be found at **wsCh7**.
3 For an interchange between Hardy and Sir F Pollock about an island custom, see **wsCh7**.
4 See J Hillis Miller, *Fiction and Repetition* (Oxford: Basil Blackwell, 1982) pp. 147–75, *Hardy the Creator* pp. 141–57, Patricia Ingham, *Thomas Hardy* (Hemel Hempstead: Harvester Wheatsheaf, 1989) pp. 96–110; and editions of the novel by Tom Hetherington (World's Classics 1986) and Ingham (Penguin 1997).
5 For a parallel in Drayton's description in 'Polyolbion' see **wsCh7**.
6 For examples of Hardyan paganism and of the ancient origins of the well-beloved, see **wsCh7**, and also the discussion of the poem with the same name below p. 172.
7 See **wsCh7** for details.
8 For 'Enter a Dragoon' see **wsCh7**.
9 See 'Topography in *The Romantic Adventures of a Milkmaid*', *The Thomas Hardy Journal* 3.3 October 1987, pp. 38–45.

8 The poetry

1 For an imaginative account of how the dual narrator might be thought to have worked in *Tess of the d'Urbervilles*, see *Proper Study* pp. 101–7.
2 Quoted by Samuel Hynes in his note on the poem in *The Complete Poetical Works of Thomas Hardy* Volume II (Oxford: Clarendon Press, 1984) p. 488; the complete letter is in *Letters of Emma and Florence Hardy* edited by Michael Millgate (Oxford: Clarendon Press, 1996) pp. 104–6.
3 A note of 1890 from *Life and Work* is relevant here: 'Christmas Day – While thinking of resuming "the viewless wings of poesy" before dawn this morning, new horizons seemed to open, and worrying pettinesses to disappear' (241).
4 At the beginning of part the fifth, chapter five, Hardy wrote of the marriage-question in the novel: 'The purpose of a chronicler of moods and deeds does not require him to express his personal views upon the grave controversy above given.'
5 It is fascinating that Hardy makes the poem's connection with *The Trumpet-Major* still clearer by revising 'In regal Budmouth Town' to 'In royal George's town' for the first edition, following the pattern of revision in the Osgood edition of the novel. In other changes made at the same time, 'The lad will mount and gallop by the cut through Yalbury Wood' became 'Let the char-wench mount and gallop by the halterpath and wood', 'Drive under tilt to Weatherb'ry' became 'Drive with the nurse to Kingsbere', 'Rain-Barrow's Beacon' became 'The Barrow-Beacon' and 'Through Casterbridge' became 'By grim Mai-Don'.
6 See chapter VIII of the novel; the text is in **wsCh8**.
7 A line in the last verse can be read to confirm that Hardy wrote the poem at the suggestion of the character: 'I cannot bear my fate as writ'.
8 For details see **wsCh8**.
9 This is as deeply a Wessex poem as *Tess of the d'Urbervilles* is a Wessex novel. It is not just that there is a list of west-of-England heights and rivers, and inns, and Wessex places, but that they are fragments of a perpetual journey, one of the deepest metaphors of Wessex; the ballad-form of the poem has its roots in traditional song and story, the date of the poem is well in the past, the footnotes are pieces of archaeological restoration, and manage at the same time to introduce the distinctively personal, a kind of realistic framework for the fiction of the poem. There is even the awkward intrusion of Blue Jimmy just because Hardy found him an individual too

fascinating to leave out. He co-authored a brief account of Blue Jimmy with his future wife Florence Dugdale, published in *Cornhill* two years later, in 1911.
10 Consideration might also be given in this context to 'A Church Romance' (I.306), 'By the Barrows' (I.317), 'The Roman Road' (I.320), 'The Noble Lady's Tale' (I.348) and 'Yell'ham Wood's Story' (I.359).
11 Another poem, 'Self-Unconscious' (II.40), might be brought into play here too. See wsCh8.
12 Parson Thirdly from *Far From the Madding Crowd* also appears in the poem, broadening the interrelation of Wessex and England.
13 *Bibliographical Study* p. 87.
14 See F B Pinion *A Hardy Companion* (London: Macmillan, 1968) p. 504.
15 Dennis Taylor calls this Hardy's Indian Summer in the epilogue to his *Hardy's Poetry 1860–1928* (New York: Columbia University Press, 1981).
16 As indeed he does not in 'The Selfsame Song' from *Late Lyrics and Earlier* (II.367).

9 Cider, Mead and Ale

1 They were all seeking 'vinous bliss' rather than 'beatitude' in the first edition. The 'night-stool' is a revision made in Hardy's study-copy of the Wessex edition: in all printed editions it is simply a 'stool'.
2 The reading in the serial and all published texts, 'wrinkled', is not a proof-revision, since it appears in the *Nottinghamshire Guardian* version, but a compositorial misreading or sophistication. (See the Clarendon Edition of the novel, p. 34, for further information.)
3 See *Proper Study* pp. 24–41 for an account of dance in Wessex.
4 The phrase 'a circle of opalized light' replaced in the one-volume edition the first edition's 'an opalized circle of glory'. In the manuscript and serials this had been 'an opalized circle or glory', and it seems almost certain that the first edition version was a compositorial error which Hardy only caught when revising for the one-volume edition.
5 The same inclusiveness on this subject can be found in *Jude the Obscure*; for a brief indication see *Proper Study* pp. 161–5.

10 Sounds

1 A second example is in *The Return of the Native*, where it is Clym's deep desire for his wife that causes his misinterpretations:

> When a leaf floated to the earth he turned his head, thinking it might be her footfall. A bird searching for worms in the mould of the flower-beds sounded like her hand on the latch of the gate; and at dusk, when soft, strange ventriloquisms came from holes in the ground, hollow stalks, curled dead leaves, and other crannies wherein breezes, worms, and insects can work their will, he fancied that they were Eustacia, standing without and breathing wishes of reconciliation. (V.vi)

11 The languages of Wessex

1 There have been a number of excellent studies of Hardy's use of dialect, some far more exhaustive than this chapter: Dennis Taylor, *Hardy's Literary Language and*

Victorian Philology (Oxford: Clarendon Press, 1993) – a wonderful book; Ulla Baugner, *A Study of the Use of Dialect in Thomas Hardy's Novels and Short Stories* (Stockholm Theses in English No 7, Stockholm University 1972); Ralph Elliott, *Thomas Hardy's English* (Oxford 1984); Patricia Ingham, 'Thomas Hardy and the Dorset Dialect' in *Five Hundred Years of Words and Sounds* ed E G Stanley and D Gray (Cambridge 1983) and 'Dialect in the Novels of Hardy and George Eliot' in *Literary English Since Shakespeare* ed George Watson (Oxford 1970). The chapter provides a different perspective from any of the above: it presents Hardy's usage chronologically, and (more importantly) it pays detailed attention to the ways that Hardy revised what he had originally written.

2 Dennis Taylor (*Hardy's Literary Language*) is particularly good in explaining the value of what have until recently been perceived by critics as the awkwardnesses in Hardy's literary dialect. My only quibble is that almost all of the examples he handles are in the narrative voice. I think it is much harder to defend the occasional eruption of such language in dialogue that is not self-evidently satirically presented – his ingenious justification as 'moral satire' of perhaps the most notorious of all, Angel Clare's 'prestidigitation', (p. 190) hardly accounts for the disruptive jolt of the word in its context.

3 There is an example of this happening in *The Woodlanders*, and others in his poetry (pp. 220–1 and 225). Such involvement in the idea seems to be the source of a fair proportion of the language in rural speakers' dialogue that was objected to by reviewers of his fiction as inappropriate. Taylor (*op. cit.* p. 42) points out a sentence in William Archer's *Daily Chronicle* review of *Wessex Poems* that describes the situation very well: 'There are times when Mr. Hardy seems to lose all sense of local and historical perspective in language, seeing all words in the dictionary on one plane, so to speak...' This seems to be more true in his poems, where Hardy was freer to think of the language as a 'translation' of the ideas of the rural speaker (as he put in a response to Archer).

4 For more examples see **wsLanguages**.

5 For some examples see **wsLanguages**.

12 Wessex rail

1 This chapter has its origin in some pages on *Jude the Obscure* in *Proper Study* pp. 168–70. More recently Charles Lock has published 'Hardy and Railways' in *Essays in Criticism* XLX (2000) 44–66, which excellent piece offers a somewhat different view of the topic, though I am glad to say he is in sympathy with my account of *Jude*.

2 For some relevant passages see **wsRail**.

3 Lock, in discussing this same passage, points out that the development of refrigeration in the 1870s was the key factor for bringing dairies in relatively remote areas like Dorset into the London market

4 See above pp. 179–80 for a comparison of this passage with Hardy's poem 'Midnight on the Great Western'.

5 Lock makes two good points in this respect: there are no pictures of railway stations in the chapter on *Jude the Obscure* in Hermann Lea's authorized guidebook *Thomas Hardy's Wessex* of 1913; and there are no railway lines marked on any of Hardy's maps of Wessex (pp. 50 and 66).

13 Conclusion: politics, guides and critics

1. His account of the relationship between Lea and Hardy is almost the only worthwhile part of Martin Seymour Smith's biography *Hardy* (New York: St Martin's Press, 1994).
2. In what follows I allow this argument for the sake of where it will take me, but it would be possible to counter the whole premise on which the essay is based by suggesting that even the least educated and cosmopolitan of the heath-dwellers has experience beyond the heath; even Christian Cantle has been to Casterbridge or to Greenhill, perhaps to Budmouth even. I think of Cain Ball's trip to Bath as an analogue here. And there is Tess's education to be taken into account; her sense of Blackmoor is moderated no doubt by a learned geography, but is still potent in her. There are even young people in the part of Georgia I live in who have no personal experience of more than a fairly few square miles, though of course the whole world is there for them on television, and they are exceptional rather than the rule.
3. The essay was published in *The Cambridge Companion to Hardy* ed Dale Kramer, (Cambridge: Cambridge University Press, 1999) pp. 19–37. I have come across two other interesting versions of Eggardon since, one dark, the other light. The former is in the first chapter of Nicolas Freeling's *The Back of the North Wind* (London 1983), a brief passage that ends 'Fuck Thomas Hardy'; the latter is a small piece by Sir Richard Eyre that may be found on the web at http://www.nationalgeographic.com/traveler/0111/sir_richard_eyre.html.

Index of Place Names

(Names in *Italic* type are English; names in Roman type are Hardy's; when Hardy uses the English name, it is in Roman type; names in **Bold** type are Hardy's, but are not found in the final revised version of Wessex, or have shifted their association with England.)

Abbot's-Cernel, 76, 93, 138
Abbotsbury, 34, 93, 130
Abbotsea, 130
Aldbrickham, 104, 126, 160, 233
Alfredston, 104, 233
Altland-Ash, 74
Alton-Ash, 74, 76
Alton Pancras, 61, 74
Ambresbury, 81–3, 150
Amesbury, 82, 150
Anglebury, 25, 70, 116, 117, 159, 162
Athelhall, 159

Basingstoke, 110
Batcombe, 76
Bath, 5, 160
Beaminster, 61, 69, 78, 245
Benvill Lane, 15, 75, 176, 249
Bere, 34, 58
Berkshire, 95
Bincombe, 130
Binegar, 14
Blackbarrow, 38, 67
Blackmore, Vale of, xiii, 27, 61–2, 66, 73–4, 76, 105, 138, 146, 221, 239, 249
Blandford Forum, 34, 58
Bloomsbury, 4
Bockhampton, 180
Boscastle, 120, 180
Bottom Pond, 129
Bournemouth, 24, 61, 150, 180
Bramshurst, 81
Bridport, 19, 43, 243, 248
Bridwick, 48
Brighton, 133
Bristol, 52, 81–2, 160
Brit (river), 73
Broadwey, 131
Bubb Down, 67, 75, 137, 138

Buckshead Hill, 5, 115
Budmouth, 12, 15, 18, 30, 35, 57, 100, 116, 131, 136, 153, 157, 180, 229, 247, 248
Bulbarrow, 63, 65, 67, 73–4, 76–7, 78, 148, 165

Cambridge, 4
Carriford, 5, 6, 7, 116
Casterbridge, xiv, 12, 15, 18, 35, 43, 45–8, 53, 63, 66, 70, 74, 92, 94, 100, 105, 115, 117, 125, 130, 133, 136, 148, 154, 157, 158–9, 160, 174, 178, 185, 217, 229, 237, 252
Castle Boterel, 119–20, 177
Cawley, 103
Cerne Abbas, 43, 75
Chalk Newton, 73, 75, 78, 157, 158
The Chase, 65–6
Chaseborough, 64, 66, 79–80, 191
Cheselbourne, 148
Chettlewood, 5
Christminster, 104, 105–7, 126, 232, 233, 250
Cliff-Martin, 59
Climmerston, 93
Cloton, 245
Coomb Martin, 59
Copsebury, 76–7
Corfe Castle, 24
Cornwall, 14–15, 43–4, 121, 161, 177
Cranborne, 61, 64
Crankhollow, 66
Crankholt, 66
Cresmouth, 30, 246
Cresscombe, 104
Creston (intended for Preston), 157
Creston (intended for Weymouth), 5, 6, 15, 116

Index 257

Cresvale, 104
Crewkerne, 43
Crimmercrock Lane, 78, 176
Cross-in-Hand, 74–6, 171–2, 249

Devon, 22, 44, 59–60, 73, 121, 162
Dogbury Gate, 137
Dogbury Hill, 75, 138
Dole's Ash, 75
Dorchester, xiii, xiv, 4, 6, 8, 19, 34, 43, 45, 75, 89, 92, 94, 118, 130, 132, 136, 184, 226
Dorset, 6, 10, 14–15, 22, 23, 24, 34–5, 41–3, 56–7, 58–9, 62, 64, 68, 77, 88–9, 123, 128, 129, 137, 143, 162, 176, 184, 226
Drouse, 225
Duddle Hole, 246
Dummerford, 46
Dunster, 133–4
Durnover, 157

East Chaldon, 34, 58
East Wake, 98
Easton, 98
Egdon Heath, 27–8, 31, 38, 45, 47, 48, 53, 56–7, 60, 67, 69–70, 78, 80, 97, 111, 127–9, 156, 177, 178, 200, 225, 239, 246
Eggardon Hill, 243
Elsenford, 159
Emminster, 15, 69, 74–5, 78
Endelstow, 21, 22, 121
Evershead, 75
Evershot, 75
Exbury, 229
Exe (river), 162
Exeter, 15, 161
Exonbury, 59, 105, 230

Falmouth, 161
Farnfield, 126
Farnham, 126
Fawley, 103
Fawn Green, 103
Fensworth (also Fenworth), 104
Ferly, 81
Flintcomb-Ash, 73–7, 78, 85, 249
Flychett, 30, 246
Fordington, 19
Forne, 98

Fortuneswell, 96
Fountall, 157
Froom (river), also Frome and Var, 8, 67–9, 70, 73–4, 85, 129, 159, 162, 165, 247
Froominster, 5–6, 7, 8

Galworth, 5, 117
Giant's Town, 161
Great Hintock, 138
Greenhill Fair, 18, 34, 45, 62, 68, 77, 246, 247
Greenhill Regis, 68

Hambledon (hill), 78
Hampshire, 60, 95, 123
Harefield, 126
Harefoot Lane (also Hartfoot Lane), 62
Hazelbury Bryan, 72, 77, 148
Helterton, 133
Henstridge Cross, 180–1
High-Stoy, 74–5, 137, 138
Hintock, 47
Hintock Abbas, 43, 47
Hocbridge, 4
Hod Hill, 78
Holloway Lane, 43
Holworth, 34, 58
Hugh Town, 44, 161
Humdon Castle, 5

Ibbesly, 150
Idmouth, 162
Ingpen Beacon, 164, 165
Ivell, 73, 157

Jersey, 15

Kennetbridge, 104, 105, 232
King's Hintock, 75, 154, 249, 250
Kingsbere-sub-Greenhill (also King's-Bere), 60, 62, 68, 77, 79, 252
Kingston Maurward, 7, 8, 116, 180
Knapwater House, 5, 6, 7, 114–16
Knollsea, 25, 57, 126

Laystead, 5
Leddenton, 105
Lewborne Bay, 5
Lewgate, 18, 92
Little Hintock, 53, 55, 136–7, 230

Lodmoor, 131
London, 4, 14, 15, 16, 31, 62, 81, 96, 126, 131, 159, 162, 199, 210–11, 226, 227, 228, 231
Long-Ash Lane, 74–5, 157
Longpuddle, 91–2, 93, 130
Lullstead, 57, 62
Lulworth, 24, 34, 57
Lyonnesse, 177
Lyonnesse, Isles of, 161

Mai-Don, 252
Maiden Newton, 73, 245
Markton, 47, 132–4
Marlborough, 160
Marlbury Downs, 160
Marlott, 58, 62, 63–6, 73, 77, 78–9, 148, 249
Marnhull, 61, 65
Marshwood Vale, 73
Martley, 80
Marygreen, 103, 104, 105, 106, 233
Melbury Down, 149
Melbury Osmond, 53, 75, 154
Melchester, 25, 81–3, 96, 105, 130, 154, 159, 160, 162, 168, 232
Mellstock, 12, 15, 18, 47, 48, 69, 92, 93, 99, 116, 157, 158, 159, 169, 177, 178, 181, 185, 189, 197, 225, 248
Middleton Abbey, 76
Milborne St Andrew, 19, 129
Millpond St Jude's, 62, 66, 129
Milton Abbas, 53
Mixen Lane, 48–50, 89
Monksbury, 93
Moreford, 129
Moreford Pool, 129
Moreton, 70, 129
Mousehole, 44, 161
Muckleford, 246
Mundsbury, 5, 7, 115, 117

Netherbury, 245
Nether-Mynton, 34, 53
Nettlecombe Tout, 73–4
Newbury, 232
Norcombe, 21
Norcombe Hill, 18
Norfolk, 126

Nuttlebury, 72, 76
Nuzzlebury, 72, 76

Oker's Pool, 129
Oldbrickham, 95
Overcombe, 34–5, 47, 53, 95, 130, 146
Owermoigne, 34
Oxford, 126

Palchurch, 5, 7
Paris, 131
Peakhill Cottage, 5
Pentridge, 64–6, 100, 160
Penzance, 44, 161
Pen-zephyr, 161
Piddlehinton, 92
Piddletrenthide, 75, 92
Pilsdon Pen, 166
Pitstock, 246
Plush, 76
Plymouth, 5, 14, 162, 227
Port-Bredy, 48, 73
Portisham, 34
Portland, Isle of, 34, 96–8, 131, 154–5, 245
Portwich, 48
Pos'ham, 131
Puddle-sub-Hedge, 248
Puddle-sub-Mixen, 248
Puddletown, 19, 20, 34, 92, 125, 129, 130, 181
Pumpminster, 58

Quartershot, 105

Radipole, 131
Rainbarrow, 67
Ranborough, 64
Reading, 5
Redruth, 44, 161
Redrutin, 161
Reforne (or *Reform*), 98
Rimsmoor Pond, 129
Ringdon, 160
Ringstead, 34, 57
Ringsworth, 57
Ringwood, 149, 160
Roy-Town, 159
Rubdon Hill, 67, 74, 138

St Clement's Isle, 44
St Eval's, 14
St Juliot, 14, 44, 120
St Kirr's 14, 22, 121
St Launce's, 121, 177
St Maria's Island, 161
St Mary's Island, 44, 161
St Michael's Mount, 44
Salisbury, 82, 130, 159, 168, 232
Sandbourne, 25, 70, 79–80, 105, 149
Scarborough, 127
Scilly Isles, 44, 133
Scrimpton, 94
Shaftesbury, 62, 65, 105
Shaston, 58, 62, 64, 65, 79, 105–6, 250
Shawley, 103
Sherborne, 43, 52, 75
Sherton Abbas, 47, 62, 74, 138, 162, 221, 230
Shottsford-Forum, 76, 77–8, 79, 154, 159
Sidlinch, 160
Silverthorn, 162
Slopeway Well, 96, 155
Snoodly-under-Drool, 20
Solentsea, 127
Somerset, 14, 15, 58, 123, 133, 222
Southampton, 5, 81
Southerton, 30, 47, 129
Springham, 246
Stagfoot Lane, 62, 72
Stickleford, 47, 71, 99, 162, 249
Stinsford, 7, 12, 115, 118, 178
Stoke-Barehills, 105, 110, 250
Stonehenge, 61, 83
Stourcastle, 61, 63, 66, 77, 180
Stranton, 22
Street of Wells, 155–6
Sturminster Marshall, 19
Sturminster Newton, 27, 61, 63, 148, 180
Sussex, 143
Sutton Poyntz, 95, 130
Swanage, 24, 25, 34, 57, 180
Swenn (river), 56, 67, 159, 162, 247

Talbothays, 67–70, 77, 223
Tarrant Hinton, 65, 93, 100
Tincleton, 7, 99
Tivworthy, 162
Toller Down, 176
Tolpuddle, 92
Toneborough, 59, 92, 133–4

Tor-upon-Sea, 161
Tranton, 93, 100
Trantridge, 58, 64–6, 79–80, 100, 146, 149, 191, 249
Troominster, 115, 117
Trufal, 161
Truro, 44, 161

Upper Joggingford, 92
Upper Joggington, 92
Upper Longpuddle, 92
Upper Trentripple, 92

Verton, 75
Vindilia Island, 156

Wakeham, 98
Warborne, 38, 47
Wareham, 116
Warm'll, 58
Waterstone, 93
Weatherbury, 18, 19, 20, 22, 47, 66, 72, 125, 129, 130, 159, 181–2, 189, 225, 248, 252
Weatherbury Castle, 19
Welland, 37, 47
Wellbridge, 62, 70–2
West Endelstow, *see* Endelstow
West Stafford, 8
Weydon Priors, 45, 49
Weymouth, 4, 5, 6, 7, 12, 15, 30, 34, 58, 116, 130–1, 153, 180, 245
White Hart Vale, *see* Blackmore, Vale of
White Lackington, 92
Whitesheet Hill, 176
Wiltshire, 22, 60, 123
Wimborne, 43, 180
Wingreen, 149
Wintoncester, 58, 84
Woodhill, 67
Wool, 70
Wooland, 77
Wylls-Neck, 164–5

Yalbury, 225
Yalbury Bottom, 136
Yalbury Wood, 18, 92, 252
Yell'ham Bottom, 165
Yell'ham Hill, 184
Yellowham Wood, 19
Yeovil, 43, 75

General Index

apples, 118, 131

Barnes, Robert, 247
Barnes, William, xii, 18, 173, 212, 215, 221, 224, 225
   Poems of Rural Life in the Dorset Dialect, 204–6, 217
   'The Water Crowfoot', 68
Barrell, John, 239–40
Barrie, J M, xiii
Baugner, Ulla, 254
Beaton, David, 249
bees, 13, 21

cider, 9, 43, 131
copsework, 54, 137

Dalziel, Pamela, 3, 245, 247
Draper, Jo, xvii
Drayton, Michael
   Poly-Olbion, 249

Elliott, Ralph, 254
Eyre, Sir Richard, 255

farm work, 20–1, 73–4, 85–6
farm machinery, 51, 85
Fowles, John, xvii
Freeling, Nicholas, 255
furze-cutting, 86

Gosse, Edmund, 111, 220–1
guidebook language, 71–2

HARDY, THOMAS
   collected editions of his work, history of, 112–14
ESSAYS:
   'The Dorsetshire Labourer', 41–3, 48–9, 50, 55, 85–6, 104, 226, 249
LIFE:
   acquaintance with William Barnes, 204–5, 217
   as architect, 1, 14, 43, 104, 120
   at Sturminster Newton, 27
   at Wimborne, 247
   birth and early life, 1
   courtship of Emma Gifford, 14, 120
   death of Emma, 176
   in Dorchester, 43, 217
   in London, 33
   negotiating for first collected edition, 112–13
NOVELS:
   Desperate Remedies, xiii, 3–11, 12–13, 14, 16, 112, 233; railways in, 6, 8, 12, 117, 226–7; in collected editions, 114–17; revision in 1889, 115; sound in, 198–9; dialect in, 205–7
   Far From the Madding Crowd, xiii, 13, 15, 16–23, 25, 45, 48, 62, 66, 69, 86, 119, 142, 147, 166, 218, 233, 253; in collected editions, 122–5, 159; drinking in, 188–9; sound in, 198, 200–1; dialect in, 209–10; railways in, 227–8
   The Hand of Ethelberta, xiii, 23–7, 36, 56; the first fully Wessex novel, 23; in collected editions, 126–8; language in, 202–4, 210–11
   Jude the Obscure, 26, 102–11, 165, 167, 178, 202, 250; the essential railway novel, 104; takes Hardy's fiction beyond Wessex, 110–11; in collected editions, 152–3; and 'Midnight on the Great Western', 179–80; dialect in, 223–4; drinking in, 253
   A Laodicean, 31, 35–7, 38, 84, 233; barely in Wessex, 35–6; in collected editions, 132–4; dialect in, 215–16; railways in, 227–8
   The Mayor of Casterbridge, xiii, 45–52, 56, 67, 69, 88, 89, 119, 248; site of a new development in Wessex, 46–8; in collected editions, 135; drinking in, 189; sound in, 198, 199; dialect in, 217–20

A Pair of Blue Eyes, xiii, 14–17, 100, 177; railways in, 14, 227; in collected editions, 119–21; sound in, 196; dialect in, 208–9
The Poor Man and the Lady, 3, 10, 11–12, 15, 16
The Return of the Native, 7, 27–33, 34, 35, 38, 45, 46, 48, 53, 55, 56–7, 67, 70, 80, 86, 88, 99, 204; in railways in, 31, 228–9; collected editions, 127–9, 148–9; sound in, 200, 253; dialect in, 211–13
The Romantic Adventures of a Milkmaid, 40–1, 56, 162–3, 181; sound in, 198, 247
Tess of the d'Urbervilles, xiv, 2–3, 56, 58, 59–60, 61–90, 93, 95, 102, 104, 160, 173, 174, 247; the essential Wessex novel, 61, 232; railways in, 66, 69, 79–80, 230–2; in collected editions, 144–51; poems extend ideas in, 170–1, 180; drinking in, 189–94; language in, 215, 222–3
The Trumpet-Major, 31, 53, 89, 97, 100, 215, 245, 252; combines England and Wessex, 34–5; in collected editions, 129–31; a poem voiced for character in, 168; language in, 213–14
Two on a Tower, 31, 37–41, 58; in collected editions, 134–5; dialect in, 216–17
Under the Greenwood Tree, xiii, 11–14, 15, 17, 18, 20–1, 39, 45, 48, 55, 67, 69, 86, 92, 93, 99, 112, 125; in collected editions, 117–19; poems extend, 169, 181–2; drinking in, 188; sound in, 197, 198; dialect in, 207–8
The Well-Beloved (earlier 'The Pursuit of the Well-Beloved'), 96–8, 165; in collected editions, 153–6; a poem explores the central concept of, 172; sound in, 199–200; dialect in, 223
The Woodlanders, xiii, 52–6, 60, 61, 67, 75, 86, 93, 112, 143; in collected editions, 136–9; poems explore, 169–70; sound in, 197–8; dialect in, 220–1, 254; railways in, 229–30

early paperback editions of, 113
linked together by common characters and places, 14, 15–16, 18, 47–8, 100
multiple narrative voices in, 14, 46, 50–1, 53, 165, 193–4, 252
realism in, 110, 179–80
POETRY:
The Dynasts, 173
Human Shows, xiv, 182–4
Late Lyrics and Earlier, xiv, 178–9, 180–2
Moments of Vision, xiv, 178–80, 183–4
Poems of the Past and the Present, 172, 200
Satires of Circumstance, 176–8
Time's Laughingstocks, 169, 170, 173–6
Wessex Poems, 167–9
Winter Words, xiv, 184–7
'After the Club-Dance', 175
'Afternoon Service at Mellstock', 178
'Afterwards', 186
'The Alarm', 168–9
'At Castle Boterel', 196
'At the Mill', 225
'At the Word "Farewell"', 180
'The Ballad-Singer', 174
'Beeny Cliff', 120, 177
'Before Marching and After', 178
'The Blow', 180
'The Bride-Night Fire', 224–5
'By Henstridge Cross at the Year's End', 180–1
'By the Barrows', 253
'Channel Firing', 83, 178
'The Child and Sage', 180
'The Choirmaster's Burial', 180
'A Church Romance', 253
'The Country Wedding', 181–2
'The Curate's Kindness', 225
'The Dark-Eyed Gentleman', 78, 175
'The Darkling Thrush', 187
'The Dead Quire', 169
'Discouragement', 184
'The Farm-Woman's Winter', 225
'The Fiddler', 175–6
'Former Beauties', 175
'Friends Beyond', 169
'Great Things', 180, 188
'Hap', 1–2

HARDY, THOMAS – *continued*
  'The Homecoming', 176
  'Ice on the Highway', 184
  'The Impercipient', 167–8
  'In a Ewelease near Weatherbury', xii
  'In a Museum', 180
  'In a Wood', 169–70
  'In Front of the Landscape', 176
  'In Weatherbury Stocks', 225
  'Julie-Jane', 175
  'A Last Journey', 182, 225
  'Let Me Enjoy', 174
  'Life and Death at Sunrise', 182–3
  'The Lost Pyx', 171–2
  'Midnight on the Great Western', 179–80
  'The Milkmaid', 172–3
  'Mismet', 180
  'The Moth-Signal', 177
  'Neutral Tones', 2
  'The Noble Lady's Tale', 253
  'Nobody Comes', 187
  'Old Excursions', 178
  'On Sturminster Foot-Bridge', 180
  'The Paphian Ball', 182
  'The Pine Planters', 170, 225
  'The Pity of It', 225
  'Poems of 1912–13', 177
  'The Rash Bride', 169
  'The Recalcitrants', 178
  'The Revisitation', 174
  'The Roman Road', 253
  'The Ruined Maid', 172, 225
  'Sacred to the Memory', 182
  'The Sailor's Mother', 180
  'The Second Visit', 185
  'Self-Unconscious', 253
  'The Selfsame Song', 253
  'The Sheep-Boy', 182
  'Shortening Days at the Homestead', 184, 248
  'A Sunday Morning Tragedy', 174, 225
  'Tess's Lament', 170–1
  'The Third Kissing-Gate', 184–5
  'A Trampwoman's Tragedy', 173–4, 225; as essential Wessex poem, 252–3
  'The Two Wives', 180
  'An Unkindly May', 185–6
  'Valenciennes', 168, 225
  'Wagtail and Baby', 109
  'We Field Women', 225
  'Weathers', 7
  'The Well-Beloved', 172
  'Wessex Heights', 164–7, 174, 176, 225; heights places where poetry might be written, 166
  'The Wind Blew Words', 180
  'Winter Night in Woodland', 182, 184
  'Yell'ham Wood's Story', 253
  audience for his poetry, 166, 167
  ballads, 174–5, 176
  double-vision in, 176
  religion in, 167
  repetition-with-variation in, 174
  requirements for writing fiction irksome, 165–6, 167, 250
  reviews of his work, 11, 22–4, 33, 35, 52, 89–90, 100, 110–11, 219–20, 220–1
  STORIES:
    A Changed Man, 43; in collected editions, 158–63
    A Group of Noble Dames, 58–9, 100; in collected editions, 143
    Life's Little Ironies, 100; in collected editions, 151–2
    Wessex Tales, 57–8, 67, 112; in collected editions, 140–3, 249
    'Absent-mindedness in a Parish Choir', 93
    'Benighted Travellers', 44, 59, 247
    'A Changed Man', 157
    'A Committee-Man of the "Terror"', 153–4
    'Destiny and a Blue Cloak', 245
    'The Distracted Young Preacher' (later 'The Distracted Preacher'), 34, 53, 57, 142–3
    'The Duke's Reappearance, 154
    'Enter a Dragoon', 158, 252
    'Fellow-Townsmen', 180, 215, 247, 248
    'A Few Crusted Characters' (earlier 'Wessex Folk'), 91–3, 100
    'The Fiddler of the Reels', 99, 169, 226
    'The First Countess of Wessex', 75, 249
    'For Conscience' Sake', 59, 101
    'The Grave by the Handpost', 157, 160
    'The History of the Hardcomes', 93

'The Honourable Laura', 58–9
'An Imaginative Woman', 142, 250
'Interlopers at the Knap', 43, 75, 143, 248
'The Melancholy Hussar', 58, 131, 152, 195–6, 249
'A Mere Interlude', 43–4, 133
'Netty Sargent's Copyhold', 93
'Old Andrey's Experience as a Musician', 93, 152
'On the Western Circuit', 95–6, 105
'The Son's Veto', 95
'The Three Strangers', 214–15, 247
'To Please His Wife', 180, 250
'A Tradition of Eighteen Hundred and Four', 142–3, 247
'A Tragedy of Two Ambitions', 58, 222
'The Waiting Supper', 67, 159–60, 222
'What the Shepherd Saw', 160–1
'The Withered Arm', 56–7, 128, 141–2
Hetherington, Tom, 250
'Holland, Clive' (Charles Hankinson), 237–8
Hutton, Richard, 22–3, 52, 90
Hutton, John, 22
Hynes, Samuel, viii, 252

Ingham, Patricia, 250, 252, 254
Irwin, Michael, 195, 196, 199–201

Johnson, Lionel
  The Art of Thomas Hardy, 102, 224–5

Kay-Robinson, Denys, 238
Keith, W J, xvii

lawn-tennis, 36
le Gallienne, Richard, 89–90
Lea, Hermann, 238, 254, 255
Lively, Penelope, 250
Lock, Charles, 238, 254
Lodge, David, xvi

Macbeth-Raeburn, Henry, 112–13
Macdonell, Annie, 100–2
McIlvaine, Clarence, 112
Macquoid, Katharine, 245
Miller, J Hillis, xvi, 252
Millgate, Michael, xvi, 235, 238, 244, 248
Morris, Mowbray, 90

New, Edmund, 236–7
Nicholl, Robertson, 93

Oliphant, Margaret, 90
Osgood, James Ripley, 112

Parsons, Alfred, 91
Paul, Charles Kegan, xv, 19, 23–4, 41, 251
  author of 'The Wessex Labourer', 124
Pearson, Raymond, 245
pig-killing, 26, 108–9
Pinion, Frank, 248, 253
poems extend the life of novels, 168–72, 173, 175, 177, 178, 185–6, 253
Pollock, Sir Frederick, 252
Purdy, Richard Little, 162

Rabiger, Michael, 244
Ray, Martin, 160, 250
reddlemen, 31, 39

shepherding, 20–1
Sherren, Wilkinson, 244
Stowe, Lucy, xv, 4, 6–7, 12–13, 14, 15, 18–19, 20–2, 23–5, 27–32, 34–7, 43, 45, 49, 52–3, 58–60, 62–3, 75, 77, 87, 92–3, 100, 101, 230, 240–1, 246

Taylor, Dennis, 253–4
Taylor, Richard, 246
Tennyson, Lord Alfred, 227
Tyndale, Walter, 237–8

website, viii, 100, 128, 155, 164, 188, 238
WESSEX
  apparent deviations from, 35–7, 44, 100
  as a way of knowing, 239–40
  as a way of seeing the world, xiii–xiv, 10–11, 27–9, 46, 88, 97, 107–8, 146–7, 184
  as copyright mark, 57, 110
  as dream-country, 124–5, 142
  as history, 147
  as style, 46
  at the *fin-de-siècle*, 96, 98, 107–8, 157
  causality, the way things happen in, 1–2, 10–11, 32, 52, 88, 173, 180
  choice of the name, 18, 42, 122–3

WESSEX – *continued*
- class in, 3, 10, 16, 25–6, 36, 39–41, 49–50, 56, 87–8, 90, 95, 121, 204, 208, 210, 217, 218–19
- a county, 24, 27, 56, 58–9, 61, 128
- critics and reviewers identifying English places in, 23–4, 35, 52, 94, 101–2, 236–8
- culture, 8–10, 141
- customs, 9–10, 13–14, 25, 31, 87, 98, 155
- destruction of houses in, 49, 56, 93, 104, 138–9, 249
- dialect, 10, 44, 109, 160, 163, 202–25
- division into separate counties, 58–60
- drinking in, 188–94
- expansion of, 43, 47, 95, 120, 122–3
- first use of, 17–18
- gentrification in, 209–10, 246
- guides to, 94–5, 101, 145, 236–8
- Hardy's attitudes to, 31, 41–3, 48, 57, 60, 82, 110, 122–5, 145–6
- Hardy's weariness with, 147, 166, 179–82
- historical Wessex in fictional, 51, 83, 84, 101
- history in, 35, 37–8, 56, 57, 83–4, 98, 99, 100, 106
- illustrations of, 92, 112–13
- in embryo, 15–16
- labourer's point of view in, 17, 39–40, 50, 109–10
- labourers criticised, 22–3, 245
- labourers defended, 23
- landlords in, 17
- landscape and objective reality in, 2–3, 28–9, 45
- local history in, 55–6, 106, 117, 119, 130, 141–2, 152
- maps of, 28–30, 95, 101, 113, 147, 161, 237, 246
- morality of revision within, 162, 181
- music and dance in, 87, 93, 96, 99, 157, 175, 191
- nationalism, 234–6
- new Wessex, 63, 68, 80, 87, 102, 110, 118, 123, 125, 141–2, 143, 166–7, 229; first signs of, 49, 57–60, 229; decisively embodied in map, 113; consequences of for Hardy's early fiction, 114–43 *passim*; anomalies caused by, 116–17; dilemma of, 127–31; Hardy's description of, 145–7; as Frankenstein's monster, 147; in poetry divides into Wessex-in-England and Wessex-in-fiction, 166–7, 168, 175, 176, 186–7; the effect of assessed, 240–2
- personal names in, 119, 160
- place and memory in, 2–3, 106–7, 196
- railways, 6, 8, 12, 14, 31, 38, 39, 100, 104, 108, 117, 165, 173, 179, 187, 226–33, 247; as metaphor for change in Wessex, 230–1
- relationship between place and character, nature and humans, in, 28–9, 32–3, 39, 45, 53–5, 86–7, 97, 109, 180, 182
- relationship with England, 7–8, 12, 14–15, 18–20, 23–4, 31, 46, 49, 51, 52–3, 56–7, 67–8, 69, 72, 74–6, 77, 90, 100, 104, 106–11, 116–17, 119, 127, 132–4, 147, 152, 168–9, 176; development summarized, 88–9, 122–5; exchange between Wessex and England made automatically, 166
- religion in, 21, 31, 83–4, 104, 156–7, 252
- rural and urban life contrasted in, 3, 16–17, 21–2, 25, 41–3, 54, 70, 86, 107, 108, 210–11
- seen ironically, 36–7
- a site of simultaneously held opposing views, 57, 193–4
- sounds of, 195–201
- summary of development of, xii–xv
- travelling folk in, 105, 109
- witchcraft in, 57
- women in, 21, 39, 86–7, 172–3, 228
- work, 8–9, 13, 20–1, 42, 54, 85–6, 104–5, 108–9

Widdowson, Peter, 238, 240, 245
Williams, Raymond, xvi, 238, 239
Windle, Bertram, 236–7